KATHERINE'S MARRIAGE

KATHERINE'S MARRIAGE

D. E. STEVENSON

LARGE PRINT

Oxford

Copyright © D. E. Stevenson, 1965

First published in Great Britain 1965
by
Collins

Published in Large Print 2014 by ISIS Publishing Ltd.,
7 Centremead, Osney Mead, Oxford OX2 0ES
by arrangement with
the Author's Estate

CIP data is available for this title from the British Library

ISBN 978–0–7531–9270–2 (hb)
ISBN 978–0–7531–9271–9 (pb)

Printed and bound in Great Britain by
T. J. International Ltd., Padstow, Cornwall

Part One: Ardfalloch

CHAPTER ONE

1

September is one of the most beautiful months of the year in the Scottish Highlands; perhaps the most beautiful of all, to those whose home it is. The gorgeous purple heather has faded and the hills are brown and tawny; there are little wisps of mist in the valleys which drift gently in the breeze and turn golden before they disperse in the rays of the sun . . . best of all, the visitors have departed and the land belongs to the Gael.

This particular morning was clear and bright with a slight nip in the westerly breeze. The jagged mountain tops were outlined against the blue sky as sharply as though they had been cut out of cardboard with a keen-edged knife; here and there were patches of fir trees, dark against the brown hillside, and little burns ran down amongst bright green mosses, leaping merrily from rock to rock, throwing up sparkling spray and finally plunging into the loch where the peaty stain spread out in a fan-shaped ripple before merging into the clear water.

It was a scene to delight the heart of a poet, but Dugal MacFadyen was so familiar with the hills and burns and mountains that he never noticed their beauty. He had been born and bred in a small cottage at the edge of the loch and had seen them every day of his life and in every kind of weather. To Dugal this was a good day for the sheep, no more and no less.

Dugal had been out since the first grey of dawn; he had been all round Ben Falloch and as far west as Ben Lithie, which was the limit of his hirsel. It was twenty miles or more, but his springy hill-man's stride took him over the heather and through the beech-brown bracken with the least possible effort. His faithful companion, a collie bitch, ran at his heels, alert and untiring.

Dugal was a small brown man, tough and wiry as the heather stems on his native hills. All his life had been spent tending sheep; counting them and rounding them up for dipping; searching for sheep which had got into trouble amongst the rocks. The hardest time was in April when the black-faced ewes were lambing, but there was no time of the year when a conscientious shepherd could sit back and take his ease. To-day, for instance, he had discovered two well-grown lambs stuck in a boggy place and had managed to drag them to safety (not an easy task, for they embogged themselves more deeply in their frantic struggles to escape from their rescuer). Then Fawn had found a ewe lying helpless and terrified in a crevice between two boulders — unfortunately her leg was badly broken so there was nothing to be done for the creature except to end her troubles quickly.

After that distressing incident the two friends went on together — and for a while there was a sadness on them.

Dugal's next adventure was different altogether: who should he see striding across the moor, but the laird with his gun? This was the best sight in the world, for there was nobody like MacAslan, and to exchange a few words with him — in the Gaelic, of course — was enough to make Dugal happy for the rest of the day.

Iain MacAslan had been born and bred at Ardfalloch. The moors and mountains, the sea-loch and the river — not to speak of the little burns — had all belonged to his family for hundreds of years. The people of Ardfalloch were his people and he loved them. As the chief of his clan the correct manner of addressing him was "MacAslan," and he certainly would not have given up this proud title for any other title under the sun. But despite his traditions and possessions there was no arrogance in the man; he was human and kindly and approachable . . . so Dugal was pleased, but not surprised, when he saw his idol turn and wait for him on a grassy knoll.

Dugal hastened towards him.

"*Tha là math ann an duigh*, Dugal!" cried MacAslan, waving his hand cheerfully.

"*Tha sin ann gu dearbh*, MacAslan," returned Dugal.

Having thus agreed that it was a fine day — indeed it was — Dugal was eager to inform MacAslan that he had just seen a small covey of grouse feeding peacefully on the farther slope of the hill.

"Good," said MacAslan. "I shall make a detour and come at them down wind. I want a brace for the house and so far I have had no luck; the birds seem unusually scarce this year."

"I have noticed that, MacAslan — and they are very wary," replied Dugal.

Time was when the Ardfalloch moors provided excellent sport, but for the last few years things had not been so good. MacAslan was badly off and in order to keep his property in order he was obliged to let the shooting for a month every year. He let it to a syndicate — which paid him well — but the big grouse drives played havoc with the game and when the laird returned home, as he always did about the middle of September, there was not much sport to be had.

When he was young, MacAslan had enjoyed a well-organised grouse drive as much as anybody, but now that he was older his tastes had changed and killing for killing's sake did not appeal to him any more; he much preferred to go out by himself with his gun and his spaniel and get a brace of birds for the pot. He wished that he could have made ends meet without letting his moors to strangers, who slaughtered his birds unmercifully and sent their miserable little carcasses to be sold to hotels in London, but he had to have the money, so it was useless to bewail.

All this he explained to Dugal, and Dugal listened and sympathised and voiced his opinion that it would be a good day for Ardfalloch when MacAslan became rich and there would be no strangers coming for the shooting (but as MacAslan saw no prospect of becoming rich this did not comfort him much).

"They are pleasant gentlemen," Dugal admitted. "They are generous too, but there is a different feeling when they are here. We are all happy when they pack up and go away and the place belongs to ourselves."

This was exactly what MacAslan had been feeling all morning. "*An là thuirt thu e!*" he exclaimed (which might be interpreted, "You've hit the nail on the head!").

They smiled at each other.

"But we are lucky here," said Dugal, and proceeded to inform MacAslan that his brother Fergus, who was a shepherd over near Inverquill, was greatly troubled with "campers" — strange people who walked over the hills disturbing the game, knocking down dikes and setting fire to the heather. These people were in the habit of sleeping in small canvas shelters and they left behind them piles of rubbish including broken bottles.

"Broken bottles?"

"Yes, indeed, MacAslan," nodded Dugal. "Fergus lost his dog, a good dog and clever with the sheep. His paw was cut and poisoned by a piece of broken glass — and he sickened and died. Campers are bad people."

"Some of them are bad," agreed MacAslan. "It certainly is very bad to leave broken glass on the hill. If Fergus knew who they were they could be punished by law."

During this conversation the two bitches had been sitting in the heather some distance apart and had taken no notice of each other; the collie because she

7

had been told to sit and was too well-trained to dream of disobeying orders; the spaniel because she was a snob.

"Oh, MacAslan, that is the spaniel from Miss Finlay of Cluan," said Dugal.

"She is indeed," replied MacAslan. "I am training her to the gun and she is not bad at all. She would be better if she did not get so much petting at home. Miss Phil spoils her."

Dugal made no comment; it was not for him to criticise his chief, but to waste a promising gun-dog by allowing it to be petted by women-folk was a thing he could not approve. "I am hoping Miss Phil is in good health?" he inquired politely.

"She is in very good health," replied her father. "I am hoping Carstiona is well?"

"Yes, indeed, MacAslan, there is never anything wrong with Carstiona."

They chatted for a few minutes longer, exchanging family news, and then took leave of each other; MacAslan shouldering his gun and striking off across the side of the hill on a northerly slant to pursue the wily grouse and Dugal continuing on his round.

Twice Dugal stopped and turned to watch the slender upright figure in the faded kilt and grey tweed jacket. It was to be hoped that the covey was still there on the sheltered slope and had not suddenly taken a fancy to fly away over the hills to some other place. Dugal was anxious about it, and continued to be anxious until he heard two shots. After that there was

8

no need for any further anxiety; MacAslan did not miss his birds.

2

Dugal had been out since dawn and was now on his way home. Glancing at the sun he saw that it was long past noon, which meant that Carstiona would be watching for him and his dinner would be ready. He quickened his pace down the hill and turned left along the rutty road (it was little more than a cart-track) which skirted the loch and led to his cottage. There was a small quarry at the edge of the road. Dugal's father had told him that the stone to build the cottage had been taken from here; before that, the MacFadyen family had lived in a turf hut.

If you had asked Dugal how long he had lived here he would have replied in his polite manner, "I am not knowing how long, but we are living here on MacAslan's land in the time of the Great Frost when the loch was frozen over from shore to shore." Further inquiries would have revealed the fact that this Great Frost which clamped down upon the hills and froze the sea-loch of Ardfalloch was the same Great Frost which froze the Thames in the year 1683.

Dugal had many stories about the Great Frost which had come down to him by word of mouth, and probably had lost nothing in the telling, but it had happened so long ago that it was like a fairy-tale. The building of his cottage interested him more. The cottage was his home . . . and here in the quarry was the same pinkish-grey stone of which the cottage was built, lying about on the ground and jutting out between green ferns and brown heather from the face of the cliff.

Carstiona, who was "fanciful" in her husband's opinion — though admittedly a good sound cook — had uncomfortably fanciful ideas about the quarry and had said more than once that it gave her a queer feeling to know that their home had come from a hole in the ground; she wondered if some day there would be a terrible storm and a flash of lightning and the stones would all fly back to their original places . . . and she and Dugal would be left sitting at the table with no house around them to keep them warm. Or maybe it would happen in the middle of the night, suggested Carstiona, and they would find themselves lying in bed in the open air with the wind blowing about their heads.

It was a foolish fancy and Dugal had told her so. There was no sense in it at all . . . but he wished she had kept it to herself. The fact was that although the idea seemed foolish in the day-time (a woman's havers and nothing more), it did not seem quite so foolish on a stormy night in winter with a north-easterly gale howling in the lum.

This afternoon in the bright sunshine Carstiona's fancies seemed ridiculous; Dugal smiled as he was passing the quarry . . . and then stopped dead in surprise. A motor-car was standing there — a large shiny motor-car! Fawn was sniffing round it, growling softly in a manner that betokened disapproval, so Dugal went near to have a look . . . and the nearer he got the more he was convinced that this was the biggest and shiniest motor-car he had ever seen in all his life. He peered in and saw that the back seat was stacked with suitcases and there was a tartan rug lying on the floor.

Where had it come from, Dugal wondered. This place was so out of the way — six miles off the main road down a rutty cart-track — that very few strangers ever came here. In fact nobody ever came here except an occasional hiker and, once a week, the van from which Carstiona bought what she needed in the way of stores — and every time it came the van-man used bad language about the road. Indeed if the van-man had not happened to be a second cousin of Carstiona's brother-in-law he would not have come at all. He had said so more than once. Could this beautiful shiny monster have made its way down that dreadful road? It must have done so, because there was no other way it could have come unless it had been dropped from the skies.

Well, here was the motor-car standing in Dugal's quarry, but where was the owner? There would be no difficulty in finding him, of course — Fawn would seek him out — and perhaps it would be just as well to make sure that he was not up to any mischief. There were queer things in the papers nowadays, so there were. Dugal stood and thought about the matter for a minute or two (although by no means a stupid man he was a slow thinker); he had just decided to put Fawn on the trail when there was a rattle of stones behind him and he turned to see a man coming up the path from the loch. Dugal had no time to mark the details of his clothes — which was a pity, because they were well worth attention — but he realised that the man was well-dressed, much too well-dressed for scrambling about on the hills.

"*Là math leibh!*" said Dugal, betrayed into his native Gaelic by astonishment.

"*Mar sin leibh féin*," returned the stranger, adding quickly, "But that's just about all the Gaelic I know, so I'm afraid unless you speak English we shan't get much further."

"It wass well said," declared Dugal in his careful English.

"Good," nodded the stranger. "As a matter of fact my nurse taught me to say it when I was a child and I've never forgotten it. She came from Skye. She taught me to sing 'The Nut Brown Maiden' — but I shan't offend your ears by endeavouring to sing it to you — and she was full of stories, some of them positively hair-raising. I loved her dearly and cried buckets when she went away. She cried too, of course. It must have been an affecting scene."

Dugal had been nearly sure that this was "a chentleman"; he was quite sure now. Only "chentlemen," like MacAslan's friends and the members of the syndicate who rented Ardfalloch, spoke in this queer way. In Dugal's opinion "chentlemen" were all slightly wrong in the head — but there was something nice about them all the same. You could not help liking them.

"Where would you be going?" inquired Dugal.

12

"Going?"

"There iss no through road. If you had kept to the main road it would have taken you to Inverness. Now there iss nothing for it but to turn your motor-car and go back the way you came."

"But supposing I don't want to go back the way I came?" asked the gentleman, taking a small key out of his pocket and opening the door of the car.

"I am saying thiss road does not go to any place," said Dugal, trying his best to explain the matter clearly. "It iss a ferry bad road . . ."

"You're telling me!"

". . . and soon it gets worse. Soon there iss no road at all but chust the moor."

Dugal stopped. Instead of getting into his motor-car and driving away, as Dugal had expected, the gentleman had dived into it head first and was pulling out the suitcases. "I'm staying here," he explained.

"But there iss no place to stay! There iss a ferry nice hotel on the main road. If you turn your motor-car and —"

"I know, but I'd rather stay here."

"There iss no place to stay," repeated Dugal. "You would not be wanting to sleep on the hill."

"Yes, that's the idea."

He was a "camper," thought Dugal, gazing at him in dismay. A camper! Who would have thought that this well-dressed man, who looked and spoke like one of MacAslan's friends, could belong to that detested tribe?

"You've no objection, have you?" asked the strange gentleman.

"Would you be leaving broken bottles on the hill?"

"Definitely not, nor empty tins, nor dirty paper; not even orange skins. Look here, you're worried — and you've every right to be worried. I wouldn't like strangers to come and camp in my garden without knowing who they were. As a matter of fact I wouldn't like *anybody* to come and camp in my garden," declared the gentleman frankly. "It would be most annoying and I should probably ring up the police. But never mind that — it isn't the point. The point is you want to know a bit about me before giving me the all-clear. I'm quite a respectable person, I'm a lawyer in Edinburgh; a W.S., if you know what that means."

It was obvious that Dugal did not. It was obvious that Dugal was having a good deal of trouble in following the explanation at all. The matter would have to be explained slowly in simple words.

"I am a lawyer," repeated the gentleman. "I live in Edinburgh. My name is Maclaren."

Dugal nodded. "The rug in the motor-car iss Maclaren."

"Quite," agreed its owner. "I see you accept that as proof. It isn't, of course. I might have bought it because I liked the colour — people do, you know — but as it happens the rug was given to me as a birthday present by my sister. She had it specially woven for me."

"Your sister iss here, Mister Maclaren?" inquired Dugal, looking up the hill as if he expected the lady to appear from behind a boulder.

"Goodness, no! This sort of thing wouldn't appeal to her at all. She's touring in France with some friends,

14

staying at the very best hotels and eating quantities of unsuitable food which will probably give her indigestion. That's what she enjoys."

Dugal's brow was wrinkled in perplexity. "Are you saying that your sister enjoys having the indigestion, Mister Maclaren?"

"I suppose I did — but it wasn't what I meant," replied Alec Maclaren smiling.

Dugal was silent. It was bad enough trying to understand what Mister Maclaren was saying — he spoke so quickly and said such extraordinary things — but if he did not say what he meant it was hopeless.

By this time all the suitcases had been taken out of the car. Their owner chose two and put them aside; he packed the others back where they had come from. He was now opening the boot.

Dugal approached nearer. "You have a canvas shelter for sleeping?" he inquired.

"A tent? No. The cave will be more comfortable."

"The cave!" exclaimed Dugal in dismay.

"There's a cave up there amongst the rocks. Didn't you know about it? I should have thought —"

"Och, I am knowing about it. I wass chust wondering how you would be knowing."

"I fell into it one day when I was out shooting."

"You were shooting on the Ardfalloch moors? But the moors are belonging to MacAslan. Maybe you are a syndicate chentleman?" asked Dugal anxiously.

"Heaven forbid!"

"You are not a syndicate chentleman?"

Alec Maclaren paused in his labours and smiled. It was a shame to tease the little man. "I'll tell you all about it," he said. "It happened like this: I was staying at my sister's cottage on the shore of Loch Ron — it's about thirty miles from here."

"It iss twenty miles from here."

"Twenty as the crow flies perhaps."

"It iss twenty walking over the hills," said Dugal firmly. "I have walked there often, Mister Maclaren."

"All right — you know best. Anyway I was staying there with my sister. A friend of mine happened to be staying with MacAslan for the shooting and they wanted another gun so I was asked to come over for the day. There were about six of us as far as I can remember. Have you got that, Donald?"

Dugal nodded. He said, "But my name iss Dugal, Mister Maclaren. Brown Dugal iss what they are calling me."

"Brown Dugal is a good name — couldn't be better. Now listen, Dugal. It wasn't a grouse drive; we walked miles over the hills and we had good sport, but I wasn't in good training, so by lunch-time I had had enough. I explained this to MacAslan and he was very decent about it; he told me to walk back to the bothy where we had left the Land-Rover and go home. I thought I would be clever and take a short cut across the hill, but I was tired and didn't look where I was going. I put my foot on a loose stone and took an almighty toss, rolling over and over down the hill. Finally I rolled over a small cliff and fell flat on my back on a nice soft piece of turf. I was shocked and winded, but that was all the damage

16

— pretty lucky, really! When I recovered I found myself in a hollow. It was a beautiful place: a stretch of green turf sloping gently down to the burn, sheltered all round by rocks and tumbled boulders . . . and there, in the cliff, was a cave. I had never seen such a delightful place for camping. I sat there for a bit until I had recovered and then I got up and went on my way. I made up my mind that some day I would come back. That's the story."

Alec Maclaren had told the story slowly, so Dugal had followed it fairly well. At any rate he had understood the most important part of it.

"Och, if you are a friend of MacAslan it iss all right," he declared with a sigh of relief.

"Well, not a friend, exactly. I mean I never saw him before — or since. I was just one of the shooting-party."

"You are knowing MacAslan, so it iss all right. There iss no harm at all if you wish to sleep in the cave. I would sooner sleep in my bed." Dugal looked round and added, "It will be a fine night and it iss not cold. The wind iss in the west, so the cave will be sheltered. Will you be after making a fire, Mister Maclaren?"

"Yes, but I'll be very careful. There's a sort of stone fireplace, you know. People must have lived there at one time."

"In the bad times after Culloden there wass men sleeping in the cave."

"Prince Charles, perhaps?"

"I would not be knowing that," said Dugal cautiously. "If Prince Charlie wass sleeping in all the caves where they are saying he wass sleeping it would be a queer thing . . . but they were Prince Charlie's men — that iss certain. They were men, broken in the battle and fleeing from their enemies. It was my granda that told me — and his granda told him — so it iss true, Mister Maclaren. Some of the soldiers were sorely wounded, but in those times the women-folk were skilled in healing and they gathered mosses from the bogs to dress the wounds."

"Sphagnum?" suggested his interested listener.

Dugal nodded. "There iss great healing in sphagnum. I am wondering why they would not be using it to-day in the hospitals."

"Yes, it seems silly not to."

"There iss a great many silly things in the world. Things that I cannot be understanding at all," declared Dugal emphatically.

"Tell me more about the cave. Did the wounded men stay there safely until they had recovered?"

"They were safe till they could be taken away in boats. It was MacAslan that arranged it. He wass our MacAslan's great-great-granda, you understand, and at that time he wass living in the castle on the island. It wass before the new house wass built. There wass other people too that helped with the boats — big people and small people."

"Go on, Dugal."

"The cave wass a good place," continued Dugal obediently. "It iss near the loch and the men could lie there in safety till it wass all arranged. The cave wass known to few people and they did not speak of it. The cave iss a ferry secret place, Mister Maclaren, and not easy to find. It wass my father showed it to me when I wass a laddie and it wass his father showed it to him. I wass thinking it wass forgotten and nobody wass knowing about it at all — except me."

"I'll keep your secret," said Alec Maclaren. He said it in a solemn tone but his eyes were twinkling.

"I would be sorry if a lot of people wass knowing about it," admitted Dugal.

By this time there was a pile of things on the ground beside the car: two suitcases, a large wooden box, a bulging kit-bag and a very large roll of fleecy brown blankets . . . not to speak of a pair of field-glasses and a stable-lantern.

Alec looked at them ruefully. "I shall have to make two journeys," he said.

Dugal said nothing but, seizing the wooden box, the lantern, the roll of blankets and one of the suitcases, he made off up the hill.

"Decent little brute — and as strong as an ox!" murmured Alec under his breath. He stayed to lock up the car, and then followed with the remainder of the gear.

3

They had not far to go, but it was a stiff climb and Alec was hot and breathless when he reached the outcrop of black rocks. It was then that he realised how fortunate he was in having the shepherd's help, not only as a porter but also as a guide. Alec had been sure that he knew the exact position of the cave, but the entrance was so well hidden that he might have searched the hillside for hours without finding it. He saw the shepherd ahead of him — and the next moment the man had vanished! When Alec reached the stunted rowan-tree where Dugal had disappeared he poked about amongst the rocks, but it was not until he had pushed aside the gnarled branches that he discovered the secret. The piece of cliff behind the rowan, which appeared solid and continuous, was composed of two large slabs of rock overlapping each other; between them was a sideways slit — a sort of narrow passage. It was difficult to get through, laden with the suitcase and other impedimenta, but Alec managed it somehow and found himself in the hollow by the burn. It was just as he remembered it, beautiful and peaceful, sheltered by the cliff and the piled-up boulders. The cave was even more delightful than his remembrance of it, with an arched entrance and a floor of yellow gravel.

"Lovely!" exclaimed Alec, taking out his handkerchief and mopping his heated brow. "And, my goodness, you were right about it being difficult to find! Of course I didn't come in by the passage when I came here before: I rolled over the cliff. I'd never have found the way in through the rocks."

"It iss ferry secret," agreed Dugal. "Many people have searched for it. At the time I wass speaking of there wass soldiers searching the hillside for two whole days and neffer finding the way in."

"I must have gone out that way," said Alec in perplexity. "There's no other way out — but I suppose

I was a bit muzzy in the head after the fall. Well, never mind; here we are and it's perfectly splendid. Nothing could be better."

While he was talking he had been looking round, and now he saw that the arched doorway of the cave had been built up on either side with large stones to make the place more comfortable.

"It wass done long ago," explained Dugal. "It wass done by the men I wass telling you about."

Alec was interested. He tried to imagine what it would feel like to be one of those men, "broken in the battle." They had been here, hiding in the cave while their enemies were searching for them on the hill. Perhaps they had heard the sounds of the hunt, soldiers scrambling over the rocks and shouting to each other. He went into the cave and found that by stretching up he could touch the roof with his hand; he paced the floor, measuring it, and trying to decide how many could sleep here in comfort . . . perhaps six.

Dugal, watching him, was pleased that Mister Maclaren appreciated the cave and was so interested in it.

When Alec had finished his measurements they came out together and stood looking at the pile of camping equipment. It seemed to Dugal that it was a lot of stuff for the requirements of one man.

"You will not be feeling the cold with so many fine blankets," remarked Dugal pointing to the bundle which he had carried up the hill. He added a trifle wistfully, "There iss nothing so warm as a good brown blanket."

"I'm afraid they're very heavy — it was good of you to help me, Dugal."

"It wass nothing at all, Mister Maclaren. I am used to carrying sheep over the hills. A dead sheep iss a ferry heavy burden."

Alec could well believe it. "All the same I'm very grateful," he said, and taking a five-pound note out of his pocket he bestowed it upon his new friend.

Dugal looked at it incredulously, "Mister Maclaren!" he exclaimed. "Mister Maclaren, it iss too much altogether."

"Not a bit," declared the donor cheerfully. "You see, this is my lucky day. As a matter of fact, between you and me and the gatepost, this is the luckiest day of my life. Take it, Dugal, and buy yourself a big brown fleecy blanket to keep you warm and cosy when the snow comes."

"Well, if you can be sparing it . . . But I wass not looking for anything. No, indeed, it was a pleasure to be helping! Och, it iss wonderful!" declared Dugal examining his treasure in delight. "Carstiona will be opening her eyes when I am showing her thiss — indeed she will! We will be thinking kindly of Mister Maclaren when the snow iss on the hills."

"That's the stuff," said Alec.

"*Cordal math duibh.*"

"What does that mean, Dugal?"

"I am saying have a good sleep," explained Dugal, and calling to Fawn, who had been an interested spectator of these unusual proceedings, he disappeared through the hole in the rocks.

22

CHAPTER
TWO

1

No sooner had Dugal gone than Alec seized one of the suitcases and rummaging through the contents found an old kilt and a flannel shirt with an open collar. He changed hastily and, leaving the rest of the stuff to be dealt with later, started off down the hill at a pace more suited to a lad of nineteen than a staid Edinburgh lawyer.

She had been asleep when he left her but he had been away longer than he had intended — half an hour at least — and, although he had left a note (torn from his diary) to say he had gone to fetch something from the car, she might be worried. She might be frightened if she had awakened to find herself alone.

Anything might have happened, thought Alec remorsefully. He had wasted time talking to the shepherd . . . well, perhaps not *wasted,* because if he had not chatted to the man and made friends with him the man would not have carried all that heavy stuff up the hill. It would have taken Alec much longer if he had had to carry it up himself — and he would never have found the entrance to the cave — so the time had not been wasted. All the same he should not have left her for so long. Supposing a stray tinker had found Katherine lying asleep on the bank — and frightened her!

I'd kill him, that's all, thought Alec as he crashed on down the hill.

Fortunately, however, nothing untoward had happened, and as Alec approached he saw her sitting on the grass at the side of the loch looking about her. When she heard the noise of his scrambling feet she turned and waved cheerfully.

"You weren't frightened, were you?" gasped Alec as he leapt over the bank and flung himself down beside her on the green turf.

"Frightened? Of course not! Why should I be frightened? I found your note so I knew you'd be back soon. You've changed!"

"More comfortable like this — but it took longer than I expected."

"You're frightfully hot!"

"I know," he agreed, wiping his face. "I'm in poor training for careering about the hills. Did you have a nice sleep?"

"It was awful of me to go to sleep."

"It was sensible. You were very tired — and no wonder."

"Yes, I was tired. It's been quite a day, hasn't it?"

"The most wonderful day of my life."

Katherine held out her hand and he took it in a firm warm clasp.

For a few minutes there was silence.

Alec lay back on the soft turf and looked at Katherine. She was gazing across the loch and he could see her head outlined against the blue sky: her charming profile and the mass of brown curls, her graceful neck and one little ear (like a shell, he thought) delicately tinted.

It had been March when he first saw her and now it was September; not very long, really, but he knew quite a lot about her because all that time he had been thinking about her and loving her and every little bit of information had been treasured up in his mind. She had been married before — happily married for four years. She had told him about Gerald the second time he saw her. She had told him of the misery she had suffered when Gerald died and how she had floundered for weeks in the Slough of Despond . . . and how she had climbed out of the slough because she realised that she was making Gerald's children unhappy. He had loved her for her courage; he had loved her for the fortitude she had shown in facing life alone and bringing up the children on a very inadequate income. It had been a struggle — he knew that — but the anxiety and the daily grind had not dimmed her gaiety of heart. He loved her for a hundred reasons . . . but chiefly because she was herself.

Alec had learnt about Katherine not only from his own observations but also from her children. Simon, her stepson, had been an especially valuable source of information. Simon (a schoolboy at an English public school) was devoted to Katherine and needed very little encouragement to talk about her. Alec had seen in

Simon a way to Katherine's heart; he had made friends with the boy with that in mind, but very soon he had come to love Simon for his own sake. Yes, Simon was exactly the boy that Alec would have liked as his son — and you couldn't say more than that. Now, Simon was his son — his step-stepson, to be exact — and also his friend, which was even better. The twins, Daisy and Denis, were Katherine's own children and in Alec's eyes they were almost perfect. In fact they were perfect in his eyes for, even if he could have done so, he would not have altered a hair of their heads. In marrying Katherine he had acquired a ready-made family. He had been a lonely man, so the ready-made family delighted him.

Alec had seen Katherine with her children, he had visited her in her tiny flat in Edinburgh — a cramped and uncomfortable abode, in Alec's opinon, but in spite of that, a real home. Indeed the little flat had often reminded Alec of a nest, full of cheerful nestlings.

All these things put together had helped to make a picture of Katherine. The picture was not complete — perhaps it never would be — there would also be more to discover: fresh beauties of mind and spirit. He would go on making these discoveries as long as he lived. He hoped he would live for a very long time so that he could go on enjoying Katherine. She was his; his very own. Only a few hours ago they had stood before the altar in the little church at Inverquill and he had sworn to cherish her (it was a lovely word and described his feelings exactly). He had sworn to cherish Katherine until death parted them. Death! No, he would not think of that. Why should he? Think of Life instead. Life was Katherine.

Suddenly she turned her head and looked at him and he saw with dismay that her eyes were full of tears. She said, "Alec, promise me something."

"Darling! Of course — anything —"

"Promise not to die — or at least not until we're both very old. It's a silly thing to say, isn't it?" she added in a shaky voice.

It was silly, of course, but he understood. "I'm terribly strong and healthy," he said seriously.

"You are so good to me," she declared, smiling at him through the tears. "You're good to me even when I'm silly. What were you thinking about when I interrupted you with my silliness?"

"Hoping we would both live to be very old."

"The same thing! How queer!"

It was not really queer. People who have suffered a great deal of unhappiness through death or loneliness are often beset by the fear of losing their dear ones.

"Well, don't let's talk about that," said Katherine, pulling herself together. "Let's talk about this morning. It was a lovely wedding; you were quite right when you said we should be married quietly in that dear little church."

"Neither of us wanted a big Edinburgh wedding with all our friends there, gazing at us, did we?"

"No, indeed!"

"It had to be one or the other and it was better for the children to be simple and quiet."

"Much better. Alec, you aren't worrying, are you? The children are quite happy about — about us."

"I hope so."

"You know they are! The very first day when we told them that we were going to be married they were terribly pleased and excited. You were afraid Simon might be jealous, but he wasn't a bit. He said it would be 'smashing,' don't you remember?"

"I shall never forget it," declared Alec with an involuntary chuckle. He added seriously, "But all the same we shall have to be careful. They were excited that morning and they hadn't really thought of what it would mean. Daisy and Denis are all right, but I think Simon got a bit of a shock when he realised that you were going away with me — and he was being left behind."

"Saying good-bye is horrid, isn't it? Simon is always sad when he goes back to school. He's quite happy when he gets there and meets all his friends."

Alec was silent.

"Listen," said Katherine earnestly. "I had a talk with Simon and explained it all carefully. I told him that I had loved his father dearly — and still loved him — but that I had found it very lonely and difficult struggling along by myself, especially when he was away at school. I told him that you and I had discovered that we loved each other and needed each other and that this had made us both very happy — so we were going to be married. I've told you the same, Alec. You don't want me to forget Gerald, do you?"

"No, darling. If you could forget Gerald you wouldn't be you — and I love you just as you are. See?"

She nodded. "I couldn't forget him if I tried; it's the way I'm made, I suppose. I wanted to say this to you because . . ."

"Because what?"

"Because I don't want there to be any secrets between you and me. I want to be able to talk to you about Gerald sometimes."

"Yes, of course."

"You understand, don't you?" she said anxiously. "If I felt it was making you uncomfortable I wouldn't be able to talk about him — and that would be a sort of — a sort of barrier."

"You must talk about him whenever you feel inclined. I shall be glad to hear all you can tell me about him. He must have been a fine man."

Alec had found this a little difficult to say, but he was rewarded. She took his hand and held it against her cheek. "Darling Alec," she said softly.

Thus encouraged Alec continued, "I'm glad you spoke to me about it. I've been thinking about it, too. We must talk about Gerald quite naturally, not only for our own sakes but because of the children; they must never be allowed to feel that their father is forgotten."

"Wise Alec," said Katherine. "What a lucky woman I am!" She paused, and then added in a different voice, "Aunt Liz told me I was a very lucky woman."

"She's a splendid person. It was good of her to come to the wedding — such a long way!"

"She wouldn't have missed it for the world. She looked splendid, didn't she? New and smart from head to foot!"

"I like your Aunt Liz immensely."

"She's your Aunt Liz now."

"I know, and I'm very proud of my new relation. I think she likes me — at any rate she made no objection when I kissed her."

Katherine laughed. "In that case she must like you very much; Aunt Liz isn't a kissing person. When did you kiss her, Alec? I wish I had seen it happening."

"It happened when you were saying good-bye to the children," replied Alec, chuckling. "I felt I wanted to kiss somebody and I couldn't kiss the Rector — or the MacRams — could I?"

"I kissed dear little Mrs MacRam," said Katherine reflectively. "Her nice fat rosy face smelt of soap."

Alec laughed.

"We're wasting time," said Katherine, coming to herself and sitting upright. "We must go and unpack the car and get settled."

"It's done."

"Alec, how naughty of you!"

"I got a brownie to help me."

"Why didn't you waken me? I meant to help you — and you went and did it all yourself!"

"I didn't. A brownie appeared — a most useful brownie. These hills are full of brownies, you know."

"No, but really —"

"Yes, really. A wee brown man in the guise of a shepherd. He was a little put out when I told him I was going to sleep in the cave — it's a 'ferry secret place,' you see — but I promised not to leave any broken bottles lying about and I talked to him in his brownie language, so we made friends."

"The Gaelic? I didn't know you had the Gaelic!" (Katherine had learnt from little Mrs MacRam that this was the correct manner in which to refer to the language of the Gael. She had learnt many other things as well — most of them useful.)

Alec smiled and replied, "All the Gaelic I have could be written upon a sixpence, but it showed the right spirit, if you see what I mean."

"There's an awful lot I don't know about you," said Katherine thoughtfully.

2

They walked slowly up the hill arm-in-arm, and as they went, he told her more about the brownie.

"He's small and brown, of course," said Alec. "All brownies are small and brown. His friends call him Brown Dugal — which isn't surprising. His hair is a sort of rusty colour; his face is tanned and weather-beaten; his eyes are like chestnuts and he smells of peat smoke. He has a brown dog, mostly collie, which follows him like his shadow, and he has a wife called Carstiona — I haven't seen her but I expect she's brown too. Last but not least he's tremendously strong; you should have seen him beetling up the hill, laden with boxes and bundles, and me panting along after him like an old-fashioned steam engine."

Katherine had not *quite* believed in Alec's brownie, but these details of his appearance, proclivities and possessions convinced her that he was real. "I'd like to see him," she said.

"I wish I could call him up for you. The trouble is I don't know how to do it. My nurse, who came from Skye, told me a lot about brownies but she never told me how to summon them when you needed their services. It was very remiss of her."

They had arrived at the black cliff . . . and, although Alec had been here little more than half an hour ago, the entrance to the little sanctuary was so well hidden that it was difficult to find. There were several rowan-trees growing from the base of the cliff, all of them gnarled and stunted by the winds, and Alec tried two of them before he found the right one.

"Ah, here we are!" he exclaimed, and holding the branches aside he showed Katherine the narrow opening between the two slabs of slimy black stone.

"Through there!" she exclaimed, drawing back in dismay.

"Yes, this is our front door," replied Alec cheerfully.

For a moment Katherine hesitated (this was worse than her gloomiest fears); but Alec was smiling encouragingly and waiting for her, so there was nothing for it but to master her repulsion and do as he wanted. She stepped over the roots of the rowan-tree and went through the narrow passage and found herself in the grassy hollow.

"Oh!" cried Katherine. "Oh, what a lovely place! Who would ever have thought . . ."

"It's surprising, isn't it?"

"It's — amazing!"

Katherine had been very doubtful about this idea of Alec's: this idea that, instead of occupying the luxurious suite which he had booked at Gleneagles for the first week of their honeymoon, they should camp in a cave in the hills. The idea had not appealed to Katherine at all. To her "a cave" conjured up the vision of a dark eerie sort of hole inhabited by bats — and she had been looking forward to Gleneagles. But Alec was so kind and dear and had given her so much that she had banished the fleshpots of Gleneagles from her mind and had accepted Alec's plan with a good grace. All she had asked was that nobody should be told — especially not Aunt Liz, who would have thought it crazy. As a matter of fact it seemed crazy to Katherine (why camp in a cave when you could dwell in luxury?), but of course Alec had dwelt in luxury all his life, so he did not appreciate it.

Now that Katherine saw the sheltered hollow, the stretch of green grass and the little burn running past, trickling from pool to pool in tiny waterfalls with a happy soothing sound, her feelings underwent a sudden change.

"Oh, what a beautiful place!" she cried. "No wonder you wanted to come here." She ran across to the cave and looked in. "Oh, lovely!" she exclaimed. "It's a delightful cave — so dry and airy! With a golden carpet of gravel."

Alec followed her and saw a huge pile of dry brown bracken which had not been here before. No, most certainly it had not been here — he could take his oath on that — for he had paced to and fro across the cave to measure its dimensions.

"The brownie!" he exclaimed. "Oh, good and faithful brownie, blessings upon your rusty head!"

"You mean he brought it here?"

"He must have! He must have cut it and brought it in while we were talking beside the loch."

CHAPTER
THREE

1

"We had better see about supper, hadn't we?" asked Katherine. "If you give me the things you've brought for supper I'll cook them."

"You will not," declared Alec. "I'm cook. I rather fancy myself at camp-cooking. First I must gather some dry sticks and get the fire going."

"There are sticks here and some bits of coal and peat."

"The brownie again!" exclaimed Alec, going over to the stone fireplace and looking at the fuel in delight. "I told you it was a good thing to make friends with a brownie."

There was not only fuel but also some dry moss, so Alec kneeled down and started the fire without any difficulty. Katherine was surprised to see him so deft; he had always had plenty of money, and people to look after his comfort, so she had expected him to be helpless. Yes, there was a lot she did not know about Alec.

Having lighted the fire, Alec proceeded to open the wooden box and to produce the necessities for the meal . . . and here again she was surprised, for she had expected to be fed out of tins.

"Go and sit down; you're making me nervous," said Alec. "Of course there are no tins, it's all going to be real food. This is a real place and you and I are real people."

She went and sat down on the soft turf with her back against a boulder and thought of what he had said. He wanted everything here to be real. There was to be nothing artificial in this little sanctuary. It was a curious idea but the more she thought about it the more she liked it. The bracken was real too, of course. She wondered what it would be like to sleep on.

Then she began to think about her children: Daisy and Denis would be getting ready for bed. They were staying with Aunt Liz at her flat in Edinburgh, and probably at this very moment — half past six — they would be leaving their baths, superintended by Aunt Liz, or perhaps Bella. If it was Bella there would be lots of fun and splashing.

Katherine felt just a tiny bit homesick when she thought of the twins — but that was silly, because they were always perfectly happy with Aunt Liz. Simon, who by this time was on his way back to school, would not be happy. She sighed; Simon, though not her own child, was especially dear and precious. Had Simon been a little more sad than usual when she kissed him good-bye? Had Simon's bear's-hug, which almost cracked her ribs, been a little more desperate? It shan't make any difference, thought Katherine. I don't love Simon a bit less because I love Alec. Now that Simon is getting older he needs a man — and Alec is so fond of him and so understanding — it couldn't be better. It's idiotic of me to worry, so I shan't worry any more.

She had just reached this sensible decision when she was summoned to the meal.

"Sit there," Alec told her. "The potatoes aren't ready yet but we can eat them afterwards. Here's your plate. The stuff smells good, doesn't it?" He helped her to a steak which was sizzling in the frying-pan together with mushrooms and tomatoes.

The steak was delicious; everything was delicious and it was all real food. Katherine discovered she was hungry, and demolished her large plateful with zest. She was given a wholemeal scone which undoubtedly had been baked by Ellen — Alec's faithful housekeeper.

"What did Ellen think of all this?" inquired Katherine.

"She thought it was a bit mad, but she's used to my madness. She said she would have everything ready for us any day. Of course she meant that we would very soon get tired of camping. We can go home to The Cedars, or we can go to Gleneagles if you'd rather."

"We'll stay here," said Katherine.

Sitting opposite to her, and watching her enjoy the food which he had cooked with his own hands, Alec thought he had never been so happy in all his life. (It is wonderful to be happy, but to know you are happy is absolute bliss.)

When they had finished their first course Alec produced the potatoes in their jackets which had been baking at the back of the fire. They ate them in their hands with salt and lots of butter. Then they had coffee, made in a fireproof jug.

"When we go home we shall have to see about a little car for you," said Alec. "You can drive, can't you?"

"I used to, but I haven't driven for ages and it really won't be necessary. There's such a good bus service from Barnton."

"Wouldn't you like a little car?"

"Yes, but ... Oh, Alec, you've given me so many presents!"

"I shan't give it to you. You'll have to buy it yourself."

She glanced at him to see if he were joking, but he seemed perfectly serious. She said in bewilderment, "But I haven't any money. I told you before we were married —"

"What have you done with it all?"

She was silent, gazing at him in alarm.

"I'm penniless," said Alec cheerfully. "I'm a pauper. Even these clothes I'm wearing don't belong to me."

"You're — joking —"

He shook his head. "No, I'm not joking. I've given away everything belonging to me. I did it this morning. You heard me, didn't you? I said 'with all my worldly goods I thee endow'."

"Oh, that!" she exclaimed, laughing in relief. "But that doesn't mean anything."

"Doesn't mean anything? It means exactly what it says. Nothing could be plainer."

"But Alec, every man says that when he's married. It means nothing. Think of all the married people you know."

"It may mean nothing to other people, but to me it means that everything I possessed belongs to you."

"I don't want it!" she exclaimed breathlessly. "I give it all back. Alec, please don't be silly. You're — you're upsetting me."

He took her outstretched hand and held it firmly. "I didn't mean to upset you, darling. I just wanted you to understand. I've been thinking about it seriously. When I said it I meant it — every word of it in plain English — so it's all yours. If you want to go shares with me it's for you to say."

"Yes. Yes, of course."

"It's a bargain," said Alec squeezing her hand. "We'll share. I just want you to remember that I've given you everything I possess and you've given half of it back."

For a few moments there was silence.

"I never thought about it seriously before," said Katherine at last. "Everybody who gets married says those words but nobody means them."

"It seems funny," agreed Alec. "However, we needn't worry about other people. When we get home I shall make over half my capital to you — and a half-share of The Cedars."

"And you are to be the children's guardian; don't forget that."

He nodded. "I spoke to my partner, Andrew Firth, about it and he agreed it would be wise, especially in the case of Simon."

They had discussed this before, so Katherine understood; Simon was her stepson and therefore Alec's step-stepson — if such a thing could be. His father's people were unfriendly so it was essential for him to have a legal guardian; all the more essential because Simon's grandfather, Sir Mortimer Wentworth, was a baronet and Simon was his heir. Some day, when his grandfather was dead, Simon would inherit the title and also the large estate of Limbourne which had been in the Wentworth family for several hundred years.

"There will be a lot of things to arrange when we go home," added Alec with a sigh.

"But we aren't going home for a whole fortnight, so let's forget all about it and enjoy ourselves," suggested Katherine, smiling.

2

They had lingered over the meal, talking of one thing and another. Alec lighted one of his small cheroots and smoked happily. The little sanctuary was so sheltered that the blue smoke drifted lazily and scented the still air with the aroma of good tobacco. By this time it was too dark to wash the supper dishes (Katherine stacked them behind a boulder to be washed in the morning), but the bed had to be made so she took the stable-lantern and went into the cave. Meanwhile Alec found a piece of soap and a towel and his pyjamas and went down to the burn.

The idea of washing in ice-cold water made him shudder, but he was hot and sticky so there was nothing else for it. Until now he had been completely happy, but now, suddenly, all the happiness ebbed away and he was miserable. Why had he been such a fool as to bring her here to this isolated spot? He should have taken her to Gleneagles, where she would have had every comfort devised by civilised man: a comfortable room, a private bathroom, a soft bed with fresh sheets — and all the rest of it. Why had he done it? Because he was selfish, of course. Because he had wanted to cook food with his own hands and watch her eat it. Because he had wanted to have her all to himself. He was not only selfish, he was a fool, the biggest fool in creation.

He stripped off his clothes and washed thoroughly. The water was even colder than he had expected, and a vigorous towelling did nothing to warm him. The fire had died down so he heaped some dry sticks on the embers and sat down to dry his hair.

Alec was still shivering — and not only because he was cold — when he felt two soft warm hands round his neck; a voice said, "Darling, you're as cold as ice! What on earth have you been doing to yourself?"

"Washing."

"Oh, Alec! In the burn, I suppose."

"There was nowhere else. I was mad to bring you here — mad and selfish. We should have gone to Gleneagles. Katherine, listen, it's quite early. Shall we dress and go? We could be there before midnight. It would be more comfortable for you — much more comfortable. We could leave everything here and come back to-morrow —"

One of the hands slid over his mouth. "Darling, you're talking nonsense. You're tired and cold, that's what's the matter. It's a lovely comfy bed and I've filled a hot-water bottle — see?"

He kissed the hand and removed it so that he could speak. "I'll get warm first."

"You'll come *now*," said Katherine firmly. It was her "no nonsense voice" which her children knew must be obeyed. She was gratified to find that it had the same powerful effect upon her new husband.

3

Katherine was awakened by the golden beams of the rising sun shining straight into the cave. For a few moments she could not think where she was . . . then she remembered and sat up and looked about her. Alec was not here, but she heard him whistling cheerfully, and presently he appeared at the entrance to the cave with a towel over his arm.

"Oh, you're awake!" he exclaimed. "It's a lovely morning. The sun rose in a blaze of glory from behind the ben. What time is it? I forgot to wind my watch."

Katherine looked at her watch. It was a little gold watch on a golden bracelet — one of Alec's many gifts to his bride. Alec had wanted her to have one set with diamonds but she had chosen this dear little plain watch with its clear bright face. Unfortunately its clear bright face told her nothing, because she had forgotten to wind it last night.

When they had finished laughing at themselves they decided to have breakfast.

"Time doesn't matter here," Alec pointed out. "If you feel like breakfast we can have it now. I've got lots of bacon but no eggs; I meant to stop at a farm and buy some but it went clean out of my head."

It did not take long for them to dress and get the fire lighted; soon the little sanctuary was redolent with the smell of frying bacon. Alec and Katherine sat near the fire and helped themselves from the pan; there is no better way to eat bacon than to choose your own crisp rasher, to lift it out of the pan and eat it really hot . . . Unfortunately the milk had turned slightly sour, which gave the coffee a curious taste.

"I wonder where those men kept their food," said Alec looking round. "They must have had a cool place."

"Those men" had become very real. The Maclarens had found various signs of the previous occupants of the cave; amongst them two rusty hooks driven into the rock on either side of the entrance. They had decided that those men must have had a curtain to hang across the doorway to keep the cave warm when the wind blew from the east, and probably they had used it when darkness fell so that they could light a candle inside their abode without fear of the glow shining out and betraying them to their enemies.

"They must have had a larder," agreed Katherine. "I believe I know where it is. I noticed a broad shelf over there near the little passage; it faces north so it would be cool and shady."

Alec rose and went to look at the "larder"; he returned with a jug in one hand and a basket in the other. For a few moments he stood there and they looked at each other.

"Oh!" exclaimed Katherine in amazement. "Oh, it's *too* kind! Why does he take all that trouble? We shall have to — to give him a present or — something, won't we?"

"Yes — well — as a matter of fact I *did* give him a little pourboire for helping me to carry up the stuff."

"I might have known!"

"But that was just — just for helping me to carry up the stuff. I never thought . . . I never intended . . . I mean there was no need . . ."

"Of course not," she agreed. "Your brownie is an angel in disguise. What's in the basket?"

"Eggs. Five beautiful eggs; brown, of course."

"Oh, of course. As long as the milk isn't brown . . ."

"It's golden," said Alec, peering into the jug. "It's almost cream. Let's boil two eggs and have them now — and some more coffee."

They had practically finished breakfast but the hill air had made them hungry so they set to and had another.

"I wonder why five eggs," said Alec thoughtfully. "Five is a curious number. Perhaps it means something special to a brownie."

Katherine, more practical and less romantic, felt pretty certain it meant that the brownie had given them all the eggs his hens had laid that morning, but it would have been a pity to spoil Alec's illusion so she kept her idea to herself.

"What a pretty jug!" she said as she helped herself to the milk that was almost cream.

"Great Scott!" exclaimed Alec. "If it isn't Limoges I'll eat my hat." He held the jug above his head and looked at the bottom of it. "Yes, it's got the mark."

"You mean it's valuable?"

"I do," he replied, putting it down as if it were made of eggshell. "I'll have a proper look at it later, when it's empty, but I'm almost sure —"

"What a lot of things you know!"

"Not a great deal about china, but there was a man at Cambridge who used to collect good pieces. He had a jug very like this, but his had a little chip out of the handle. This one is perfect — not the tiniest crack as far as I can see."

Katherine looked at it and agreed. "They ought to be careful with it," she said.

"Careful! Mr and Mrs Brown Dugal ought not to be using it at all. It's a collector's piece. It ought to be in a cabinet with a glass door."

"They don't know, of course!" exclaimed Katherine in alarm. "We must tell them. Perhaps they would like to sell it. You could buy it from them, couldn't you?"

"No, I couldn't. I wouldn't know how much to give him. It should be sent to Sotheby's if he wants to sell it."

"I expect the money would be useful."

"I expect it would," agreed Alec in thoughtful tones. "I wonder where the dickens he got it."

Katherine was so impressed that she emptied the remains of the milk into a jug which Alec had brought with him and put the brownie's jug carefully aside.

When they had finished their second breakfast Alec collected all the dishes he could find and took them down to the burn. As she made the bed tidy, Katherine could hear him clattering the plates and swishing them about in the water, humming cheerfully the while.

"Oh lord, there's a cup gone west!" he exclaimed. "Never mind, I brought several cups in case of accidents. We must dig a hole and bury the pieces. Perhaps you had better wash the brownie's jug; I'm a bit heavy-handed at this sort of game."

"Perhaps I had better," agreed Katherine, laughing a little. She had never had the slightest intention of allowing Alec to perform the delicate operation.

CHAPTER
FOUR

1

It was delightfully warm in the little hollow amongst the rocks, so warm and sunny that Katherine had taken off her frock and was sun-bathing in a pale-green nylon petticoat and bare legs and feet. Alec had gone for a walk; he had wanted her to go with him but she had refused, saying she was a little tired. This was true — yesterday had been a long tiring day — but there were other reasons for her refusal: she thought it would be good for Alec to have a long walk by himself and she wanted peace to think.

Certainly it was peaceful and quiet here; there was no sound except the trickling of the burn.

Last night Alec had told her a great deal about the cave: how he had found it when he was out shooting with MacAslan and how beautiful it had seemed to him and how he had made up his mind that some day he would come back. He had told her that he often dreamed of it. This place had taken hold upon Alec's imagination; it was a sanctuary, a place of rest and peace, and he had wanted to share it with her. He said,

"We are lost to the world, here." It was true; they were lost to the world.

Alec had wanted the first few days of their married life to be spent in this peaceful spot, amongst the hills which he loved, and not — most definitely not — in a luxurious hotel amongst a crowd of strangers. It was a romantic idea.

The curious thing was Katherine had valued Alec's friendship because she had believed him to be "solid and sensible"; they had been friends for months before she had discovered that his heart was full of romance. Last night she had been worried: at first on her own account (she had been afraid that perhaps — well, perhaps the thought of Gerald might upset things), and then she had been even more worried about Alec. It had been all right, of course, but Katherine realised that she would have to be very careful of this brand new husband. He appeared solid and sensible but, inside this shell, he was unsure of himself and as sensitive as a boy.

Yes, thought Katherine, poor Alec was full of fears and forebodings . . . it was Zilla's fault.

Zilla was Alec's sister; she had lived with him for years at The Cedars (his beautiful house at Barnton, near Edinburgh). She had been surrounded with every luxury, but in spite of this she had been discontented and bored; she had grumbled and complained and nagged at Alec on every conceivable occasion. Everything that Alec did was wrong. Few men would have stood such treatment, but Alec was kind and gentle and he had believed it to be his duty to look after Zilla. He believed her to be very delicate; he believed her to have some curious heart condition which might prove fatal . . . so he had given in to her and allowed her to trample upon him and to make his life a burden. Katherine had been to The Cedars quite often and had seen Zilla's behaviour with her own eyes.

Well, it was over now. Alec was never going to be trampled upon again. His wife would see to that. His wife intended to make it clear to Alec that everything he did was right, so he would regain his self-confidence.

One had to be sorry for people like Zilla, thought Katherine rather sadly. They did a great deal of harm in the world and they, themselves, were miserable. Now, at this very moment, Zilla was in France with her friends, the Carews, doing a tour of the Loire valley. It sounded delightful, of course, but somehow Katherine could not believe that they were enjoying themselves. When they returned Zilla was going to New Zealand to stay with some cousins and after that she intended to live in London.

Zilla's plans were cut and dried — which was just as well. It would have been disastrous if she had decided to remain in Edinburgh; there would have been no peace for Alec and Katherine, no chance of a settled married life. However, it was needless to worry, for Zilla had said over and over again that she was miserable at The Cedars — she never felt well in Edinburgh — so perhaps she would be able to make a new beginning and be happier.

Katherine, herself, was making a new beginning. She had been lonely and sad; she had been so busy cooking and scrubbing and cleaning her little flat that she was always tired . . . it would be different now. She was looking forward eagerly to her life at The Cedars with Alec and the children. Ellen was a capable housekeeper and an excellent cook; she had been with Alec for years and Katherine had no wish to interfere with her arrangements. There would be very little for Katherine to do in the house. How lovely to have leisure! How lovely to have time to read, to potter in the garden or go for a walk!

2

While she was thinking of all these various matters Katherine had been sitting in the sunshine, but now she took the brownie's jug, which she had hidden from Alec, and went down to the burn. She washed it very carefully and dried it and put it back on the stone shelf. Then she found last night's supper dishes, which Alec had forgotten, and proceeded to wash them too.

Katherine had been burdened with chores for years, but this was different and enjoyable. Instead of bending over an ancient sink, which no amount of scrubbing would whiten, she was kneeling on soft turf, washing the dishes in a delightful pool beside a tiny waterfall, the drops from which were splashing round and glistening in her hair . . . and, lo and behold, there was a blue forget-me-not tucked into the crevice where she had put her soap-dish!

"You're quite wrong," said Katherine, looking at the little flower severely. "This is the end of September so you have no business to be flowering like that . . . but all the same you're sweet and I love you."

At that very moment she felt a touch on her arm and a soft silky head was thrust confidingly against her. It was a dog; the brownie's dog, of course! She had a vague feeling that Alec had said the brownie's dog was a collie, but she must have misunderstood him because this was a spaniel.

"Oh, you darling!" she exclaimed. "Where have you come from? What are you doing here?"

Alec also had said — she was sure of this — that the brownie's dog followed him like his shadow, so where was the brownie? She particularly wanted to see Brown Dugal, to thank him for his gifts and to tell him that his jug was very valuable, so she rose from her knees and looked towards the passage which led to the outside world.

A man was standing there, looking about with interest. When he saw her he stepped backwards and leant against the rock.

They gazed at each other in silence for at least half a minute — which is quite a long time.

He was tall and slender and splendid — yes, splendid was the word in spite of his faded kilt and well-worn tweed jacket. If Katherine had been a trifle more romantic and less matter-of-fact she might have taken him for one of "those men," come back to look at the sanctuary where he had hidden from his enemies, and perhaps to resent the intrusion of strangers. The idea did just flash across her mind . . . but it was gone in a second. No, this was a being of flesh and blood, and although not young, he was quite astonishingly good-looking, with perfectly chiselled features and dark hair powdered with silver as if touched with hoar frost. His dark eyes were staring at her, staring and staring in bewilderment.

Katherine was the first to recover her powers of speech. She said, "Oh, I was surprised! You see I was expecting to see Alec's brownie, who brought the milk . . . but of course you're not. Would you like to come and sit down? This is a beautiful place, isn't it?"

He neither moved nor spoke. Could he be deaf? She went forward and repeated her invitation louder, adding, "I was just going to have coffee. Would you like some?"

"That's very kind," he said vaguely.

Katherine remembered suddenly that she was unsuitably attired to receive visitors but as this was a cave amongst the hills she decided that it did not matter. What mattered was that she should receive her visitor kindly and put him at his ease. He seemed to be recovering his wits but he still looked a trifle queer. Perhaps he was feeling ill.

"We haven't any chairs but you could sit on the box, couldn't you?" said Katherine, smiling at him.

He did as she suggested. "Are you . . ." he began and stopped.

"I'm Mrs — er — Mrs Maclaren," she told him. It was the first time she had called herself by the new name and it felt very odd indeed. "Mrs Maclaren," she repeated more confidently.

"Oh, I see. I didn't know . . ."

"Perhaps you expected to see Alec. He has gone for a walk this morning."

"Dugal told me Mr Maclaren was camping here but I thought he was alone. Dugal doesn't understand English very well; that's the trouble. I thought I would call and have a chat with Maclaren and see how he was getting on."

"It's a perfect place to camp."

"Yes, it's very sheltered. As a matter of fact I haven't been here for years. My father knew about the cave, of course; he showed it to me one day when we were out shooting together. I had forgotten all about it until Dugal mentioned it to me this morning. It took me quite a long time to find the way in. Eventually Hero found it."

"Hero? Is that her name?" asked Katherine who had been fondling the spaniel's silky ears.

"She belongs to my daughter. Phil said she must be called Hero because her sire was Leander. That doesn't seem a very good reason, I admit."

"I know who you are!" exclaimed Katherine. "You're our — our landlord. Is that right?"

He smiled. "Well — yes. I suppose you might call me your landlord. But I'm afraid I haven't provided the usual amenities."

"Oh, you have!" she cried. "Who could ask more than a lovely dry cave and a bed of bracken? — and look at the view! — and there's running water laid on. You've even provided me with a forget-me-not in my soap-dish."

He laughed.

Katherine was pleased to see that the bewildered expression had vanished. She continued to babble in her benevolent attempt to put him at his ease. It seemed queer that this should be necessary when the hills, the craggy mountains, the placid loch and all the little burns belonged to him. "Perhaps you don't believe in the forget-me-not," she suggested. "But quite honestly it's true — a dear little blue flower in a crevice by the burn. It's quite the wrong time of year so I felt it was blooming specially for me."

"It was," he said, nodding gravely. "Naturally it thought you were a naiad. I thought so myself when I saw you rising from the burn in that very pretty green dress with diamonds sparkling in your hair."

"Was that why . . ." she began, smiling to hear her nylon slip described in this man-like fashion. "I mean do you really believe in water-fairies?"

"'Ye nymphs, called naiads, of the wandering brooks'."

"Oh, I'm very human," declared Katherine. "I'm the mother of a family."

"Really?" asked her visitor in surprise. "That just shows how bad I am at arithmetic. While we've been talking I put two and two together — and made five."

54

He opened his hand and disclosed some pink paper rose-petals and a couple of tiny silver horse-shoes.

"Oh goodness!" she exclaimed. "Where did you find them? But you could have found them anywhere — our clothes were full of the stuff. It was the children. They thought it was fun. Your five was right, of course. Alec and I were married yesterday at Inverquill."

After this somewhat incoherent explanation there was a short silence.

"I believe I've solved the mystery," said MacAslan at last. "You were married before. The children belong to your first marriage."

She nodded. "I didn't mean to be mysterious; I'm just a bit muddled. My first husband was Gerald Wentworth. We had four happy years together — and then he died. I was miserable for a long time. Then I met Alec and we became friends. Alec was very, very good to me and to the children, but I just wanted him as a friend. We were friends for months before I suddenly found that I was — was fond of him. It was quite, quite sudden," declared Katherine, taking Hero's ears and folding them across Hero's eyes. "It was the most sudden and unexpected thing that ever happened to me . . . and yet I had known him for months."

"Sometimes it happens like that."

"I don't know why I told you. I seem to be behaving rather strangely."

The fact was she felt a little nervous. She had asked the man to come in under the impression that he was a stranger; she had offered him a seat and a cup of coffee because she thought he looked unwell. It was disconcerting to discover that he was king of all he surveyed. Her difficulties were augmented by the fact that she did not know what to call him. Alec had talked about "MacAslan" and had explained that this was the correct way to address him — he was the chief of his clan. That had sounded all right at the time but now that Katherine was face to face with this fine-looking man, a great deal older than herself, she found it impossible to address him as "MacAslan." He ought to be Sir Somebody MacAslan, thought Katherine. Then it would be quite easy.

Fortunately the coffee was ready so she poured it out and handed him a cup.

"This is delightful," he said. "You mentioned that your first husband was Gerald Wentworth. Was he any relation to Peter Wentworth, a major in the Gunners?"

"Oh yes! Do you know Peter?"

"We know him well. He comes and stays with us sometimes for the grouse shooting. His father, Sir Mortimer Wentworth, asked me to go to Limbourne for the pheasant shooting but I couldn't go."

"What a pity! Limbourne is a beautiful old house in a lovely part of the country. It's within easy distance of London so perhaps you'll be able to go some other time."

"Well, perhaps." MacAslan said it in such a manner that his hearer realised he had no intention of accepting Sir Mortimer's invitation. She wondered why.

"Tell me about the family," said MacAslan after a short silence. "I'm interested because I'm fond of Peter. Was your first husband Peter's cousin?"

"No, he was Peter's brother. Sir Mortimer had four children: Henry, Florence, Gerald and Peter."

"I didn't know that! I knew Peter had an older brother called Henry and I've met his sister, Florence Godfrey, but I don't think they ever mentioned Gerald . . . in fact I'm sure of it. How strange!"

"It wasn't strange, really. I mean they wouldn't mention Gerald. There was a family quarrel — that was the reason. It happened long ago, before I met Gerald, but of course Gerald told me; we had no secrets from each other. Gerald was sorry; he had no wish to quarrel with his family." She paused.

"Perhaps you would rather not talk about it, Mrs Maclaren?"

"I don't mind in the least, but it's rather complicated," replied Katherine. She was sitting on the grass at MacAslan's feet drinking her coffee. "It was like this," she continued, drawing up her knees and putting her arms round them. "Long ago when Gerald was quite young — he had just left Oxford — his father wanted him to live at home and manage the estate, but Gerald had taken good degrees in history and archæology and wanted to make a career for himself. It would have been different if he had been the heir, but of course he wasn't."

"Henry was the eldest son?"

"Yes, he was a lawyer in London. Later he became a barrister and a very successful one. That was why Sir Mortimer wanted Gerald to stay at home. There was a good deal of unpleasantness about it but Gerald felt he must get away so he went to Rome as assistant to a well-known archæologist who was excavating at Pompeii."

"It sounds an interesting job for a young man."

"Yes, it was — and it suited Gerald. While he was in Rome he met a beautiful Italian girl and married her."

"That was the quarrel?"

Katherine nodded. "His parents were furious with him; they cut him off completely and returned his letters unopened."

"What an extraordinary thing!"

"Sir Mortimer is an extraordinary man."

"Yes, I was aware of that."

"He likes people to do exactly as they're told."

"So I gathered. Last year when Peter was staying with us his father wired to him to come home at once. It so happened that Peter had been asked to shoot at Froy; it was a big grouse drive and he particularly wanted to go, so he rang up his father and explained. Apparently there was no real reason why his father wanted him to go home but all the same he had to go — and started off at dawn next morning."

Katherine nodded; she was not surprised.

"Peter was extremely angry," continued MacAslan. "No wonder he was angry! You can't treat your family in that tyrannical way. I shouldn't dream of treating Gregor like that and he's only seventeen. Peter is a major in the Gunners — a very distinguished officer with war-service — so it's quite ridiculous that he should be at his father's beck and call."

Katherine looked thoughtful. She said, "I quite agree that you can't treat your children like that if you want their love. If you want them to grow up into whole people, good and true and straight you must give them their freedom. Sir Mortimer hasn't got their love but only their obedience."

"A poor substitute," said MacAslan. "As I told you, Peter was angry; he said a good deal about his father and his family. It was obvious that he had no affection for any of them — it seemed all wrong and I felt very sorry about it —"

"It *is* all wrong," Katherine declared emphatically.

"Oh well, I suppose it can't be helped," said MacAslan with a sigh. "People have got to work out their own lives according to their natures."

"You believe that?" asked Katherine. "I mean if you are born with a tyrannical nature you can't help being a tyrant?"

MacAslan smiled. "You're going a bit too deep for me. Let's leave that to the psychiatrists to decide. Tell me what happened to Gerald Wentworth and his Italian wife. Were they happy?"

"Yes, very happy. They lived in Rome until Simon was born and Violetta died. Gerald couldn't bear Rome after that so he came back to Oxford with his baby son and did some research and coaching. It was in Oxford that I met Gerald . . . and we were married."

"So Simon is your stepson."

"Yes. He was seven when I married Gerald; now he's sixteen. It's an interesting age, isn't it? At least it is in Simon's case. One moment he seems a child and the next moment you realise that he's almost a man."

"He's a curious mixture," MacAslan reminded her. "His father was descended from a very old English family and his mother was an Italian. I'd like to meet Simon."

"You would like him," said Katherine smiling.

"Let's see now," continued MacAslan. "Henry Wentworth died last February — I saw a notice of his death in *The Times* — so I was under the impression that Peter had become the heir; I didn't know he had an older brother."

"They never mentioned Gerald. They had cast him off completely."

"They had severed all connection with Gerald because of his marriage, but they couldn't really cast him off completely. I mean Gerald's son, Simon, is heir to the baronetcy — whether they like it or not."

"Yes, I told you it was very complicated, didn't I? Simon is heir to the baronetcy — and to Limbourne. The property is entailed. Fortunately Sir Mortimer is very hale and hearty so we don't need to worry. I mean Simon is much too young for — for that sort of thing."

MacAslan laughed. "Much too young. Let's hope Sir Mortimer will live to a ripe old age. Go on, Mrs Maclaren."

"Do you really want to know more?"

"I want to know about you," he replied. "You said you met Gerald Wentworth in Oxford and married him."

"Yes, we were married and lived in Oxford for four years. I was much younger than Gerald — only nineteen — but we were very happy. We had twins: a boy and a girl. Then when Gerald died I came to live in Edinburgh with the children. My aunt lives in Edinburgh; she wanted us to be near her and it seemed the best thing to do. You see my parents died when I was a baby and my aunt brought me up and looked after me so I'm devoted to her. She's my only relation."

"But what about the Wentworths? Didn't they —"

"Goodness, no!" exclaimed Katherine. "All the time we heard *nothing* of Gerald's relations. To tell you the truth I had almost forgotten they existed. It wasn't until Henry Wentworth died that they took any notice of us at all. Then — and not till then — Sir Mortimer wrote to Simon and asked him to go to Limbourne. He wanted to see Simon because Simon had become the heir."

"Did Simon go?"

"Yes, but he said his father wouldn't have gone to Limbourne unless I was asked too, so he wouldn't go unless his grandfather was prepared to be friends with me. I tried to persuade him to go alone, but he wouldn't."

"Simon was perfectly right."

"I suppose he was," said Katherine with a sigh.

"So all's well that ends well. The feud is over."

"I'm afraid it isn't. In fact the feud has taken a new lease of life."

"There was trouble during your visit?"

Katherine shook her head. "No, it wasn't that. Sir Mortimer was kind to us. As I said before he's very kind if you do exactly as you're told. He wanted Simon to promise to go to Limbourne when he leaves school and learn to look after the estate. It seemed a sensible arrangement and at first Simon thought he would like to do it; he would have had a full and interesting life — hunting, and a car of his own and holidays abroad — but afterwards he changed his mind and decided that he couldn't bear it."

"You mean because his grandfather was so difficult?"

"Yes, that was the reason. The whole atmosphere of Limbourne is — is unhappy."

"So the feud continues."

"Worse than ever," said Katherine regretfully. "The only bright spot is Peter. Sir Mortimer sent Peter to see me to try to persuade me to *make* Simon go to Limbourne, but I managed to get Peter to see Simon's point of view."

"That was clever of you!"

"Not clever — just sensible. I merely asked him if he would like to live at Limbourne and be absolutely dependent upon Sir Mortimer — for everything."

"And Peter said, 'Not on your life!'?"

"Words to that effect," agreed Katherine, smiling reminiscently. "At any rate he saw the point and we made friends. We write to each other occasionally which keeps us in touch. Of course Sir Mortimer doesn't know; he would be furious with Peter if he knew that we corresponded."

"Sir Mortimer must be an absolute monster!"

"And yet there's something nice about him," said Katherine in a very thoughtful voice. "He was kind to us when we were at Limbourne — really kind — and he liked Simon. If only he were a little less arrogant . . ."

"He must be an unhappy man."

"Yes, unhappy and — and rather lonely. He has nobody to love him, you see." She added, "It's very strange how history repeats itself. Gerald felt that he must leave home and make a career for himself because he wanted to be free; now the same thing has happened again. When Simon was telling me that he couldn't bear to go and live at Limbourne he said, 'I must be free — to breathe'."

MacAslan nodded. "Yes, it's interesting but I think it's quite natural and only to be expected under the circumstances. There are people who can bear to live under the rule of a dictator and there are others who feel they must be free to breathe. One needn't be surprised to find that Gerald's son resembles him."

There was a short silence, but this time it was quite a comfortable silence. Katherine and her visitor had become friends.

At last MacAslan said, "I wonder if you could give me Peter's address, Mrs Maclaren."

"He's in Germany," replied Katherine. "I wrote to him to tell him I was going to marry Alec. It was rather a difficult letter to write but I wanted to tell him about it myself. I had a very friendly letter in reply and a beautiful silk scarf as a present. It was nice of him, wasn't it? I'm afraid I can't remember his address in Germany. If you write to The Naval and Military Club they'll forward the letter."

"Yes, I'll do that."

Katherine offered her guest some more coffee but he shook his head and rose.

"I'm afraid I must go," he said. "Phill will be annoyed if I'm late for lunch. Not that it matters about me, of course, but Hero has four puppies and they get in a frightful state if their mother is out too long."

"They must be darling puppies."

"Yes, they're very attractive, but rather a nuisance," said MacAslan. He added with old-world courtesy, "Thank you very much for your hospitality, Mrs Maclaren. It has been a great pleasure to meet you. I should like to renew my acquaintance with your husband, so if you would care to come across the loch and have lunch with us some day while you're here we shall be delighted to see you."

"It's very kind of you, but I don't quite know —"

"Leave it," said MacAslan smiling. "I had forgotten for the moment that you were honeymooning."

"Oh, it isn't that!"

"Well, never mind. Just do as you like about it. Meanwhile please accept my very best wishes and tell your husband that I shall be delighted if he cares to shoot some birds. They're a bit scarce, and wary, but if he stalks them carefully he might get a brace for the pot."

"Alec didn't bring a gun but I'll tell him what you said and I know he will be very grateful."

They shook hands.

"Good-bye, Mrs Maclaren."

"*Là math leat*, MacAslan," said Katherine. She blushed and added, "Alec taught me to say it last night."

64

MacAslan smiled. "Excellent! He must teach you some more. Come, Hero, we must go home."

3

When MacAslan had gone Katherine helped herself to another cup of coffee; she had talked so much that she had allowed her first cup to get cold. Perhaps she had talked too much — but he had seemed interested in the Wentworth family and had kept on prompting her to tell him more. She could not have refused.

Katherine still had no idea what time it was — why hadn't she asked her visitor? — but as the sun was high in the sky it must be getting on for noon. So far the brownie had not come for his jug and his basket but he might come at any minute so perhaps she had better dress. It would be a pity if she were to frighten the brownie out of his wits. She put on a nylon blouse and a tweed skirt and sat down to watch for him; she had not long to wait. There was no sound of his coming but she saw the small brown figure emerge from the passage with the collie at his heels.

"Good morning," she said. "You're Dugal, aren't you? Mr Maclaren has gone for a walk. I'm Mrs Maclaren."

"Och, I did not be knowing he had a woman!" exclaimed Dugal, taken aback.

Katherine laughed and said, "He hasn't had me very long."

Dugal stood and gazed at her with his chestnut-coloured eyes. He was in every particular exactly as

Alec had described: his rusty hair, his weatherbeaten face and his general appearance of brownness.

"Thank you very much for the milk and the eggs," added Katherine. "It was very kind of you —"

"Och, it iss nothing. It wass a pleasure to be bringing the food."

"It was very, very kind."

"Carstiona iss ferry happy about the blanket. Will you be saying that to Mister Maclaren? Carstiona can be getting a ferry big brown blanket from the second cousin of her brother-in-law that drives the van."

"How nice," said Katherine. She was completely bewildered; what *could* be the connection between the milk and eggs and "a ferry big brown blanket"? However, Dugal was already sidling towards the passage and she had not told him about the jug.

"That's a very beautiful jug," she said. "You shouldn't have brought the milk in it, Dugal."

"It iss the best we have got, Mistress Maclaren."

Katherine was so touched by the simple explanation that for a moment she could not speak.

"It was because of the blanket," added Dugal, as if that explained all.

"But, Dugal, it's a *valuable* jug. It's worth a great deal of money."

He nodded. "I am knowing that. There wass two men came up the glen — it would be a week ago or more — and they wass wanting to buy the chug for five pounds. When Carstiona wass saying no they wass offering seven pounds for the chug . . . but Carstiona wass not wanting to sell it so they went away. The big

66

one wass saying they would come back another time and Carstiona wass to think about it."

"They were trying to cheat you!" exclaimed Katherine indignantly.

"The chug is worth more than seven pounds?"

"Much more. Mr Maclaren says it is worth a lot of money. You must never sell it to people like that. If you want to sell it you must tell Mr Maclaren and he will send it to — to a big place in London where they sell very valuable things."

"To London?" asked Dugal incredulously.

"Yes. Mr Maclaren will do it for you and see that you get enough money for it. Do you understand, Dugal?"

He nodded. It was easy to understand Mistress Maclaren; she spoke slowly and used simple words. "It iss ferry kind of Mister Maclaren to be taking the trouble. I will be telling Carstiona, but it iss in my mind that she iss not wanting to sell the chug whateffer. It hass been belonging in her family a long, long time."

"That's right," agreed Katherine nodding. "She ought to keep it, but tell her to keep it very carefully. You see, it's perfect. I mean there are no chips or cracks. If there were one tiny chip in the jug it wouldn't be nearly so valuable."

She looked at him to see if he had understood and saw that he had. He took the jug off the shelf very carefully indeed.

"Tell Carstiona to put it away safely," she added.

"I will be telling her . . . but we are not using the chug in the house, Mistress Maclaren. Carstiona iss

67

keeping it wrapped in a shawl in the big kist. It wass chust because of the blanket that I wass bringing the milk in it to-day." With which enigmatic statement Dugal vanished through the passage and was gone.

CHAPTER
FIVE

1

The Maclarens were very happy in their mountain fastness; the weather was kind and day succeeded day with bright sunshine and westerly breezes. Every morning a jug of milk — a plain white jug — and a few eggs appeared as if by magic in their larder. Sometimes when Dugal called to fetch the jug they saw him and chatted to him; in this way they learned a good deal about the district. Katherine had been told about "the ferry big brown blanket" so she felt able to accept Dugal's offerings without feeling too beholden to him.

One morning when they had been living in the cave for nearly a week Alec suggested that they should take their lunch and picnic upon the small island in the middle of the loch which long ago had been the dwelling place of the MacAslan family. Dugal had assured them that it was well worth seeing . . . in fact Dugal was so eager for them to see the ruins of the old castle that he told them about it every time he spoke to them. He had offered several times to row them across to the island and show them round.

"We shall have no peace until we've seen it," said Alec with a smile.

Katherine laughed and agreed. The brownie, having taken them under his wing, was anxious that their stay at Ardfalloch should be thoroughly enjoyable. He was benevolence itself.

Dugal was not visible when they walked down to the loch but he had made them free of his boat, which was lying moored to the little jetty, so they got in and pushed off.

It was a day of golden sunshine, there was scarcely a breath of wind, but Ardfalloch is a sea-loch and, although apparently surrounded by hills, it has an outlet to the western ocean. For this reason the water is never completely calm; there is always a slight movement in it. The water is salt, of course, but so clear that in shallow places one can see little shells on the bottom and seaweed moving lazily and tiny darting fish.

On this particular morning there was more movement than usual in the clear water; the tide was beginning to flow. Here and there, on the shore, a tiny wave splashed feebly or ran along the side of a rock in a silver undulation.

Katherine pointed this out to Alec.

"There's no wind here," he replied. "But there must be a swell in the sea. It's beautiful, isn't it?"

"Beautiful," echoed Katherine with a sigh of bliss.

Dugal's boat was an old tub, he used it "for the fishing," it was heavy to row but there was no hurry so Alec did not exert himself unduly; he could row and watch Katherine sitting in the stern; he could see that she was completely happy which was all that mattered.

Dugal had told them where to land so they beached the old boat on the north side of the island and made the painter fast to a convenient stump. Then they took their lunch-basket and walked up the grassy slope.

The island was warm and peaceful, the sun streamed down upon the green grass and trees and bushes and upon the ruins of the castle. The huge tumbled stones were covered with ivy and patches of yellow lichen.

They chose a sheltered hollow in which to have their lunch and, leaving the basket, went to explore. In the outer courtyard was a deep well, the sides were uneven and covered with brown fungus and pale green ferns. Far down they could see the glimmer of water.

"A fresh spring," said Katherine in surprise.

"It would have to be," Alec replied. "Rather wonderful when you think of it, but they couldn't have lived here without fresh water." He took her hand and added, "Don't lean on the wall, it doesn't look safe."

They went through an archway into the great hall, which was roofless. Two huge oak-trees overhung the thick walls so that the sunshine fell on the uneven stone floor in flickers of golden light. The ruined windows were masked with thick growths of ivy which made the place dim and mysterious.

Alec said in a low voice, "Look at the thickness of the walls. It must have been an impregnable fortress in the old days."

Katherine shivered, partly because it was cold and damp in the ruined hall and partly because there was

71

something eerie about it. "It's terribly sad," she said. "It's like a — like a dead giant. Let's go out into the sunshine."

"Just a minute. I want to explore."

Katherine did not want to explore the bones of the dead giant so she went out to the sheltered place where they had left the basket and sat down on the soft turf. It was some time before Alec joined her.

"This place is frightfully interesting," he said. "It's a huge place, far bigger than I thought. I found part of a staircase and there are stone passages — all ruined, of course — but I discovered a large room at one end of the castle where the roof has been mended; there's a fireplace with logs ready for lighting and a big oak settle. Perhaps MacAslan comes here sometimes and dreams about his ancestors."

"It would be all right for him," said Katherine. "He's one of the family. I feel we aren't welcome here."

"I had the same feeling," admitted Alec. "But we're friends of the family — I mean we feel friendly towards them. An enemy of the MacAslans would get short shrift. If you feel uncomfortable about it we can have lunch somewhere else."

"Would it be silly to have lunch in the boat?"

Alec did not think it would be silly so they returned to the boat and had their lunch afloat in the calm water.

As they were now within sight of Ardfalloch House they decided that this would be a good opportunity to call on their landlord. It was only polite in view of the fact that they were camping on his ground and he had asked them to lunch. The house looked quite near, on

72

the south side of the loch, but a breeze had sprung up so it was a hard pull for Alec.

"Never mind," he said. "We had better do it to-day; then it will be done. We needn't stay long and the wind will blow us home."

All the same he was glad when they reached the shelter of the jetty where MacAslan kept his boats. There was a motor-launch and a sailing-skiff and an old rowing-boat tied up to the little pier.

The house lay in a small strath, all about it were pinewoods; in front ran a burn, dropping from pool to pool with a splashing sound. There was a bridge across the burn and the two visitors stood here for a few moments.

Ardfalloch House was built of grey stone, with high windows and a close-fitting roof; not a beautiful house but thoroughly sound and in harmony with its surroundings.

"It looks friendly and comfortable," remarked Katherine. "Dugal said they built this house when there was no further need to protect themselves from their enemies. They must have been glad to leave the castle."

"This certainly is much more convenient, but they must have had regrets when they said good-bye to their old fastness which had been their home for hundreds of years."

2

The front-door bell of Ardfalloch House was of wrought-iron. Alec pulled it and they heard it jangling

73

in the distance; the door was opened by a young girl in a white apron who showed them into the drawing-room.

To Katherine the house seemed different from other houses . . . though in what way she could not have explained. The hall was wide with a bare, polished wooden floor; there were several stags' heads on the walls; the drawing-room was beautifully proportioned. There were a few good pieces of furniture in it, a sofa covered with faded cretonne, and several easy-chairs. Here, too, the floor was of polished wood with a large and very beautiful Persian rug near the fireplace. The whole effect was spacious and uncluttered — not exactly a comfortable room but quiet and dignified.

"No electric light," said Alec in a low voice. "Just lamps. That's funny, isn't it? They could make it so easily with power from the burn."

Katherine was about to reply when the door opened and a girl came in, followed by four puppies.

"Oh, how do you do," she said. "Daddy is out, I'm afraid, but I expect he'll be back soon. I'm Phil."

They shook hands and Katherine said, "We're Mr and Mrs Maclaren."

"I know," said Phil, nodding. "You're camping. Daddy told me about you. I've always wanted to camp but Daddy won't let me camp by myself — or with Gregor. He's my brother. We have a half-brother, called Richard, who is much older but he's in Canada. Richard has promised to go camping with me when he comes home. You're camping in the cave, aren't you? I've never seen it, but I've heard about it, of course."

"The cave is lovely," Katherine told her.

"I've tried to find it several times," said Phil.

Alec smiled and said, " 'It's a ferry secret place.' Dugal was quite worried when I told him that I knew about it."

"How did you find it?" asked Phil eagerly.

While Alec was explaining how he had found the cave, Katherine had time to look at their hostess. She was like her father, Katherine thought. She was as slender and graceful as a silver birch and really beautiful, with dark curls and hazel eyes and a smooth skin tanned by the sun, but unlike her father she was vivacious and full of life — as friendly and natural as the puppies which were tumbling on the floor.

"They're Hero's puppies, aren't they?" said Katherine, looking at them in amusement.

"Oh goodness! They oughtn't to be here," exclaimed Phil. "Please, Mr Maclaren, catch that one for me. Janet would be livid! They still make pools occasionally . . . but they *will* follow me wherever I go, especially when their mother is out."

Alec went on his knees and caught the puppy while Phil managed to gather up the other three.

"Oh, thank you," she said. "Tea is nearly ready. We don't have it here unless it's a party. Daddy's study is so much cosier. You don't mind, do you?"

"We just called," said Katherine. "I'm afraid we can't stay for tea."

"Oh, but you must!" she cried. "You can't go away without having tea. Daddy will be coming and I know he wants to talk to Mr Maclaren."

"Are you sure?"

"Of course I'm sure. Daddy said he had asked you to lunch, but he didn't think you would come because you were quite happy by yourselves."

The Maclarens looked at each other and smiled.

"Yes," admitted Katherine. "But it was so kind of your father, and we're enjoying ourselves so much that we wanted to thank him."

"And there's something I want to speak to him about," added Alec.

"Then you must stay and see him," said Phil, nodding.

They followed her across the hall and down a short passage to a shabby comfortable room lined with bookcases. There was a round table laid for tea; an oak desk stood in the corner; a peat fire with a black kettle sitting on it flickered in the open hearth.

"It's in an awful mess," said Phil apologetically. "When Daddy and I are alone we use this room for *everything* and neither of us is very tidy. Of course if I'd known you were coming I'd have had tea in the drawing-room." She dumped the puppies into a big basket and rushed round putting things to rights, clearing a pile of books off a chair and shaking up the cushions.

Alec had sat down near the basket and was looking at the puppies. "They're beautiful little creatures," he said.

"Yes, they're very well-bred. Miss Finlay of Cluan gave me Hero and we mated her with a very good dog. Miss Finlay is my godmother; she's going to help me to sell the puppies. I want a lot of money for them. It's horrid to be poor, isn't it?"

"Horrid," agreed Katherine fervently . . . but the MacAslans were not poor, of course, not really poor. They owned mountains and rivers and the house was full of beautiful things.

"That's one reason why it was so silly to send me to school," explained Phil. "It was terribly expensive and I hated it and Daddy was lonely all by himself. It's silly to spend a lot of money and make two people miserable."

"Everybody has to go to school," said Alec smiling.

"No," said Phil, shaking her head. "I had a governess for years and it worked very well. Then people began worrying Daddy and telling him that he ought to send me to school — so at last he did. I stuck it for one term but I refused to go back after the holidays. I refused point-blank. I'm fifteen, but I look older, don't I? You thought I was older didn't you, Mrs Maclaren?"

Katherine smiled and nodded. It was not so much that she looked older but that she seemed older. Phil was no gawky adolescent, she was a finished person.

"Education is important," said Alec.

"Oh, I agree," declared Phil. "Education is very important indeed, but being with Daddy is a much better education than a girls' school. Did you go to school, Mrs Maclaren? Did you like it?"

"I didn't enjoy my first term."

"Oh, I see what you mean! But I don't think I should ever have got used to it. The girls were so childish. That was one of the things I couldn't stand. You see when Mummy died — three years ago — poor Daddy was so terribly lonely and miserable that I had to grow up quickly and be a companion to him. It wasn't easy at

77

first but if there's something you want to do and you try your very hardest you can do it. Don't you agree?"

"Yes, I do," said Katherine who had learnt the truth of this from experience (and although she had been acquainted with Miss MacAslan for less than half an hour it was obvious that she was of the kind who could accomplish practically anything if she gave her mind to it).

"I did it in various ways," said Phil thoughtfully. "Fortunately Miss Donaldson was no good at Latin so I asked Daddy to teach me. That was a beginning. I didn't enjoy it at first, and neither did he, but soon we both got interested. We still read Latin together . . . and I read all the books that Daddy gets from the library so that we can talk about them. He likes biography and travel. I'm not an ignoramus, Mr Maclaren."

"I never thought you were," said Alec hastily. "I just thought — I mean most girls like school."

She laughed. " 'Your schooldays are the happiest days of your life'? Well, if that's true I must be different from other girls."

The kettle on the hearth was boiling, sending out puffs of steam, so Phil knelt down with the tea-pot in her hand and made tea very efficiently. "We always make tea ourselves," she told them. "It saves Janet a lot of trouble. Janet is old and we can't afford to give her much help. Besides she's a Lowland woman and doesn't get on well with Highland girls — she has no patience with them — which makes things a bit awkward. That's another reason why it was senseless to send me to school. I'm the only person who can oil the wheels and keep the house running smoothly. Poor Daddy nearly went mad with all the bother."

They sat down round the table and ate exceedingly good scones and greengage jam.

"What else do you do, Miss MacAslan?" asked Alec, who was always interested in people's doings.

"Call me Phil — everybody does," said Phil smiling. "My real name is Philomela; it's a family name which belonged to a great-great-grandmother. What do I do? Well, I do so many things, but the most important is looking after Daddy. I practise singing and playing the piano and I do a little cooking and rifle-shooting. I try to keep Janet from upsetting the girls and I read a lot, of course. Sometimes I go with Daddy to Inverness in the car and sometimes I take the boat and go to lunch with my godmother at Cluan. Whenever I have time I visit some of the women who live in very isolated places; for instance Carstiona MacFadyen."

"She's Dugal's wife, isn't she?" asked Katherine. "Ought we to go and see her?"

"Well, I don't know," Phil replied doubtfully. "She's terribly shy with strangers and her English is very poor, so perhaps it wouldn't be much use. It's rather a problem, really."

"You mean the language problem?" asked Alec.

"Yes. Of course there aren't many people nowadays who can't get on pretty well in English. The children learn to speak it at school, but people like Carstiona, who live at the back of beyond, never hear it spoken so they forget all they learnt."

"What about wireless?"

"Hopeless," said Phil. "It's terribly bad because of the hills; besides if you aren't very good at a language it's a bother trying to listen. You would think it was dull, wouldn't you? But Carstiona is perfectly happy doing her work and thinking her own thoughts. You see she's so much alone that she has plenty of time to think, and all sorts of strange ideas come into her mind. Carstiona is fey."

Alec said, "I've often wondered what that means — exactly."

"Fey? Well, it's a bit difficult to explain in plain English. There's a thick curtain which veils the future from most people but in Carstiona's case the curtain is thin . . . and there are holes in it."

"I think you've explained it very well," said Alec. "It must be rather uncomfortable. I'm glad my curtain is thick and solid."

"Yes, it isn't a good thing to be fey." Phil hesitated and then added, "Of course we're all inclined to be fey but if you keep your mind busy you can prevent it from bothering you. Oh, there's Daddy!" she cried, jumping up. "Will you excuse me for a minute while I run and tell him you're here?"

3

The Maclarens had heard no sound of their host's arrival at Ardfalloch House — Phil had been on the alert. However, they sat and waited until Phil reappeared with her father and Hero. Immediately all was confusion: the four puppies came tumbling out of the basket and rushed to greet their mother, yapping and whining. Hero barked and frisked about playfully. The room seemed full of dogs.

"Catch them!" cried Phil. "Oh, Hero, don't be silly! Come here at once, you bad girl! Daddy, quick, there's one under the desk! Oh, thank you, Mrs Maclaren! Put him into the basket."

At last the puppies were all caught and put back into the basket with their mother . . . and there was peace.

"Really, Phil," said MacAslan. "This place is like a bear-garden. You should keep the puppies in the gun-room."

"Oh no, Daddy! It would be so dull for the poor darlings. If they feel dull they chew the carpet and Janet gets cross."

"This is a nice way to treat guests!"

"You needn't talk!" exclaimed Phil. "You haven't said how-do-you-do to Mr and Mrs Maclaren."

As they had all been crawling about on the floor trying to catch the wriggling balls of golden silk the etiquette of greeting had been forgotten but, having been reminded of his manners, MacAslan laughed and shook hands.

"Better late than never," he said. "How do you do? It was very good of you to come, especially as it must have meant a long hard row in Dugal's tub. If you had let me know I would have come for you in the launch."

"The exercise was good for me."

"Are you an oarsman?"

"No, cricket was my game and now it's golf. We stopped at the island on the way. As a matter of fact we intended to have lunch there."

"Why didn't you?"

Alec hesitated.

"Because I was silly," said Katherine.

"I find that difficult to believe."

There was a short silence. Then Katherine said, "I had a curious sort of feeling that we weren't welcome, that's all."

While they were talking Phil had been making a fresh pot of tea.

She turned and said, "Oh Daddy, do you remember those people who camped on the island?"

"That was different," replied her father frowning at her and shaking his head. "They weren't our friends . . . if people are so foolish as to climb about in a tumble-down ruin they have only themselves to blame if they get hurt."

Katherine would have liked to ask how and when and why, but MacAslan changed the conversation abruptly by asking if they liked living in the cave and whether they were able to get supplies of food. "We could let you have some eggs, couldn't we, Phil?" he added.

"Dugal has been very kind to us," said Alec. "He has brought us milk and eggs every morning."

"I gathered that you had been very kind to Dugal. There was some talk of a big brown blanket — if I remember rightly."

82

"Oh, I gave him a little present, that's all. I wanted to talk to you about Dugal. The first morning he brought us milk in a Limoges jug. It's a valuable jug and we told him so. He had no idea of its value."

"Do you mean really valuable?"

"It's a collector's piece, quite perfect."

"That's interesting."

"I've seen it," put in Phil. "Carstiona showed it to me one day; it's her greatest treasure. She keeps it in her oak kist wrapped up in an old shawl. It's a beautiful jug but I didn't know it was really valuable."

Katherine said, "Two men came up the glen the other day and wanted to buy it. Dugal told me that they offered seven pounds for it and when Carstiona refused to sell it they said they would come back. I told Dugal that they mustn't sell it to people like that."

"They mustn't sell it," Alec declared emphatically. "If they want to sell the jug, Dugal must let me know and I'll see he gets the proper price for it. The only thing is I wondered if he would be able to write to me."

"Not very easily," replied MacAslan. "In any case he would probably be too shy to make the attempt. If they want to sell the jug they must tell me and I can write to you. It's most kind of you to take the trouble."

"I should hate him to be cheated," said Alec frankly. "It makes my blood boil when I think of the way dealers go about the country picking up valuable furniture and pewter and china for half nothing and making hundreds on the transactions."

"You don't mean Dugal's jug is worth hundreds?" asked MasAslan incredulously.

"Quite honestly, I don't know; but I should be surprised if it isn't worth a good deal of money."

"I'm sure Carstiona won't sell it," said Phil. "It's an heirloom — and she has a 'feeling' about it. She would think it would bring ill-fortune if she were to sell it . . . but, oh Daddy, I've just thought! We've got some old furniture and china and all sorts of things in the attic — things we never use — why don't we sell them and make lots of money?"

"There's nothing of any value in the attic."

"How do you know?" asked Phil eagerly. "You haven't been up there for years — and even if you looked at it you wouldn't know whether it was valuable or not. Mr Maclaren knows about things like that."

Alec denied this hastily. "I'm afraid I don't. I just happened to know about the jug because I'd seen one very like it before. If you wanted an opinion about old furniture it would be essential to get an expert; a thoroughly reliable man who would give you an estimate of its worth."

"There's nothing in the attic except junk," said MacAslan. The subject was closed but Katherine had seen Phil's look of determination and felt certain that it would be reopened later.

They talked about various other matters; Alec asked his host if he had ever considered using hydraulic power to make electricity.

"Yes, I've thought of it," replied MacAslan. "I let this place for a month every summer and I could let it more easily if we had electricity."

"It would be lovely!" cried Phil. "We could have a deep freeze and a vacuum cleaner and all sorts of gorgeous things."

"The trouble is that it would cost a great deal of money."

"It shouldn't if the burn has a good fall," said Alec. "I went into the matter some years ago, when my sister thought of putting it into her cottage at Loch Ron, but unfortunately the burn wasn't suitable."

"Does the cottage still belong to your sister?" asked MacAslan.

"No, it belongs to Katherine," replied Alec smiling at his wife.

"It's a dear little cottage," Katherine said. "Alec's sister lent it to me for the summer holidays. The children and I had a very happy time there and I liked it so much that Alec bought it and gave it to me. We mean to come there for week-ends and for the holidays. Alec is fond of fishing."

"That's Crag an Ron, isn't it?" said Phil. "Some people called Mitchell had it for a month last summer. The Mitchells were an awful nuisance."

"Phil!" exclaimed her father warningly.

"Well, they were," declared Phil. "You know they were, Daddy. Mr Mitchell asked you to give him some shooting — straight out, just like that. You were soft enough to say yes."

"What else could I say?"

"You could have said no," Phil pointed out. "You wished afterwards that you'd said no, because he brought three untrained dogs with him and they wrecked your day."

"Only half the day."

"Yes," agreed Phil, nodding. "I remember now. One of them got a few pellets into him and Mr Mitchell had to take him to the vet at Inverquill. It was an accident, of course."

She waited until her elders had finished laughing and then added, "You didn't laugh so much at the time, Daddy."

"You were just as soft as I was," retorted her father. "Mrs Mitchell asked you to tea — and you accepted. When the day came you were as cross as a bear at having to go."

Phil chuckled. "We were both soft, but you're older than I am so you ought to have more sense."

As they had finished tea by this time the two men went off together to have a look at the burn.

"Oh, I do hope it will be all right," said Phil. "It would be so marvellous to have a deep freeze. I expect you've got all sorts of electrical appliances in your house, Mrs Maclaren. You live in Edinburgh, don't you?"

For a few minutes they talked about various gadgets which were obtainable to make life easier for the housewife. Then Katherine asked what had happened to the people who camped on the island; she had been longing to know the whole story.

"It was a party of men and women," replied Phil. "Awful people! Daddy keeps some food in tins in a cupboard in the tower-room and sometimes when he

86

goes to the island he makes a fire and cooks himself a meal. He keeps a bottle of whisky there too. None of our people would touch it, of course, but these awful people found the cupboard, helped themselves to the food and finished the bottle of whisky. Then they put the empty bottle on a rock and threw stones at it and smashed it to bits."

"How frightful!"

"Yes, wasn't it? There was broken glass all over the place . . . but that wasn't all. They had a gramophone with them and played jazz; we could hear them screaming and yelling like lunatics. Daddy and Donald and some of the other men were very angry. You see the castle is very special. It was the home of our family for hundreds of years so it means a lot to us."

"Didn't your father go and turn them out?"

"He meant to go over in the morning and take some of the men, but there was no need. The people left in a hurry in the middle of the night. We never heard exactly what happened but Donald's cousin lives at Inverquill and he told Donald that two men had been brought into the hospital. One had a broken leg and the other had 'head injuries' — and, can you believe it, Mrs Maclaren? — they blamed Daddy for having an 'unsafe ruin' on his estate." She paused and then added, "The dear old castle did it on purpose."

"Of course."

Phil looked at her in surprise. "You think so too?"

"I'm sure of it. We didn't misbehave ourselves, but all the same . . . well, I just felt . . . unwelcome."

"I'll take you some day, Mrs Maclaren. It would be all right if you came with me."

Katherine did not reply. She had no desire to revisit the old castle either with or without a member of the MacAslan family.

Presently a tall thin old woman came in to clear away the tea.

"This is Janet, Mrs Maclaren," said Phil. "Janet is part of Ardfalloch, she has been here longer than Daddy. Haven't you, Janet?"

"I was here before he was born," admitted Janet. "I came to Ardfalloch when MacAslan's grandmother was alive and I've been here ever since. There's been times when I've wearied to get home to my own folk but I've never managed it."

"You love us too much," said Phil.

"Well, maybe," admitted Janet with a little smile. "But I've a lot to put up with. Will Mr and Mrs Maclaren be staying for their supper?"

"Oh yes!" cried Phil eagerly. "You'll stay to supper, won't you, Mrs Maclaren? We don't call it dinner because we just have a simple meal in the evening, but to-night we've got lovely fresh mackerel."

"There's enough and to spare," said Janet hospitably.

"It's very kind of you, but I'm afraid we must go back — and we ought to start soon. We've a long way to go and the boat is rather heavy."

"Oh, we'll take you home! That goes without saying. We can take you in the launch and tow Dugal's boat. It will be quite easy. Please stay; it's so nice for Daddy to have a man like Mr Maclaren to talk to."

Katherine was doubtful. She did not know whether Alec would want to accept the invitation; he had said that they must not stay too long.

"We'll go up to the burn and see what they're doing, shall we?" asked Phil.

Obviously she was eager to go — she had set her heart on having electricity — so they went out together and found the two men examining a small waterfall.

"I'm not an engineer but I should think it could be done fairly easily," Alec was saying. "The fall seems good and it isn't far from the house. I can't tell you what it would cost. The house would have to be wired."

"I'm afraid it's a pipe-dream," said MacAslan regretfully. "It takes me all my time to keep my property in order."

"It would *save* money," declared Phil. "Really it would. If we had a deep-freeze cabinet we could buy things when they were cheap and they wouldn't go bad."

"And what would a deep-freeze cabinet cost?" asked her father. "No, Phil, it's out of the question."

Katherine was about to suggest that she and Alec must go home when she discovered that Alec had received an invitation to stay to supper and, subject to her approval, had accepted it. This being so there was no need to hurry back and they walked on together through the pine-woods and up the hill behind the house. There was a beautiful view from here. The loch lay before their eyes, deep blue, with little ripples glinting in the sunshine. In the middle of the loch lay the island like an emerald-green gem.

Katherine was surprised to see that Ardfalloch House was not as isolated as she had imagined; on this side of the loch there was a perfectly good road which wound along eastwards to a village and beyond that to a larger village which boasted a church and a little station.

"The small village is Ardfalloch and the big one is Balnafin," said Phil. "Yes, there's a church and a railway. We don't know how long there will be a railway, of course. Look, Mrs Maclaren," she added, pointing to a large white building on the other side of the loch. "That's Cluan Lodge where my godmother lives. I told you about her, didn't I? Her father died some years ago; he was very rich so everything at Cluan is in perfect order. There's a lovely garden, very sheltered; they can grow all sorts of wonderful plants. People come from far and wide to see it."

"They have very good salmon fishing in the river," added MacAslan.

"What is it like here in winter?" asked Alec.

"Everybody asks that!" exclaimed Phil laughing. "Janet would say, 'Whiles it's bad and whiles it's worse.' But last winter it was lovely; there was deep snow and sunshine for weeks on end."

"Phil spent most of her time ski-ing," put in her father.

"I love it," said Phil nodding. "It's like flying — terribly thrilling. Sometimes we have bad storms. You wouldn't think so to-day, would you? They come quite suddenly; the wind howls and screeches and lashes the

90

loch into an absolute frenzy. There's something rather thrilling about that, too."

"A bit too thrilling," said MacAslan dryly. "Last winter we had a frightful storm and I lost several hundred young pines which were just reaching maturity." He glanced at his watch and added, "We're having supper early; I know you will want to get back to your primitive abode before dark."

The Maclarens were given an excellent supper of fresh-caught mackerel and apple-pie and were taken back to their "primitive abode" by their host and hostess in the motor-launch. By the time they started, the sun had begun to sink behind the western mountains amongst a flotilla of small white clouds.

MacAslan was steering, Katherine was sitting beside him in the stern.

She said, "How beautiful and peaceful it is!"

"Yes. I've travelled a good deal — my wife was fond of travelling — but I never saw any place more beautiful than Ardfalloch. I admit I'm not entirely unprejudiced."

"Ardfalloch belongs to you, so naturally —"

"I belong to Ardfalloch," he replied. "I belong to the hills and the moors and the mountains — but perhaps most of all to the people. There's something about this feeling of 'belonging' that I find difficult to explain." He added in a different tone, "I hope you will come and stay with us some day. Your husband might like some shooting and it's good for Phil to have company. I feel a little worried about Phil."

"Why are you worried?"

"Everybody told me I should send her to school but it wasn't a success. Poor Phil was miserable. She absolutely refused to go back when the holidays were over. I'm afraid I've spoilt Phil a little; she has been such a wonderful companion."

"She's happy here — and useful."

"It's good to be happy and useful, I agree; but it isn't a normal life for a girl. My friend and neighbour, Meg Finlay, is very angry with me; she says I'm selfish. She says Phil is too old for her age and never has any fun." He sighed and added, "Of course I realise that Phil ought to mix with other young people, but how can I manage it?"

"Would you like to come and stay with us for Christmas?" The invitation came out involuntarily. Katherine was amazed when she heard herself offering it. She was even more amazed when she saw that MasAslan was considering it seriously.

"It's very kind of you," he said. "Do you really mean it, Mrs Maclaren?"

"Of course I mean it! Perhaps Alec told you that our house is at Barnton, near Edinburgh. Simon will be home for the holidays and we know quite a lot of young people so there will be parties. Phil would enjoy that, wouldn't she?"

"I'm sure she would. The fact is I have been thinking about plans for Christmas. Usually we're all at home together but this year my stepson is in Canada and my son, Gregor, has been asked to go to Switzerland with a school-friend so it would be a very dull Christmas for Phil at Ardfalloch. I thought Phil and I might go to a hotel for a few days (I intended to ask Meg Finlay where we should go) but if you really think you could put up with us it would be much better in every way. It would be delightful. May I think about it and let you know later?"

"Think about it and talk it over with Phil. We should love to have you. It will be fun to have lots of children in the house for the Christmas festivities."

"Lots of children?" asked MacAslan in surprise.

"The twins," Katherine explained. "They're seven years old and rather stirring; when they get excited there seems to be more than two of them — if you see what I mean — but the house is quite big and you can retire to Alec's study if you want a little peace."

MacAslan laughed and said he was used to children; Phil was quiet when she was alone but when she and Gregor got going there seemed to be more than two of them in the house.

CHAPTER
SIX

1

The MacAslans landed their guests at the jetty where
Dugal kept his boat. They parted with many
expressions of good will. Phil said she wished she could
see the cave so her father promised to bring her on
Saturday morning for a cup of coffee. Alec and
Katherine stood on the jetty and waved as the launch
turned and sped off down the loch.

It was getting dark now, but there was still enough
reflected light in the clear sky for the cave-dwellers to
find their way home. They walked up the hill
arm-in-arm, talking about all that had happened.

"They're delightful, aren't they?" Alec said. "I was
thinking all the time what a beautiful relationship it is:
father and daughter in perfect harmony. It was fun to
see them teasing each other." He sighed and added,
"My father didn't bother much about me."

"I don't remember mine," said Katherine. "I didn't
really miss my parents because I never knew them —
and Aunt Liz was such a tower of strength — but I
quite agree that the MacAslans have something very
precious and wonderful. I'm glad you think them

delightful because I've done a most extraordinary thing."

"What have you done?"

"Asked them to come to The Cedars for Christmas."

"What!" exclaimed Alec in amazement.

"I know," said Katherine apologetically. "It was quite mad, wasn't it? The invitation popped out before I knew what I was saying."

"They won't come."

"I think they will. He said he would think it over. Do you mind awfully, Alec?"

"I don't mind at all. It's just — just surprising. Somehow I can't imagine MacAslan anywhere except here. I like him immensely and we have a great deal in common so I expect we should get on all right. Why do they want to come to Edinburgh for Christmas?"

Katherine told him. She was very much relieved to find that Alec was pleased at the prospect of the MacAslans' visit.

The following day was Thursday. Alec and Katherine had been camping in the cave for a week; although Alec had brought quantities of food their supplies were getting low, so on Thursday morning they took the car and returned to the main road. Here they found a village where they could buy all they needed: meat and vegetables and potatoes and a large stock of groceries. Katherine thought they were buying far too much, but as Alec pointed out, the road to Dugal's quarry was in such a deplorable condition that it was better to have enough food to last until they were going home.

"You aren't tired of being a troglodyte, are you?" asked Alec.

Katherine laughed and shook her head. "Let's stay another week if the weather lasts. It wouldn't be much fun if it rained."

"It isn't going to rain," said Alec.

"The glass is steady," agreed the grocer who had become intensely interested in the affairs of his customers.

All this took time; it was nearly one o'clock when they had finished their purchases and as there was a small fishing hotel in the village — highly recommended by the grocer — they decided to have lunch before returning to the cave. Katherine noticed a telephone-box in the hall so after lunch she rang up Aunt Liz and was reassured to hear that the twins were well and happy and had gone back to school.

She returned to the lounge where Alec was sitting and told him her news. The lounge was a somewhat dreary apartment but as it was empty except for themselves they were able to talk freely.

"That's good," said Alec. "Did you tell Aunt Liz we were camping?"

"No, she thinks we're at Gleneagles, but it doesn't matter. I can ring her up again in a few days. There's sure to be a telephone at Balnafin and we can go across in Dugal's boat. Hadn't you better ring up Ellen?"

"Perhaps I should."

Alec was away a long time . . . at least it seemed long to Katherine. She sat at the window looking out at the garden; a garden full of scrubby yellow grass interspersed with mossy paths and flower-beds choked with weeds. There are few sights more depressing than a neglected garden. She had just decided that she could bear it no longer and had risen to go and look for Alec when he returned.

It was obvious that he had received bad news. "Alec, what's the matter?" she exclaimed in alarm.

"Zilla," he replied grimly. "Zilla is in London. She rang up Ellen last night and said she was coming home on Saturday and Ellen was to have everything ready for her."

"I thought she was going to New Zealand to stay with your cousins?"

"So she was; I booked a stateroom for her. Now she has changed her mind. She told Ellen she wasn't going to New Zealand, she was 'coming home'."

"I expect she just meant that she was coming back to The Cedars to collect some of her things. The Cedars has been her home for five years, so —"

"It isn't her home any more," said Alec, subsiding into a chair as if every bit of strength had gone out of him.

"Of course not! She doesn't want to live at The Cedars; she never liked it — she said so over and over again. She intended to go to New Zealand for six months and then come back and find a flat in London. That's what she wanted."

Alec did not seem to be listening. He said, "The Cedars was her home for five years — nearly six — and she made it almost intolerable. She complained about everything; she said it was dull and dreary; she said the weather was wretched; she nagged me until I nearly went mad. She nagged Ellen too. I don't know why Ellen stood it."

"She stood it because she's devoted to you."

"I bore it all," Alec continued miserably. "I bore it because I thought she was ill. If ever I did anything that displeased her she threw one of those heart attacks and frightened me out of my wits. Then the doctor told me there was nothing the matter with Zilla's heart; it was all put on to make me do as she wanted. Hysteromania, he called it."

"I know, darling," agreed Katherine. "You had a frightful time with her, but it's over now. Zilla will find a flat in London. She's just coming back to The Cedars to collect her things." Katherine spoke calmly and with conviction but she did not feel calm or convinced; Zilla was an unknown quantity, she changed her mind from one moment to another; you never knew what she would do next.

"Perhaps you're right," said Alec doubtfully. "She certainly said she wanted a flat in London and asked if she could have some furniture from The Cedars; of course I told her she could." He walked to the end of the room and back.

"What else did Ellen say?" asked Katherine.

"She said a lot. She was in an awful state of fuss. Zilla had no idea that we were married and Ellen didn't dare to tell her!"

"What? But you wrote to Zilla and told her!"

"Of course I did. I wrote to the address she gave me in Biarritz and told her we were going to be married —

and all about it — but apparently she never got the letter."

Katherine gazed at him in dismay.

"Poor Ellen didn't know what to do," continued Alec. "You see Zilla asked to speak to me on the phone, so Ellen just said I was on holiday somewhere in the north, and she didn't know my address . . . which was perfectly true as far as it went. Ellen says there's a letter from Zilla waiting for me at The Cedars; it came last week but she didn't know where to send it."

"Alec, how frightful! Zilla will be furious."

"I know," he agreed. "It isn't my fault, of course — I wrote and told her — but that won't count with Zilla. We shall have to go home. I told Ellen we would come to-morrow."

"There's nothing else to be done," agreed Katherine. She said it regretfully for she had been looking forward to another peaceful week, alone with Alec, "lost to the world" in the little sanctuary amongst the hills. Now the world with all its cares and worries was crowding in upon them and, although they might return some day, it would never be quite the same.

"All that food!" said Alec. "I ought to have rung up Ellen before we bought it, but I never thought . . ."

"The food doesn't matter, we can give it to Dugal and his wife, it will be just the right sort of present for them. Don't worry, Alec. It's unfortunate that we've got to go home to-morrow but it isn't a major disaster."

Alec tried to smile. "It will be all the same a hundred years hence — is that what you mean?"

"It will be all the same a year hence," she replied. "Let's face the disappointment as cheerfully as we can and think of what we must do. We shall have to start early to-morrow morning so we had better stop at Dugal's cottage on the way back to the cave and give them the food."

"We shall have to let the MacAslans know. Phil will be very disappointed about Saturday."

"Yes, I'm afraid so," agreed Katherine. She sat down at the writing-table and added, "I'll write to her now. Dugal can take the letter to Ardfalloch House."

Alec watched her. Yes, this was the proper way to treat a disappointment: to accept it and get on with the job. He thought of his sister — she was very much on his mind at the moment — Zilla would have moaned and groaned and bewailed her fate and made herself and everybody else miserable. He said, more cheerfully, "I'll go and get the car. I'd better fill up with petrol and check the tyres for to-morrow's run."

2

Dugal was out when they called at the cottage; they were received politely by Mrs Dugal who resembled a small brown mouse. Katherine put the letter on the chimney-piece and explained slowly and clearly that Dugal was to take it to Ardfalloch House to-morrow morning. Meanwhile Alec carried in the parcels and packets and paper-bags and stacked them on the kitchen table.

"That iss for uss?" asked Carstiona incredulously.

Katherine nodded, "We thought it would be useful for you and Dugal."

For a moment Carstiona was dumb . . . then she burst into a torrent of Gaelic.

Katherine smiled and shook her head.

"Ach, I am sorry," said Carstiona. "I am saying thank you a hundred times, Mistress Maclaren. I am not ferry cood at the English. Dugal could pe thanking you petter. Dugal iss out in the poat. He will pe thanking you tomorrow."

"We are going away," said Katherine, resisting the inclination to shout.

"You are going away? Dugal wass saying you wass happy."

"We're very happy but we've got to go home."

"You haff got to go home," nodded Carstiona. "I will pe telling Dugal. He will pe sad."

"We're very sad," Katherine told her. "You've been so kind to us — you and Dugal — thank you very much indeed for the milk and eggs. We've had a lovely holiday and we hope to come back some day."

Carstiona gazed at her helplessly. "I am not ferry cood at the English," she repeated.

Katherine hesitated. She was anxious to find out whether or not Carstiona intended to keep her beautiful jug or wanted to sell it. Phil had been sure that she meant to keep it.

"Your jug is very valuable," said Katherine slowly and clearly. "You must keep it safely."

"I am keeping it ferry safe," replied Carstiona. She went over to a large oak chest which stood in the corner of the room, opened it and took out the jug wrapped in an old shawl. "Ferry safe," she repeated, holding it out for Katherine to look at.

"It's lovely," said Katherine. "You must never sell it."

"Not sell my chug, neffer," declared Carstiona, shaking her head.

Katherine smiled; she was glad that the beautiful thing was to remain in Carstiona's possession. Phil had said that Carstiona did not care for books and never listened to the wireless so it was good that she had something of her very own which she valued . . . and it was obvious by the way she was holding the jug and looking at it that it gave her a great deal of pleasure.

I shall remember the little brown mouse and her "chug" when I'm far away, thought Katherine as she watched the treasure being wrapped up and put away in the chest.

There were other things that Katherine would have liked to say to the little brown mouse; it would have been nice to talk to her about Phil, who was her friend, and to tell her how much they had enjoyed their visit to Ardfalloch House, but she realised that it would be too difficult so she held out her hand and said, "We must go now. *Là math leat*, Carstiona."

This valediction was still the only Gaelic she had; how lucky that it had come into her head at the right moment!

Part Two: The Cedars

CHAPTER
SEVEN

1

Alec and Katherine packed all they could the night before their departure and left the cave very early in the morning. The sun rose from behind the mountains as they went down the hill to the car but despite the early hour Dugal was there to thank them for their presents. Carstiona had given him the letter — he had it in his hand — and he assured Katherine that he would take it over to Ardfalloch House.

"Ach, I am sad," said Dugal regretfully. "MacAslan will be sad too . . . but you will come back some day."

"Yes, we shall come back," said Katherine.

They shook hands with their little friend and said good-bye and drove off down the bumpy road.

Alec drove carefully and did not talk much; he was depressed and worried. The news about Zilla had come as a shock for he had been living in the present and enjoying every moment. Their honeymoon had been idyllic; now it was over and they were going back to the world.

There was going to be serious trouble — Alec knew that — and he was upset at the idea of subjecting

Katherine to the unpleasantness which was bound to ensue from Zilla's return to The Cedars. It had seemed to fit in so well (Zilla's decision to part company with him, her trip to New Zealand and her intention to make her home in London), but now it was all in the melting-pot; Zilla had told Ellen that she was "coming home." Although Katherine was of the opinion that Zilla was coming back to The Cedars to collect some of her belongings, Alec was not so sure. The situation was further complicated by the fact that Zilla had not received his letter so she would arrive at The Cedars in ignorance of his marriage. Alec had no illusions about Zilla's attitude to his marriage with Katherine; she had done all she could to keep them apart . . . to the extent of telling deliberate lies.

With so much brewing in his mind it was no wonder that Alec was silent.

They stopped on the way for lunch but did not waste much time. It was barely five o'clock when they arrived at Barton and as Alec turned in at the gates of The Cedars his spirits rose, for he was coming home to the house he loved and bringing Katherine with him. There was a mellow autumnal look about the old grey house and the virginia creeper which covered the front façade was more beautiful than it had ever been before, it was like scarlet flames leaping up to the roof.

Ellen had been listening for the car and ran to open the door. Alec seized his bride in his arms and strode over the threshold. He put her down in the hall and said, "Welcome home, darling."

Katherine was laughing, she had been taken by surprise. "How strong you are!" she exclaimed. Then she looked round and added, "It's a lovely house — I've always thought so — but it seems lovelier than ever."

"Because you have come home," declared Alec.

"That's true," agreed Ellen. "The house is happy because you've come home. I just knew, the very first time I saw you, that you were the right one for Mr Maclaren. I've told him so — more than once."

They were all laughing now. Katherine shook hands with Ellen and complimented her upon the beautiful vase of autumn flowers in the corner of the hall.

"Och, it's nothing," declared Ellen. Unfortunately she was so excited that the set speech of welcome which she had memorised most carefully had vanished from her mind.

There was a pile of letters upon the hall table; Katherine expected Alec to open them at once, instead of which he went into the drawing-room and through the glass doors which led to the veranda and the garden.

Katherine and Ellen looked at each other.

"He's dreadfully upset about — about Miss Maclaren," said Katherine.

"I thought that was it," nodded Ellen. "When he's upset he always makes for the garden. There'll be trouble to-morrow when Miss Maclaren comes — and he can't abide trouble. Maybe I should have told her you were married when she rang up, but I just didn't dare — and that's the truth."

"I feel rather guilty. I mean this has been her home —"

"That's silly — if you'll excuse me saying so, Mrs Maclaren. This was her home but she was never done girning and wishing she was somewhere else. It was decided that she was to take a flat in London long before there was any thought of Mr Maclaren getting married. And why shouldn't he get married and have a bit of happiness like other gentlemen? There's not been much happiness for him here . . . nor for me neether," added Ellen under her breath.

Katherine, who was following Ellen upstairs, did not know how to reply to this downright statement but after a few moments' thought she said, "Yes, Ellen, you're right. It was silly of me."

"I shouldn't have said it."

"I'm glad you said it. I shall remember every word and it will help me to take a firm line when — when Miss Maclaren comes."

"A firm line is what she needs; just you stand up for yourself. Look, I've put you and Mr Maclaren in the big spare room. It's not the best room (Miss Maclaren has that, herself, and all her things are in it) but there's a nice view over the garden and a bathroom next door. Mr Maclaren can use his own room as a dressing-room — that's what I thought. We can alter it later if you'd like it arranged different."

It was quite perfect in Katherine's opinion. She went round all the rooms with Ellen and admired everything. At one end of the broad passage there were five steps up to a small landing and here there were two small rooms and a bathroom. These had been newly painted and papered for the twins. Another larger room had been prepared for "Mr Simon."

"You've thought of everything," Katherine said.

"Well, I've tried to," admitted Ellen. "Dinner will be ready at eight so there's plenty of time for you to have a bath and a nice rest. I've put a bottle in the bed. You'll have been up early this morning, no doubt."

2

Shortly after eight o'clock Alec and Katherine were sitting at the dining-room table, its polished mahogany laid with shining silver and lighted by candles with rose-coloured shades. There was champagne in long-stemmed glasses and silver dishes filled with crystallised fruits. Both Alec and Katherine were dressed as befitted the occasion: "in full fig" as Alec put it.

They had finished their soup and had been served with sole — small pieces rolled up and stuffed with mushrooms — when Katherine began to laugh.

Alec smiled in sympathy. "Yes, it's rather different," he said. "I don't know what you feel about it, but —"

"It's lovely!" she cried. "I enjoyed the cave and I'm enjoying *this*."

"So am I," nodded Alec. "My bath was marvellous."

"Mine was heaven. Ellen prepared it for me. I haven't had a bath prepared for me since I was a child. When I went into the bathroom the scented water was steaming gently and it was just the right temperature — so hot that I had to get into it slowly, bit by bit. I'm clean now," she added smugly.

"So am I," said Alec chuckling.

"But all the same I loved the cave and I want to go back some day."

"We shall," Alec agreed. "I loved the cave and I'm enjoying this. I like things to be real, like the cave, or else highly civilised. I don't like things that are in-between — if you know what I mean."

She knew what he meant only too well; she had lived for years in the "in-between" condition, trying her best to be civilised but not succeeding very well. It is impossible to be what Alec called "civilised" when you live in a small flat with three children and have to do all the work yourself.

"I hope I shall be able to keep up the standard," she said apprehensively. "It will be awful if I can't make you comfortable."

"Make me comfortable? I'd live in a slum quite happily if I had you to live with me."

"Nonsense! You'd be miserable."

"I wouldn't," he declared. "Nothing would matter if I had you."

She smiled and shook her head in disbelief so he was obliged to get up and come round the table to kiss her. He was still kissing her when Ellen came in to remove the plates.

"Don't mind me, Mr Maclaren," said Ellen cheerfully. "It's a funny thing if a gentleman can't kiss his wife in his own dining-room."

"She's priceless, isn't she?" said Alec when she had gone.

"Worth more than her weight in gold," Katherine replied seriously.

They had finished dinner now and so far Alec had not opened his letters; he picked them up as he went through the hall and took them into the drawing-room.

"There's nothing here that matters — except Zilla's," he said. "I don't want to open it, Katherine."

She said nothing — what could she say? — but busied herself pouring out the coffee; after a few moments' hesitation Alec opened the letter and read it.

Presently he said, "It's a very friendly letter all about the various châteaux they visited in the Loire valley — and there's a lot about 'the grey lady,' the ghost of the *Comtesse* who was immured in a damp dungeon by her abominable husband. She appeared to Zilla and tried to speak to her . . . Zilla told me about it before in her last letter, but she has told me the same thing again — in more detail. It seems to have made a great impression upon her."

"There was some idea of her joining a 'circle' in London which goes in for psychic phenomena, wasn't there?"

"Yes, but she doesn't mention that. She has probably changed her mind. She changes her mind every five minutes. I'll give you the letter and you can read it all for yourself. The only important thing is that the letter is written from Perpignan. She says, 'I have enjoyed this tour immensely in spite of the silly way the Carews bicker with each other. I find it best to laugh and tell them to stop behaving like a couple of children. We have decided not to go to Biarritz as we had planned. Madeline has suggested Spain, which will be much more interesting, so we shall be crossing the Pyrenees tomorrow or next day. Our destination is uncertain. Madeline wants to go to the Costa Brava and sunbathe; Jack is keen to go to Madrid where he has a friend in the British Embassy. He says we should be asked to lots of parties and have a rattling good time. We are still discussing it. I have come to the end of my money but Jack seems to be able to wangle as much currency as we want. He refuses to tell me how he does it but just laughs and produces! Of course I am keeping an account of what he gives me and will settle up with him when I get home. I will let you know later if I can give you an address, but Madeline says the post in Spain is slow and erratic. I have definitely decided not to go to New Zealand this year but will just come home when our wanderings are over.'

"There you are," added Alec, handing Katherine the sheets of thin paper written in Zilla's somewhat illegible scrawl.

"I find her writing difficult to read," said Katherine. "Anyhow you've told me the most important part. Zilla didn't go to Biarritz; that's why she didn't get your letter. People who disappear into Spain without leaving an address can't complain if they find unexpected things have happened during their absence."

"Zilla will complain."

112

"Don't let's worry. Sit down and have your coffee, darling. I want to talk to you about something important."

"Something important?" asked Alec, sitting down as requested and lighting a cheroot.

"It's about Ellen. She has her niece to help her, of course, but I think when the children come she will need more help. She knows a girl who can come daily. Will that be all right?"

"Of course! When are the children coming?"

"Yes, that's another thing. We had better leave them with Aunt Liz for a few days longer until we discover what Zilla means to do."

CHAPTER
EIGHT

1

During the night the weather broke and the next morning was wet and misty; however, Alec and Katherine wanted to do some shopping so they took the car and went into Edinburgh and got what they wanted. They returned home to lunch and then settled down comfortably by the fire. They had bought some books (Katherine had discovered a book entitled *Astronomy for Beginners*). They intended to read but found themselves talking instead.

"It wouldn't be very nice in the cave to-day," said Katherine, looking at the streaming window-panes.

"But all the same I'd rather be there than here."

Katherine did not need to ask why. "She didn't say what time she would arrive, did she? If she comes by that midday train she won't be here until after dinner."

"She will probably fly. If I knew what time I could meet her at Turnhouse and get the worst of it over. Ellen was too upset to ask. What's that book you've got?"

"It's about stars," replied Katherine. "I want to know about them because they're so beautiful. Now that I shall have more leisure I mean to improve my mind."

Alec laughed. He came over and sat beside her on the sofa so that they could look at the book together. It was an illustrated book with pictures of the constellations. For a time they were quite happy looking at the pictures and talking about them; then suddenly Alec rose and began to walk about the room.

"I'm sorry," he said apologetically. "I can't sit still."

"Alec, why not put on your waterproof and go for a walk?"

"She might come while I was out."

"If she comes while you're out I can talk to her and tell her everything."

"I may be a coward but I'm not such a coward as that. Do you really think I would go out and leave you to face Zilla alone? It's because of you I'm funking it."

"She can't eat me. Do go out, Alec."

"Nothing will induce me to go out . . . but that has given me an idea. Listen, Katherine —"

"If your idea is that I'm to go out you can think again," said Katherine, smiling at him. "I shall sit in my own drawing-room beside my own fire. I suppose it *is* my own drawing-room? Half of The Cedars belongs to me. That's what you said, didn't you?"

"Yes, of course!" exclaimed Alec. He stood and looked at her for a moment and then repeated in a different tone of voice, "Yes, of course. That makes it easier."

"Why?"

"I don't know — but it does. What a good thing you reminded me! I shall stand no nonsense from Zilla. No nonsense," repeated Alec firmly.

Katherine was about to encourage him further when they heard the sound of a car coming up the drive.

"Oh heavens, that's Zilla!" cried Alec in dismay. "I had better meet her at the door."

"I'll come," said Katherine rising.

"No, don't come. Please don't! I'd rather get it over alone."

Katherine hesitated and then sat down. Perhaps it was better this way.

2

When Alec opened the front door Zilla was getting out of the taxi.

"Hallo, Alec!" she exclaimed. "What a nice surprise to see you! Ellen said you were away from home. She didn't know your address and seemed a bit het up about it."

"I got back yesterday," he replied. "Don't bother about the taxi — I'll pay it. I'd have met you if I'd known when you were arriving."

"I came by air." She kissed him and added, "You're looking splendid. Have you been shooting or what?"

"I've been getting married," he replied. "I wrote to the address you gave me at Biarritz, but apparently you didn't get my letter. How much?" he asked, turning to the driver of the taxi.

Zilla had stepped back and was leaning against the wall. She was speechless. It was not until the taxi had gone and Alec had shut the front door that she found her voice.

"Alec, it isn't true!" she cried.

"It's perfectly true. Aren't you going to congratulate me, Zilla?"

"Congratulate you? You've ruined yourself! It's Kit, of course. I knew she was after you but I thought I'd saved you from her clutches by letting her have the cottage. I suppose she's here — with all her brats. Heavens, what a fool you are! I can't turn my back for a moment without you getting into a mess . . ."

They were still standing in the hall. Alec shut the drawing-room door and let her rave. The raving had to come out so it was better to get it over.

Alec used to be frightened when Zilla raved like this, but now he stood there and looked at her . . . and wondered why he had put up with her for so long. He had endured so many storms of temper that he had grown a sort of shield and was able to "not listen." He was not listening now but was just looking at her with detachment. Her face, usually pale, was the colour of a beetroot; her curious yellow eyes were blazing. (She has eyes like a lion, he thought. I wonder why I didn't notice that before.)

When she paused for breath he said, "I told you all about it. If you had gone to Biarritz, as you intended, you would have got my letter. I told you we were going to be married at Inverquill."

"A hole-and-corner wedding!"

"We were married at the Episcopal Church. Katherine's aunt was there — and the children. We wanted a quiet wedding but as I told you in my letter we would have been very pleased if you would have come."

"I wouldn't have come."

"No, I don't suppose you would."

"Why didn't you write to me at Madrid? You knew I was going to Madrid with the Carews. I told you."

He took her letter out of his pocket. "This is the last letter I had from you — from Perpignan. Listen, Zilla, 'We have decided not to go to Biarritz as we had planned . . . Madeline wants to go to the Costa Brava . . . Jack is keen to go to Madrid where he has a friend in the British Embassy . . . we are still discussing it . . . I will let you know later if I can give you an address but Madeline says the post in Spain is slow and erratic.' Take it and read it for yourself."

She took it and threw it on the floor. "You could have written to the British Embassy at Madrid."

"You didn't say so. Anyhow what are you worrying about? You say you wouldn't have come to the wedding, so —"

"I would have flown straight home and prevented it."

"I don't see how," said Alec, picking up the letter and putting it back in his pocket. "Katherine and I are both of marriageable age and there was no just cause or impediment."

"I would have prevented it somehow," cried Zilla furiously. "You've ruined yourself — that's what you've done. You've allowed yourself to be trapped by a designing woman. You're the biggest fool on earth. Have we got to stand here in the hall?"

"Of course not. There's a fire in the drawing-room, but perhaps you'd like to go to your room and tidy up. You look a bit dishevelled," said Alec, surveying her critically.

"Very well. You can bring up my dressing-case. It's the spare room, I suppose."

"Your own room is ready for you. Katherine and I are in the big spare room. Later, when you have moved into a flat in London, we can have your room done up and refurnished."

"Who said I wanted a flat in London?"

"You did. You said it to me and you said it to the Carews. You asked me if you could have some furniture from The Cedars. Don't you remember?"

"I suppose I can change my mind?"

"You can live anywhere you like — except here," said Alec firmly. "I'm married now so I can't offer you a home."

"You're married now!" cried Zilla as she ran upstairs. "It's a wonderful marriage! What will your friends say? You'll be the laughing-stock of the whole place. Can't you hear them talking about you, sniggering behind your back? 'Poor old Alec has been had for a mug.' That's what they'll say."

Alec had picked up the luggage and was following her. "I don't care a rap what they say," he declared. "I've been miserable for years and now I'm happy. That's all that matters to me."

"You're insane," she told him.

"What is insane about it?"

"First, to marry a woman like Kit, and second to marry in that hole-and-corner way. You've got to live here, haven't you? If you were determined to get married and ruin yourself you should have been married here, in Edinburgh . . . a proper wedding with all your friends there."

"I told you we wanted a quiet wedding. Neither Katherine nor I wanted a lot of fuss and nonsense." He put down the suitcases and unstrapped them.

"What was her other wedding like?" asked Zilla. She threw back her head and laughed. Her throat was thin and scrawny like the throat of an old woman. The thought crossed Alec's mind that it would be very easy to strangle her.

"Did you hear what I said?" she asked.

"Yes, I heard. Katherine and Gerald were married in Oxford. I think it was in New College Chapel but I'm not sure. You had better ask Katherine if you really want to know. Come down when you're ready, Zilla. We shall be in the drawing-room."

3

Katherine was sitting in the chair by the fire — just as Alec had left her. He knelt down and buried his face in her neck. She turned and put her arms round him.

"I didn't come," she said. "You told me not to. I heard her voice going on and on. Alec darling, you're shaking all over!"

"It upsets me."

"I know, but she can't do anything. It's all right — really it is. She won't stay long. We shall just have to bear it."

"Not listen," he whispered.

"Not listen," she agreed. "We're so happy — and she's so miserable. We must remember that and try to — to make allowances. People who are miserable are always — difficult. Alec, darling, she can't do *anything*. We're married."

"Yes, thank God," said Alec reverently.

They were silent for a few minutes and then they heard Zilla's high heels tap-tapping on the polished floor of the hall, so when she opened the door and came in Alec was standing upon the hearth-rug in front of the fire.

Katherine rose and said, "Oh, here you are, Zilla! Did you have a good trip? What a horrid wet day for you to come home!"

"Did you say 'home'?" asked Zilla. "I haven't got a home. You've kicked me out of my home! That's a nice return for all my kindness to you!"

"But you never liked it!" Katherine exclaimed. "You hated this house. You said so over and over again."

"Dear, beautiful room," said Zilla, looking round. "How many happy hours I've spent here!"

"You're fond of this house, are you?" asked Alec.

"Of course I'm fond of it! Who wouldn't be fond of it — and the lovely garden? It has been my home for six years. We planned it together, didn't we, Alec? We altered it all and made it just as we wanted. We built on the veranda and made new bathrooms; we put in central heating. All these improvements were my idea, and you approved of them, didn't you, Alec? I chose the furniture and the carpets and curtains . . . I spent hours and hours choosing the furnishings. It was a labour of love. Everyone has admired this house, everyone who has seen it has said it was perfect — and so it is. The Cedars is my creation."

"In that case you can have it. Katherine and I will give it to you just as it stands — lock, stock and barrel — provided you undertake to live here for at least nine months in the year. What do you say, Katherine?"

"Yes, of course, Alec," said Katherine. She felt absolutely dazed; she could scarcely take in what he had said, but she realised that he wanted her to agree.

"Yes, of course, Alec'," said Zilla sneeringly. "What a dutiful wife! She promised to obey you, I suppose — or did you have the new service?"

"We had the old service in which I endowed Katherine with all my worldly goods, so The Cedars belongs to Katherine. She will give it to you, won't you, Katherine?"

"Yes, of course," Katherine said. "You must have it, Zilla. We don't want to turn you out of your home. I thought — we both thought that you wanted to live in London."

"How kind of you to offer it to me! But of course you wouldn't offer it if you thought there was the slightest chance of the offer being accepted."

"The offer is absolutely genuine," Alec told her. "Katherine and I can easily find another house. We

122

might buy one at Gullane. What do you say, Katherine?"

Katherine nodded. "The offer is absolutely genuine," she said, repeating Alec's words.

"Is it?" asked Zilla, still in that sneering voice. "In that case I've a good mind to accept it — with thanks. It's far too big for me to live in by myself but I can shut it up and let it stand empty."

"No, I'm afraid not," said Alec. "You've forgotten that I made a proviso. I told you that you could have The Cedars provided you undertook to live here for nine months in the year."

"You would find it difficult to make me do that."

"Not difficult at all. Houses are often bequeathed as legacies with conditions of that nature."

Katherine was more and more bewildered. She said, "But you're fond of the house, Zilla. You want to live here, don't you? It's all a mistake. We thought you didn't like it. When Alec and I were married we thought —"

"You managed it, didn't you?" Zilla interrupted. "I wonder how you managed to catch him. I knew you were after him but I never imagined he would be such a fool as to let himself be caught. You're clever, aren't you, Kit? I wonder why you were so anxious to marry Alec. Was it the man — or his money bags?"

"It was the man," replied Katherine, looking up at the man with her heart in her eyes. "I know you never appreciated Alec, but I love him dearly and I shall do my best to make him happy."

"Very pretty," said Zilla. "Most affecting. Another thing I'd like to know is why it was all done in such a hurry. It seems funny to me but perhaps there was a Good Reason for the haste."

Alec was rising up and down from his toes to his heels and back again. It was a little mannerism which betokened his intention of making a cogent remark. (His partner, Andrew Firth, knew it well and had once said to his wife, "When Alec begins to see-saw you can look for trouble." Katherine also knew it and was alarmed.)

"It's all right, Alec," said Katherine. She said it under her breath but Zilla's ears were sharp.

"'It's all right, Alec'," mimicked Zilla. "There isn't any need for you to speak. You've got a wife to do all the talking — isn't that nice? She has talked you into marrying her and supporting her and her brats for the rest of your life. 'It's all right, Alec'."

"Zilla," said Alec. "Listen to me for a moment. You've always said what you liked to me — and I've borne it — but if you say another unkind word to Katherine I shall strangle you."

There was silence. The two women gazed at him incredulously.

"It would be quite easy," he added. "My hands are very strong." He held out his hands, clenching and unclenching them; they looked very strong indeed.

"Alec!" exclaimed Zilla in alarm.

"You needn't be frightened," he told her. "I just thought I'd warn you, that's all. It seems only fair to warn you. Katherine is my wife, you see, and I've sworn in church before the altar to cherish her all my life. Cherish is a nice word, it means to love and comfort and protect, so it's my duty to protect Katherine and I shall use my strength to do so."

"You've gone mad," said Zilla in a shaky voice.

"I've gone sane," replied Alec. "I was mad for years — mad to give in to you and let you trample on me — but that's all over. I wasn't brave enough to protect myself but I'm brave enough to protect Katherine. You needn't be frightened," he repeated, smiling kindly. "As long as you're pleasant and agreeable to my wife you're perfectly safe."

Katherine had been listening in dismay, but now, suddenly, she was threatened by a hysterical fit of giggles. She could feel the bubbles beginning to bubble inside her. It was Zilla's face! Incredulity was struggling with alarm. Just so might a woman look at a worm upon the garden path which had turned upon her and bitten her foot . . .

Don't think about that, Katherine adjured herself. Think about something terribly sad. She was trying to find something terribly sad to think about when the door opened and Ellen came in with the tea-tray.

"Oh, tea!" exclaimed Katherine ecstatically. "How lovely; I've been longing for tea. I'll clear the table for you, Ellen. We'll have it here, near the fire."

The table was cleared; Alec had pushed in a chair for Zilla and was now on his knees piling wood on the fire.

"It's cold to-night," he said.

"Frightfully cold," agreed Katherine. "It feels like snow."

"Don't you think it's a bit too early for snow?" asked Alec.

"Yes, I suppose it is," agreed Katherine. She added, "You like your tea with lemon, don't you, Zilla?"

"Not unless there's China tea," replied Zilla ungraciously.

There was China tea. Ellen had remembered and had made two pots. She had also produced — goodness knows how — a plate of cucumber sandwiches which Zilla adored.

When Katherine had finished pouring out tea (China for Zilla and Indian for Alec), she began to babble. "You must tell us about your adventures, Zilla. Alec said you had seen the ghost of a grey lady at the château in the Loire valley. Weren't you frightened?"

"There was nothing the least alarming about the *Comtesse*."

"I should have been terrified."

"You wouldn't have seen her. The spirits of the departed appear only to those with whom they are in tune."

"Have a cucumber sandwich, Zilla," said Alec, handing her the plate.

She hesitated for a moment . . . and then accepted one.

"Take two while you're about it," he suggested.

"No, thank you."

Alec put the plate beside her and helped himself to a scone.

"You were in tune with the *Comtesse*," said Katherine with interest.

"Absolutely in tune. I could feel her reaching out to me, asking for help. I knew she was trying to communicate with me — but just at that moment Jack Carew walked in, talking and laughing with two American women, so she vanished."

"How dreadful!" exclaimed Katherine. "You'll never know what it was that she wanted to tell you."

"Perhaps I shall, some day," replied Zilla, taking another sandwich without realising what she was doing. "I went to a man in London — a wonderfully psychic man called Mr Guest. He was introduced to me by a friend of the Carews. Mr Guest's circle is very select, he doesn't accept everyone; in fact it was only when I told him about the *Comtesse* that he accepted me as a member. He thinks I may be able to get in touch with the *Comtesse* which would be very wonderful, of course."

"But she's earth-bound in the castle, isn't she?" asked Alec.

"You don't understand," said Zilla.

"I know. That's why I'm asking."

"I don't understand either. Do tell us about it," said Katherine.

Thus encouraged Zilla took another sandwich and attempted to explain the curious ways of psychic phenomena. Her audience listened with rapt attention, but, whether it was that Zilla did not really understand the subject herself or that she was unable to put her information clearly, the fact remained that Alec and Katherine were no wiser than before.

Afterwards when they were upstairs dressing for dinner they discussed the whole conversation in private. Katherine wanted to know whether Alec had been sincere in offering his sister The Cedars.

"Absolutely sincere," replied Alec. "As a matter of fact I was pretty certain she wouldn't take it if it meant that she would have to live here for nine months in the year, but if she had accepted the offer we could have cleared out and found another house."

"She didn't say definitely that she wouldn't take it."

"No, but she has joined Mr Ghost's circus."

"Alec, don't call it that! You might do it by mistake when Zilla was there."

"Well, anyway, she has joined it so she'll want to live in London. That's obvious, isn't it?"

"Yes, of course! I never thought of that."

"I wonder how much he rooked her. Mr Ghost's circus is very select so I expect she had to pay through the nose."

"You're being very naughty," said Katherine, trying not to laugh.

"I know," he agreed. "I'm feeling full of beans because I've managed to stand up to Zilla. The spell is broken and I'm not frightened of her any more. All the time she was talking I was looking at her and thinking what a fool I had been. Did you see her wolfing the cucumber sandwiches? She finished the lot."

Katherine was sitting in front of her dressing-table, brushing her hair. She turned and said, "Alec, I wish you would explain it to me in simple words. You understood all that she was saying about psychic phenomena, didn't you?"

"I?" exclaimed Alec. "It was such awful rubbish that I didn't even try to understand."

"There's something in it," said Katherine thoughtfully. "But people like Zilla who talk about it in that silly way make it sound silly. I'm quite prepared to believe that Zilla saw the *Comtesse* in the château, but if that man makes her appear to Zilla at a séance in London . . . well, I can't believe that."

"He will," said Alec. "They do it with mirrors."

CHAPTER
NINE

1

The Maclarens had thoroughly enjoyed their first evening at home together. Their second evening was not so good; Zilla was there, sitting at the table with them and making a most unwelcome third. The meal was harmonious, due to the efforts of Katherine who was aware that if Zilla could be induced to talk about herself and her own affairs she would go on talking. A few leading questions from Katherine, and Zilla was off on an account of her travels in France: where they had stayed, what the hotels were like, and all about the interesting things they had seen.

Katherine listened and made the right responses; Alec sat in silence.

After dinner they settled down round the fire in the drawing-room. "Hadn't you better go and write those letters, Alec?" said Katherine.

"Letters?" asked Alec in surprise. "Oh yes! Yes, of course. If you'll excuse me I'll go and write to — to one or two people."

"If you write them now you can post them to-night. The rain has stopped."

"Yes, I'll do that," he agreed, rising with alacrity. "I'll post them to-night. I'll walk to the village and post them."

As the door closed behind him, Zilla laughed unpleasantly. "You've got him where you want him, haven't you, Kit? I wonder why you want to speak to me alone."

The question was difficult to answer because Katherine had no desire to speak to Zilla alone. She hesitated and then said, "Alec and I have no secrets from each other."

"How delightful!" said Zilla. "In that case why did you send him away?"

"I thought he was gettting a little bored," replied Katherine truthfully. She unrolled some more wool from her ball and continued to knit.

For a few moments Zilla was dumbfounded; she tried to think of a cutting remark which would put Kit in her place but could find nothing to say. When at last she found her voice she changed the subject. "Do you ever hear from the Wentworths?" she inquired.

Katherine hesitated; she had not expected the question and she disliked telling lies . . . but she saw in a flash that it would be most unwise to reveal the fact that she was on friendly terms with Peter.

"Didn't you hear what I said?" asked Zilla irritably. "Do you ever hear from the Wentworths? I remember you told me that you had quarrelled with Simon's relations and I advised you to make it up."

"You remember incorrectly," declared Katherine. "I didn't say I had quarrelled with them. I said they had quarrelled with Gerald long ago — long before Gerald and I knew each other. It was because Gerald went to Italy and married an Italian girl."

"It comes to the same thing. Why don't you make it up? The Wentworths could be very useful to Simon."

"The quarrel *was* made up. Sir Mortimer wrote to Simon (I thought you knew that, Zilla) and Simon and I went to Limbourne last July. Everyone was very friendly while we were there but after we left there was a disagreement and things are much the same as before."

"So you've had another quarrel? What was it about this time?"

Katherine was silent; her temper was beginning to rise.

"I think you're mad," declared Zilla. "Surely you can see how important it is for Simon to be on good terms with his father's relations. Sir Mortimer liked Simon and was willing to accept the boy as his heir. He wanted Simon to go to Limbourne and learn to look after the property — but you were jealous and refused to let him go."

"I was jealous?" exclaimed Katherine in amazement.

"Yes, jealous. You didn't want Simon to go to Limbourne so you quarrelled with Sir Mortimer and —"

"Zilla, I don't know what you mean!"

"Oh, you needn't pretend to be so innocent," said Zilla smiling maliciously. "Madeline Carew met Mrs Godfrey and heard all about it. Madeline and I agreed that it was very foolish of you."

"If you knew all about it why did you ask me?"

"I wanted to see what you would say."

132

"I say this," Katherine declared angrily. "Florence Godfrey's story is untrue. I was not jealous and I had no wish to quarrel with Sir Mortimer. I hate quarrels; I would do almost anything to avoid them." She paused and then added significantly, "I'm very long-suffering, Zilla, but it annoys me when people are underhand."

"Underhand?"

"Yes, underhand. If you wanted to know what had happened why didn't you ask me straight out instead of pretending to know nothing? You tried to trap me, Zilla. I don't like that sort of thing."

Zilla's eyes flashed; obviously she was furious . . . but it was no part of her policy to quarrel irretrievably with Katherine so she controlled her temper and said with a laugh, "Goodness, what a fuss about nothing! I was teasing you, that's all."

Perhaps it was just as well that at this moment the door opened and Alec came in. He said cheerfully, "I'm just off to the village. Have you got any letters you want posted?"

Katherine had written a letter earlier in the day and by the time she had found it in her desk and stamped it and given it to Alec the storm in her bosom had subsided and she was able to speak to Zilla with her usual civility.

2

Several days passed. On Monday morning Alec returned to his office and found plenty of work to keep him busy. Katherine was glad of this; it was easier to get on with Zilla when Alec was away. For years Alec had been under Zilla's thumb, but now — as he had said — he was not frightened of her any more and when Zilla annoyed him he showed his annoyance plainly. Unfortunately Zilla annoyed him frequently so Katherine found herself in the position of a buffer state, which was exhausting to say the least of it. She had explained this to Alec in private, and expostulated with him, but to no avail.

"How long have we got to put up with her?" he asked. "What are her plans? Is she going to Mr Ghost's circus or does she intend to stay here for the rest of her life?"

"I don't know," admitted Katherine. "She has several friends here and in Edinburgh and she wants to see them. She has accepted an invitation to a luncheon-party next week."

Alec groaned. "Next week! Look here, if you can't find out her plans I shall ask her straight out how long she intends to stay."

"You mustn't do that! Zilla is our guest."

"She doesn't behave like a guest."

"Let's wait and see. We don't want to quarrel with your sister, do we?"

It was natural that Zilla should have friends in the neighbourhood; she had lived at Barnton for nearly six years, and now that she had returned she found it pleasant to ring them up and arrange to see them. Her car was still in Alec's garage so she was free to come and go as she liked. She went out to tea on Monday

134

and to lunch on Tuesday; on Wednesday morning she announced that she was going in to Edinburgh to do some shopping. It did not seem to occur to her that Katherine might like to go with her.

"You should get Alec to buy you a car," said Zilla as she got into her own car and shut the door.

It was a fine morning, sunny and bright with a pleasant autumnal nip in the air, so Katherine decided to spend it in the garden. First she snipped off some dead roses and then she settled down to do some weeding.

It is easy to think while weeding and Katherine had a good deal to think about: so far she had managed to keep the peace between Alec and Zilla but she might not be able to do so much longer. Could she, or could she not, give Zilla a gentle hint? The children presented another problem: they were still with Aunt Liz, of course, but they could not be left with her indefinitely — it was not fair to Aunt Liz who was elderly and had her own interests — besides, Katherine was longing to see her darlings. Could she have them home while Zilla was here?

Katherine considered the matter. Daisy and Denis were perfect pets — in their mother's opinion — but they were natural children; they ran about and chatted in an uninhibited manner . . . in fact the house seemed full of children when Daisy and Denis were there. This was all to the good, of course (Katherine would not have liked it if they had been mouselike in their behaviour), but Zilla was not used to children and the liveliness of the twins would probably annoy her. Daisy was especially lively so it would not be easy . . . and things were difficult enough already.

She had worked for some time and had begun to feel more peaceful when she heard Ellen shouting to her from the veranda.

"Telephone!" shouted Ellen, beckoning frantically.

Katherine scrambled up and ran across the lawn.

"It's Mrs Carew," said Ellen. "She's wanting to speak to Miss Maclaren but she said you would do."

"Oh, is that all?"

"That's all."

Katherine hesitated on the steps of the veranda. She was reluctant to take the call, not because the message was ill-mannered (she knew Ellen pretty well by this time and was aware that all messages entrusted to Ellen suffered a sea-change and were transmitted in her own downright words) but because, although she had never met Mrs Carew, she had heard a great deal about her . . . and, of course, Mrs Carew has heard a great deal about me, thought Katherine apprehensively.

"You better hurry; it's a trunk call," said Ellen.

Thus adjured, Katherine went into the study, took up the receiver and said, "Katherine Maclaren speaking."

"Oh, Mrs Maclaren," said a voice in honeyed accents. "This is Madeline Carew. I'm *so* sorry to bother you, but it really is *most* frightfully important. Zilla asked us to find a flat for her — you know that, of course — and Jack and I have been hunting high and low. We've simply worn ourselves to *skin and bone*. We had begun to feel *hopeless* when I happened to meet

136

Lady Fotheringay Massington in Harrods — quite by accident — and she told me that the flat below hers is being vacated next week. *Wasn't* it lucky? My dear, we went straight off then and there — and it's perfect, quite fabulous! When we had been all over it and poked into every cupboard Jack and I just *looked* at each other! Of course there are literally *hundreds* of people after it — all offering the *earth* — but Jack put down five hundred pounds and they've promised to hold it over until to-morrow night."

"How kind of him!" exclaimed Katherine.

"Zilla must *come at once*. You see that, don't you?"

"Yes, of course. I'm sure she'll be very grateful to you for taking so much trouble."

"Jack and I *want* Zilla to take it," Mrs Carew explained. "Not only because it's so *absolutely* perfect — a service flat in Chelsea with a view over the river and *exactly* the right accommodation — but also because . . . well, because Jack and I would *like* Zilla to be settled in a flat of her own. Of course Zilla can come and stay with us whenever she likes, but she isn't a very *easy* guest, is she?"

"Not very."

"Alec is a perfect saint — he bears anything — but Jack gets annoyed if people contradict *every* word he says. I find it difficult. Do you know what I *mean*?"

"Yes, I do."

"Our tour wasn't *all* joy and bliss," said Mrs Carew regretfully. "Zilla knows *too* much. Then there was the ghost. Did Zilla tell you about the ghost, Mrs Maclaren?"

"Yes, she told us about it."

"I suppose she told you that Jack frightened it away? Zilla was *terribly* angry with Jack; she behaved in a *most* extraordinary fashion. There were two American women with us at the time — delightful creatures, so gay and friendly — and they thought Zilla was *raving mad*."

"How dreadful!"

"Mrs Maclaren," said Mrs Carew earnestly. "I'm *sure* this flat would suit Zilla. Lady Fotheringay Massington has the flat above — which is exactly the same — and she says the whole place is *perfectly* managed and the service is quite *too* marvellous for *words* . . . and Zilla particularly wants to be in Chelsea because of Mr Guest. I expect she told you about Mr Guest?"

"Yes."

"Well, Mr Guest *lives quite near. Isn't* that lucky?"

"Yes, very lucky indeed."

"So you'll tell her all about it, won't you? Flats are *terribly* difficult to find and if she misses this one she may not be able to find another for *months*. Tell her she *really must come to-morrow*, otherwise it will be snapped up by someone else."

Katherine hesitated.

"It's *urgent*," said Mrs Carew urgently.

"Yes, I know," agreed Katherine. "I quite understand, Mrs Carew. Alec and I are just as anxious as you are to see Zilla comfortably settled in a flat of her own — and it sounds quite perfect — but it wouldn't be a good plan for me to tell her about it."

"Not a good plan?" asked Mrs Carew in dismay.

"For me to tell her," explained Katherine. "It would be much better if you told her yourself. Perhaps you could ring up about one o'clock — she's sure to be home by then — and speak to her and — and perhaps *not* tell her that you've spoken to me."

"Oh, I see! Yes, *of course!* It was a bit dim of me, wasn't it? I'm not surprised that you're having trouble. As a matter of fact —"

"There are the pips," said Katherine, who was anxious to terminate the conversation.

"Oh, I never bother about the pips — and I haven't *nearly* finished talking to you. Jack and I are *so* glad that Alec is married. *Poor* Alec *deserves* a little happiness — he had a dog's life with Zilla — and it *was* so clever of you to do the deed while she was away."

"Mrs Carew, I really think —"

"Oh, I *know* I'm being indiscreet, but that's just *me*. I'm the *most* indiscreet woman in the world — *positively* — and the worst of it is I don't care. If anyone is listening they're *quite* welcome to listen to every word. If it amuses them so much the better! I want to tell you that Jack and I both think you're the *right woman* for Alec — no matter *what* Zilla says."

"Oh thank you, Mrs Carew, but I've never met you, so how —"

Mrs Carew laughed. "Ah, but I've seen *you!* We saw you and Alec one day when we were lunching at a hotel in Moffat (you didn't know us from Adam and Eve, of course, and Alec was *much too interested* to notice us). Jack and I thought you looked gay and charming; *just* the right woman for solemn old Alec — and obviously *Alec thought so too.* If you take my advice you'll stand up to Zilla and —"

"Hold on a minute!" exclaimed Katherine. "I think that's Zilla's car. Yes, it is! I'll just say you've rung up and want to speak to her. You understand, don't you?"

"*Perfectly,*" said Mrs Carew.

Katherine summoned her sister-in-law to take the call and went and sat down in the drawing-room. Mrs Carew had given her a great deal of information — some of it rather surprising — and she wanted to think it out. She had plenty of time because Zilla was shut up in the study for at least fifteen minutes.

It will cost pounds! thought Katherine. Fortunately it was the Carews' pounds — not Alec's — but even so Katherine felt uncomfortable about it (she had not yet become used to the idea that pounds were unimportant) but, on the other hand, the longer the conversation lasted the more hopeful it was; Zilla could not have taken fifteen minutes — or more — to say No.

Presently the door opened and Zilla came in.

"That was Madeline Carew," said Zilla. "She and Jack have found a flat that they think might suit me. They want me to go and see it."

"What a bother for you," said Katherine sympathetically.

"Yes, but I suppose I must. Madeline wants me to go to-morrow."

"But you're going to that luncheon-party next week, aren't you?"

"Really, Kit!" exclaimed Zilla crossly. "You don't seem to understand *anything*. The luncheon-party doesn't matter. What matters is that the Carews have managed to find a flat and they'll be very angry if I refuse to look at it. Flats in London are almost unobtainable; it was only because Lady Fotheringay Massington told Madeline about it and they rushed off and saw it at once that they were able to get the first refusal. I shall have to fly south early to-morrow morning. Alec must come with me of course; there will be a lot of business matters to arrange."

When Alec returned home to lunch he was delighted to hear that his sister intended to fly south to-morrow but not pleased when he discovered that he was expected to accompany her. He hoped for Katherine's support in the argument that ensued; in this he was disappointed.

"Of course you must go," said Katherine firmly. "It will be so nice for Zilla to have you with her, and you want to see the flat, don't you?"

Alec did not want to see the flat; he would very much rather have stayed at home with his wife. He began to explain his feelings and then, catching his wife's expressive glance, changed his mind and agreed to go.

CHAPTER
TEN

1

After lunch Alec went back to his office; Zilla spent the afternoon in her room, looking out her clothes and packing them in suitcases with quantities of tissue paper; Katherine wrote to Simon and walked to the village to post the letter.

Katherine was a little worried about Simon. He had always been a very good correspondent; he wrote every Sunday, and his letters were usually full of amusing details about all he was doing. This term his letters had been quite short and, somehow, *not like Simon*. There was no glimmer of Simon's personality in them. Perhaps he was very busy (the beginning of term was always busy and it was difficult to settle down to work after a long holiday), or perhaps it was because he disliked rugger. Katherine was aware that Simon was never very happy in the Christmas term. Cricket was his game. It must be that; what else could it be?

When Katherine returned home at four o'clock she was surprised to find that Ellen had laid tea in the dining-room for five people and had provided an enormous spread of cakes and scones; she was on her way to the kitchen to find Ellen and ask her what was the meaning of these elaborate preparations when the front door burst open and Daisy and Denis rushed into the hall and flung themselves upon her with shrieks of delight.

"We've come!"

"He brought us in the car!"

"Aren't you pleased to see us?"

Taken by surprise at the onslaught, Katherine was nearly knocked over; she was so smothered with hugs and kisses that she was speechless.

Alec followed the children into the hall with their suitcase, he put it on the floor and said, "It was Ellen's idea, really. She thought you'd be lonely while I was away."

"Oh yes," gasped Katherine. "It was a wonderful idea. Oh, my darlings! Oh, what a lovely surprise!"

"Aunt Liz seemed to think it a good plan," said Alec. "So we got their things packed — and here they are."

"Aunt Liz was glad to get rid of us," said Denis cheerfully.

"Denis!" exclaimed his mother in alarm. "You weren't naughty, were you? I told you —"

"We weren't naughty," replied Denis reassuringly. "But you can't be *perfectly good* for twelve whole days."

"We argued a bit now and then," explained Daisy. "It was when we were arguing that the vase of flowers got upset."

"An accident isn't naughty, it's just unlucky," Denis pointed out. "And Aunt Liz needn't have made such a fuss, because the vase wasn't broken at all. It wasn't even cracked."

"And Bella mopped up the water in two minutes," added Daisy.

"Five minutes," said Denis who liked to be strictly accurate.

Katherine was so delighted to see them and to discover that they were just as dear and funny as ever that she was obliged to hug them again.

"I'll tell you something," announced Daisy, emerging somewhat breathless from her mother's embrace. "He says we can call him Alec."

"Oh," said Katherine doubtfully. "Alec, do you think . . ."

"Well, what?" asked Alec.

"Simon calls him Alec," said Daisy.

"Yes, I know, but Simon is a lot older than you are."

"We're getting older every minute," said Denis.

"They asked me and I said they could," Alec explained.

"He said we could! He said we could!" sang Daisy, capering round the hall in her usual exuberant fashion.

Katherine saw that the matter was settled and as she had no suggestions to offer she held her peace. She was still thinking about it when Zilla, who had heard the noise of the children's arrival, came downstairs looking somewhat glum.

Urged by their mother the twins shook hands with her and Denis said, "How do you do, Miss Maclaren."

"You had better call me Aunt Zilla, I suppose," said Zilla ungraciously.

144

The suggestion was received by the twins in silence and their mother was dismayed to see what she thought of as "the mulish look" appear on both their faces. She had always thought them as different from each other as two children could possibly be: Daisy was fair and plump with golden pigtails and very blue eyes; Denis was small and thin with dark hair and eyes, but the mulish look was the same and, just for a moment, Katherine saw a resemblance between them.

"You must come and wash before tea," she declared, herding them into the flower-room near the front door where there were facilities for washing.

"We've washed," objected Denis, hanging back. "Aunt Liz made us wash before —"

"You must wash again," said Katherine, handing him the soap. "And you should have thanked Aunt Zilla for saying you could call her 'Aunt Zilla.' It was very kind of her."

"But we don't want to — do we, Den?" said Daisy.

"We don't like her," explained Denis, taking the soap and giving his hands a perfunctory rinse under the tap.

"And she doesn't like us," added Daisy, who usually had the last word.

2

The conversation at tea did not interest the children so for a time they were silent, enjoying all the good things which Ellen had made for their benefit. Zilla talked about the wonderful time she would have in London.

"I shouldn't like to live in London," said Alec, rather unwisely. "It's too crowded and noisy and there's no fresh air."

"You're stuck in a rut," replied Zilla. "London is a delightful place to live. There's always something going on — never a dull moment — and of course the climate is so much better than it is here. In Edinburgh it's either raining cats and dogs or else there's a biting east wind."

Alec was about to reply heatedly to this unfair aspersion upon the climate of his beloved city . . . but Katherine managed to get in first.

"How lucky that the Carews heard about the flat!" she exclaimed.

"Yes, wasn't it?" agreed Zilla. "It will be very pleasant to have Lady Fotheringay Massington as a neighbour."

"You talk as if the whole thing was decided," Alec said.

"Of course it's decided."

"But you haven't seen the flat yet. You may not like it."

"Oh, Madeline says it's exactly what I want."

"How does she know?"

"Because she has been helping me, of course. What a relief to know that the search is over!"

Katherine looked at her and saw that she was smiling happily. Had she forgotten all that she had said on Saturday or did she suppose Katherine had forgotten? "You've kicked me out of my home. That's a nice return for all my kindness to you!" These words had

146

upset Katherine so profoundly that she would never forget them.

Suddenly Denis said, "Will you have another scone, 'Aunt Zilla'?" and handed her the plate. His face was perfectly solemn but he had said "Aunt Zilla" in a curious way — as if it were not her real name but just a sort of joke. To Katherine, who knew him, it sounded impertinent but nobody else seemed to have noticed. "Aunt Zilla" accepted the offering and continued to talk:

"I particularly wanted a flat in Chelsea because Mr Guest lives quite near — just round the corner, Madeline said — and his circle meets in a large room not ten minutes' walk from the flat. He has accepted me as a member so I can go regularly."

"D'you mean you can go to the circus whenever you like?" asked Daisy. Fortunately she was so excited at the mere idea that she had spoken with her mouth full of scone and honey.

"Only once a week," replied Zilla. "But there are books to study and Mr Guest gives his members little exercises in relaxation to carry out at home."

"What sort of exercises?" asked Daisy eagerly. "We do exercises at school. I'll show you afterwards —"

"Alec," said Katherine loudly. "Did you manage to get all your business settled satisfactorily?"

"Nearly all," he replied. "I've just gone back to the office, of course, and it's a bit difficult to get away again so soon."

"What nonsense!" said Zilla. "Surely your partners can carry on for a few days without you. Didn't you explain to them that it was important business?"

"Naturally I explained. It will be quite all right, but I shall have to go to the office to-morrow morning just to —"

"But I told you!" cried Zilla. "I want to go by the early plane. Madeline is expecting us to lunch."

"There's a plane about twelve; I've booked our seats."

"I want to go by the early plane," repeated Zilla angrily. "I told you distinctly. Oh Alec, what a fool you are!"

"Aren't you frightened to say that?" asked Daisy. She was leaning forward across the table gazing at Zilla with large round blue eyes.

"What do you mean?"

"Don't you know that people who call their brothers a fool are in danger of hell fire?"

"You're a very rude child!" Zilla exclaimed.

Denis flew to the rescue. "She isn't rude. She's just telling you. It's *kind* to warn people about things like that. We had it at school in our Scripture lesson; I can say it from the beginning." He took a long breath, "'Ye have heard that it hath been said by them of old time — '"

"Not now, old chap!" interrupted Alec. "You can say it to me later."

"It's true, anyhow," declared Daisy. "It *must* be true because Jesus said it Himself."

Zilla rose and left the room.

148

There was a short silence after her departure. Katherine was trying to decide whether or not you could punish a child for quoting from Scripture when her cogitations were interrupted by Alec seizing a knife and brandishing it in the air.

"Who's ready for a piece of Ellen's chocolate cake?" he inquired, smiling cheerfully.

"Me!" cried Daisy, holding out her plate.

"And me," added Denis, cramming the last fragments of a cheese-cake into his mouth.

3

It was not until the children had gone to bed, after a session of somewhat noisy games with their stepfather, that Katherine found an opportunity of speaking to Alec in private.

"You've given them a very happy time," she said. "But you mustn't spoil them, you know."

"I don't spoil them; we have fun together. I enjoy it as much as they do. Why shouldn't we have fun?"

"They ought to have been punished."

"Punished? Why on earth should they have been punished?"

"For saying that to Zilla. She was very upset."

"They only said what was true."

"But they must learn not to upset people."

"And what about Zilla?" asked Alec. "Wouldn't it be a good thing if she learnt not to upset people? I'm a bit tired of being called a fool — by Zilla. She has done it frequently, for years, but perhaps she'll be more careful in future."

"I'm sorry for Zilla," said Katherine sadly.

"I'm not. What's more if she doesn't behave herself I shan't go to London with her."

"Oh Alec, you must! You must *make* her take that flat — whatever it's like."

"She'll take it — whatever it's like," said Alec, chuckling. "Mr Ghost lives round the corner."

Katherine sighed, "I wish you wouldn't be naughty about Zilla. Why can't you bear her for just a little bit longer?"

"I don't know," he replied thoughtfully. "Perhaps it's because I've borne her for nearly six years."

Dinner went off quite smoothly. Zilla was unusually silent; there was no mention of the incident which had taken place at tea-time, there was no talk of going to London by the early plane. It was left to Katherine to carry the burden of the conversation. She began to talk about Ardfalloch and described the old castle on the island. It seemed a safe subject.

"Katherine felt uncomfortable there," said Alec smiling. "She had an idea that the spirits of the dead-and-gone MacAslans were unfriendly."

"Really?" asked Zilla, pricking up her ears. "Did you see any manifestations?"

"We saw nothing except huge ruined walls covered with ivy."

"Perhaps if you had stayed there alone, at night, with your psyche attuned to the delicate emanations —"

150

"I wouldn't have stayed there alone at night for anything under the sun," Katherine declared emphatically.

"How interesting!" said Zilla. "I must tell Mr Guest about it. I wonder if the MacAslans would allow the matter to be investigated."

"You and Mr Gh — Guest might spend the night there," suggested Alec. "I dare say MacAslan would agree, provided you didn't leave broken bottles lying about or play jazz music on a gramophone."

"Alec is teasing you," said Katherine hastily and, since there was nothing else for it, she proceeded to tell her sister-in-law about the party of campers who had behaved in an unseemly manner and been punished for their sins.

"*Most* interesting," said Zilla. "I must certainly tell Mr Guest. There would be no difficulty in getting permission from the MacAslans. I could do it through the Mitchells."

"The Mitchells?" asked Katherine doubtfully. "Do you think —"

"Yes, my friends the Mitchells are very intimate with the MacAslans. Edna Mitchell told me that when they were staying at Craig an Ron the MacAslans kept on asking them to go over to Ardfalloch until it became quite a bore."

"Did they ask the dogs too?" inquired Alec.

"I don't know what you mean," said Zilla crossly.

Again Katherine was obliged to intervene and change the subject. Fortunately it was easy to do so —

she had only to mention the flat — but the strain of being on the alert was beginning to get her down.

After dinner Zilla said she must finish her packing, and went upstairs, so the remainder of the evening was pleasant and peaceful except for Alec's lamentations over the prospect of being torn from the bosom of his family and "carted off to London."

CHAPTER
ELEVEN

1

It was very peaceful at The Cedars. When Katherine had seen the children off to school in a taxi (ordered by Alec) she had all the time in the world at her disposal. She was glad to rest after the strain of Zilla's visit and thoroughly enjoyed her unaccustomed leisure.

Various snags had appeared in connection with the lease of Zilla's flat and it was nearly a week before Alec managed to straighten things out but at last it was done and he flew home on Wednesday. He looked tired and complained that there was "no fresh air in London."

Katherine heard about the snags at dinner that night and listened like a dutiful wife — it all seemed very complicated — but there were other matters in which she was more interested and when they had settled down by the fire she asked if Alec had seen Simon. "Perhaps you hadn't time," she added.

"I rang him up," replied Alec. "I intended to go down to Barstow on Sunday and take him out to lunch but he had arranged to go out with his friend Mark Butterfield."

"Oh, what a pity!" Katherine exclaimed. "Why didn't he put it off and go with you? Simon is so fond of you — and he can go out with Mark any time; Mr Butterfield often takes the two boys out to lunch."

"I suggested that, but he didn't seem keen."

"Didn't seem keen? I can't understand why he —"

"Oh, it was quite natural," said Alec hastily. "The arrangement had been made so it would have been difficult for Simon to back out at the last moment."

Katherine sighed; she was sorry that Alec had not seen Simon. It would have been nice to hear first-hand news of Simon — whether he seemed well and happy — his letters were still short and unsatisfactory.

"I didn't see Mr Guest either," continued Alec. "Zilla was very anxious for me to meet him but she couldn't arrange it. I think he was away or something."

"What about Lady Fotheringay Massington?"

"Oh, I saw her. We met her one day going up in the lift and Zilla introduced me."

"Is she good-looking?"

"I don't know."

"You don't know?" asked Katherine, surprised.

"Her face was covered with white paint," Alec explained. "It was just like a mask . . . in fact she reminded me of a clown in a circus except that she hadn't a red nose. She's very grand — or thinks she is."

"I wonder how she'll get on with Zilla."

"I wonder."

"Were the Carews nice?"

"Yes, very pleasant and helpful. I liked them better than before."

154

Katherine would have been interested to hear a great deal more about Alec's visit to London — all the little details about what he had seen and done each day — but very few men are able to supply this sort of information and Alec was not one of them.

She asked a few more questions and then gave it up.

"I had better order the van," said Alec after a short silence.

"Oh yes," agreed Katherine. "Zilla wants us to send her the furniture from her bedroom."

"I think she would like a few other things as well. I told her she could have anything she wanted so she said she would let you know."

"She'll write to me, I expect," said Katherine.

Zilla's letter came on Monday morning; she had enclosed a list of all the things which were to be sent to her from The Cedars and asked that they should be packed and sent off as soon as possible. Katherine did not grudge Zilla her bedroom furniture, which was too ornate to be comfortable, but she was sorry to part with some of the other things. She could not consult Alec, he had gone to Perth to see a client, but as he had told his sister that she could have anything she wanted Katherine decided to get on with the job . . . and went round the house sticking labels on to the various pieces of furniture and marking them off on the list.

Ellen followed, grumbling. "What right has she to say she'll have this and that and the other? It's a piece of nonsense; they're Mr Maclaren's things. Some of them he bought himself — he knows about good furniture — and others came from the old house. I've looked after

155

them and cleaned them and polished them for years and years."

"Mr Maclaren told her she could have anything she wanted," explained Katherine as she wetted a label with a little sponge and stuck it on to a particularly delightful mahogany table which stood in the hall.

"Mr Maclaren bought that at a sale and paid a lot for it," grumbled Ellen. "It fits into the alcove just right. It was dirty when he got it but I cleaned it and polished it — and look at it now!" Then, as Katherine moved on, she exclaimed in dismay, "Not the clock, Mrs Maclaren! You're never going to send her the clock! It belonged to old Mr Maclaren — he'll turn in his grave!"

This horrifying prophecy made Katherine pause.

"It's such a lovely clock," added Ellen, taking advantage of Katherine's indecision.

It was a lovely clock — a venerable grandfather, with an attractively decorated face and a silvery chime.

"The Cedars wouldn't be the same without that nice old clock," urged Ellen.

At that moment, as if to clinch the matter, the clock chimed eleven in its usual charming way.

"You're right," said Katherine. "I'll wait until Mr Maclaren comes home and see what he says about it."

She broached the subject after dinner that night. "Must we send Zilla everything she wants?" asked Katherine. "For instance, the grandfather clock; Ellen says it belonged to your father."

"Good heavens!" Alec exclaimed. "We can't part with the old clock — besides it would be quite out of place in a modern flat. What else does she want?"

156

Katherine produced the list and they went over it together. In addition to her bedroom furniture and the clock and the hall table, Zilla wanted all the furniture of the small spare room — a bed, a carpet, two chairs, a dressing-table and a wardrobe — she wanted two pictures out of Alec's study, two pairs of curtains, a cabinet full of Dresden china, two easy-chairs, three rugs, four Chinese jars, which were used by Ellen for flower arrangements, and the drawing-room carpet.

"She doesn't want much, does she?" said Alec sarcastically. "Let's send her the stair carpets as well. There isn't a staircase in her flat but I dare say she could cut them up and use them in some way." He paused and then added seriously, "Of course I said she could have anything she wanted but I didn't mean she could furnish the whole flat with stuff from The Cedars."

"You meant that she could have all her bedroom furniture and a few other things which she valued for one reason or another," suggested Katherine.

"Exactly. It was foolish of me not to make it clear; I might have known Zilla would be greedy. Well, anyway," declared Alec with decision, "whatever I said, I'm certainly not going to part with the clock nor the hall table — nor the pictures in my study. They're Peploe paintings and I bought them myself because I liked them."

"I've always admired them," Katherine said. "The colouring is so beautiful."

"Yes, beautiful — and Zilla isn't interested in pictures, except as decorations."

"Decorations?" echoed Katherine in surprise. It seemed a curious word to use in connection with pictures.

Alec was not listening, he was poring over Zilla's list. "The cabinet full of Dresden china," he said. "It's yours, of course. We agreed that the drawing-room was yours, didn't we? Are we to send it?"

"I suppose we had better . . . but what about the drawing-room carpet? Surely it will be much too large for Zilla's flat?"

"We can easily buy a new carpet. Let's go and choose one to-morrow. It will be rather fun."

Katherine smiled. She said, "Yes, it will be fun, but I can't go to-morrow; besides it will be much better to wait until we have sent off Zilla's things. Then we can see exactly what we want. There's no hurry about it."

"None at all," agreed Alec.

The van was ordered and arrived at the appointed time. Katherine watched it being packed and ticked off the various items on her list as they were carried out of the house . . . but despite all her care she discovered afterwards that a number of things, which should have been sent to Zilla, had been left behind.

The Bokhara rug in the hall had been taken up and packed in sacking — Katherine could have sworn that she had seen the men put it into the van. Then, at tea-time when the van had been gone for more than an hour, the rug was back in its old place, spread out in the hall. As a matter of fact Katherine was so used to seeing it there that at first she did not notice it . . . then she remembered and stopped and stared at it in amazement. The tall Chinese jars had been packed too, but reappeared in an equally mysterious manner and were to be seen in their usual places filled with autumn flowers and beech-leaves.

"Ellen," said Katherine. "Those jars have been left behind. I wonder how it can have happened."

"I needed them," Ellen replied.

"And the Bokhara rug —"

"Oh, Mrs Maclaren, I couldn't bear that rug to go to London! The colours are so beautiful — just like a stained-glass window — and the smuts and dirt would have ruined it."

"But I saw it packed!"

"I went and got it out of the van while the men were having their dinners," explained Ellen with a self-satisfied air.

"Well, I hope she won't be frightfully angry, that's all," said Katherine apprehensively.

The house looked rather empty until some of the gaps were filled but Katherine enjoyed the experience of going with Alec and choosing furniture and a new carpet for the drawing-room. Zilla's bedroom was completely empty so they had it redecorated and painted and bought a large bed, a carpet and curtains and a walnut suite. It looked fresh and charming when it was ready and they agreed that it was a great success.

2

These unwonted pleasures kept Katherine busy and filled her mind so she was taken by surprise when one evening after dinner she was summoned to the telephone and found herself speaking to her sister-in-law.

"Hallo, Zilla! How are you getting on?" she asked in a friendly manner.

"I'm here, at the flat," announced Zilla. "The van arrived more than a week ago but I haven't had time to unpack everything until to-night. You've forgotten to send half the things I wanted. You've muddled it, Kit! You really are a perfect fool. I sent you a list so there's no excuse at all."

"But Zilla —"

"The only thing to do is to hire another van and send the things immediately. There's the clock and the pictures and —"

"Zilla, listen!"

"You got the list, didn't you? I told you in my letter to be very careful about it and mark off the various things I wanted as they were put into the van. If you had done as I said you couldn't have made any mistake."

"It wasn't a mistake. You see, Zilla —"

"It's too maddening for words; I particularly wanted those pictures in Alec's study. They will fit in with my colour-scheme and they're just the right size to hang on each side of the fireplace in my drawing-room."

Despite her alarm Katherine was obliged to smile.

"Are you listening, Kit?" demanded Zilla.

"Yes, of course . . . but it wasn't a mistake. Alec bought those pictures himself. They're beautiful pictures and he intends to keep them."

160

"Oh well, I dare say I can do without the pictures — I can buy some suitable ones to-morrow — but I must have the Bokhara rug and the Chinese jars and —"

"I'm sorry, Zilla, but we need them," interrupted Katherine, borrowing Ellen's admirable excuse.

"You need them?"

"Yes."

"Tell Alec I want to speak to him at once."

"He's out, I'm afraid. He often goes out for a walk after dinner."

"He can't possibly have gone for a walk; it's pouring cats and dogs."

"Oh, it's a lovely evening here," replied Katherine, delighted to be able to stand up for the Edinburgh weather.

"Well, tell him to ring me up when he comes in — if it's not too late. Meanwhile you had better make a list of all the things you've forgotten to send. First, the clock: tell Alec I must have the grandfather clock."

"Alec has decided not to part with the clock."

"Nonsense!" exclaimed Zilla with rising temper. "Alec said I could have *anything I wanted*. I want the clock. It has a pretty chime and it belonged to my parents."

"But, Zilla, they were Alec's parents too."

"It's no good talking to you," declared Zilla in furious tones. "Give Alec my message the moment he comes in." With that the receiver was replaced with a deafening bang and the conversation was over.

A few minutes later Alec returned from his walk and was told what had happened.

161

"Oh, it doesn't matter," he said.

"Doesn't matter? She's frightfully angry; you must ring her up at once."

"I'm not going to ring her up."

"She said you were to do it."

Alec smiled. "You said that she said I was to ring her up if it wasn't too late. Well, it's too late. See?"

"But Alec —"

"Listen darling! You're always telling me that I worry too much. Who is worrying now?"

"I know," agreed Katherine with an involuntary smile. "But she really was dreadfully angry."

"Zilla is nearly four hundred miles away so it doesn't matter if she's angry." Alec took off his coat and hung it in the hall-cupboard. He added, "Where's that book of yours about stars? The whole sky is full of stars this evening."

"It's pouring cats and dogs in London."

"Good," said Alec cheerfully.

After that the little family at The Cedars settled down to a pleasant routine which was only slightly disturbed by several exceedingly disagreeable letters from Zilla. Eventually she put through a personal call to Alec and they had a short conversation. Katherine, who was sitting in the room at the time, heard Alec's side of it and was startled to hear him tell his sister that she was selfish and greedy.

"There, what do you think of that?" asked Alec as he replaced the receiver.

"Oh, Alec, you shouldn't have been so rude!"

"My goodness! You should have heard what she said to me."

"I don't like it; she's your sister —"

"Don't worry, darling. Zilla is nearly four hundred miles away so let's forget about her," suggested Alec.

It was not difficult to forget about Zilla; there were so many pleasures in Katherine's new life. She bought a little car and, after a few trial trips with Alec, her old skill in driving returned. Alec and Katherine each had friends, all of whom were eager to entertain the newly-married couple and of course the hospitality had to be returned so there were several very pleasant parties at The Cedars.

Isobel Fisher was Katherine's greatest friend, they had known each other for years, so naturally she was one of the first visitors to be invited. She came to tea one afternoon and was delighted with all she saw.

"The house is perfect," declared Isobel. "It's lovely to think of you living here instead of in that horrid little flat . . . and you look a different person."

"I'm just the same."

"The same old Kit," agreed Isobel smiling. "But I used to get terribly worried about you because you were so thin and tired. Now you look years younger — and happy."

Katherine nodded. "If I couldn't be happy, living here with Alec, I should be the most extraordinary woman in the world."

CHAPTER
TWELVE

1

Autumn passed and winter set in. One morning in early December a letter appeared upon the breakfast-table addressed to Katherine in an unknown hand.

"Who is this from, I wonder," she said as she slit the envelope.

For a few moments there was silence.

"Well?" said Alec smiling. "Who is your correspondent and what does he want? You look a little worried."

"Not worried, just surprised. I had forgotten I had asked them, that's all. There has been so much to think about . . . but it will be lovely to have them, won't it?"

"Who?" asked Alec in alarm.

"The MacAslans, of course. They want to know if the invitation is still open. We are to say quite honestly if our plans are changed; it will not matter a bit as they can easily make other arrangements. Here, Alec, you had better read it."

"No time now," he said, glancing at the clock and rising hastily. "We'll discuss it to-night. Where are the children?"

Alec took the children to school every morning on his way to the office and it was always a rush to get them ready, but when Katherine had seen her family off in the car she took up MacAslan's letter and read it again more carefully. It was just like him, she thought. It was warm and friendly but there was an old-fashioned dignity about it which she found very charming.

Katherine had not thought of the MacAslans for weeks but the letter brought them back to mind and they were in her thoughts all day. How delightful it would be to see them again! Phil was a darling — it would be fun for Simon to have a girl of his own age to go about with. There would be parties for them — and the pantomime, of course. Katherine was determined to give Phil a good time. She decided that Phil must have the pink room. The carpet had been sent to Zilla but could easily be replaced. An Indian carpet would be nice.

It was not until after dinner that Katherine found a good opportunity to discuss the matter with Alec. She found to her dismay that he did not want to have the MacAslans.

"You must write and make some excuse," he told her.

"Oh, Alec, I can't possibly do that."

"You can do it quite easily. He says in his letter that we are to be sure to say if it isn't convenient."

"But I don't understand! You seemed quite pleased when I told you I had asked them."

"I never thought for a moment they would come."

"You liked them."

"Of course I liked them."

"Then why —"

"It's so alarming. Can you see him here, sitting in this house or walking about the garden? I can't. I can only see him in his own domain, striding over his own mountains and steering his boat on his own loch."

"But, Alec, he wants to come."

"You'll have to make some excuse," said Alec desperately. "We can't entertain him here. He's like a king. His family have been kings for hundreds of years. The whole district of Ardfalloch belongs to him . . . and the people belong to him too."

"He belongs to them," Katherine said.

"What do you mean?"

"He said it himself. He said Ardfalloch and all the people didn't belong to him — he belonged to Ardfalloch. I was puzzled at first but afterwards when I thought about it I understood. It makes him less alarming, much more human."

"He's too grand for us."

"MacAslan may be 'grand' but there are no airs about him. If you're really grand you don't need to put on airs."

"Katherine, listen —"

"No, listen to me, Alec," said Katherine earnestly. "It would be much easier to entertain the Queen Mother, who is really grand, than a woman like Lady Fotheringay Massington who only thinks she's grand . . . and it would *much* more pleasant."

166

Alec was obliged to laugh. "All right," he said. "Let's ask the Queen Mother to complete our Christmas party."

Katherine laughed too; she was delighted to have won her point so easily. It would have been difficult to have found an excuse to put off the MacAslans' visit. "Seriously, Alec," she said. "We needn't worry about it. They want to come and Phil is sure to enjoy the parties and the pantomime and everything."

"It isn't Phil I'm worrying about. I shall have to entertain MacAslan. That's the trouble."

"He won't need any entertainment. We shall just be ourselves, perfectly natural and friendly — or do you intend to hire a piper to walk round the dining-room table?"

Alec chuckled. "I hadn't thought of that," he admitted. "But I had better lay in several kinds of whisky. Perhaps he would prefer that light-coloured blend with the peaty taste. I must go and consult Mr Drummond to-morrow morning."

2

"Is that you, Kit?"

It was Zilla's voice on the phone and although, as Alec had said, she was nearly four hundred miles away it sounded as if she were in the room. Usually it is pleasant to be connected with a clear line but on this occasion Katherine would have felt more comfortable if the connection had been faulty.

"Is that you, Kit?" repeated Zilla's voice in her ear.

"Yes," replied Katherine with a little gasp. "Yes, Zilla. What is it?"

"Oh, I was just wondering how you were getting on," said Zilla's voice sweetly. "It has been such awful weather, hasn't it? I hope Alec hasn't got one of his horrid colds."

"No, he's perfectly well, thank you."

"Good. Of course I've been much too busy to notice the weather; I've had such a rush getting the flat in order . . . but I'm settled now, so if you and Alec feel inclined for a little spree in town I can put you up quite comfortably."

"Oh, how kind of you! But I'm afraid Alec is terribly busy, just now."

"Come by yourself, then," suggested Zilla's voice.

The voice was so clear that Katherine could scarcely believe its owner was nearly four hundred miles away. She said, "Are you in London, Zilla?"

"Yes, of course! Where did you think I was? You'll come, won't you, Kit? I want to show you all that I've done to the flat. It's really beautiful."

"I can't come just now . . . perhaps later . . . thank you very much . . ." said Katherine incoherently. The mere idea of going to stay with Zilla took her breath away.

"Yes, later," agreed Zilla. "In the spring, perhaps."

"Perhaps," said Katherine vaguely.

"How are the children getting on at school?"

"Very well, thank you."

"Denis is so clever, isn't he? And Daisy is so pretty! Dear little things! By the way, Kit, I wondered if you and Alec had got an invitation to Eileen Dermot's wedding. She's being married on the fourteenth of December. That's next week, of course."

"Yes."

"You're going, I suppose?"

"Yes, we've accepted."

"They've sent me an invitation. The Dermots are great friends of mine and I should like to go. It will be a big wedding — everyone will be there. Do you think you could put me up for a few days?"

Katherine smiled . . . So that was the reason! She was glad that the feud was over, but what would be Alec's reaction?

"Can you put me up, Kit?" Zilla's voice was a trifle anxious. "I expect I could get a room at the club but I thought if you could give me a shake-down —"

"You must come to us, Zilla. We shall be delighted."

"Oh, splendid! It will be lovely to have a little change and a rest after all my hard work."

"We can have you for three nights, from the twelfth to the fifteenth, if that will suit you."

"It's a long way to come for three nights."

"But you can fly, can't you?" Katherine pointed out. She felt rather mean at this limitation of hospitality but for Alec's sake she must be firm. For three nights — and three days — Alec would have to bear it; she would not ask him to bear it for longer.

"Very well," said Zilla's voice, not quite as sweetly as before. "I thought I might have stayed at The Cedars over Christmas, but —"

"I'm so sorry," Katherine interrupted. "We're having the MacAslans for Christmas so the house will be full. It will be lovely to have you from the twelfth to the fifteenth. We shall look forward —"

"You're having the MacAslans to stay with you?" Zilla's voice was incredulous.

"Yes, for Christmas. MacAslan thought it would be a little dull for Phil at Ardfalloch."

There was a good deal more conversation on the much-too-clear line, but Katherine remained firm and when she put down the receiver the matter was settled: Zilla was to come for three days, no more and no less.

The news was broken to Alec on his return from the office. He was displeased and said so, frankly.

"But you must be nice to her," said Katherine in soothing tones. "You will be nice to her, won't you? Surely you can be nice to your sister for three days?"

Alec replied that he would find it extremely difficult to be nice to his sister for three minutes.

It seemed strange to Katherine that Zilla had left it so late before making arrangements to be put up for the Dermot wedding — the invitations had been sent out weeks ago — but presently she discovered that Zilla had asked several of her friends in Edinburgh to give her "a shake-down," and, having been denied this modest request for one reason or another, she had been obliged to fall back on The Cedars.

170

As has been said before, Katherine was glad the feud was over, but as the day of Zilla's arrival approached she became more and more apprehensive: Alec refused to promise to be nice to Zilla; Ellen remarked in her usual downright manner that "no good would come of Miss Maclaren's visit"; the children took the news in silence — with the mulish look very much in evidence.

All this was very worrying indeed and it was with a heavy heart that Katherine got out her little car and went off to meet her sister-in-law at Turnhouse Airport . . . but, like many events which are dreaded in advance, Zilla's arrival was unexpectedly pleasant. She descended from the plane wreathed in smiles; she approved of Katherine's new car and complimented Katherine upon her skill in driving. They had tea together in the drawing-room beside the fire (there was China tea and cucumber sandwiches, of course) and Zilla professed herself charmed with the new carpet. In fact she was so polite and kind that if Katherine had been meeting Zilla for the first time she would have liked her immensely.

After tea Zilla unpacked and produced presents for everyone in the house. "Christmas presents, of course," she explained. "So much easier to bring them with me than to send them by post. Perhaps you would like to open them now? I'm sure the children would like to open theirs . . . just one or two little things that I thought might amuse them."

It was obvious that Zilla wanted the parcels opened at once, so Katherine agreed; Daisy and Denis wasted no time in opening theirs. The "one or two little things" proved to be half a dozen delightful toys and books which were highly acceptable to the recipients. Katherine's present was a little cushion which was exactly right for her chair in the drawing-room; Ellen received a beautiful handbag. When Alec returned he found the atmosphere of The Cedars warm and friendly; he endured his sister's kiss and accepted a large book about old furniture, with sketches and coloured plates . . . and was suitably grateful.

Oh dear, what a pity she isn't always like this, thought Katherine, as she watched Zilla being pleasant and happy.

At dinner Zilla began to tell them of her activities in London and the troubles she had had in getting the flat redecorated and suitably furnished. "It's delightful now," she said. "I'm longing for you to see it. Madeline wanted me to have the drawing-room done in egg-shell blue but I decided on white walls and a pale pink ceiling. I was right, of course, it couldn't be more charming. Mr Guest complimented me on my colour-scheme when he came to lunch."

"Have you got in touch with the *Comtesse?*" inquired Alec.

"Not yet," was the reply. "Mr Guest says I have a great deal to learn about psychic phenomena before I can hope for any results. I have attended his circle regularly and I'm reading the books and practising the exercises — deep breathing and relaxation — so perhaps before long I shall be far enough advanced. Mr Guest is hopeful."

"Oh, good," said Katherine encouragingly.

172

"By the way," continued Zilla. "I told Mr Guest about the emanations you experienced in the old castle at Ardfalloch and he was *most* interested. This isn't the right time of year for an expedition to Ardfalloch — Mr Guest says it would be too cold — but perhaps as you are having the MacAslans to stay with you for Christmas you could mention it to them and ask if we might —"

Katherine and Alec both spoke at once:

"Oh, I don't think —" began Katherine in alarm.

"We couldn't possibly," Alec declared emphatically.

"But if they're staying with you it would be quite easy."

"We couldn't," said Katherine. "To be quite honest, Zilla, I'm sure they wouldn't like it. The old castle is 'a very special place' to the MacAslans. Phil said so."

"What did she mean by that?"

"She meant that Ardfalloch Castle is the cradle of their race," Alec replied in a portentous manner.

"Oh," said Zilla, somewhat impressed. Then she rallied and returned to the attack. "But that's all the more reason why they should be pleased to have the phenomena investigated by a wonderful man like Mr Guest."

"They won't be pleased."

"How do you know until you ask them?"

"Zilla," said Alec grimly. "I have no intention of asking MacAslan to allow you and Mr Guest — or anybody else — to camp upon his island. If you want his permission you had better get into touch with your friends, the Mitchells. That was what you intended, wasn't it?"

"Really!" exclaimed Zilla, her eyes flashing. "Really, Alec, you might be more co-operative! You might have more consideration for me! All I want is for you to sound MacAslan and see what he says. I'm not asking much."

"You're asking a great deal. Get this, Zilla: *I refuse to mention the subject to MacAslan.*"

They glared at each other.

Fortunately dinner was finished so Katherine rose from her chair and said, "Let's go into the drawing-room and have our coffee, Zilla. You haven't told me what you're going to wear for the wedding — a lovely new frock, I expect."

For a few moments the situation hung in the balance and then Zilla got up and stalked out of the room.

"A new frock?" asked Katherine as they sat down by the fire.

"You could do it, Kit," said Zilla, ignoring the red herring. "As a matter of fact it will be much better for you to do it."

"I'm sorry, Zilla, but I can't. You heard what Alec said."

"It's you I'm asking."

"I know, but —"

"You're putting me in a very difficult position," Zilla declared. "As I told you I spoke to Mr Guest about it and promised that I'd arrange it. I never thought for a moment that you would refuse to mention it to

MacAslan. It's very unkind of you — to say the least of it."

"I'm not the right person to ask him."

"Why? Surely it would be quite easy when he's staying here in the house?"

"It wouldn't be easy. You see, Zilla, I know MacAslan would dislike the idea so I couldn't ask him with the right sort of — of enthusiasm."

"I thought it such a good plan," said Zilla a trifle doubtfully. "There's Edna Mitchell, of course, but I have a feeling that Edna isn't on quite such intimate terms with the MasAslans as she tried to make out."

Katherine did not think so either. She said, "If you want my advice I think Mr Guest should write to MacAslan himself."

For a few moments there was silence; obviously Zilla was considering the suggestion. Then she said, "It isn't a bad idea. Mr Guest is a highly cultured man — he writes a very good letter — and of course he could explain the matter better than anyone else."

"Of course he could!" declared Katherine emphatically. "And it would be much better to ask MacAslan in a straightforward way than to do it through an intermediary."

Zilla nodded thoughtfully.

"MacAslan is a straightforward man," added Katherine, pushing home her point.

"Yes," said Zilla. "Yes, that's the best way to do it. I wonder why I didn't think of it before."

Having settled the matter satisfactorily Katherine heaved a sigh of relief and inquired once more about

Zilla's wedding garment; this time she was rewarded by a full and detailed description of its elegance.

Although Zilla's friends had refused, for one reason or another, to give her a shake-down they made up for their inhospitality by offering her lunch or tea or dinner. The telephone bell rang five times (Alec counted the calls) and by bed-time she was completely booked up for the three days of her visit. Her car had been sent to London but as Katherine's car was available there was no difficulty about transport.

"Did you say she could have your car whenever she wanted it?" asked Alec.

"I don't actually *remember* saying it," Katherine replied doubtfully.

"It's just like her cheek!" Alec exclaimed.

"Oh, I don't mind. It means that she's out all the time — and she's so much nicer when she's happy."

"You're making her too happy."

"Too happy?"

"She won't want to go away."

Thus warned, Katherine was prepared for Zilla's hints. At first they were gentle hints — there was no real need for Zilla to return to London the day after the wedding — but, when the gentle hints were ignored, the hints became stronger. Unfortunately her hostess was so dense that at last Zilla was obliged to put the matter plainly.

"I'd like to stay over the week-end," she said. "There hasn't been time for me to see the Langs — I could run over to Stirling on Sunday and spend the day with them

— and the Howdens are having a fork-luncheon on Monday, so —"

Katherine's heart was beating fast but she rushed in bravely, "I'm sorry, Zilla, but I'm afraid we can't have you any longer. I told you before, didn't I? We arranged that you were to stay from the twelfth to the fifteenth."

"But the MacAslans aren't coming till next week, so you could easily have me until they come."

"I'm afraid not. I've got a lot to do before they come — and the children will be getting their holidays. We've enjoyed having you so much," she added with less than her usual regard for the plain unvarnished truth.

This little exchange took place in the hall when they were about to set out to the wedding; Alec had gone to fetch the car round to the door.

"But, Kit, I don't see why —"

"I'm sorry, Zilla," said Katherine firmly.

There was no time for more. Alec was waiting for them; he blew his horn impatiently.

The wedding was a splendid affair; the bride was charming; the bridegroom young and handsome; there were masses of flowers, beautiful music and hundreds of elegant guests.

During the interval, while the register was being signed, Alec whispered to Katherine, "Would you have liked a wedding like this?"

She smiled at him and shook her head. "Our wedding was real — if you know what I mean."

He knew what she meant: there was something theatrical about this society wedding; he had heard one of the guests remark that it was "a very good show." In

Alec's opinion it was an exceedingly good show (he felt like taking off his hat to the stage-manager), but was it right that the Sacrament of Marriage should be celebrated in this fashion? Alec could not make up his mind about it.

CHAPTER
THIRTEEN

1

After Zilla's departure Katherine became very busy indeed; there were only nine days in which to complete her preparations for the MacAslans' visit and to buy all her Christmas presents. She had done very little before — Christmas had seemed a long way off — but now she realised that it was next week. She and Ellen got to work preparing the rooms for the guests; they had long consultations about food and made out lists of all that would be needed. Suddenly Katherine would discover that something very important had been forgotten and would dash off to Edinburgh in her little car, returning bright of eye and laden with curiously-shaped parcels. The old house which for years had been dull and melancholy became a hive of happy activity.

When the children's holidays started they were wild with excitement, rushing all over the house, laughing and talking and getting in everybody's way. Alec enjoyed the bustle and confusion; he realised that Katherine and her family had never before experienced the pleasure of Christmastide in a big comfortable house with money to spend upon presents for each other. It was natural that the joy of it had gone to their heads.

On the Saturday before Christmas Day he offered to take Daisy and Denis on a shopping expedition; needless to say the proposal was accepted with rapture.

"But, Alec, it will be frightful," objected Katherine. "You had much better go to Muirfield and play golf."

"I'd like to take them — if you don't mind."

"Oh, I don't mind," she replied. "But you have no idea what you're letting yourself in for . . . and the shops will be crowded."

Heedless of the warning Alec took the children to Edinburgh and trailed round the shops with them, listening while they made their purchases and getting a great deal of amusement out of the novel experience. The shops were crowded — as Katherine had said — but obviously the children were enjoying themselves thoroughly which was all that mattered to Alec.

Denis had a list; he was a methodical little boy. Daisy was a scatterbrain.

"Let's buy that lovely blue scarf for Mums!" Daisy cried excitedly.

"But we've got a blotter for Mums," objected Denis, referring to his list.

"She would like the scarf *much* better. We can give the blotter to Ellen. Oh, Den, look at those lovely gloves! Ellen would like those gloves — I know she would."

"But what about the blotter?"

"We could give it to Aunt Liz. Her blotter is dreadfully shabby."

"We've got an ashtray for Aunt Liz."

"It doesn't matter."

"It does matter," declared Denis. "You're messing up everything. We simply must stick to the list or we'll never get through. What's the good of making a list if you don't stick to it?"

"No good," retorted Daisy. "Making a list is silly. It's far better to buy things people will like. Aunt Liz would *like* the blotter."

"A list isn't silly."

"It *is* silly —"

"It isn't —"

The argument became so heated that Alec was obliged to intervene. "Listen," he said firmly. "Daisy can give Aunt Liz the blotter and Denis the ashtray. Now what about Simon? You thought of a book for him, didn't you?"

They had thought of a book for Simon, but on the way to the book department Daisy's eye fell upon a small travelling-clock in a green leather case.

"Simon would like this!" she cried, seizing it from the counter. "I *know* Simon would simply love this dear little clock. It's ever so much nicer than a book. Oh, we *must* buy this for Simon!"

"I'm sure it's terribly expensive," said Denis. "He would rather have a book."

"No, this dear, darling little clock! It doesn't matter how much it costs; Alec will give us the money."

Daisy was right, of course. The little clock was bought and went safely into Alec's pocket "in case of accidents." Was he spoiling them? He did not think so.

181

They bought presents for everybody except themselves; they were surprised at Alec's suggestion that they should buy presents for each other.

"We never do," said Daisy.

"We share things," explained Denis.

But soon Alec discovered that his suggestion had taken root, for when they were in the book department he felt Daisy tug his sleeve and bending down received a whispered request:

"Alec! That book over there — for me to give Den. You do it *now* when he isn't looking."

"That book over there" was a beautifully illustrated edition of *Pilgrim's Progress*. Alec thought it an excellent choice and bought it while Denis was browsing dreamily over some Boys' Annuals. The only thing that bothered Alec was the fear that Denis might be disappointed when he discovered that Daisy had a present for him . . . and he had none for her. However, all was well, for presently he was led into a corner by Denis.

"Listen, Alec," said Denis earnestly. "Do you think you could possibly afford to buy another little clock just like the one we got for Simon? Daisy liked it awfully much, didn't she? I thought I could give it to her — only I'm sure she would like a red one. I saw a red one on the shelf. Perhaps you could go and get it now, while she isn't looking; then it could be a secret. We'll wait here till you come back."

Alec hastened away on his errand — he could not refuse — but the shop was full of people so the purchase took some time and all sorts of frightful

182

contingencies occurred to him while he was waiting for the little red clock to be wrapped up. Supposing they strayed away and he could not find them in the crowd! Supposing they were kidnapped! He imagined himself returning to The Cedars and admitting to Katherine that he had lost them!

Fortunately nothing of the kind happened; they were waiting for him exactly where he had left them. They looked smug and self-satisfied and Denis had a small parcel under his arm which had not been there before.

"What's that?" asked Alec with interest.

Denis was taken aback at the question but Daisy chuckled and replied, "It's a present for somebody."

After that they went to the fancy-goods department and spent some time — and money — there. Then Alec, who was feeling extremely jaded, asked if they had finished.

"Yes," said Denis, referring to his list. "Yes, we've finished . . . and we better go home before Daisy sees something that she thinks would be nicer for somebody than what we've got."

Alec took the point and led them out of the nearest door. They had gifts for everyone in the house — Ellen's niece had not been forgotten — and, of course, they had suitable presents for the MacAslans. They were all laden with parcels; the loops of string were cutting into their fingers.

"Oh, what a gorgeous time we've had!" exclaimed Daisy as she climbed into the car.

Simon had been spending a few days with the Butterfields, at Wimbledon. Mark Butterfield was his greatest friend and it had been arranged that when Simon left school he was going into Mark's uncle's firm. Mark had been destined to go into Butterfield's export-and-import business since he was a child, and Mr Butterfield had offered an opening to Simon. The boys could start learning the business together.

It was Monday night when Simon arrived at The Cedars . . . and immediately it was apparent to Alec that he had lost Simon's friendship. Alec was distressed about it, but he was not really surprised. After the wedding when he and Katherine were about to drive away together, amidst the cheers and smiles and hand-waving, Alec had glanced at Simon, who was standing aloof, and had encountered a look which was unfriendly to say the least of it. He had tried to tell himself that he had imagined that look . . . and Katherine's conviction that Simon understood and was quite happy about their marriage had done much to reassure him. Now there was no doubt about it at all, thought Alec, as he watched Simon being received into the bosom of his family with affectionate acclamations. Simon's greeting to Alec had been polite — and no more.

There was no feeling of resentment in Alec's heart; he understood Simon and did not blame him. Naturally the boy was jealous. For years he had had Katherine all to himself and they had been very close to each other.

Then a stranger had come along and carried her off! A saint with a golden halo might have suffered a few twinges of jealousy — so Alec thought.

It will come right, thought Alec. It must come right. For Katherine's sake it must come right — Katherine would be terribly distressed! I must try to hide it from her. I must keep myself in the background and wait patiently. That's what to do.

Alec's plan, whether right or wrong, was fairly easy to carry out; all the more so because the decorations had arrived and Simon took it upon himself to hang them up. He spent most of his time standing upon a ladder surrounded with strings of coloured paper, bunches of holly and trails of variegated ivy. The twins helped — or tried to help — and Ellen emerged from the kitchen premises whenever she could spare the time and gave her advice, standing with arms akimbo and head on one side to get the general effect.

One morning Katherine suggested that Simon might like to come to Edinburgh with her and do some Christmas shopping.

"I've no time," he said. "I suppose you want the decorations ready before your guests arrive."

Katherine answered the tone rather than the words. "They're your guests too," she said quickly.

"It isn't my house," muttered Simon. "I didn't ask them to come."

"It will be fun!" exclaimed Daisy. "It will be like having a party all the time. But Simon, listen. Don't you want to go shopping with Mums?"

"I've got no money to buy presents."

"Alec will give you money. Won't you, Alec?"

Before Alec could answer Simon said quickly, "I don't buy presents with other people's money!"

Most people would have been silenced, but not Daisy.

"Simon, you must!" she cried. "You won't have any presents to give people on Christmas Day."

"I shan't be here on Christmas Day."

"Not here?" asked Daisy in alarm.

"I've been invited to spend Christmas Day with some friends, that's all. I suppose nobody has any objections."

It was obvious that Simon's family objected strongly to the plan. Katherine was silent but her face showed her feelings all too clearly.

"You can't," said Denis.

"Can't what?"

"You can't not be here on Christmas Day."

"Simon must do as he likes," said Alec. "Of course we'll all be sorry not to have him here on Christmas Day, but it will be nice for him to see his friends, won't it?"

"I think it would be nicer to be here with Mums and Alec and Den and me," said Daisy reproachfully.

3

The following evening Alec was writing letters in his study when the door opened and Katherine came in.

"Am I disturbing you?" she asked.

"Of course not!" replied Alec, putting down his pen.

"I know I'm disturbing you but I want to talk to you . . . I'm worried about Simon."

"He's all right," said Alec uncomfortably. "It's natural for the boy to want to spend Christmas Day with his friends."

"It isn't that — or at least that's only part of it. Simon is horrid to you, Alec."

"He's always quite polite."

"Oh, polite!" she exclaimed. "Yes, like the Germans when they occupied France. 'Correct' was the word."

Alec looked at her in surprise; it was exactly what he himself had thought.

"Simon ought to be down on his knees to you," declared Katherine. "We should all be down on our knees."

"I should dislike it intensely."

"I know. That's why I'm not." She was half laughing, with tears in her eyes. Then suddenly she was down on her knees beside his chair with her arms round him and her face hidden against his shoulder. "It isn't the money," she whispered. "It's you, yourself, so full of goodness and kindness and — and understandingness."

"Oh, darling, don't cry!"

"No, I won't," she said, taking out her absurdly small handkerchief and blowing her nose. "I can't stand weeping women. I shall go and speak to Simon and tell him —"

"No, Katherine! You mustn't do that; it would make things worse. This is just a passing mood. Coming

187

home from school and seeing us all here together has upset him temporarily."

"It isn't that. This mood — or whatever you like to call it — has been going on for weeks. I've had a letter from Mr Talbot, Simon's house-master, saying that he can't understand what has happened to Simon. All this term Simon has done no work; he has slacked at games; he has been 'a subversive influence in the house.' Simon! Simon, who has always been so good and sensible!"

"It will come right, darling. All boys go through a 'bolshie' phase. It's just his age."

"You didn't, did you?"

"Everybody goes through it and it's worse for Simon, because — well, because of this sudden change in his life."

"He was pleased about our marriage."

"Yes, at first he was pleased, but he didn't realise what it would mean. For years and years you've belonged to him — and him alone. I think you should be specially kind to Simon to show him that it has made no difference."

"I don't feel kind."

This was worse than Alec had feared. He said, "But he's all right with you, isn't he?"

"I've lost contact with Simon. There's no warmth in him, if you know what I mean. The children have noticed it too. They're unhappy about it."

For a few moments there was silence. Then Alec said, "I shouldn't have married you."

"Alec, how dare you say that!"

"Because it's true. Before I married you there was complete harmony in your family. I've broken something beautiful."

"You've made something beautiful," she said breathlessly. "The relationship between us — between you and me. It's real and strong and — and lovely. And what about Denis and Daisy? They love you dearly. You know that. Simon is the only one who — who —"

"Simon is the only one who resents me."

"What right has he to resent you?" she exclaimed indignantly.

"First because I've stolen a bit of your heart and second because you're all living in my house. Yes," said Alec thoughtfully. "I believe the fact that he is obliged to live in my house and eat food which has been bought with my money has quite a lot to do with it. I don't blame him. I just feel terribly sorry that I've lost Simon's friendship."

"Alec, do you really think he dislikes being dependent upon you?"

"Yes. You see it's very difficult to accept things from people unless you're fond of them."

"Then it's my fault! I shouldn't have allowed him to quarrel with his grandfather. If Simon had accepted his grandfather's offer and agreed to go to Limbourne when he leaves school Sir Mortimer would have given him anything he wanted. Anything," she repeated, "a generous allowance, a car of his own, holidays abroad —"

"Simon made his own decision; you didn't influence him one way or the other."

"Not consciously," she agreed. "But Simon knew I hated the place — that may have influenced him — and he knew I was glad when he decided not to go."

"You were glad because you knew that it would be the wrong thing for Simon."

Katherine was silent. It was true, of course; she had been sure that the queer unnatural atmosphere of Limbourne would be bad for Simon, but could anything be worse for Simon than this?

"Darling, you mustn't worry," said Alec. "If Simon had accepted his grandfather's offer he would have had plenty of money in his pocket, but no freedom. He decided that he couldn't bear the idea of being completely under Sir Mortimer's thumb like everybody else at Limbourne. You told me that, yourself. Anyhow it's over now so just put it out of your head. We've got to think of the present and do all we can to help Simon; he's very unhappy, I'm afraid."

"I think we ought to speak to him, Alec."

"No, we must just be kind and patient and wait for things to come right. You can do a lot to help him."

Katherine considered the matter. "I'll try," she said. Then she rose and added, "I must write to Simon's house-master; what am I to say?"

"Would you like me to answer Mr Talbot's letter?"

"Oh yes!" exclaimed Katherine. "What a comfort you are! You'll be able to do it ever so much better than I could." She put the letter on his desk and went away.

CHAPTER
FOURTEEN

1

It was Christmas Eve. The guests were due to arrive at tea-time so Katherine and Ellen had made a tour of the house to see if all was as it should be. They had done this several times already so naturally they found everything in perfect order: the furniture polished meticulously; the beds warm with electric blankets and the bedside lamps ready to switch on at a touch. In the bathroom, which MacAslan and his daughter were to share, there were towels and soap and bath salts. The decorations of holly and ivy and coloured paper gave the rooms a festive air and Ellen's flower arrangements in the tall Chinese jars were perfect — or almost perfect.

"Tut-tut," muttered Ellen as she stopped to pick up a tiny leaf which had fallen on the drawing-room carpet. "That's the worst of those beech-leaves; they drop off when you least expect it. What a good thing I noticed it before Mr MacAslan arrives!"

Katherine smiled. A vision rose before her eyes and she saw MacAslan's study at Ardfalloch House: books piled on a chair; papers in confusion on the desk and puppies scrambling over the floor. She seemed to hear Phil's voice saying, "When Daddy and I are alone we use this room for *everything* and neither of us is very tidy."

Ellen had been told that she must call their guest "MacAslan" because this was the correct way to address the chief of a clan, but after a moment's thought she had declared that she "couldn't do it." "I'll do anything else you like to make the Highland gentleman feel at home — but not that, Mrs Maclaren. Maybe he would like a haggis. I've a grand recipe from my cousin who's married on a crofter in Skye. Would he care for that, do you think?"

"Well, we'll see," replied Katherine. She realised that it was useless to say any more . . . and she could not blame Ellen for her reluctance to address MacAslan in the correct manner for she herself had experienced the same difficulty.

Simon and the children were out this afternoon — they had gone to a Christmas party at the Fishers' — so Katherine decided to give her guests tea in the drawing-room.

"That's what I was thinking," agreed Ellen. "It will be more restful for Mr MacAslan after driving all that long way. They'll be cold so I'll make up the fire."

Ellen was busy at the task and Katherine was standing watching her — and thinking what a good soul she was — when they heard a car coming up the drive.

"That'll be them!" cried Ellen.

Katherine rushed into the hall and opened the front door — and there they were!

Although she had been looking forward to their visit for weeks and had made elaborate arrangements for their comfort it gave her quite a shock to see them. Alec had said he could not imagine MacAslan here, at The Cedars; now, all of a sudden, Katherine realised that she, herself, had not really imagined him here . . . but here he was, getting out of his shabby old car and standing upon her doorstep. He was dressed, not in his kilt, but in a well-tailored grey suit.

"How lovely to see you!" exclaimed Katherine, giving him both her hands and smiling with pleasure. "And dear Phil," she added, turning to kiss the girl affectionately.

"Oh, Mrs Maclaren!" cried Phil. "I'm so excited that I don't know where I am."

"She's quite crazy," declared her father. "I've driven a lunatic all the way from Ardfalloch. First she would scarcely allow me to stop for a bit of lunch in case we should be late and then she was afraid we should arrive too early."

"Oh, Daddy, what nonsense!"

"Come in," said Katherine. "I'll show you your rooms and then we'll have tea."

Alec arrived while the guests were tidying up and soon they were all sitting round the drawing-room fire having tea and chatting.

"Where are the children?" asked MacAslan. "You said the house would be full of children."

"They've gone to a party," replied Katherine. "I wasn't sorry, really. It's nice for you to have tea in peace."

"This is a gorgeous house," declared Phil. "It's so warm and comfortable, and everything is shiny. Isn't it lovely, Daddy?"

He agreed that it was.

"We're going to have electricity," Phil announced. "Isn't it too marvellous for words? It's all your doing, Mr Maclaren."

"My doing?"

"It was you who told us about Carstiona's jug and of course that made me think of the stuff in our attic. Daddy got a man from Edinburgh to look at it and he found a lot of treasures. Tell them about the chest, Daddy," she added eagerly.

"Yes, that was rather curious. Phil and I found a large chest full of black jugs and vases and bowls —"

"Black?" asked Katherine in surprise.

"Quite black," said Phil with her attractive chuckle. "Janet wanted to throw away the dirty old things, but fortunately we didn't take her advice. I washed a small jug and cleaned it with polish — it was an awful job to get it clean — and it was silver! All the things are silver and very valuable. So we're going to sell them."

MacAslan was silent.

"We're going to sell them, aren't we, Daddy?"

"I suppose so," he agreed reluctantly. "I'm not very happy about selling the silver. According to some old letters it was brought to Ardfalloch by my great-grandmother as part of her dowry. She was a Frenchwoman."

"French silver," said Alec with interest. "I wonder if it was designed by Paul Lamerie. If so you should get a very good price for it."

194

"I'm not very happy about selling the silver," repeated MacAslan. "There are other things in the attic —"

"But not so valuable," interrupted Phil. "We shall need a lot of money and I'm sure Great-Great-Grandmama wouldn't mind. Her name was Philomela — I told you I was called after her, didn't I?"

"What has that got to do with it?" asked her father.

"Quite a lot," declared Phil earnestly. "I often think about her and I know what she was like. You have only to look at her picture which hangs in the dining-room to see that she was a practical sort of person. She would rather we sold her silver and used the money to make electricity instead of keeping it shut up in a chest in the attic, mouldering away and getting as black as ink. You agree, don't you, Mr Maclaren?"

Thus appealed to, Alec said somewhat diffidently, "Well, it would be different if you could use the silver, but —"

"We could never, never use it," Phil declared. "Who would keep it clean? Can you see Janet cleaning it — or Morag — or any of the girls from the cottages?"

"I'm a practical, matter-of-fact sort of person," admitted Alec. "I like things to be of use and I can't see that a chest of silver in the attic is of use to anybody."

"You're right, of course," agreed MacAslan with a sigh.

"Times have changed," said Katherine. She felt sad at the thought of MacAslan having to sell his great-grandmother's silver.

"Yes, times have changed," agreed MacAslan. "I often wish I had lived in the old times — two hundred years ago — when we resided in the old castle on the island."

"That's Daddy's theme song," explained Phil. "You would think, to look at him, that he's quite a civilised person — especially in that suit — but underneath he's a wild Highland chief, as bold as a lion and twice as fierce."

"Really, Phil!" said MacAslan smiling.

"It's true, Daddy. I've heard you say that the old days were best — when a man could take his sword in his hand and go after his enemy."

"I don't know when you can have heard me say that! There was only one occasion when I felt like murder and it was long before you were born."

There was a short silence and then Alec said, "You don't mean it seriously, of course."

"Oh yes, quite seriously," replied MacAslan. "There was murder in my heart — I would have killed my enemy with as little compunction as I would kill a venomous snake — but fate took a hand in the matter and prevented me." He looked at Alec and added, "You seem surprised, Maclaren. Can't you imagine yourself contemplating murder?"

"N-not really," stammered Alec, taken aback at the question.

"Not under any circumstances whatever?"

"No . . . at least . . . not unless somebody injured Katherine."

MacAslan sat back in his chair and smiled.

196

At that moment the door was flung open and Daisy rushed in; she was followed in a leisurely manner by Simon and Denis.

"It was gorgeous!" cried Daisy, her eyes shining like stars. "Father Christmas was there himself . . . he gave me a doll. I talked to him. I told him we were living at The Cedars now — just in case he didn't know we'd moved — but he said he knew all about it and he's coming to-night so *that's* all right. He was nice — I liked him — he had a funny gruff voice just like Mr Fisher. I'm going to stay awake to-night and see him when he comes." Daisy paused for breath.

"You've forgotten to say 'how do you do'," said Daisy's mother.

Daisy said "how do you do" politely and then continued her vivid account of all that had happened at the party. Simon and Denis greeted the guests . . . and were silent. Indeed it was impossible for anyone else to speak while Daisy held the floor. Fortunately both MacAslan and Phil were amused and were chuckling delightedly.

Katherine had always thought that Phil was very like her father; now she saw the resemblance even more clearly. For a few minutes she allowed Daisy to have her say and then she rose and swept the children off to bed.

It was a pleasant evening. The three elders sat by the fire chatting. Simon got out the card-table and he and Phil played Monopoly; both of them knew the game and were experts. The paper counters were changing hands and little green houses and red hotels were springing up like mushrooms all over the board.

Katherine saw that Simon was looking more like himself; she heard him laugh quite heartily. Phil is good for him, she thought. She is sweet and clever and full of life. She would be good for anybody.

Later, Alec went upstairs and returned with a pair of golfing-stockings and several large brown-paper parcels. "Fast asleep — both of them," said Alec smiling. "We'll get the stockings packed and then I can creep up and put them back."

"Oh, can I help?" asked Phil, looking up from the game. "I've never helped Santa Claus before."

2

It had always been the custom on Christmas morning for the twins to bring their Christmas stockings to their mother's room and unpack them upon her bed. Katherine had warned Denis that the invasion was not to take place before seven-thirty — at the earliest.

"But we'll be awake long before that," Daisy had objected. "How can we *possibly* wait for hours and hours to see what Santa Claus has brought?"

"If you can't wait you must unpack the stockings in your own rooms," replied Katherine firmly. It was her "no nonsense" voice — the voice of "She, who must be obeyed."

Katherine was awake before half past seven so she saw the door open and the two small figures appear. Each bore one of Alec's golfing-stockings, swollen to an enormous size with treasures.

198

"We didn't unpack them," said Daisy.

"We thought you and Alec would like to watch us," explained Denis.

With that they leapt on to the bed, waking Alec who had been slumbering peacefully, and proceeded to examine their loot.

They were still young enough to be pleased with the small presents: coloured balls, wooden animals, building blocks, fruit and sweets and crackers. Watching them tearing the parcels open and listening to their exclamations of delight, Katherine remembered similar scenes when Simon was a small boy. How lovely it would be if you could keep your children young for ever and ever, reflected Katherine. It was so much easier when they were like this, happy as birds in a nest . . . but even the twins were growing up. Soon Denis must go to a proper boys' school — Alec had been talking about it — so by next Christmas neither he nor Daisy would believe in Santa Claus any more. This is the last time, thought Katherine, as she watched Daisy unwrapping a doll's looking-glass and listened to her exclamations of delight.

"Look, Mums! Look, Den! It's a tiny mirror. I can see myself in it. Look, Alec! Can you see yourself?"

Alec took the toy in his large hand and looked at himself; he decided that his face was not a pleasant sight and said thoughtfully, "I wonder if Santa uses a mirror like this for shaving."

"Silly Alec!" cried Daisy, bursting into shrieks of laughter. "Silly, silly Alec! *He's got a beard!*"

It was so absurd, and Daisy's mirth was so infectious that they were all laughing uncontrollably when Ellen came in with the tray of morning tea.

"Well, you're having a merry Christmas and no mistake," declared Ellen smiling in sympathy.

Simon had left the house early to spend the day with his friends but the rest of the party met at breakfast and, although some of the presents had been given already, the table was covered with parcels, large and small. Perhaps it would have been better to wait until after breakfast before opening them — Katherine suggested this — but the children could not wait. The porridge grew cold and the bacon and eggs congealed upon their plates while they cut the string and tore the parcels open. Soon the table was cluttered with books and handkerchiefs, boxes of sweets, boxes of games and building toys and other gifts too numerous to mention. The floor was littered with wrapping-paper; everyone seemed to be talking at once.

"Oh, Mrs Maclaren, what lovely gloves!" exclaimed Phil.

"Oh, look at this dear little red clock!" cried Daisy.

"A book," muttered Denis, seizing it with avidity.

"Thank you very much, Mrs Maclaren. This will be most useful to me," said MacAslan, displaying a large chromium-plated torch.

"And thank you for this — it's charming," returned Katherine, holding up a little Dresden-china shepherdess and smiling at him.

"Just what I wanted," declared Alec as he unpacked a pigskin case of exactly the right size to hold his cheroots.

Daisy was sitting beside him; she whispered, "It says who it's from inside. You'll never guess."

He opened it and found a small piece of paper upon which was written, "From Denis and Daisy."

"Those are kisses," explained Daisy, pointing to a row of little crosses. "Your present was so expensive that we hadn't any money left to buy a proper card. But you like it, don't you?"

"It's a lovely present. You couldn't have given me anything nicer."

"Oh, thank you, Mr Maclaren!" exclaimed Phil, who had opened an envelope and discovered a card and a five-pound note. "I shall buy a pullover —"

Denis was the only silent member of the party, he was poring over the pictures in his copy of *Pilgrim's Progress*.

"He likes it," said Daisy, nudging Alec and pointing to her brother. "But he hasn't said thank you."

Alec smiled and replied, "There's no need for him to say it, you can see how pleased he is."

"I've said thank you to everybody — and I'm going to say thank you again for my gorgeous bicycle. Darling Alec, I like it best of all my presents." And with that she flung her arms round his neck and hugged him fondly.

Daisy's embraces were always whole-hearted. When Alec at last was disengaged he realised that breakfast was over. Phil was helping Katherine to tidy up the paper; MacAslan had risen and was arranging the cards on the chimney-piece.

There were still some unopened parcels. "They're all for Simon," said Katherine as she piled them on a chair. "He can open them later. Does anyone want to come to church?"

Apparently everyone wanted to go to church — with the sole exception of Denis.

"It isn't that I don't want to go to church," he explained when his mother roused him and told him to come and get ready. "It's because I would rather stay at home and read my book."

"There will be plenty of time later to read your book," replied Katherine briskly. "You like going to church; we shall have 'Hark the Herald Angels Sing'."

"And 'Once in Royal David's City'," cried Daisy, starting to caper round the room like a frisky pony.

MacAslan was laughing heartily. "How delightful they are!" he said to Alec.

CHAPTER
FIFTEEN

1

Alec's car was large enough to take the whole party to church including Aunt Liz, who was picked up from her flat in Heriot Row. St. Mary's Cathedral was beautifully decorated and full of people but Katherine had arranged to be in good time for the service so they were able to get seats together. Even more fortunately they had the children's favourite hymns.

It was still early when they returned to The Cedars — time for a glass of sherry before lunch. They all gathered in the drawing-room and chatted while the children opened more parcels, produced by Aunt Liz.

"Where is Simon?" said Aunt Liz to Katherine.

"He's spending the day with some friends."

"Who?"

"He didn't say."

"Do you mean to tell me you don't know where he has gone?"

"Oh, to the Howdens' I expect," replied Katherine hastily. "The two Howden boys are both at Barstow. It's nice for Simon to spend the day with his friends."

"Well, it seems most extraordinary to me," said Aunt Liz crisply.

Fortunately there was no time to say more, the gong boomed to warn them that lunch was ready, so they went into the dining-room and took their places at the table and ate the usual Christmas fare: turkey and ham, plum-pudding and brandy butter; pineapple and grapes and crystallised pears.

The party was a success; they all talked and laughed and enjoyed themselves . . . only Katherine felt sad. It was so strange not to have Simon here; it was so distressing to feel that she had lost him. Somehow the words of Aunt Liz had brought home to Katherine how deep and wide was the rift between Simon and his family. Hitherto she had been angry with Simon but suddenly her feelings changed and her heart yearned over the boy. Alec had said that Simon was unhappy and that she must be "specially kind." She had tried to be kind, she had made every effort to reach him, but it was useless. He looked miserable, pale and haggard, his mouth was pulled down at the corners . . . and now, to-day when all families should be together, he had chosen to absent himself; he had chosen to spend the whole day with friends. Katherine was sure he had gone to the Howdens' — or nearly sure. Where else could he have gone?

Katherine glanced round the table and saw that they were all happy; even Daisy, who adored Simon, was happy. Nobody was missing Simon except herself. Nobody was thinking about him. I wonder if Alec is right, she thought. Wouldn't it be better to have a show-down with Simon — talk to him seriously and reason with him? I've always been able to talk to Simon about everything; he has always been so good and sensible, even when he was quite a little boy. Oh darling Simon, what has happened to you?

Katherine was so engrossed in thought that she did not hear what MacAslan was saying to her. She was obliged to ask him to repeat himself.

"I just said it's a pity Simon isn't here to enjoy the fun."

"How extraordinary that you should say that!" exclaimed Katherine.

"Not really very extraordinary, Mrs Maclaren. This is a time when one is inclined to think of absent friends and to wish for their presence."

"Yes, I was wishing he were here," she admitted. "All the more so because nobody else is thinking about him."

MacAslan glanced round the table. There was so much noise going on that there was privacy to talk. He said, "I understand your feelings only too well. When you lose a beloved person through death: for a time people are sorry and then they forget and the world goes cheerfully on its way."

Katherine nodded. "They all forget . . . but you remember."

"To-day is different, Mrs Maclaren. Your guests are all happy, but you wouldn't wish it otherwise, I'm sure."

"Of course not! Simon is happy too — having fun with his friends — so I'm just being silly."

The meal was finished and the children had begun to pull crackers and to put on paper hats. Aunt Liz had a lavender bonnet and was tying the strings beneath her chin; it was most becoming and Alec was telling her so. Daisy came round the table to pull a cracker with MacAslan; there was a chief's hat inside so MacAslan put it on.

"Oh Daddy, it suits you splendidly!" cried Phil. "Oh, look at Mr Maclaren! He's got a dunce's hat."

Phil's hat was a Balmoral bonnet; she had crammed it sideways onto her dark curls and looked like the daughter of a chief — which, of course, she was.

Yes, I'm just being silly, thought Katherine, as she nodded to Aunt Liz at the other end of the table and gave the signal for the ladies to retire.

2

Alec had been apprehensive about the entertainment of his guest but he soon discovered that MacAslan needed no entertainment; he fell in quite naturally with the routine of the household. If he had nothing to do he retired to Alec's comfortable study and wrote letters or read Alec's books but most days he was out on business of his own. One morning he went off to Edinburgh by himself, saying he must see his solicitor, the next morning he and Phil went down to Leith Docks to find Iain MacFadyen (a brother of Brown Dugal) who had been born and bred in the little cottage at Ardfalloch. They had some difficulty in tracing the man but eventually discovered him in a small and exceedingly dirty ship-chandler's store.

"We *had* to find him," Phil explained to Katherine.

"Is he like Dugal?" Katherine asked.

"Not a bit. He's — he's very rough — rather bolshie, you know. At first he was rude and would hardly speak to Daddy but he soon came round. Nobody can resist Daddy . . . and of course Daddy had promised Dugal to find out if Iain was all right."

"Is he all right?"

"It depends what you mean by all right," said Phil, frowning thoughtfully. "He has got a job, selling oil and stores for ships, so that's something. You see Iain is the black sheep of the MacFadyen family; he doesn't stick to any job — or else the jobs don't stick to him." She sighed and added, "Daddy has got him out of trouble several times and given him a new start but it isn't any use."

This was the night of Alec's pantomime party so the children were very much excited. MacAslan explained that a cousin, whom he had not seen for years, had asked him to dinner and he did not like to refuse. He suggested that his ticket should be given to Ellen.

Katherine agreed that this was an excellent plan. As a matter of fact she had been wondering whether the pantomime was a suitable entertainment for MacAslan; Ellen would enjoy it thoroughly, of course, so it was all for the best.

When Katherine saw MacAslan coming downstairs, ready to go to dinner with his cousin, she was astonished beyond measure. She had always admired him but to-night, arrayed in the full evening-dress of a Highland gentleman, he was positively breath-taking. He was wearing his dress kilt and black cloth doublet adorned with silver buttons; at his throat and wrists were falls of exquisite lace. There were silver buckles on his shoes and a jewelled skean-dhu in his stocking.

"Oh, how marvellous you are!" Katherine exclaimed impulsively.

MacAslan smiled and replied, "Fine feathers make fine birds. Besides," he added with a chuckle, "between you and me and the gatepost I don't possess a conventional evening-suit."

"Oh, I'm glad you don't! *You're just right like that* . . . and it isn't true about fine feathers making fine birds. I mean, another man wearing those clothes would look as if he were in fancy dress."

"But I don't?"

"No, I've told you already that you're marvellous and I'm not going to tell you again," replied Katherine, laughing.

They were both laughing when Alec came out of his study to ask if MacAslan would like a latch-key.

"Perhaps I had better have one," MacAslan said. "I shan't be late; in fact I might be back before you are. If so you'll find me comfortably ensconced in your study."

Katherine and Alec stood at the door and watched their guest walk over to the garage to get his shabby old car.

"He looks fine, doesn't he?" said Alec. "I wonder what the Duke will think of him."

"The Duke?"

"Yes, his cousin is married to an Austrian duke. He told me the name, but I couldn't get hold of it. They're staying at the North British Hotel. MacAslan hasn't met the Duke before — that's why he didn't like to say no when his cousin asked him to dinner."

"Oh, I see," said Katherine; she was not really surprised. It was, somehow, typical of MacAslan that he should spend the morning searching for a black sheep in the neighbourhood of Leith Docks and the evening dining with a duchess.

3

In addition to the pantomime there were children's parties and "half-grown-up" parties and visits to the cinema. Phil enjoyed it all ... and she enjoyed shopping with Katherine. Unfortunately the weather had been somewhat disappointing but on Friday night there was a touch of frost and on Saturday morning the sun was shining brightly in a cloudless sky.

MacAslan announced at breakfast that he must stretch his legs (which were becoming stiff for lack of exercise) and intended to walk over the Pentland Hills.

"I wish I could come," said Alec. "I usually manage to get Saturdays off, but to-day I have to go to Haddington to see an old client."

"I could come if you like, sir," said Simon a trifle diffidently. "There are some fine walks over the hills."

"Splendid," declared MacAslan. "You can show me the lie of the land. Let's take a sandwich in our pockets and make a day of it."

Katherine glanced at Simon in surprise; it was so unlike him, in his present strange mood, to offer to do anything for anybody. She saw that he was looking better this morning — more like himself — but there was no time to think about that now. She hurried into the kitchen and started to prepare sandwiches.

Phil pursued her and offered to help.

"You might heat up the coffee," said Katherine. "You'll find a Thermos flask in the pantry."

"Oh, Daddy won't want coffee. When he goes off for the day he takes one sandwich or sometimes a couple of oatcakes and a piece of cheese."

"We'll make the coffee," replied Katherine smiling. "If they don't want to be bothered with it they can leave it in the car. What would you like to do this morning?"

Phil hesitated.

"Go on," said Katherine. "Tell me what you'd like to do."

"Well . . . I haven't been to the castle. Daddy said he would take me some time but there aren't many days left."

"We'll go this morning."

"Are you sure it wouldn't be a bother? You've seen it before, of course."

"I love the castle. I don't mind how often I see it — and the children love it too. We'll take them with us."

Somewhat to her surprise Katherine discovered that although Phil had never been within the walls of Edinburgh Castle she knew a great deal about its stormy history; in fact Phil knew more about the battles and sieges which had taken place on this very spot than Katherine herself. The children soon became tired of listening and ran off to explore; Phil and Katherine wandered round together evoking the past.

"How terribly steep the rock is!" said Phil, as she leaned over the stone battlements and looked down. "You would think it was impregnable, but it wasn't, of course. At one time there was an English garrison in the castle, and it was besieged by Randolph, Earl of Moray, who was a nephew of Robert the Bruce. He tried to take it several times and he tried to starve the garrison — but it seemed hopeless — so at last he became impatient and one dark stormy night he climbed up the face of the rock with thirty men; they had all been carefully chosen for their courage and agility. Suddenly at a signal from Randolph they leapt over the wall and overpowered the careless sentries, and opened the castle gates. What a night that must have been!" exclaimed Phil with flashing eyes. "Can't you imagine it, Mrs Maclaren? The guards taken by surprise and killed before they could make a sound . . . and Randolph rushing to open the gates."

Katherine shivered involuntarily; she could imagine it only too well.

"And that wasn't the only time we won the castle back from the English," continued Phil. "It was won by Sir William Douglas and a clever priest. They pretended that they were bringing provisions for the English garrison; they had a string of mules, laden with boxes and barrels, and the men were dressed as English sailors. When the guards saw them coming they lowered the drawbridge and raised the portcullis to let them in. Then the men threw off their disguise and rushed into the castle shouting, 'A Douglas! A Douglas!' They killed the guards and took the castle and threw the governor into the deepest and darkest dungeon."

"You would like to have been there," suggested Katherine.

"I would rather have been with Randolph," replied Phil. "His way of taking the castle was more exciting."

Katherine felt she had heard enough about battles and bloodshed so she led the way to Queen Margaret's Chapel, a small Norman building on the crown of the rock. She was rather pleased to discover that Phil knew very little about Queen Margaret's history.

"She was a Saxon princess," Katherine explained. "She came to Scotland quite by accident; it was a fortunate accident for Scotland. Princess Margaret and her brother and sister were escaping from England, from the Norman conquerors, and crossing the sea to the Flemish coast when suddenly there was a terrific storm and they were obliged to take shelter in the Forth. They asked the Scottish King for protection and he gave it to them and entertained them royally in his palace at Dunfermline. His name was Malcolm Canmore."

"You said it was a fortunate accident for Scotland."

"It was very fortunate. King Malcolm fell in love with Princess Margaret and married her. She was beautiful and cultured and deeply religious so she was able to do a lot for her husband and for the poor people of the country. Everybody adored her. It was in Queen Margaret's time that Edinburgh Castle first became a royal residence."

"You mean they lived here?"

"Yes, Queen Margaret liked it better than Dunfermline so various buildings were put up. Nobody knows what they were like because the castle has been destroyed and rebuilt several times since those days. The only building that remains is Queen Margaret's Chapel, which I'm going to show you. It was restored about a hundred years ago but part of it is actually the original building and dates from 1070 or thereabouts. Look, there it is, Phil! It's the oldest building on the rock."

"Nine hundred years, very nearly," said Phil, looking at it with awe. She added, "Isn't it wonderful to think of Queen Margaret saying her prayers here . . . all that long time ago?"

Katherine was pleased; she had often thought of this herself. She was about to tell Phil more about Queen Margaret and about her three fine sons when the children appeared and asked if Phil had seen the banqueting hall and the dungeons; on hearing that she had not, they insisted that she should come at once and be shown round.

"You'll like the dungeons; they're awfully grim and creepy," said Daisy taking her hand.

"She'll like the banqueting hall better," declared Denis.

Phil allowed herself to be led away, so Katherine went into the beautiful building which commemorates the men and women of Scotland who gave their lives for their country in two great wars. It was a favourite haunt of hers and she was quite pleased to wander round alone.

CHAPTER
SIXTEEN

1

It had become a pleasant habit for Alec and MacAslan to retire to the study when the rest of the party went to bed. They found plenty to talk about for their lives were entirely different and they were interested in each other. Alec learned a great deal about the difficulties of a big land-owner with insufficient money to spend upon the improvement of his estate; Iain MacAslan learned a certain amount about the life of an Edinburgh lawyer.

The friendship thus engendered was very satisfactory and enlarging, as all good friendships are. There was give and take not only of interesting information, and ideas about all sorts of subjects, but also give and take of essential personality. Alec felt this strongly; he looked at MacAslan, sitting at ease in the comfortable leather chair, and thought: I'm a little bit different because of knowing that man. I'm bigger, somehow. I wonder what he feels about me.

Alec had expected that to-night, after his walk over the Pentland Hills, MacAslan would want to go to bed earlier than usual, but MacAslan was used to walking all day long over his own hills so he was not in the least tired; the clock in the hall was striking twelve when he rose to say good night.

They parted in the hall. MacAslan went upstairs while Alec proceeded on his usual round of the house, making sure that all the doors were locked and the windows securely fastened. He had just finished bolting the front door when he heard a sound and, turning round, saw Simon standing behind him.

"Goodness, haven't you gone to bed!" he exclaimed. "Is something the matter?"

"I wanted to talk to you," said Simon. "I've been waiting for a chance . . . but perhaps it's too late?"

It was much too late in Alec's opinion — he was longing to get to bed — but he replied cheerfully, "Not a bit too late. There's still quite a good fire in the study. Come in and sit down."

Simon came in but he did not sit down. He stood and looked at Alec, who was poking up the fire. "I'm sorry," he said.

"What are you sorry for?"

"I'm sorry for — for everything. I've been terribly wicked. I knew I was wicked but I went on doing it."

Alec gazed at him in alarm.

"Hating you," explained Simon in a low voice.

"Oh, that! It doesn't matter, Simon: I mean I understood what you were feeling and —"

"It does matter. I want to say I'm sorry to you — terribly sorry, Alec."

"Don't worry, old chap. I knew things would come right in time. I didn't blame you in the least."

"Please say you forgive me."

"There's nothing to forgive, but if you want me to say it: I forgive you, Simon. Now everything is all right, isn't it?"

Simon came forward and they shook hands. Then he sat down on the arm of a chair. "I want to explain," he said. "There's no excuse, of course, but I'd like to explain what happened to me. It has been horrible, Alec. For weeks and weeks I've been miserable. All the time I was at school I kept thinking of you and Mums driving away together after the wedding and about you and Mums together at The Cedars. You see Mums has always belonged to me in a special sort of way . . ."

"I know. It was quite natural that you should feel a bit upset."

"Upset! I sort of went mad," declared Simon. "I couldn't think of anything else. I did practically no work and I couldn't be bothered with games. I got into frightful hot water but I didn't care. In fact I was glad. It was like a devil inside me. Yes, it was just like a devil inside me," repeated Simon.

There was a short pause, then he continued, "I quarrelled with Mark. He has been my best friend ever since we went to Barstow — we share a study, you know. Well, suddenly I wanted to be beastly to him. Mark said I was 'insufferable.' I knew I was insufferable. I was insufferable to myself as well as to other people."

Alec was silent. He had known that Simon must have been unhappy but he had not realised it had been as bad as this.

"I want to tell you everything," Simon said. "There was another thing that made me angry with you. I thought about your kindness to me, taking me to the cricket club and coaching me at the nets, and — and lots of other things."

"We were friends, Simon."

"Yes . . . but then, when I was so miserable, it came into my head that you weren't really my friend. You were just using me as an excuse for coming to tea at the flat and seeing Mums."

"Oh, Simon!" exclaimed Alec in distress. "Oh no! It wasn't like that at all. I'll tell you exactly what happened. When I first met Katherine I wanted to see her again and I thought — I thought I might be able to get in touch with her more easily and naturally through her stepson. But that was only at the very beginning, before I had seen you. When I got to know you I loved you for yourself and we became friends. There, that's the truth."

Simon nodded. "Yes, I believe you."

"I used to think I should like a son of my very own exactly like you."

"You've changed your mind now, I suppose," muttered Simon.

"Don't be an ass," said Alec, smiling at him affectionately. "We've forgiven each other, haven't we? I'm sorry you've had such a bad time but it's over now."

"Yes, it's over," agreed Simon. "It has been very bad. It was bad at school and even worse when I came home. Christmas Day was just about the worst. I felt so miserable — all mixed up — that I couldn't bear the idea of seeing you all happy, laughing and talking and

218

giving each other presents, so I had to escape. I spent the day in the Waverley Station and —"

"What!" cried Alec in amazement.

"Oh, the Howdens *did* invite me to spend the day with them — that wasn't a lie — but I refused. They would have been happy and Christmassy too."

"You spent the whole day wandering about the station?"

"Yes, I had intended to go for a long walk over the hills but it was wet and cold. I didn't want to get soaked through because — well, because you all thought I was spending the day with friends. It would have looked funny if I'd come in soaking wet. I sat in the waiting-room most of the time; it was warmer there. Nobody noticed me or minded; all the people were too busy with their own affairs. I had a cup of coffee and a bun at the restaurant."

"Was that all you had to eat?"

"I hadn't much money."

"Oh, Simon!"

"I didn't mean to tell you about it. You won't tell Mums, will you?" asked Simon anxiously.

"No, I won't. She would be terribly distressed." Alec himself was distressed at the thought of the boy wandering about the station for hours all by himself and having, as his Christmas dinner, a cup of coffee and a bun. He said again, more to comfort himself than to comfort Simon, "But it's all over now."

"Quite suddenly," nodded Simon, "I feel as if a burden had fallen off my back, like Christian in *Pilgrim's Progress*. There's a picture of him in that book you gave Denis with the ugly burden of sin falling off and rolling into the pit. After all these weeks and weeks of misery . . . it's over."

Alec wondered why it was over. What was it that had loosened Simon's burden and caused it to drop from his shoulders into the pit? He was wondering if he could ask — but there was no need to ask.

"It was Daisy who began it," said Simon in thoughtful tones. "Yesterday afternoon when I was in my room I heard the two of them in the garden. They were just under my window, talking to each other — you know the way they talk. Daisy said, 'Mums is *so* miserable.' Den said, 'He's horrid to Alec so of course that makes Mums miserable. We were all happy before he came home from school.' Then Daisy said, 'Simon didn't come home from school — it's somebody else. It's somebody nasty in dear, darling Simon's body.'

"That gave me a shock because it was true. Then Den said gruffly, 'Don't cry, you ass. It's black magic. We must think of something . . . ' Then they put their heads together and whispered so I didn't hear any more."

"What did they do?"

"I wondered what they would do," admitted Simon, smiling a little. "I kept on wondering . . . but it was nothing very desperate. When I went to bed last night there was a four-leaved clover under my pillow, that's all."

"Did you sleep on it?"

Simon nodded. "I couldn't throw it away when they had taken all the trouble of finding it, could I? Well, that was the beginning."

"So there really was magic in the four-leaved clover."

"There was a special sort of magic in what Daisy said — and in the two little donkeys hunting for the clover and putting it under my pillow. You see, when they were babies I helped to bath them and I used to give Daisy her bottle," added Simon as if that explained the matter fully.

Perhaps it did, thought Alec. He said, "Yes, I see."

"That was the beginning," repeated Simon. "Then, to-day when I was out on the hills with MacAslan, I told him the whole thing."

"You spoke to MacAslan about it!" exclaimed Alec in surprise.

"It was quite easy. He seemed to — to know there was something wrong with me; he even seemed to know what it was. He didn't make light of it, but just talked sensibly and seriously. He hasn't had an easy life himself; he told me about a thing that happened to him when he was young — at least it happened to somebody he loved very dearly. She was in dreadful trouble and he was powerless to help her. I can't tell you about it, of course, but I can tell you my trouble seemed very childish in comparison. It's because he came through such an awful time that he can understand and sympathise with other people. He's a wonderful man."

"Yes, he is."

"One of the things he said to me was that real love is unselfish, 'seeketh not her own.' Of course he meant that if I really loved Mums in the right way her happiness would be my first consideration. *That* gave me something to think about."

There was a short silence. A piece of coal fell out of the fire; Alec leant forward and put it back.

"He said a lot more," continued Simon. "He said it all in a nice friendly sort of way — not laying down the law but just asking me questions. For instance he asked me if I could look after Mums and the children. At first I didn't realise what he meant . . . but when I had thought about it for a minute I realised all right! Of course I had to say no. Then he made me see what you had done."

"What do you mean?"

"He made me see that if I really loved Mums I ought to be grateful to you for taking her out of the flat, where she was toiling and moiling and wearing herself out, and bringing her here to this comfortable house. He said that in his opinion she was the sort of woman who needed care and affection and a man to look after her — and the children needed a father. What did I think about it? Well, what could I say? I mean it was true. Then he said that you were the right man for the job."

"He said that?"

Simon smiled. "He thinks you're pretty good value, Alec."

Alec smiled too. It was extremely pleasant to know that MacAslan thought him "pretty good value."

"We had been walking fast," continued Simon. "I thought I was a good walker, but my goodness, I had my work cut out to keep up with MacAslan! You should have seen him swinging along up hill and down dale as

222

if it was no trouble at all. By this time I had come to my senses and I saw everything clearly ... saw what an almighty fool I had been. I tried to tell him and thank him for helping me but he just laughed and gave me a terrific thump on the back and said something in Gaelic. I asked him what it meant and he said, 'It means I've knocked the devil out of you, my lad.' Then he sat down and told me to go up to the top of the hill by myself and let the wind blow through me. So of course I did. If he had told me to stand on my head I'd have done it. I would do *anything* for MacAslan."

Yes, thought Alec, looking at the boy's flushed face and shining eyes. MacAslan is the sort of man that men would die for ... the sort of man to lead a forlorn hope. Even I, a staid Edinburgh lawyer, can imagine myself following MacAslan to the death.

"It was cold on the top of the hill," continued Simon. "The wind was like a knife; it blew right through me, just as he had said. I felt as if I had no clothes on. I felt ... well, I felt clean. Presently I heard him shouting to me so I went down and we sat in a sheltered place and ate our lunch together. He gave me a nip of whisky out of the flask which he had in his pocket. It had rather a nasty taste — a queer peaty sort of taste — but it warmed me up like anything. He talked a lot while we were having lunch; he was most awfully kind. He wants me to go and stay at Ardfalloch for part of the Easter hols. You and Mums wouldn't mind, would you?"

"Of course not. It would be a splendid holiday for you."

Simon nodded. "I'd like you to tell Mums all that I've told you, Alec — at least nearly all. Perhaps you had better water it down a bit."

"Yes, perhaps I should."

"Well, that's the whole story," said Simon with a sigh of relief. "When MacAslan and I had finished our sandwiches and were coming away I said I was going to tell you everything and ask you to forgive me. He said, 'Yes, first make your peace with Alec and then make your peace with God'."

There was quite a long silence; then Simon rose. "It's frightfully late," he said. "I expect you want to go to bed."

Alec put the guard on the fire. "Yes, it's late," he agreed. "However, to-morrow is Sunday — it's to-day, really — so you can have a good long sleep. You look as if you needed it."

"Oh, I'm not tired. I'm going to church at eight o'clock. MacAslan said it would be all right if I was really sorry. I shall go in the bus — it will be quite easy — but I may be a bit late for breakfast."

2

Katherine was asleep when Alec went up; he was glad (I can tell her in the morning, he thought), but she was not very fast asleep for when he got into bed she stirred and murmured, "Simon . . ."

He had expected his own name on her lips and for a moment he drew back with a queer pang in the region of his heart. Then he smiled a trifle grimly; so this was what jealousy was like!

"Oh, Alec!" said Katherine, opening her eyes. "What a long time you've been! I was trying to keep awake because I wanted to talk to you — there never seems to be time to talk during the day — then I went to sleep and I had such a horrid dream."

"Go to sleep again, darling. It's nearly two o'clock."

"I was dreaming about Simon. He was standing on the other side of a deep ravine — a ravine with black rocks and a river at the bottom — and I couldn't get to him."

"It's all right. You'll be able to get to him now."

"What do you mean?" she exclaimed, raising herself on one elbow and gazing at Alec in surprise.

"We had a long talk, Simon and I. That's what made me so late. He has had a miserable time but it's all over. We're friends."

"Alec, really? Do you mean you spoke to him?"

"I didn't say much; Simon did most of the talking."

"Tell me all about it."

Alec hesitated; he was very tired but he saw that he had said too much — or too little. It was natural that Katherine should want to know what had happened . . . so he told her. He "watered it down a bit" as Simon had suggested and left out the inessentials. Shorn of its trimmings the story did not take long to tell.

"How wonderful!" Katherine exclaimed. "What a relief to know it's over! We ought to have talked to Simon ourselves when he first came home from school. I thought so at the time, but you said —"

"No, darling. Neither you nor I could have talked to Simon; it had to be somebody outside the trouble; it had to be a man of heroic stature with an understanding heart . . . in fact it had to be MacAslan. I don't believe anybody else could have done it."

"What a lot we owe him!"

"Yes, indeed."

"I wish we could thank him, but I suppose —"

"We mustn't mention the subject," interrupted Alec. "The whole affair is between him and Simon."

"What shall I say to the children? They'll notice Simon is different and they'll wonder why."

"You've forgotten the four-leaved clover."

"Oh, I see," said Katherine. "But perhaps I ought to explain. It isn't good for them to believe in magic."

"Say nothing," replied Alec, stifling a yawn. "A belief in magic will do them no harm. They'll soon outgrow it." He was about to turn over and go to sleep when he felt a hand on his shoulder.

"Alec, are you *sure* Simon is all right?" asked Katherine.

"Quite, quite sure," he replied, yawning uncontrollably.

"Simon is Simon again . . . our own Simon . . ."

She realised that already Alec was half asleep so she kissed him gently and said no more. For a long time she lay and listened to his rhythmic breathing. She was too happy to sleep.

CHAPTER
SEVENTEEN

1

The MacAslans stayed on for a few days longer than they had intended; they stayed for the New Year celebrations and then left to spend a couple of nights with a cousin who had a sheep-farm in the Grampians (their cousins were as the sands of the sea). They were sorry to go and their hosts were sorry to part with them; it had been a most satisfactory visit.

"It isn't good-bye, dear darling Mrs Maclaren," declared Phil, as she kissed Katherine fondly. "You're coming to stay at Ardfalloch as soon as ever we get our electric light. You promised, didn't you?" Then Phil kissed everybody else, including Simon, who looked a trifle embarrassed but by no means displeased.

MacAslan repeated his daughter's invitation and reminded Simon that they were expecting him to visit them in the Easter holidays. Then he shook hands with everybody — except Daisy, who leapt into his arms and gave him one of her "special hugs."

After that the MacAslans got into their car and drove away.

No sooner had they gone than Katherine began to look out Simon's school clothes which as usual were found to be in a well-worn condition and much too small. However, this did not matter; she could take him to Edinburgh and buy him everything he needed.

"I don't like Alec paying for my clothes," said Simon as he got into the car beside her.

"Alec isn't going to pay for them," replied Katherine — and she proceeded to expound Alec's views about the marriage vows and to show Simon her cheque book. It was delightful to be able to talk to Simon like this. In very truth he was once more her own dear Simon.

"Well, I'm jiggered!" Simon exclaimed. "I see it now, of course. Everybody says, 'with all my worldly goods I thee endow' but nobody means it — except Alec. He always means what he says, doesn't he?"

"Yes," said his wife.

"So you're rich beyond the dreams of avarice, Mums?"

"Yes — or at least I've got more money than I can spend."

"How funny!"

"Very funny indeed, when I think of the way I had to pinch and scrape and make do with clothes which were literally falling to pieces."

"You never seemed unhappy."

"I tried not to be — but it was such a worry," she explained. "I had nothing to fall back on, so the smallest accident was a major disaster. For instance when I dropped the casserole into the sink and smashed it to bits I sat down and cried. Silly, isn't it?"

"I never realised it was as bad as that," said Simon uncomfortably.

There was a short silence while Katherine overtook an enormous lorry with six cars anchored upon its back. Then she said, "I want you to go to Cambridge when you leave school. It would be so much better than going into business."

"But Mums, Butterfield's is a very good business. Mark's uncle says it's a splendid opening for a young chap who is willing to put his back into the work. Mark and I are going into it together, starting at the bottom to learn the ropes."

"I know," agreed Katherine. "It's an exceedingly good plan for Mark to go into his uncle's business — Mark will stay in the business and can look forward to being a director — you have quite a different future before you. Some day Limbourne will belong to you and you'll have to look after your property. Nothing that you learn at Butterfield's will be the slightest use to you."

"I see what you mean. Is that why you're so keen for me to go to Cambridge?"

"It's one of the reasons."

"What are the others?"

She hesitated — it was so important to put it to Simon in the right way — then she replied, "The principal reason is that your father would have wanted you to have a university education. I couldn't have managed it before but now that I've got money I can do it for you. That's why I'm keen on it, Simon."

"It's true," said Simon thoughtfully. "Both reasons are good. Mark will be disappointed but he'll understand when I explain it to him."

"You'll go to Cambridge?"

"It would be silly of me to refuse, wouldn't it?"

"You've made me very happy," said Katherine.

There was no need to say more which was just as well because by this time they had arrived at the car park.

2

Katherine and Simon had a busy morning and were late in getting home; they were carrying in the parcels and cardboard boxes when Alec came out of the dining-room.

"Here you are!" he exclaimed. "The children were hungry so we started lunch. You seem to have been buying Simon a trousseau."

"Yes, we rather let ourselves go," admitted Katherine.

"Good! It's important to have nice clothes." He added, "That telegram came for Simon a few minutes ago."

"For me?" exclaimed Simon in surprise. "Who on earth can have sent me a telegram?"

"Open it and see," Alec suggested.

Simon tore it open and read the message. He looked at it for a few moments in silence. Then he said, "How awfully queer! Grandfather is ill and wants me to come."

"Your grandfather? Is he very ill?" asked Katherine apprehensively.

Simon handed her the form and she read it aloud: "SIMON WENTWORTH THE CEDARS BARNTON EDINBURGH SIR MORTIMER ILL WOULD LIKE YOU TO COME FLECKER."

"Flecker is the doctor," explained Simon. "He came one day to see Aunt Florence. I don't know how he knew my address — unless Nitkin told him."

"Who is Nitkin?" asked Alec.

"Oh, the groom," replied Simon. "He's an awfully good chap; he has been at Limbourne for forty years — I used to ride with him every morning — so I sent him a Christmas card. Nobody else at Limbourne knows that we're living at The Cedars."

By this time Alec had taken the telegram and read it. He said, "Why didn't the doctor tell us more, I wonder."

"Why didn't he phone?" exclaimed Katherine.

"He couldn't phone. Simon's name isn't in the telephone book. But we can ring up and find out —"

"I'll have to go," interrupted Simon. "I mean I can't *not* go when he's ill and wants to see me."

"Of course you must go," agreed Alec.

Katherine had been about to say that of course Simon could not possibly go. It was an instinctive reaction; she hated Limbourne and all it stood for; but quite apart from that there were practical reasons why Simon could not go; there was little more than a week of his holidays left; his school clothes were not ready; they had made an appointment for him to see the dentist ... but suddenly she realised that Simon's clothes and teeth, however important, were of secondary consideration compared with Sir Mortimer's illness so she held her peace.

"I don't think you need worry unduly," Alec was saying. "If he were very ill the doctor would have said, 'Seriously ill come at once.' All the same we had better go to-morrow, hadn't we?"

"Do you mean you'll come with me?"

"Unless you'd rather go by yourself; in which case —"

"Oh Alec, you *are* decent!" cried Simon joyously. "I was just thinking how frightful it would be. It isn't the journey I mind, it's getting there and — and everything."

"Well, that's settled. You had better ring up and say we're coming to-morrow. We'll go by road," added Alec. "It will be just as quick and the car may be useful when we get there."

Naturally enough the conversation at lunch was concerned with the visit to Limbourne.

"Why does he want Simon to go?" asked Daisy. "I thought he was very angry with Simon."

"Perhaps he's sorry," replied Alec. "At any rate if somebody is ill and wants to see you it would be very unkind not to go."

"He hasn't asked you," Denis pointed out. "Why have you got to go?"

"I'll tell you why," said Alec seriously. "When Mums and I were married we decided that it would be a good thing for me to share her responsibilities, so we signed some papers and I became your guardian. Do you understand?"

Denis nodded. "Guardian is nice. If I was in a fix you would have to look after me — that's what it means."

"Yes."

"Simon is in a fix so you've got to look after him."

"Yes."

Katherine had listened to all this in silence. She thought (as she had often thought) that Alec was wonderful with the children, and especially with Denis. The two understood each other, they were both rather serious-minded, and it was never too much trouble for Alec to answer questions. Denis had always been a delicate little boy, and sometimes difficult to manage, but in the last few months he had improved in every way. Was it Ellen's nourishing food or Alec's "understandingness"? Katherine decided that it was a bit of both.

3

Alec sat on the bed and watched Katherine brushing her hair. She brushed it for two minutes every night and it gave him pleasure to watch the performance. He enjoyed the intimacy of the scene. The white peignoir fell aside from her white, rounded arm as the brush swept through her brown curls. From where he sat he could see her face in the mirror, serious and intent.

"Why do you always sit there when I'm brushing my hair?" asked Katherine.

"Have you ever noticed how a very small thing can give you an enormous amount of pleasure? You don't know why it should; but it just — just makes you happy. That's the answer."

"Yes," replied Katherine thoughtfully. "Yes, I know what you mean." Then she sighed and added regretfully, "This time to-morrow night you'll be at Limbourne."

"There's nothing else for it. We can't let Simon go alone."

"I hope you won't have to stay very long."

"I shan't stay a moment longer than I need," Alec declared emphatically. He added, "You had better tell me something about the place and the people."

"Perhaps you'll see the Heaths," said Katherine. "He's the vicar. He showed me over the church and asked me to tea. Mrs Heath was very kind to me — they're both darlings."

"I want to know about Limbourne."

"But I've told you!"

"You've told me a certain amount but it would be helpful to get a complete picture — as far as possible. You don't often talk about it, do you?"

"I was utterly miserable there — that's why I don't like talking about it — but I'm willing to tell you all I can. What do you want to know?"

"Just imagine that I know nothing about the Wentworth family and tell me about them," Alec replied. He was wearing what Katherine always thought of as his "lawyer face" and had produced a pencil and a notebook from the pocket of his dressing-gown.

"Anything I say will be taken down in evidence against me," suggested Katherine in a teasing voice. Then she put down her hair-brush and began her story.

The week which Katherine had spent at Limbourne last July had seemed more like a month. The atmosphere of the place had oppressed her; everyone was terrified of Sir Mortimer who ruled his subjects with a rod of iron. The household had consisted of Sir Mortimer, his daughter Florence Godfrey (who had been a widow for years) and Florence's grown-up son and daughter. There was also old Miss Wentworth, but she had been ill when Katherine was there so Katherine had seen her only for a few minutes. Most of Katherine's time had been spent with Florence, listening to her endless complaints. If there was a more foolish and tiresome woman in the whole wide world Katherine had not met her.

"She's your sister-in-law, of course," put in Alec.

"Yes, she's Gerald's sister — but it's hard to believe. I had the greatest difficulty in calling her Florence."

The two young Godfreys were both at Limbourne. Lance was some years older than Simon but the boys had made friends and had gone about together on Lance's motor-bike; Anthea had been anything but friendly. All the same Katherine had felt sorry for Lance and Anthea; they had lived at Limbourne ever since they were children and had been domineered over by their grandfather to such an extent that they could scarcely call their souls their own. They had been "chained up" — as Simon had put it — and this treatment had led to deceit and evasions. They had been obliged to find an outlet for their pent-up energies and had found it by getting into serious mischief.

"Serious mischief!" exclaimed Alec. "You didn't tell me that."

"It was a secret," Katherine replied. "However, I don't suppose it matters telling you now. Lance and Anthea belonged to a sort of club which was run by a young man called Oliver Wade. I don't know how many young people belonged to it. They went out at night in cars and — and smashed traffic lights and telephones and — and things like that."

"Great Scott! I saw an account of it in the papers, but I never thought . . . Katherine, how did you hear about this?"

"Simon told me. He got mixed up in 'the fun' — as they called it — but it wasn't fun to Simon. He was distressed and horrified. I think that was one of the reasons why he felt he couldn't accept his grandfather's offer and promise to go and live at Limbourne. Not because of the vandalism — that's all over now — but because he realised that the vandalism was the outcome of frustration."

"You say the vandalism is all over now. Does that mean 'the club' is defunct?"

Katherine nodded. "Lance was caught smashing up a car but fortunately the owner didn't prosecute him.

Peter got him a job on an orange farm in South Africa; he's there now, I suppose."

"What happened to the ring-leader, the chap who ran the whole thing?"

"Oliver Wade. He was caught setting fire to a barn and sent to prison."

"Arson! Good lord!" murmured Alec, looking at Katherine in amazement. He was shocked not only by the unlawful activities of the Godfreys and their friends but also by the discovery that Katherine — his very own Katherine — had known of these unlawful activities and had never mentioned the subject.

"I couldn't tell you before," explained Katherine. "You see I had promised faithfully not to tell anybody. Of course it worried me a lot; I *wanted* them to be punished — especially Oliver Wade. Then Simon gave his uncle a hint about what was going on so after that I knew it would be all right and I didn't worry any more. To tell you the truth I haven't thought about it for months," she added in a surprised tone of voice.

"Simon's uncle? You mean Peter Wentworth, of course."

"Yes, I've told you about Peter. He's the only reasonable member of the Wentworth family. I showed you the lovely handbag he sent me for Christmas, didn't I? Perhaps Peter will be at Limbourne when you get there."

"It seems unlikely."

"Why? He may be on leave."

"If he had been there he would have rung you up, wouldn't he?"

"Of course! How silly of me!"

"It seems strange," said Alec in thoughtful tones. "Why should the doctor send the telegram? Why didn't Sir Mortimer's sister send it — or his daughter, or his niece?"

"Oh no! You don't understand. None of them are capable of doing anything sensible."

Alec chuckled involuntarily. "Really, Katherine! It sounds as if Limbourne were a home for mental deficients."

"Well, it is," said Katherine quite seriously. "Limbourne is a beautiful house, and very well run, but the people who live in it are all queer — in one way or another. You'll see when you get there."

This seemed to bring the conversation to an end. Alec rose and said, "Look at the time! And I've got to be up before dawn. We had better go to bed."

Part Three: Limbourne

CHAPTER
EIGHTEEN

1

The roads were in splendid condition so Alec had been able to press along at a good pace and it was still early in the afternoon when they approached Limbourne. Simon had gone to sleep; he looked so comfortable curled up in his corner that it seemed a pity to waken him. Alec lost his way and stopped twice to ask for directions. The second time he was told by a postman that Limbourne was "just up the road." Soon after that he came to a large place surrounded by high stone walls; there were trees inside the walls and on either side of the gateway there were massive stone pillars with queer stone beasts on the top of them.

"Wake up, old chap," said Alec, shaking his passenger gently. "I think we've arrived. This is your ancestral home, isn't it?"

Simon sat up and rubbed his eyes. "No, this isn't Limbourne. This is Hurlestone Manor. It belongs to the D'Artingtons who came over with William the Conqueror."

"Ten sixty-six and all that."

"Yes, and one of them was a crusader — there's a stone effigy of him in the church — but in spite of that they're very nice and not a bit sidey. Limbourne isn't much farther. Straight on, Alec."

"Are the D'Artingtons your nearest neighbours?" asked Alec, not that he really wanted the information but because he wanted Simon to wake up thoroughly before they arrived

"Yes, I'll tell you about them: there's old Lord D'Artington — Grandfather goes and plays chess with him sometimes — and there's his son, Major D'Artington, who was badly wounded in the war . . . and there's *his* son, Wilfrid, who's a year older than I am."

"Did you meet Wilfrid when you were here?"

"No, I didn't," said Simon regretfully. "They asked me to go over to tea but Grandfather wouldn't let me."

"Why not?"

"Oh, there was no sensible reason. Grandfather doesn't like people to make their own plans. If he had made the arrangement it would have been all right. Grandfather is very kind if you do exactly as you're told — but if you don't do as you're told there's trouble."

"Rather cramping," suggested Alec.

"You're telling me!" exclaimed Simon. "That's why I felt I couldn't go and live at Limbourne. I don't mind doing what I'm told if there's a good reason; it was the unreasonableness that got me down."

"But you liked him?"

"Yes, I liked him quite a lot," replied Simon in thoughtful tones. "When I was staying at Limbourne he

242

used to call me into his room and talk to me and show me his books. He has travelled a great deal and he's really very interesting. If only he wasn't so — so unreasonable and autocratic he would be grand. I believe you'll get on with Grandfather rather well."

"I'll take care not to tread on his toes."

"Yes, that's the idea," agreed Simon. "Look, Alec, that's the village on the right! And there's the church! It's a beautiful little church, very old and full of interesting things — I must show it to you some time. When we were here in July, Mums and I went to the eight-o'clock service on Sunday morning. Mr Heath, the vicar, is a dear old man with silver hair; he has got a son in the Navy."

"You've met the son, have you?"

"No, but I'd like to. He must be terrific. Here! Hi! Slow down, Alec! Those are the Limbourne gates . . . on the left."

The Limbourne gates were of wrought iron and very beautiful. Alec was about to stop for Simon to get out and open them but, as the car approached, the gates opened automatically, swinging back slowly in a manner which was extremely impressive.

"Open Sesame!" cried Simon gleefully. "Were you surprised? I didn't tell you because I wanted to give you a surprise."

Alec professed himself astounded. He was amused and touched at the boy's excitement; it was natural, of course. This had been the home of his family for generations and some day it would belong to him. Certainly it was a home to be proud of: the green park with its lovely old trees; the long winding avenue; the house itself, large and stately, with tall chimneys and rows of windows, glittering in the afternoon sunlight.

"Everything in Limbourne is tip-top," said Simon. "It's nice to come back — really. I suppose, as Grandfather has sent for me, it means he has forgiven me and wants to be friends."

"It couldn't mean anything else," replied Alec with conviction.

"That's nice too," said Simon. "Perhaps he would let me come to Limbourne in the holidays for a week or ten days, I'd like to do that."

The car swept up the smooth avenue and stopped in front of the door.

Simon got out, ran up the steps and rang the bell. Then he turned and grinned mischievously. "Don't unpack the car. It's not the right thing."

Alec smiled and followed Simon up the steps.

The door was opened by an elderly butler, a portly individual with grey hair and a round solemn face.

"Oh, Mr Simon, it's you!" he exclaimed. "We weren't sure when you'd be arriving. Sir Mortimer *will* be pleased; he's been asking for you."

"Hallo Bassett, how are you?" said Simon. "This is Mr Maclaren. He's my stepfather, you know. You'll get the car unpacked, won't you?"

"Yes, of course, Mr Simon. Your rooms are all ready; Mrs Sillett has seen to that. The London doctor is here at the moment.

"The London doctor?"

244

"Dr. Flecker wanted another opinion," explained Bassett, obviously quoting. "Very anxious to have another opinion, Dr. Flecker was, so he got the London doctor to come. You'd better go up, Mr Simon; Sir Mortimer said you were to go up the minute you arrived. The nurses are there so they'll tell you when you can see him. Just go straight up."

"All right," said Simon. He ran up the stairs and disappeared.

During this colloquy Alec had been looking round the hall and admiring the beautiful furniture, the thick carpets and the general air of comfort and opulence. The walls of the hall were panelled and adorned with oil paintings, depicting long-dead members of the Wentworth family. Two of them were mediocre, to say the best, but there was one in the corner that looked remarkably like a Peter Lely. Alec would have liked to inspect it closely but Bassett was holding open a door.

"There's a nice fire in the library, sir," he said invitingly.

"Is Major Wentworth here?" asked Alec as he went in.

"No, sir, he was here last week but he has gone back to Germany — his leave being over. He has been telegraphed to by Dr. Flecker, but there has been no word when he's coming. Mrs Godfrey is ill in bed and Miss Anthea is ski-ing in Austria with a party of young ladies and gentlemen. There isn't anyone in charge, sir. It's a bit awkward not having anyone in charge; people take advantages that they wouldn't dare if Sir Mortimer was up and about. If you'll excuse me I'll go and see that your luggage is being brought in correctly."

Alec turned away to hide an involuntary smile. It was all too good to be true. How amazing that this sort of set-up should still exist in the modern world of pop singers and beatniks! He felt as if he had walked straight on to the stage in the middle of an Edwardian play.

The library did nothing to shatter this illusion. In Alec's opinion it was a most satisfactory apartment; there was a thick green carpet on the floor, comfortable leather chairs, an enormous sofa, a large desk in the corner and an even larger table, standing in the middle of the room. Before the table stood a massive oak chair with a green velvet cushion on the seat — Sir Mortimer's throne? All round the room were glass-fronted bookcases, full of books. Alec wandered round, looking at the books, which were all in perfect order: travel, biography, history and classical fiction. He would have liked to examine some of them but the bookcases were all locked. This was not to be wondered at, thought Alec; he was pretty certain that some of the books were first editions — that row of Dickens for instance!

Alec yearned to take one out and hold it in his hands. Oh well, he couldn't . . . and it was not much fun looking at the books through the glass. He had just decided to ring and order tea (obviously Limbourne was the sort of establishment in which tea, or anything else, could be obtained by pressing a bell) when the door opened and the "London doctor" walked in.

246

Nobody could have mistaken the gentleman for anything but a Harley Street specialist.

"Oh, good afternoon, sir," said Alec. "I'm Simon's stepfather. Maclaren is my name."

"How do you do, Mr Maclaren. I am Sir Reginald Woodhall. Dr. Flecker invited me to see his patient."

They shook hands.

"I was just going to ring for tea," said Alec. "May I offer you tea or would you rather have something stronger?"

"No time, I'm afraid," replied Sir Reginald, glancing at his watch. "I have to get back to town for a meeting. Are you — um —"

"Well, yes," said Alec, smiling. "I think I'm sort of — in command at the moment. There doesn't seem to be anybody else. How did you find the patient, sir?"

"I found Sir Mortimer fairly comfortable," replied Sir Reginald. "It is a cardiac embolism, of course, so —"

"It's serious, then?" asked Alec in alarm.

"Sir Mortimer's condition is — um — serious but by no means critical. We can deal with the condition quite satisfactorily nowadays provided the patient is co-operative. Rest and quiet and drugs is the correct treatment and in most cases it is successful. Dr. Flecker has engaged two experienced nurses; I have spoken to them and they understand that the patient must on no account be excited or disturbed."

"Is it wise to allow him to see his grandson?"

"We thought it best. Sir Mortimer seems very much attached to his grandson and has been asking for him.

Dr. Flecker (who, of course, knows his patient a great deal better than I) is of the opinion that once he has seen the boy for a few minutes he will settle down more peacefully; which is what we want." Sir Reginald smiled and added, "Patients are human, Mr er — Maclaren. They cannot be treated like machines. It would be a great deal easier for their medical advisers if patients were like motor-cars; one could remove a faulty plug or replace a big end — you see the idea?"

"Yes, I do," replied Alec, smiling. He was a little surprised to discover that Sir Reginald was human.

"Sir Mortimer's general physical condition is excellent," continued Sir Reginald. "There is no superfluous adipose tissue, which is unusual in a man of his age."

"All the same I suppose it's likely to be a long illness?" asked Alec. To tell the truth he was wondering when he would be able to get home.

Sir Reginald nodded, "These things take time. One cannot foresee the future but if all goes well I should expect Sir Mortimer to be confined to bed for about a month. After that he could begin to get up for a brief period daily. One cannot expect a complete recovery, of course; he will always have to 'go slow' — as the saying is. However, Dr. Flecker will keep an eye on him."

"Dr. Flecker understands the case?"

"Perfectly. He is most efficient . . . perhaps just a trifle inclined to be pessimistic, but we need not quarrel with him on that account. Dr. Flecker and I are in complete agreement as regards the treatment; everything that can be done is being done; you may rest assured of that."

"Good."

"Dr. Flecker tells me that he has sent for Major Wentworth. When do you expect him?"

"We haven't heard when he's coming. He's in Germany so it may take a few days before —"

"Who was your informant, Mr Maclaren?"

Alec hesitated. He was unwilling to disclose the fact that his information had been obtained from the butler.

"No matter," said Sir Reginald, brushing it aside. "I merely asked because I happened to see Major Wentworth yesterday in Regent Street."

"Do you mean he's in London?"

"He was in Regent Street yesterday morning. I have no idea where he is to-day," declared Sir Reginald, a trifle testily.

"You didn't speak to him, did you?"

"I did not."

"How very strange!" said Alec thoughtfully.

Sir Reginald was putting on his gloves. "I can easily run down and have another look at Sir Mortimer if necessary but, as in all these cases, the most important factor is the nursing; a light diet, complete rest and freedom from anxiety. I can't say more."

In spite of this, Sir Reginald found that he could say a good deal more, but as most of it was very technical Alec was little the wiser.

Eventually Sir Reginald glanced at his watch again, gave an exclamation of dismay and departed in haste.

Alec rang the bell and sat down on the large sofa by the fire. When Bassett appeared he ordered tea.

"Yes, sir," said Bassett. "Would you prefer India or China?"

"Indian tea in a china teapot, please."

"And hot buttered toast, sir?"

"Nothing to eat, thank you."

Bassett withdrew. He reappeared in a surprisingly short time with a large silver tray upon which was arranged a silver milk jug and sugar basin, a silver hot-water jug, a silver box containing biscuits, a china teapot and a delightful old Worcester cup and saucer. He fetched a small table and put it beside the sofa with the tray upon it, then he knelt down and made up the fire.

"Will there be anything else, sir?" he asked.

"Yes," said Alec. "First of all your name is Bassett, I believe."

"Yes, sir. Edmund Bassett."

"I expect you've been here a long time."

"I have been in Sir Mortimer's service thirty years."

"Of course you know that Sir Mortimer is seriously ill."

"Yes, sir, I was afraid of that. The staff have been wondering. The staff haven't been told *nothing*," said Bassett plaintively.

"Sir Mortimer is seriously ill," repeated Alec. "It's an embolism, Bassett. I'm not a doctor so I don't understand about it very well but I gather that it's a clot of blood which has lodged near his heart. With perfect rest and quiet and the right medicine the clot can be dissolved."

"It's wonderful what they can do nowadays, isn't it sir?"

"Yes, but it will take a long time."

"Perhaps it won't take as long as they think. Very strong Sir Mortimer is — very wiry — never nothing the matter with him. Last winter when the whole house was laid low with influenza Sir Mortimer never turned a hair. He takes a pride in keeping fit; gets up and goes round the place before breakfast — in the summer, that is. You don't know Sir Mortimer, do you, sir? If you knew Sir Mortimer you would —"

"You know him well, of course," said Alec, interrupting the saga. "That's why I want to speak to you, Bassett. Your knowledge of Sir Mortimer's likes and dislikes will be very helpful. The London specialist says that absolute quiet is essential."

"Absolute quiet, sir?"

"Yes, it's very important that nothing should be done to upset or annoy Sir Mortimer."

"There's a lot of things that annoy Sir Mortimer! For instance there's the vacuum cleaner. Perhaps I'd better tell them not to use it."

Alec nodded. "I was sure you would be able to help," he said encouragingly.

"And there's his toast," said Bassett in thoughtful tones. "His toast annoys him if it isn't just right — crisp but not hard. I'd better see to his toast myself."

"What else?"

"There's quite a lot of things — doors banging drives him mad — I'll speak to the staff."

"That's the idea."

Bassett hesitated and then said, "Will you be giving the instructions, sir?"

"What do you mean?"

"The instructions about — about everything. There's so many trays needed with Mrs Godfrey in bed — and Sir Mortimer — and the nurses. We're very short of trays, sir."

"You had better get some."

"Sir Mortimer always —"

"Ask Mrs Sillett to get three trays in Wandlebury."

"Yes, sir. Medlam was wondering if he could order a couple of barrows."

"Medlam is the gardener, I presume."

"The head gardener, sir. There are three gardeners not counting the boy."

"Oh, I see. Well, tell him to order his barrows." Alec hesitated and then added, "I don't want to throw my weight about but I'm Mr Simon's legal guardian so I suppose if you want any instructions you had better ask me. When Major Wentworth comes he'll take over."

"Yes, sir, that's a great relief to my mind. You see Sir Mortimer gives all the instructions himself, so now that he's ill we're all at sea."

Of course you are, thought Alec. That's exactly what happens when a dictator drops the reins. Aloud he said, "About Major Wentworth, are you sure he's in Germany?"

"Yes, sir. His leave was over so he had to go back to his battery. That was the day before Sir Mortimer was took ill. If you would give me a few instructions, sir, it would be a help."

Bassett had numerous problems requiring attention and Alec dealt with them to the best of his ability. Some of them seemed to him very paltry and could be settled offhand (did Sir Mortimer really concern himself with trays and barrows and new curtains for the servants' hall?); other matters could be put off until the arrival of Major Wentworth, but there was one matter which he felt should be investigated. Mr Friece had rung up and had been "very put out" when he heard that Sir Mortimer was ill.

"Mr Friece is Sir Mortimer's lawyer," explained Bassett. "Mr Friece wanted a dockyment out of the top of Sir Mortimer's desk. He was very urgent about it — very urgent indeed. He asked to speak to Mrs Godfrey but Mrs Godfrey didn't feel well enough to speak on the telephone. So then he told me that I was to get it and post it to him — but of course I couldn't take it upon myself to do that. I couldn't have done it if I'd wanted because Sir Mortimer always keeps everything locked up. Mr Friece was annoyed about it and he said that if anyone with any sense came to Limbourne they were to ring him up . . . so perhaps you'd better, sir."

"Perhaps I should," said Alec with reluctance.

"As a matter of fact it's been worrying me a bit," admitted Bassett. "I was wondering if the dockyment he wanted was the one that Mrs Sillett and I signed."

"You signed something, did you?"

"Yes, sir. It was the night Sir Mortimer was took ill. Sir Mortimer taking ill — and everything in such a muddle — put it right out of my mind."

"Quite natural," said Alec sympathetically. "No wonder you forgot all about it. What was the document? Was it a lease or something like that?"

Bassett nodded. "I dare say it was. Sir Mortimer didn't say. He just told me to get Mrs Sillett and we came into the library — just here, it was. Sir Mortimer signed his name and showed us the place where we were to sign our names. It was a big important-looking dockyment written on thick paper. Sir Mortimer folded it up and put it in a yellow envelope; he sealed the envelope with red sealing-wax and pressed it with his seal, that he has on a gold chain, and slipped it into the top of his desk. Then he said, 'Well, Bassett, you've signed your death warrant.' It gave me quite a turn but it was just a joke, of course; he was sort of excited. That was the last words he said to me before he was took ill."

"Was he taken ill here, in the library?"

"Oh no, sir. He went upstairs to dress for dinner and I was going up after him as usual to see that he'd got all he wanted. When he was half-way up he fell and hit his head on the banisters. I thought he'd just fallen — if you see what I mean. I thought it was the bang on the head that had knocked him out."

"I'm afraid it was more serious, Bassett."

CHAPTER
NINETEEN

1

Alec was enjoying his tea. It had been a little difficult to get rid of Bassett — the man was a gas-bag — but even gas-bags have their uses and this one had provided quite a lot of information, some of it rather intriguing. For one thing: where was Peter Wentworth? Bassett was perfectly certain he had returned to Germany; Sir Reginald Woodhall was equally certain that he had seen him in Regent Street. Which of them was right? Then there was the "dockyment." Having listened to Bassett's account of the signing of the document Alec was no longer in doubt as to its nature . . . but how odd, thought Alec as he poured out his third cup of tea, how very odd that Sir Mortimer should have chosen his butler and his housekeeper to witness his signature! In Alec's experience an important person like Sir Mortimer preferred to sign his will in his lawyer's office with two of the partners standing by to witness the testator's signature, to fold the document with reverent care, to tie it with pink tape and put it away securely in the client's deed-box. What a fuss there had been when Lord Z — signed his last will and testament, thought

Alec smiling to himself at the recollection. When the deed was safely locked up — but not before — a bottle of sherry had been produced by the senior partner. It was a fitting conclusion to the ceremony and had gone down well; his lordship liked old-fashioned manners. He had been very affable, not to say jovial!

From what one had heard of Sir Mortimer Wentworth one would have expected him to have received the same sort of V.I.P. treatment from his legal advisers.

By this time Alec had finished his tea. He had begun to wonder where Simon was and what he was doing when the door opened and Simon came in.

"Alec!" he gasped. "Thank heaven I've found you! I've been looking for you everywhere . . ."

"I've been here all the time, waiting for you," said Alec in surprise. Then he turned and saw the boy's face. "Goodness, what's the matter?" he exclaimed.

Simon was as white as a sheet; he looked distraught; he was clinging to the back of a chair, shaking from head to foot like a nervous colt.

"What's the matter?" repeated Alec.

"He's . . . d-dead," stammered Simon.

For a few moments Alec was absolutely speechless; then he realised that he must do something to help Simon so he pulled himself together and rose and took a firm grip of the boy's arm. "Brace up, old chap," he said encouragingly.

"I c-couldn't find you. I n-never thought you'd be here."

"Come and sit down. Come and tell me what happened."

"It was awful," said Simon, allowing himself to be led across the room to the sofa and sinking on to it in a crumpled heap.

"Tell me about it."

"Yes, I'll tell you. I want to t-tell you. That's why I was l-looking for you. I went up, but I had to wait for a bit because the doctor was there. Then he came out and told me I could go and talk to Grandfather for ten minutes or so, but I mustn't excite him. I didn't excite him — honestly I didn't! It was the nurse who excited him . . . but that was afterwards . . ."

"You went in and talked to him."

"Yes, I sat on a chair beside his bed. He seemed all right — quite like him — except that he was a bit thin and pale. He talked just like he always does. He asked me to do something for him and I said I would. He didn't mention the row — just said it was good of me to come so quickly. I said I *wanted* to come when I heard he was ill. That's true, isn't it?"

"Perfectly true."

"I could see he was pleased. He smiled and said, 'Good boy.' I was glad about that. I'm even more glad now."

"Yes, of course you are."

"He talked for a bit and then he said, 'Tell me about Katherine and your new stepfather.' I was just beginning to tell him when the nurse came in and said he had talked enough and I was to go away. He said, 'I'm not talking, I'm listening. It's good for me to see a reasonable human being for a change.' That made her a bit cross and she began to argue with him; she said it was time for him to rest. He said he would rest later — but she wouldn't leave him alone. She went on trying to persuade him, talking in a smarmy sort of way — as if he were a child. I could see he was beginning to get angry — boiling up, you know — and I didn't wonder; it was enough to make anybody angry. He said, 'Go away and leave me in peace. I want to talk to my grandson.' Then the nurse said, 'Now you're getting excited, Sir Mortimer. That won't do. Doctor wouldn't be a bit pleased' — and she signed to me to come. Well, I couldn't. He had taken hold of my hand — he was gripping it tightly — so I couldn't get away. I couldn't drag my hand away by force, could I?"

"No, indeed, it would have made him angry."

"It would have made him furious," declared Simon. "I *knew* it would make him furious, so I couldn't do *anything*. If only she had gone away I could have got him soothed down and it would have been all right. I could have made a little joke about it and promised to come back later. I could have persuaded him quietly — I *know* I could. It would have been *all right* if she had been sensible and gone away . . . but instead of that she beckoned to me again and told me to come at once.

"Then it happened! I knew it would happen — and it did. He boiled over. He sat up in bed and swore at her; he called her names — frightful names — and told her to get out and stay out. She turned and rushed out of the room."

258

"Good heavens!"

"Alec, it wasn't my fault — really it wasn't. What could I *do*?"

"Of course it wasn't your fault. The nurse must be an absolute idiot."

"She didn't know him, you see. I mean I know him, so of course I knew he was boiling up."

"Yes, but all the same —"

"It was awful," declared Simon, beginning to shake again. "He was holding my hand t-tight — like I t-told you — and saying that they n-needn't think he was going to die — because he wasn't going to. He didn't intend to die — he was getting better — they were a pack of fools. That's what he said, 'They're a pack of fools, the whole ruddy lot of them.' Then suddenly he sort of choked and — and he had gone."

Alec took Simon's hand and held it firmly.

"He had gone," repeated Simon in a trembling voice. "His body was . . . empty. I mean he wasn't there . . . any more. He had gone somewhere else. He wasn't dead (if you see what I mean). He hadn't been b-blown out like — like a candle. *He had gone somewhere else.* Where had he gone, Alec? That's the awful thing. He didn't believe in God or — or anything. He was rather — rather wicked, I suppose, but I was fond of him all the same. I was fond of him even when he was angry with me. I couldn't help . . . being . . . fond of him," declared Simon and he burst into a flood of tears. "Gosh, what a fool I am!" sobbed poor Simon.

A large white handkerchief was pressed into his hand.

"Oh, thank you!" sobbed Simon. "You are — decent to me, Alec. I'm sorry I'm such a fool. It's just — that it was — so awful."

"I know. It must have been awful; no wonder you're upset."

What an extraordinary chap he is! thought Alec as he sat there holding Simon's hand. Sometimes he seems quite grown-up and the next moment he's a child. (What was I like at his age? I wasn't as adult as Simon — and I wasn't as young. I was just an ordinary schoolboy, mad on cricket and not bothering much about anything else . . . but of course I hadn't all this to contend with. It must have been a frightful shock. Yes, he's suffering from shock, that's what's the matter with him. Goodness, I wish Katherine were here!)

"It's all right, old chap," said Alec. "It was enough to upset anybody. You'll feel better soon."

"I was fond of him," repeated Simon, weeping bitterly. "I don't believe anybody else was fond of him. He was difficult and — and queer, but sometimes he talked to me so — so *kindly*. He was like a different person when he talked like that — all about the family and about Limbourne. He liked me, you know. He did really, Alec."

"I'm sure he did. He wouldn't have sent for you to come if he hadn't been fond of you."

"He didn't want to die. He was determined not to die . . . and then suddenly he had gone. Where did he go? That's what's making me so miserable . . . and sort of . . . f-frightened. Alec, do you believe in Hell?"

"Not really."

"Not burning for ever?"

"No, I don't. What would be the sense of that?"

"No," agreed Simon, blowing his nose. "Not much — sense — really."

"No sense," declared Alec emphatically.

"Well, what do you believe?"

"Perhaps people go to some place where they can learn. God doesn't waste anything, Simon."

"What do you mean?"

"I mean nothing is wasted. Leaves wither and fall off the trees but there's good in them so they become leaf-mould to nurture the soil. It would be a waste of the good in your grandfather not to do something useful with it. There *is* good in him. You wouldn't have been fond of him if there hadn't been good in him. You saw the good in him, didn't you?"

"Yes, I did."

"Well, if you saw the good in him you may be quite sure God saw it."

Simon was beginning to recover. "Yes, of course," he said. "I hadn't thought about it like that. In fact I hadn't really thought about it at all — until now. When Dad died I was terribly miserable but I knew he would be all right because he believed in God. He liked going to church — he was really good, all through. He was kind and gentle and everybody loved him. You see what I mean, don't you?"

Alec saw exactly what he meant. There was only one thing he could find to say and he said it: " 'The Lord is full of compassion and mercy, long suffering, and very pitiful, and forgiveth sins, and saveth in time of affliction'."

"That's nice," said Simon. "It's sort of comforting. Say it again."

Alec said it again.

2

Now that Simon was calmer Alec felt he could leave him, so he went to find Bassett and discovered him in the pantry. It was obvious from the man's white face and dazed appearance that the news of Sir Mortimer's death had reached the staff. For a few minutes Alec condoled with Bassett and listened patiently to an account of Sir Mortimer's numerous virtues, interspersed frequently with the assertion, "But of course you didn't know Sir Mortimer, did you, sir?" At last Alec felt that the decencies had been observed, so he put a stop to the eulogy by asking Bassett to make fresh tea and bring it to the library adding that Simon was very much upset by his grandfather's death and some food might do him good.

On returning to the library Alec found Simon sitting bolt-upright with an expression of dismay upon his face.

"Alec!" he exclaimed. "I've just thought of something frightful. I'm a baronet."

"Yes, I suppose you are."

"Alec, I don't *want* to be a baronet — it's silly. It would be all right if I were older, but — but it's silly for *me*."

"I don't think it need worry you."

"Not worry me!" cried Simon in anguished tones. "Of course it's worrying me. It'll be frightful to go back to school — I don't know how I shall bear it."

"There are other baronets at Barstow, aren't there?"

"Yes, two — but I don't like either of them."

"You don't need to bother about them. You've got —"

"Could I give it up?"

"Give it up? What do you mean?"

"Renounce it, like Sir Alec Douglas-Home. He gave up his title, didn't he?"

"You couldn't; besides —"

"Why? Why couldn't I? If he could do it why couldn't I?"

"Listen, Simon," said Alec firmly. "Listen to me for a moment. You couldn't give up your title until you are of age and by that time you'll have got used to it and you won't want to. By that time you'll be proud of your long line of ancestors and —"

"Oh, I'm proud *now*," declared Simon. "It isn't that at all. I wouldn't mind being a baronet when I was older — in fact I'd like it — but *not now*. Don't you understand? I'm too young to be called Sir Simon Wentworth; it sounds silly. Oh gosh, I wish Dad hadn't died! Everything would be all right if Dad were here, wouldn't it?"

Alec found himself unable to agree. He sat down beside the new baronet and said comfortingly, "It won't be as bad as you think."

"It will! There will be all sorts of snags. For one thing the wrong sort of people will suck up to me."

This was only too true.

"I've seen it happen," declared Simon. "I've seen people go all goofy."

"You needn't bother about the wrong sort of people; you've got your own friends, haven't you?"

"Oh, Mark will be all right, of course. It won't make any difference to him. He knows I can't help it."

Alec hid a smile. He had heard a good deal about Mark Butterfield, Simon's greatest friend and staunch ally at Barstow. "Well, that's all right," said Alec. "With Mark on your side you can face up to anything, can't you? I think I'll leave you now," he added. "Bassett will bring your tea in a minute; I must go and see what has to be done."

"What have you got to do? Can't somebody else —"

"There's nobody else to do anything," replied Alec a trifle irritably. "There doesn't seem to be a creature in this house with a grain of initiative. They've all been told exactly what to do for so long that they've ceased to use their brains. When you cease to use your brain it becomes atrophied."

"Grandfather decided everything," said Simon, nodding. "He liked to keep everything in his own hands, he used to say that if he left things to other people they 'always made a mess of it.' I can see him sitting in that big chair and saying those very words.

264

You know, Alec," added Simon with a little quiver in his voice, "you know I can't help thinking that if it hadn't been for me — and all that fuss — he'd be alive now."

"I want to tell you something," Alec said seriously. "While you were upstairs I had a talk with the heart specialist and he told me that even if your grandfather recovered from this attack he would always have to go slow. He wouldn't have liked that, would he?"

"He would have hated it! I can't *imagine* Grandfather going slow."

There was silence for a few moments and then Simon added, "That makes me feel a bit better about it."

Alec had hoped it might.

They talked for a few minutes longer and then Bassett came with fresh tea and hot buttered toast and various other comestibles including a large and luscious chocolate cake.

"Oh, good!" exclaimed Simon, his eyes lighting up at the sight. "I'm terribly hungry for some reason or other. I hope it wasn't a bother for you, Bassett."

CHAPTER
TWENTY

1

There was a great deal to be done and, as Alec had said, there was nobody but himself to do it. First he went upstairs and found that Dr. Flecker had arrived and was talking to the nurses. He explained who he was to Dr. Flecker and arranged various matters with him. Then he went to his bedroom and, finding a telephone there, decided to use it for some necessary calls. He remembered that the vicar's name was Heath so he found the number and rang him up.

Mr Heath was considerably upset at the news of Sir Mortimer's sudden death. "Oh dear me, how dreadful!" he exclaimed. "I had heard he was unwell, but I had no idea it was anything serious. I should have called. It was very remiss of me not to have called. As a matter of fact I thought of calling but I was not sure that he would care to see me. My wife thought *not*. I am sorry now that I did not call and inquire. I could have left a few Christmas roses; my *Helleborus niger* is very beautiful this year. Yes, I should have done that. How very distressing it is!"

Having made suitable rejoinders to Mr Heath's lamentations Alec asked for help.

"Yes, indeed!" cried Mr Heath. "I am only too pleased to do anything in my power, Mr — er —"

"Maclaren is my name. You don't know me, of course. I'm Simon's step-stepfather and guardian."

"Did you say you were Simon's stepfather, Mr Maclaren?"

"Two steps," explained Alec. "It's a bit complicated, I'm afraid. You see I married Simon's stepmother in September. You saw her when she was staying here, didn't you?"

"Mrs Gerald Wentworth? Yes, of course we saw her. She came and had tea with us at the Vicarage — a charming lady!"

"She told me that you and Mrs Heath were very kind to her."

"Not at all, it was a great pleasure to meet her — a charming lady!" repeated Mr Heath. "Dear me, how exciting to hear she is married! My wife and I were enchanted with her. I cannot tell you how pleased I am — Helena will be delighted when I tell her — all the more so because we both felt that she was a little — a little lonely. Please accept my warmest congratulations, Mr Maclaren."

"Thank you. Yes, I know I'm frightfully lucky."

"And my best wishes — in which I am sure Helena would like to join — our very best wishes for a long and happy life together."

"Thank you very much, Mr Heath."

"Well, now," said Mr Heath in a different tone of voice. "You asked for my help. What can I do?"

Alec explained his predicament. He had expected that Mr Heath would be sympathetic, but he was surprised to find him capable and understanding.

"Yes, I see," said Mr Heath. "It must be very difficult for you, but what a good thing you are here! I shall be very pleased to officiate at the funeral, of course. I think we should arrange to have it on Monday. There are a good many things to be done; the opening of the family vault, for instance. Would you care to leave that to me?"

"Yes. Yes, of course," said Alec. "I didn't know — I mean I shall be very grateful if you will see to it. I suppose it's all right to go ahead without Major Wentworth?"

"We had better — er — 'go ahead.' Yes, I really think so, Mr Maclaren. You may hear from Peter at any moment, but it seems pointless to wait. It really is very strange about Peter. Of course Sir Reginald Woodhall might have been mistaken, but may I suggest that you ring up Peter's London club? I happen to know that Peter's club is the Naval and Military; he was kind enough to invite me to have lunch with him there. It was an excellent lunch."

"Yes, that's a very good idea."

"Perhaps I should come and see you," said Mr Heath anxiously. "I have a boy with me at the moment — I am giving him some instruction in Latin — but I could easily send him away."

"It's very kind but I shouldn't dream of troubling you. To-morrow will be time enough and by then I may have heard from Major Wentworth."

268

"Very well. Let it be to-morrow. Would you and Simon care to come and have tea at the Vicarage? It would be a great pleasure. You and I could have a little talk in my study about the arrangements in church. It had better be a full choral service."

"Yes, certainly."

"And flowers. It is a difficult time of year for flowers, I'm afraid, but —"

"We must order them from London if necessary. We must have lots of flowers."

"Yes, I see. Would you like to leave the flowers to us, Mr Maclaren? Helena usually arranges the flowers in church."

Alec accepted the offer gratefully. He also accepted the invitation to tea at the Vicarage. Mr Heath had a good deal more to say and Alec was obliged to explain that he was very busy indeed before he could ring off.

His next call was to Mr Friece, the lawyer.

Mr Friece was suitably horrified at the news of his client's death. "It must have been very sudden," he said. "Sir Mortimer seemed in very good health when I saw him last week. Was it an accident?"

"It was heart failure," replied Alec, who felt disinclined to go into particulars on the phone.

"Most people die of heart failure," said Mr Friece snappily.

"There was some trouble about a document," suggested Alec. "You left word that somebody was to ring you up."

"Yes, I was exceedingly worried about it, but Sir Mortimer's death means that I must come to

Limbourne myself, so the matter of the document can be deferred until I come. You will wait until I come before looking through Sir Mortimer's papers, of course. Nothing must be touched. Please arrange for me to be met at Wandlebury station to-morrow morning at eleven-fifteen."

Alec agreed to send a car; he was slightly nettled at the dictatorial manner in which he had been given his orders, but decided that this was because he had just been speaking to Mr Heath whose manner was so very different. Then he rang up The Cedars and told Katherine the news.

"Oh, Alec, how awful!" exclaimed Katherine. "I had no idea he was as ill as that. Goodness, what about the estate? Who is to look after things? Florence is quite helpless, isn't she? Will Peter be able to come? Alec, why did he die so suddenly? Did Simon see him?"

"Which question shall I answer first?" asked Alec, stifling a most unseasonable chuckle.

"Did Simon see him?"

"Yes, and Sir Mortimer was very friendly indeed. All was forgiven and forgotten."

"Oh, I'm so glad!"

"Simon was glad, too."

"What about the funeral?"

"It's to be on Monday. You had better send my clothes; Ellen will help you to look them out."

"Yes, I'll send them to-morrow. Simon can hire clothes from that place in London. He got evening clothes from them when we stayed at Limbourne, so they'll have his measurements."

270

"Good! I was wondering about that. Simon will have to be properly dressed for the occasion."

"Oh dear, I'd forgotten!" exclaimed Katherine. "He's a baronet, of course. Is he — is he pleased about it?"

"Not very, but he'll soon get used to it," replied Alec cheerfully.

There was a short pause.

"Alec, do you think I ought to come?" asked Katherine in reluctant tones. "I suppose I could, if necessary, but —"

"There's no need for you to come; I've got everything under control."

"It *is* good of you," said Katherine warmly. "I feel awful about having let you in for all this. Poor darling, are you having a frightful time?"

Alec had been having a frightful time but it was no good worrying Katherine. He said, "I'm very comfortable here — or at least I would be if I didn't miss you so dreadfully."

The conversation continued for quite a long time but nothing was said that was of any importance except to the two people concerned.

2

After his chat with Katherine, Alec felt a good deal better. He went back to the library and found Simon fast asleep in the corner of the big sofa. Poor laddie, thought Alec looking at him compassionately, he's worn out — and no wonder!

However, in spite of his exhaustion Alec's ward had made an exceedingly good meal before going to sleep — there was not much left of the substantial tea which Bassett had provided — so that was satisfactory. Alec, himself, felt exhausted for they had left Edinburgh before dawn that morning and a great deal had happened ... it was difficult to believe it had all happened in one day.

Alec made up the fire very quietly and went to find Bassett and to tell him that Simon must not be disturbed. In the course of the conversation Bassett let fall the information that Miss Wentworth was coming down to dinner. Miss Wentworth had a suite of rooms in the west wing; she had her own maid and, more often than not, she preferred to have her meals sent up to her — but to-night she was coming down. Bassett added that Miss Wentworth was Sir Mortimer's eldest sister and very deaf.

The news depressed Alec considerably. He went upstairs, had a bath and a shave and arrayed himself in evening-dress (he would very much rather have arrayed himself in pyjamas and gone to bed). Then he went downstairs and found Miss Wentworth in the drawing-room ... and even if he had not known that this was Miss Wentworth he could not have mistaken her for anyone else. She had the same shape of face which Alec had noticed in all the portraits of the Wentworth family.

Miss Wentworth was sitting bolt-upright in a straight-backed chair and enjoying a cigarette. "How do you do," she said. "You are Mr Maclaren, of course. Would you care for a glass of sherry?"

There was a tray of bottles and glasses standing on a table in the corner.

"May I give you something?" Alec inquired.

"Amontillado, please," she replied.

He poured out two glasses, took them across the room and sitting down beside Miss Wentworth offered his condolences on her brother's death. Remembering that she was deaf he spoke clearly but not loudly and was glad to find that she heard him perfectly.

"Thank you, Mr Maclaren. Yes, it is very sad," she agreed. "Mortimer was not old — and he was remarkably strong and healthy — but these things happen and must be accepted with fortitude. I have no patience with people who are unable to face the vicissitudes of life. Florence has retired to bed."

"I hope Mrs Godfrey isn't ill."

"Florence always retires to bed when anything untoward occurs. However, I went in to see her, to make sure she was being properly looked after, and observed a tray being carried into her bedroom. If people are able to enjoy large meals there is not much the matter with them," added Miss Wentworth trenchantly.

Alec had not been looking forward to having dinner *tête à tête* with a deaf old lady, but although at first she seemed somewhat alarming she was an unexpectedly pleasant companion, interesting and interested. He found himself telling her about Katherine and the children.

"You have a good voice," said Miss Wentworth approvingly. "Young people nowadays have no idea how to produce the voice correctly."

Alec was pleased.

"I don't dislike your Scotch accent," she added.

Alec was not quite so pleased. He rather prided himself upon his diction. He had read Law at Cambridge and believed that he had managed to eradicate all trace of his native idiom. It was true that unless he was careful he still had some trouble with "woulds" and "shoulds" but apart from this it was his own private opinion that he spoke better English than the inhabitants of Mayfair. They thanked you for the lovely flahs; they asked you to shut the daw and to come near the fah, and when they referred to Wales you could never be certain whether they were speaking of the principality or the larger species of Cetacea.

"I don't dislike your accent at all," repeated Miss Wentworth kindly. "Tell me more about the children. You were saying that it was delightful to have acquired 'a ready-made family' but I hope you intend to add to it, Mr Maclaren. This modern idea of limiting families is against the laws of Nature and the vows of marriage. We have been given a shining example of what is right and proper by our dear Queen."

Alec was slightly taken aback; it flashed across his mind that Miss Wentworth was referring to Queen Victoria — it sounded like that — but of course she was not. "Oh, yes," he said. "Yes, of course. As a matter of fact Katherine — er — likes babies, so we have every intention of — er — er —"

274

"Good," nodded Miss Wentworth. "Now perhaps you will be so kind as to tell me what is going to happen."

"What is going to happen!" echoed Alec in bewilderment.

"What is going to happen to Limbourne, Mr Maclaren?"

"Oh, I see. I'm afraid I can't tell you at the moment."

"It is important to me," explained Miss Wentworth. "I have lived here all my life — my brother was good enough to provide me with a suite in the west wing — but if the house is to be shut I shall have to — to look for — another — home." The clear contralto voice faltered and the heavily-ringed fingers were busy crumbling a roll of bread.

"Miss Wentworth, I hope there will be no need for anything of that sort," said Alec earnestly. "I can't promise, of course — I can't say anything definite at the moment — but I'm Simon's guardian and what I should like to do is to put in a competent manager and keep the place running with a skeleton staff until Simon is of age. In that case it would be a great advantage to have you on the spot to keep an eye on things."

"Thank you, Mr Maclaren. It is kind of you to say so. I am not as young as I was but I still have my faculties unimpaired."

"You have, indeed. To be quite frank it all depends upon the conditions of Sir Mortimer's will — and how much money there is. You understand, don't you?"

She nodded. "My brother was very well off and I happen to know that his will was just and generous to all his family and dependents, but last week when Peter was here there was some — some unpleasantness. My brother was annoyed and sent for a lawyer — not our own family lawyer — and made a new will, which was neither just nor generous."

"You mean your brother was annoyed with Major Wentworth?"

"Yes, and also with me. He was annoyed with the whole family — except Florence, of course. Florence took no part in the discussion; she never by any chance disagreed with her father. I have often wondered whether this was due to fear or foolishness — or possibly to an innate shrewdness. She *appears* to be an exceedingly foolish woman."

"But she always comes out on the sunny side of the wall," suggested Alec.

"An apt analogy," declared Miss Wentworth with the ghost of a smile. "Florence is already making plans to live with her sister-in-law, Miss Godfrey, who has a house in Kent. They will do very well together; both are fond of rich food and neither has any brain at all."

This seemed to dispose of Mrs Godfrey, thought Alec. He said, "Of course Sir Mortimer was very much annoyed with Simon for refusing to promise to come to Limbourne when he leaves school."

"He was exceedingly angry with Simon — for a time," agreed Miss Wentworth. "But he was beginning to soften. It was obvious to me — I knew him well, of course — that he intended to forgive Simon and make up the quarrel. In fact he mentioned, in a casual manner, that Simon might come here for part of the summer holidays."

"That was good."

"Yes, he was fond of Simon — and proud of him. Simon is a remarkably handsome boy, he has the Wentworth looks. Then last week when Peter was here the whole matter was reopened and my brother became even more angry with Simon than before."

"But Simon wasn't here. Simon had nothing whatever to do with it!"

Miss Wentworth sighed. "It is a little difficult to explain because you did not know my brother. You see, Mr Maclaren, Mortimer was businesslike and capable and his ability to organise and run his property was outstanding — but his brain was not logical. He said several times most emphatically that if Simon had not changed his mind and decided *not* to come and live at Limbourne the unpleasantness would not have arisen. Therefore it was all Simon's fault."

"I'm afraid I don't understand."

"Mortimer has always wanted a member of his family to come and live at Limbourne and help to look after the estate. The same trouble has divided the family before. First there was Gerald; then Simon; now it is Peter."

"Oh, I see. He wanted Major Wentworth to retire."

She nodded. "It was ridiculous of Mortimer; he had no right to ask Peter to do such a thing. Peter has made the Army his career, he has served his country with distinction and is due for promotion. Naturally he refused to retire."

"So that was what the — the unpleasantness was about?"

"Yes."

"And you backed him up, I suppose?"

"Yes," said Miss Wentworth. She smiled and added, "I backed him up."

Alec smiled too. The slang phrase sounded very funny on Miss Wentworth's lips . . . but in reality it was no smiling matter. The estate was entailed, but Alec would have liked to know how much capital went with the estate. Sir Mortimer had been very well off — one had only to look at the place to see that — but possibly a good deal of the money which had been lavished upon Limbourne was Sir Mortimer's own private fortune which he could dispose of as he pleased.

"There are farms, aren't there?" said Alec. "Have you any idea whether the estate is self-supporting?"

Miss Wentworth was no fool. She said, "Mr Maclaren, I cannot believe that my brother would leave his heir insufficient means to keep Limbourne in perfect order."

"No," said Alec, very thoughtfully indeed. "But all the same . . ."

There was a short silence.

"Where is Simon?" asked Miss Wentworth.

Alec told her what had happened.

"Poor boy," she said. "You were right to let him sleep. Sleep is a wonderful healer, especially for the young. Simon will probably waken extremely hungry — in spite of his large tea — and I should advise a light

278

nourishing meal, a warm bath and bed. I shall give you a small and perfectly harmless sleeping-tablet for him, Mr Maclaren."

Alec replied that in his opinion the treatment prescribed could not be bettered and he would see that it was carried out in every detail. He was extremely grateful to Miss Wentworth for her sympathy and began to tell her so, but she cut short his thanks by saying she was a little tired and would retire to her rooms and rest. Alec opened the door for her and watched her walk across the hall, an upright and indomitable old lady. He admired her immensely. I shall see that she doesn't suffer for her courage, he decided.

<h2 style="text-align:center">3</h2>

By this time Alec was quite dazed with exhaustion; however, there was still a duty to be performed. He ordered a "light nourishing meal" for Simon and watched him eat it. The "small and perfectly harmless sleeping-tablet" was brought in a pill-box by Miss Wentworth's maid and presented to Simon with implicit instructions that he was to take it with a little water when he was in bed — but not before.

"It's from old Aunt Prissy," said Simon looking at it doubtfully. "Do you think I should take it?"

"Of course! It will give you a good sleep."

"I only saw her for a few minutes — and she wasn't feeling well — but she seemed a bit dotty."

"Your impression was erroneous," said Alec dryly. He added, "Buzz off and have a warm bath and go to bed. I'm going to bed myself."

"Right!" agreed Simon, turning to go.

"And don't forget to take your tablet."

"Right oh!"

Alec followed him upstairs; he shut the door of his room and proceeded to undress . . . and now at last he had peace to review the events of the day. He had been so worried about Simon and so busy with one thing and another that he had not had time to think seriously about Sir Mortimer. Alec had never met him so it would have been hypocritical to pretend that he was grieved at the man's death, but it seemed rather dreadful that nobody should mourn his loss. Nobody really cared, thought Alec; nobody was heartbroken. Simon had shed tears but had soon recovered; Miss Wentworth was more concerned with her own affairs than unhappy at the loss of her brother; Mrs Godfrey had retired to bed but was reported to be eating well and making plans for the future; Bassett had been upset, but it was shock at the sudden loss of a master who had seemed larger than life — practically immortal — rather than sorrow for a human being whom he had served for thirty years.

Sir Mortimer had been respected and feared but nobody had loved him — perhaps he had not wanted love. He was like the rich man in the parable whose ground brought forth plentifully; he had ruled supreme in his little kingdom and was making plans for the future . . . then, without a moment's warning, his soul had been required of him: "Then, whose shall those things be, which thou hast provided?"

Sir Mortimer had been torn from his comfortable surroundings and — as Simon had put it — he had "gone somewhere else." Alec had been sincere in his comforting words to Simon; he believed that God wasted nothing and was merciful, but all the same it was an awesome thought that a man who had openly denied the existence of his Maker should have been taken suddenly in the middle of a fit of rage without any opportunity for repentance.

By this time Alec was ready for bed so he knelt down to say his prayers and included an earnest petition for the soul of Mortimer Wentworth, wherever it might be.

CHAPTER
TWENTY-ONE

1

The next morning was bright and sunny with a nip of frost in the air. Alec and Simon met at breakfast and consumed bacon and eggs. Both had slept well and felt refreshed and cheerful.

"What have we got to do this morning?" asked Simon. "I was thinking about what you said last night — I mean having so much to do and nobody to help you — and I decided I must help you. I suppose it's about — about the funeral?" He hesitated and then added, "Listen, Alec, it will have to be a terrific splosh; he would have liked that, you know."

"Yes, I know. I'll see to it, Simon."

"Lots of people and flowers and — and all that."

"Masses of flowers."

"A slap-up service in the little church."

"Yes, I've spoken to Mr Heath about it."

"Oh good! I suppose I shall have to — to —"

"Don't worry, Simon. I'll tell you what you'll have to do when the time comes."

"All right," nodded Simon. "Well, what can I do to help you?"

"There's nothing much at the moment. Why not go for a ride? It's a pity to waste such a lovely morning."

"Would that be all right?"

"I wouldn't ride through the village but there are lots of other places to go, aren't there? I'd like to go with you but I can't because that lawyer fellow is coming."

"Alec, who do the horses belong to? I mean do they belong to me?"

Alec smiled. "I can tell you that definitely when the will is read, but it doesn't matter. It will do them good to be exercised."

"I'll nip over to the stables and find Nitkin," said Simon joyfully. He rose to go and then paused. "Oh, look here, Alec! You'd better keep this for me; I might lose it or something."

"This" was a short gold chain with a seal and a small key attached to it. Simon dropped it on the table and made for the door.

"Where did you get it?" asked Alec.

"Grandfather gave it to me. He had it under his pillow. I'll tell you all about it some time."

With that Simon vanished. The front door banged and there was the sound of racing footsteps on the gravel sweep.

Alec examined the seal with interest. The Wentworth crest was the head of a horse; it was deeply cut in a large translucent yellow stone. Obviously it would make an exceedingly good impression; he must try it on wax when he had time. The key interested him too; it was about the size of an ignition key but, although small, it looked strong and it had very curious wards. Alec had never seen such a queer little key before. He put the chain in his pocket and went into the library.

Sir Mortimer's massive oak chair stood in front of Sir Mortimer's gigantic writing-table. On the table stood impedimenta for writing letters and carrying on the business of the estate. Everything was outsize except the telephone which, though an ordinary standard instrument, looked small and humble.

Alec took up the receiver and put through a call to Major Wentworth's club. At first the hall porter was unwilling to disclose information about the movements of the members, but when the reason for the inquiry was explained he became sympathetic and co-operative. No, Major Wentworth was not staying at the club, but he had been in for lunch yesterday. No, the hall porter had no idea where he was staying nor when he would be back. "But you could leave a message, sir," he suggested. "I'll see Major Wentworth gets it if he comes in. Did you think of trying his bank?"

"Where does he bank?"

"I don't know sir . . . but wait a minute. They might know at the office because of his cheques. I'll go and ask."

"Good man!" exclaimed Alec.

The hall porter was away for some time. As Alec waited he noticed that there were two drawers in the left-hand side of the writing-table; the top drawer had a ring of brass round the lock and a brass flap over the key-hole. He took the chain out of his pocket and slipped the key into the lock; it slid in and fitted snugly with an audible click — but it would not turn. He tried it one way and then the other without success

That's funny, he thought. It seems as if it ought to be the key — but obviously it isn't.

The key fitted so tightly in the lock that it was difficult to withdraw but at last he got it out and returned it to his pocket.

No sooner had he done so than the hall porter came back with the information that Alec wanted; he added that if the bank was unable to contact Major Wentworth it would do no harm to try his tailors, Carton and Whitehead.

Alec thanked the man for the trouble he had taken and rang off. He tried the bank — and left a message — and then rang up Messrs. Carton and Whitehead. Mr Whitehead was there himself so Alec spoke to him and told him what had happened.

"Good gracious!" exclaimed Mr Whitehead. "How very distressing! We have known Sir Mortimer for years. He was in here last week and ordered a new suit — he was looking extremely well."

"Have you seen Major Wentworth lately?"

"Yes, indeed. He came in yesterday afternoon — I had a chat with him myself — but he didn't say anything about his plans. If he happens to come in again I shall see that he receives your message. We aren't expecting him, but you never know. Have you tried his club?"

"Yes, and his bank."

"Try Asprey's," suggested Mr Whitehead. "Major Wentworth is well known there. Oh, and I believe he has his shoes made at Dunne's."

2

Alec had just finished telephoning to these London shops — without success — and was sitting looking at the telephone and wondering what else he could do when the door was opened widely, with a flourish:

"Major D'Artington, sir!" announced Bassett.

It took several moments for Major D'Artington to walk in; he was lame and leant heavily upon a stick. This gave Alec time to collect his thoughts: D'Artington? Of course! That big place with the stone beasts on the gateposts ... ten-sixty-six ... crusaders ...

"Oh, how do you do, sir!" exclaimed Alec. "My name is Maclaren. I came here with Simon and —"

"I know," said Major D'Artington, smiling and shaking hands. "The grape-vine flourishes in this part of the world, so we heard all about the affairs of our neighbours. I really called to leave letters of condolence for Miss Wentworth and then I decided that it might be a good plan to see if there was anything I could do for you."

"I'm delighted to see you, sir. Come and sit down."

"I prefer a high chair if possible."

"Yes, of course," said Alec, pushing the furniture about and placing Sir Mortimer's throne beside the fire.

"Thank you," said Major D'Artington. He sat down and added, "I've never sat in this majestic piece of furniture before."

"It's Sir Mortimer's chair, I suppose."

"Yes — and it suited him."

In Alec's opinion it suited Major D'Artington. Now that he had time to look at his visitor properly Alec decided that he must be the exact replica of his crusading ancestor. He was tall and gaunt with strong features which were stern in repose but were softened and irradiated by his smile . . . and he had the same worn look as a crusader who had endured the privations of a campaign against the enemies of Christendom.

"You didn't know Mortimer, did you?" asked Major D'Artington.

"No," said Alec. He was becoming slightly annoyed at this question.

"In that case I needn't commiserate with you. I mean you don't really regret his death."

"It would be hypocritical to say that I do," Alec replied frankly. "At least not in the way you mean . . . but it seems sad that nobody is very sorry about it. To tell you the truth I regret his death but only because it's going to throw too much responsibility upon Simon — and upon me, as Simon's guardian. I'm afraid that may sound rather heartless."

"I prefer sincerity to sentimentality, Mr Maclaren. Mortimer was a curious man, difficult to understand. I got on with him quite well but other people found him unattractive. He inspired respect but not affection; he was friendless. Strangely enough my feeling for him was . . . pity."

He had paused before the last word and Alec had wondered what was coming. He was taken aback by the word that came.

"I see you're surprised," said Major D'Artington. "Perhaps it is rather surprising — and nobody would have been more surprised than Mortimer himself! — but he was terribly lonely, or so I felt. Oh, he was surrounded by his family, of course, but none of them was much use to him. I believe he was more attached to Simon than to anyone else. I believe the reason he was so furious with Simon was because he was fond of the boy."

"That sounds rather queer."

"It isn't, you know," said Major D'Artington thoughtfully, "I don't know whether you ever read Coleridge. I can't get about much so I read a good deal.

And to be wroth with one we love
Doth work like madness in the brain.

There you have it in a nutshell."

"Yes, it's true — horribly true," agreed Alec.

"As you say, horribly true. Well, anyhow, I've always thought that Mortimer was one of the loneliest men in

288

the world. It was his own fault but that didn't make it any better. He had no faith in anything or anyone; he was completely self-sufficient — or thought he was — but occasionally when he was off-guard I've seen a hungry soul looking out of his eyes. What can one feel for a man like that except deep compassion?"

Alec could find nothing to say.

"Well now," said Major D'Artington in a different tone. "Is there anything I can do to help you?"

Alec explained that Major Wentworth was in London and detailed the efforts which had been made to find him. "As you know I'm a stranger here," he said. "I'm pretty much at sea. The funeral is on Monday — I've fixed that with Mr Heath — and I'm sure it would be the wish of the Wentworth family that you should be a pall-bearer."

"I'm glad you mentioned it. I should have been pleased to accept, of course, but I'm too crippled to officiate in that capacity. I intended to suggest that my son should represent our family. He's just a year older than Simon and it seemed to me that it would be a help to Simon to have a boy of his own age to back him up."

"Yes, that's an excellent plan."

"Is there anything else you would like to know?"

"Yes, there is," said Alec. "Who else should be asked and how am I to do it?"

"It would be better for Peter to ask them."

"Of course it would — if only I could get hold of him!" exclaimed Alec. "What on earth am I to do if he doesn't come? I'm almost demented."

"Don't worry too much, Mr Maclaren. You've done your best to get hold of Peter, nobody can do more, and of course he'll see the notice in *The Times*."

"That's another thing. I haven't sent the notices yet; I've been waiting for Major Wentworth because I was afraid of not getting it right. If you would be good enough to tell me exactly —"

"I'll do it for you if you like."

"How kind of you, sir!"

"Not at all. I'm only too pleased to be of use." He rose and added, "Oh, there's just one other thing! I suppose you've got in contact with Mr Sandford."

"Mr Sandford?" repeated Alec in bewilderment.

"Mortimer's lawyer," explained Major D'Artington.

Alec was about to ask for more information but there was no time; Major D'Artington was on his way to the door so Alec ran to open it for him . . . and Bassett was waiting in the hall with his coat and hat and gloves. In the slight confusion of Major D'Artington's departure there was no opportunity to to speak to him privately.

"Good-bye, Mr Maclaren," said Major D'Artington. "I'll see to those notices — and don't become *quite* demented, will you?"

"Good-bye, sir — and thank you very much indeed," said Alec.

Helped by his chauffeur Major D'Artington got into his car and was driven away.

CHAPTER
TWENTY-TWO

1

Mr Sandford, thought Alec as he went back into the library. *Now* what am I to do? Does Mr Sandford know about Mr Friece and the new will — or does he not? Do I ring up Mr Sandford and explain? No, it's impossible . . . besides I don't understand the matter myself. I had better wait for Mr Friece and hear what he has to say.

Alec still felt demented, so he walked about the room and tried to compose his thoughts. He was walking about the room when the door opened and Bassett ushered in Mr Friece. There was no flourish for this visitor, Alec noticed.

"Oh good! I'm very glad to see you," said Alec, going forward and shaking hands. He *was* glad, of course; anything was better than hanging about waiting for the telephone bell to ring; but when he had time to look at Mr Friece he was disappointed and surprised. Not unnaturally he had expected Sir Mortimer's lawyer to be a cultural man, a polished member of the legal fraternity; this man was small and rather shabby, worse still his eyes did not meet Alec's frankly but seemed to be fixed on something behind Alec's left shoulder. I don't like him, thought Alec in alarm. Aloud he said, "Are you Sir Mortimer's lawyer?"

"Yes, of course," replied Mr Friece. "I suppose you're Mr Maclaren. You spoke to me on the telephone last night. Have you got the keys of Sir Mortimer's desk?"

"No, I'm afraid not."

"Where are they, then?" asked Mr Friece and he began trying the drawers of the big desk in the corner. They were all locked.

"Perhaps Bassett would know," suggested Alec.

"The butler knows nothing. He's a fool," replied Mr Friece.

The words were scarcely out of his mouth when the door opened and Basset came in with a bunch of keys on a silver salver.

"You were asking for keys, sir," said Bassett. "Mrs Sillett found these in a drawer in the drawing-room cabinet."

"Ha!" exclaimed Mr Friece. "I wonder which of them fits the top of the desk."

Alec went over and looked at the bunch. He said, "Those keys are an odd lot."

"An odd lot? What do you mean?"

"They haven't been in use for years, some of them are rusty. From what I've heard of Sir Mortimer I should think he would keep all his keys carefully oiled and labelled."

"He did," replied Mr Friece. "He kept all his keys in a drawer in his writing-table, but the key of the drawer is lost. These keys are probably duplicates."

292

Alec put his hand in his pocket . . . and then paused. Why should he produce the key? For one thing Simon had asked him to keep it safely; for another thing he did not trust Mr Friece a yard; besides, he had tried the little key in the drawer of the writing-table and it would not turn the lock.

Strangely enough Alec was beginning to enjoy himself. He stood on the hearth-rug with his back to the fire, watching Mr Friece; it was obvious that Mr Friece was not enjoying himself at all. Mr Friece was trying one key after another in the lock which secured the top of the big desk and becoming more red in the face every moment. It was some time before he gave up the struggle but at last he was forced to admit defeat. He threw down the keys in disgust.

"Sir Mortimer kept everything locked," said Alec conversationally. "Even the bookcases. I don't blame him in the least. There's a very fine collection of rare books in this room — I should like to have a look at them some time — besides, apart from that, it's annoying when people borrow books and forget to return them."

"There are more important things than books."

"Such as?"

"Such as his will," snapped Mr Friece. "He made a new will only last week. I prepared it for him and left it with him but I don't know whether he signed it or not."

"I rather think it was signed."

"You rather think? What do you mean? Who told you?" asked Mr Friece eagerly.

"Bassett told me that he and Mrs Sillett witnessed Sir Mortimer's signature to 'a big important-looking document written on very thick paper.' The idea occurred to me that it might possibly have been Sir Mortimer's last will and testament."

"Of course it was. Where did he put it?"

"Bassett said 'he slipped it into the top of his desk.' Obviously you know that already."

"I didn't know for certain," replied Mr Friece, picking up the bunch of keys and starting to try them all over again.

"You're wasting your time," said Alec. "As I told you before those keys are an odd lot."

"I know that as well as you do," retorted Mr Friece. "I just thought one of them might fit — but it's hopeless. What I want is a small key on a gold chain which Sir Mortimer always kept in his pocket. The nurses say he kept it under his pillow, but it has disappeared. Someone must have taken it — and for no good purpose. I wish I knew —"

"Perhaps this is what you're looking for."

"Of course that's it! Where did you get it?"

"Sir Mortimer gave it to his grandson just before he died. I really don't know whether I'm justified in letting you have it."

"Nonsense! Of course I must have it," declared Mr Friece, taking it from Alec's hand. "This is the master-key. It's the key of the top drawer of the writing-table which contains all Sir Mortimer's keys. Look, it fits the lock perfectly!"

Alec watched with interest. The key slid in as it had done before but again refused to turn. Mr Friece fiddled with it in growing irritation. "I can't understand it," he muttered. "This is the key — I've seen it in Sir Mortimer's hand — but it won't turn the lock."

"Bad luck," said Alec, sympathetically.

"There's something gone wrong with the wretched thing. Someone has been trying to force the lock — that's what's happened. I must get this drawer open somehow; all the keys are here — the keys of everything in the house. I shall have to get a locksmith. What's the name of the locksmith in Wandlebury?"

"I'm a stranger here so I can't tell you."

Mr Friece stretched out his hand to the telephone. "The police will be able to give me the name of a good —"

"Mr Friece," said Alec. "Nothing of that sort can be done without permission from the Wentworth family."

"Oh, well — perhaps not," said Mr Friece, hesitating.

Silence fell. It was quite a long silence. Alec fixed his eyes upon an elegantly-shaped pottery jar which stood on the top of one of the bookcases but he saw it with his eyes only and not with his mind. Although he appeared perfectly calm and collected he was thinking hard, wondering what on earth to do . . . and then in the distance he heard the sound of horses trotting up the avenue — Simon and Nitkin were returning from their ride. It would be very much better if Simon and Mr Friece did not meet, but how could it be prevented?

"If you will excuse me for a moment —" began Alec.

He was too late. Before he had reached the door it burst open and Simon appeared.

"Alec, I've had a splendid ride —" he began excitedly.

"Good," said Alec. "This is Mr Friece, Simon. I told you he was coming, didn't I?"

"Oh yes, how do you do, Mr Friece."

"You are Sir Mortimer's grandson, I suppose," said Mr Friece.

"Yes."

"Well, in that case I should like your permission to send for a locksmith to break open this drawer."

"That drawer?" asked Simon in surprise. "But there's no need to —"

"It is absolutely necessary. I must look through Sir Mortimer's papers. There is one especially important document which must be found at once."

"He wouldn't like it," said Simon quickly. "I mean Grandfather wouldn't like anyone to mess about with his papers. That's why he told me to do it."

"Do you mean that your grandfather told you to 'mess about' with his papers?" asked Mr Friece, smiling sarcastically.

"No, of course not. It was just something special he wanted me to do. You see, when he was taken ill he sent for me to come. There were two reasons why he sent for me: he wanted to see me to — to make up a quarrel we'd had and he wanted me to do something for him. He said he couldn't ask anybody else because the house was full of fools. Of course I said I would do anything he wanted, so then he told me — and I did it. That's all."

"What did he ask you to do?" inquired Mr Friece.

Simon remained silent.

"Did you hear what I said?" demanded Mr Friece.

"It was a private thing. It has nothing to do with you."

"If it had something to do with Sir Mortimer's papers — as you seem to imply — it is most certainly my business."

"Not your sort of papers."

There was a short silence. At last Alec said, "Simon, I think you should tell Mr Friece what he wants to know."

"Do you?" asked Simon in doubtful tones. "Grandfather said I wasn't to tell anybody — but perhaps it doesn't matter now."

"I think you should tell us the whole story."

"Everything?" asked Simon, still hesitating.

Alec nodded. "I'm quite certain you've done nothing to be ashamed of."

"Oh no, it isn't that! It's just because Grandfather wanted it to be a secret."

"Go on, old chap," said Alec encouragingly. "Begin at the beginning."

"Well, if you say so, Alec." Simon paused to collect his thoughts and then continued, "When I arrived I went in to see Grandfather. He was propped up with pillows and he looked a bit pale, but he talked quite happily so I knew he had forgiven me. Then he asked me to do something for him. I told you that. Of course

I said I would. Then he took the little gold chain with the seal and the key from under his pillow and gave it to me and told me what to do. When he had told me *exactly* what I was to do he made me repeat it. Then he said that it was a secret and I wasn't to tell anybody and I was to do it when nobody was in the library. He was very earnest about it. He had just finished telling me and we had begun to talk about — about something else when the nurse came in and said I was to go away. She said it was time for him to rest — and all that — and Grandfather was angry. I told you that, didn't I, Alec?"

"Yes, you told me," agreed Alec, coming to the rescue. "He was angry because he wanted to talk to you. He shouted at the nurse . . . and a few moments later he died, holding your hand. That's right, isn't it?"

"Yes, that's what happened. It was awful. It was so awful that I forgot about the key — and everything."

"You were very upset," put in Alec.

"Yes, I was. It seemed so — so awful for him to die — like that. I was so upset and wretched that I forgot all about the key until I was undressing to go to bed. Then I found it in my pocket and of course I remembered. I felt an absolute beast for having forgotten to do what he had asked me to do, so I put on my dressing-gown and came downstairs and did it."

"Did what?" barked Mr Friece.

"I did exactly what Grandfather had said. I opened the drawer in the writing-table and I found the key of the top of the desk — it was marked with a little tag. I opened the desk and found the envelope; it was a very thick yellow envelope, sealed with red wax, and was lying on the top of some red books. Grandfather had said I wasn't to open the envelope, so of course I didn't; I put it in the fire just as it was. That's what —"

"You burnt it!" cried Mr Friece in furious tones.

"That's what Grandfather said," explained Simon. "The fire was a bit low and the envelope was so thick and heavy that it took some time to burn, but I poked it a bit and waited until there was nothing left but black ashes — Grandfather had told me to be very particular about that. Then I locked the top of the desk and put the key back in the drawer. Grandfather had told me exactly what I was to do — and I did it.

"I felt happier after I had done it," added Simon. "I mean it was awfully nice being able to do something for him."

There was a long silence. Simon was looking pleased with himself at the recollection of a task completed without a hitch. Mr Friece had sat down suddenly in the nearest chair — apparently stricken dumb.

Alec, who was still standing in his favourite spot on the hearth-rug, suddenly became aware that he was on the verge of laughter. He was almost overpowered by spasms of unseemly mirth . . . almost, but not quite. He controlled himself with difficulty and, taking a cheroot from his pigskin case, lighted it with a match. The soothing aroma of tobacco completed his cure and fortified him for future developments.

At last Mr Friece found his voice. He said huskily, "To destroy a will is an indictable offence, especially when the testator is deceased."

"I don't understand what you mean, sir," said Simon frankly.

"You had no right to burn your grandfather's will."

"Oh, was it his will?" asked Simon in surprise. "I didn't know what was in the envelope — I told you that — but even if I *had* known I would have done it just the same. Grandfather asked me to burn that envelope; it was almost the last thing he said . . . so I burnt it."

Mr Friece held out the gold chain with the key attached. "Is this the key that was given to you?"

"Yes, that's it."

"Kindly open that drawer and show me where you found the will."

Simon took the key and opened the drawer without any difficulty. "It's quite simple when you know how," he explained. "And this is the key of the top of the desk. Shall I open it?"

"Please do so."

Simon did so.

Mr Friece at once began to rummage feverishly in the top of the desk.

While he was thus engaged Alec went forward, shut the drawer containing the keys, took the small key on the gold chain and put it in his pocket. He winked at Simon and returned to his stance on the hearth-rug.

"Yes, the will has gone!" Mr Friece exclaimed.

"I told you," said Simon. "It was lying on the top of those red books — just as Grandfather described."

"You're sure it was here?"

"Yes. A big thick yellow envelope. It's no good asking me any more about it because I've told you everything

". . . and that's the gong for lunch," added Simon cheerfully.

It was indeed the gong, booming through the house in its usual peremptory manner.

"Just a moment," said Mr Friece. "You don't seem to realise the gravity of the matter. Lunch can wait. The will may be in one of the drawers of the desk."

"It isn't. It was there — just as I told you."

"All the same I intend to look for it." Mr Friece went back to the writing-table and found the drawer locked; he held out his hand to Simon and said, "Give me the key. I shall have to go through all the drawers and —"

"I have the key," said Alec. "We can go through all the drawers another day — we shall have to, of course — but I prefer to wait until Major Wentworth is with us."

"We must do it to-day."

"Not until Major Wentworth comes."

"I insist upon it."

"No," said Alec, shaking his head.

"What right have you to interfere?" asked Mr Friece furiously. "I am Sir Mortimer's lawyer."

"I am Sir Simon's guardian," replied Alec calmly.

Sir Simon made a curious choking noise and rushed out of the room.

2

There were just the three of them at lunch in the big dining room; Miss Wentworth was reported to be lunching upstairs. The food was excellent, as it always was at Limbourne, but the company was poor. Alec would have preferred a dinner of herbs with his beloved . . . probably at this very moment she was having lunch in the dining-room at The Cedars. He was thinking of her — and wishing he were there — so he did not hear the beginning of the conversation between his companions; he came to himself to hear Simon say defiantly, "I don't care. You can prosecute me if you like. I shall stand up in the dock — or whatever it's called — and tell the judge exactly what I've told you. Judges are sensible so he would understand that I *had* to do what Grandfather asked me to do."

"Are you threatening to prosecute my ward, Mr Friece?" asked Alec in an interested tone of voice.

"I have every right," declared Mr Friece angrily. "There are severe penalties for destroying a will. If you knew anything at all about law you would be aware of that."

"But Alec is —" began Simon. He was stopped by a somewhat painful kick.

"As Sir Simon's guardian," said Alec thoughtfully, "I have no objection to raise. It would be interesting to see the result of such an action. Go right ahead, Mr Friece."

Mr Friece glowered fiercely but said no more; the meal was finished in silence except for the curious noises made by Mr Friece masticating his food.

It seemed incredible that Sir Mortimer had entrusted the drafting of his will to a man like Mr Friece. Alec thought it over, trying to get it clear. Miss Wentworth had said that her brother was "very much annoyed and sent for a lawyer — not our own family lawyer — and made a new will which was neither just nor generous." Then came Bassett's part of the story: Bassett and Mrs Sillett had witnessed Sir Mortimer's signature, had watched him put the document into an envelope, seal it up securely and "slip it into the top of his desk." Almost immediately afterwards Sir Mortimer had been taken ill and (laid low upon his bed of sickness) had come to his senses and taken steps to destroy the document. The unjust will had been well and truly burnt, but where was Sir Mortimer's previous will which was "just and generous to all his family and dependents"?

Major D'Artington had mentioned Mr Sandford — and, of course, Mr Sandford's address could be obtained from Miss Wentworth — but the fact was Alec shrank from approaching the Wentworth's family lawyer with this extraordinary story. Mr Sandford might — or might not — have the will in his possession, but it was very certain that he would be displeased when he heard what had happened.

Lunch was over by the time Alec had got the matter straightened out in his mind. Mr Friece made another attempt to persuade Alec to give him access to Sir Mortimer's papers — but without success. Alec repeated calmly but firmly that he preferred to await the arrival of Major Wentworth and as the all-important key was in Alec's pocket there was nothing to be done. The car was ordered to take Mr Friece to Wandlebury to catch his train and he departed in a state of fury and frustration.

Alec and his ward stood on the steps and watched the car drive off.

"Golly," said Simon. "Nasty piece of work, isn't he?"

"Most unpleasant."

"You fairly twisted his tail," added Simon with ghoulish glee. "I nearly burst with laughing when you said you were 'Sir Simon's guardian' — I had to dash out of the room."

"I noticed that."

"He said he was going to prosecute me. Do you think he will?"

"Not unless he's a bigger fool than I take him for."

"I wouldn't mind," said Simon thoughtfully. "You needn't be frightened of a judge if you've done the right thing."

Alec agreed that British judges were famed for their wisdom and integrity.

"It would be rather fun," said Simon, smiling at the idea. "Bennington mi. had to appear in court when his mother was divorced and everybody at school thought it was a frightfully good show. The lawyer told him exactly what he was to say beforehand. It would be different for me. All I shall have to do is to tell the truth the whole truth and nothing but the truth."

"Quite," agreed Alec, somewhat dryly. "But I very much doubt if you will be given the opportunity. Tell me, Simon; did you know what was in the envelope?" This was a point which had intrigued Alec more than a little and he waited with interest for the answer to his question.

"Of course not!" exclaimed Simon. "I told you I didn't know what was in the envelope, but naturally I wondered. As a matter of fact I thought perhaps it was . . ." He paused.

"Well, go on. What did you think it was?"

"A packet of love letters," said Simon. He added indignantly, "It's all very well for you to laugh like that, Alec, but he seemed so anxious that I shouldn't open the envelope and see what was inside. He made me promise not to. He said they were 'private papers.' Well, love letters are private, aren't they?"

CHAPTER
TWENTY-THREE

1

It was a lovely afternoon. Alec would have liked to go
for a good long walk and explore the policies of
Limbourne but by this time Major Wentworth might
have received one of the messages and ring up to say
when he was coming. Alec decided to stay at his post.

"It's sickening for you but perhaps you'd better,"
agreed Simon. "What about tea at the Vicarage?"

"You'll have to go by yourself."

He had expected objections from Simon, but there
were none. On the contrary Simon seemed quite
pleased at the idea. "I'll go for a walk and drop in at the
Vicarage on the way home . . . unless you want me for
anything."

"Off you go; it's no use for us both to fug indoors,
but I'd like a book to read if it's all the same to you."

"A book?" asked Simon, looking round at the
close-packed shelves. "Won't any of those do?"

"They're all locked up."

"Oh, I see. The keys will be in the drawer, of course.
I'll show you how it opens; it's rather cute, really."

The secret of Sir Mortimer's master-key was decidedly "cute." Instead of sliding the key well home, as was one's natural inclination, one slid the key half-way in, gave it a half-turn clockwise, then slid it up to the hilt and turned it anti-clockwise. As Simon had said, it was quite simple when you knew how. The drawer was full of keys, all neatly labelled, so Alec was able to open the bookcases without any trouble at all. For a time he browsed about contentedly amongst Sir Mortimer's treasures; then he found a travel-book about an expedition to Peru so he settled down to read.

The book was extremely interesting; there were pictures of the fabulous Maya temples; there was a large coloured plate of the ruins of Machu Picchu, the lost city of the Incas; there was a photograph of part of the wall of a fortress made with huge stones. Even more interesting, the book was annotated in small neat writing — presumably by Sir Mortimer himself. Beside the picture of the enormous wall he had written, "Some of these stones weigh nearly 20 tons. It would be interesting to know how they were transported to the site without wheels and erected without a crane." In another place, beside the picture of some stone slabs, he had written, "The carvings on these slabs are 2,000 years old — toads and monkeys and a goat with horns. One of the monkeys was exactly like Brown. I told him so!" There were annotations on nearly every page (some of them extremely witty) which gave Alec a new light upon the strange and varied character of the late baronet.

During the afternoon the telephone bell rang twice. The first time the caller was a gentleman who wished to order four tons of the best coal and was annoyed to discover that Alec was not a coal merchant; the second time the caller was a lady who had heard that Sir Mortimer was ill and hoped he was better.

The afternoon seemed very long indeed. Basset brought tea at half past four — Indian tea in a China teapot — and made up the fire. He said, "Major Wentworth will have got the telegram by now. It doesn't take long to Germany, does it, sir?"

"Major Wentworth isn't in Germany."

"Not in Germany?" asked Bassett in surprise. "He must be in Germany. His leave was over and he had to go back."

"He's in London," said Alec, putting down the book with a sigh. "He has been seen in London by several people who know him well, but I can't get hold of him anyhow. I've tried his club; I've tried his bank; I've tried his tailor. Have you any idea as to how I could find him, Bassett?"

It was obvious that Bassett had no ideas at all; his face was completely blank.

"Well, never mind," said Alec irritably. "Brilliant ideas don't seem to be your strong point, but if you ever happen to have an idea as to how I can find a man who has vanished without trace in a city of between eight and nine million inhabitants just let me know, will you?"

Alec was slightly ashamed of this outburst but it rolled off Bassett like water off a duck's back. Bassett was used to harsher words than these.

"There's the wireless, sir," he suggested.

308

"The wireless?"

"Yes, sometimes they puts out calls for people that have disappeared . . . but I doubt if the Major would like it."

"He would not," said Alec and took up his book.

Bassett went away and closed the door very quietly.

It was six o'clock when Simon returned from his tea-party; he came in looking pleased and excited.

"Alec, he was there!" exclaimed Simon. "I hoped he might be on leave — and he was."

"Young Heath, I presume?"

"Yes, I told you about him, didn't I?"

"You said 'he must be terrific.' That was all."

"Oh well, I thought perhaps Mums might have told you . . ."

"She told me about 'the club,' if that's what you mean."

"Yes, that's what I mean. It was Adam Heath who found Lance smashing up his car and, instead of telling the police which would have made an awful scandal, he gave Lance a thrashing with his own hands. Uncle Peter told me that Lance was absolutely beaten up and Adam Heath hadn't a mark on him. That's pretty terrific, isn't it?"

"Yes, it is," agreed Alec, smiling.

"Then this afternoon Adam told me all about how he and Uncle Peter caught Oliver Wade. They waited outside his house for several nights and at last he came out and buzzed off in his car — so they followed him. He made for a big farm about five miles from here and hid his car in a field. Uncle Peter went to warn the farmer while Adam kept watch. It was a very dark night so it was a bit difficult to keep track of Oliver without getting too close but presently Adam saw the reflection of a dark lantern so he ran after it and was just in time to see it disappearing into a huge barn. The field was very rough; he took a frightful toss over a tussock of grass but he picked himself up and ran on. When he got to the barn and pulled the door open he found that Oliver had set fire to a pile of straw so he blew his whistle as loud as he could and went for Oliver with his fists. Fortunately Uncle Peter and the farmer heard the whistle and rushed in and beat out the fire before it had done much damage. Meanwhile Adam had given Oliver a hiding and tied him up with ropes. Sailors are pretty good with ropes and I bet Adam made a good job of it. The farmer was furious of course; he said the barn was five hundred years old and very valuable; it would have made a tremendous blaze — and there were cows in a byre next door! Uncle Peter told the farmer to ring up the police — so he did. Gosh, I wish I had been there to see the fun!"

"You don't like the young man?" suggested Alec.

"Oliver Wade? He's an absolute wart. He has done the most awful things — especially with fire."

"Arson."

"Yes, that's the word. Adam said he had a sort of flamethrower which he had made himself, that's how he got the fire going so quickly."

"Had he used it before?"

Simon nodded. "I don't know how often, but I happen to know that one night he set fire to an empty house and then rang up the fire brigade. When the engines arrived Oliver helped them to put out the fire and got a lot of kudos for it. What do you think of that?"

"Horrible."

"Yes, horrible — but I think the worst thing of all was the way he got people to join his club and taught them to destroy things. There wouldn't have been a club at all if it hadn't been for him."

"You mean he influenced young people?"

"Yes, he ruined Lance and — and Anthea too, really — but I don't think I'd better tell you about that. He had a very strong influence on people. He influenced me into giving him a five-pound note for his beastly club. Of course that was before I knew what kind of a club it was, but all the same I shouldn't have done it. He just held out his hand and I gave it to him without thinking. The next moment I realised what a fool I had been . . . but it was too late."

Simon looked so enraged at the recollection of his folly that Alec was obliged to hide a smile. He blew his nose and said, "Oh well, he's in prison now, I suppose."

"Yes, he got six months," replied Simon with relish.

2

Miss Wentworth came downstairs to have dinner with Alec and Simon; it was a pleasant meal. When they had finished they went into the library which, in Alec's opinion, was much more comfortable than the drawing-room.

Miss Wentworth remarked casually that she had never sat in this room before and when Alec showed surprise she explained that her brother preferred his own company. "It looks comfortable," she admitted, "but the chairs are too large and reclining."

She certainly did not look comfortable sitting upright in the big leather chair so Alec seized two cushions and arranged them behind her back, a small attention which was greatly appreciated. They had coffee and talked for a while and then Miss Wentworth asked if Simon were fond of cards.

"Yes, rather," replied Simon. "Mums and I sometimes play piquet in the evenings; it's a very good game for two people."

Miss Wentworth was surprised and delighted. Bassett was summoned and produced cards and a card-table and the game started without delay.

For a time Alec watched them; he found it interesting and amusing, for although Miss Wentworth was old and Simon was young there was a strong resemblance between them (Wentworth faces, thought Alec) and the resemblance was enhanced by their absorption in the game. Alec had never played piquet but he could see that this was a hard-fought battle between two evenly-matched antagonists.

"Point of six," declared Simon in ringing tones.

"Good," said Miss Wentworth.

"Quarte major."

"No good," said Miss Wentworth.

"Trio of aces," said Simon.

"No good," said Miss Wentworth complacently.

312

"No good?" asked Simon in dismay. "Gosh, Aunt Prissy, you *are* awful!"

She smiled and said, "I have a quatorze of knaves. I admit I was lucky. Go on, Simon. It is your turn to play."

The game continued. Alec watched and listened; he took up the evening paper and read for a little and then put it down. He was becoming more worried with every hour that passed. What can I do? he wondered. Surely there must be some way of finding the man. Surely somebody must know where he is. Should I ring up Mr Sandford? But I can't — I simply can't explain what has happened. It would be so much better for Major Wentworth to ring him up and explain. On the other hand I mustn't leave it too long. The funeral is on Monday; to-morrow is Saturday and I haven't fixed up about pall-bearers or anything. I don't know who to ask. If this were Scotland I wouldn't be so frightfully at sea. If this were Scotland I'd ask Nitkin — the man has been here for forty years — but I don't know about this place. It might not be the right thing. If Major Wentworth doesn't turn up before Monday . . . but he must, thought Alec desperately. There must be some way of getting hold of him. Is there anything that I haven't thought of? . . . No, there's nothing. I must just wait patiently and try not to worry.

In spite of this sensible resolution it was impossible to sit still so he rose and made another tour of the bookcases and, finding a copy of *Northanger Abbey* with the most delightful illustrations, he settled down to read.

At ten o'clock Miss Wentworth's maid came to take her to bed. Simon also went to bed and Alec was left alone. For a time he read quite happily — it really was a delicious book, he had forgotten how amusing it was — and then the telephone bell rang.

Alec leapt from his chair and took up the receiver; he was sure it was Peter Wentworth.

There was some delay on the line; then a woman's voice said, "Is that my call at last? I've been waiting for ten minutes."

"This is Limbourne."

"You sound about a hundred miles away. It's a very bad connection."

"This is Limbourne," repeated Alec loudly.

"Who?"

"Limbourne. Is Major Wentworth there?"

"Do you want to speak to him?"

"Yes, I do. It's very urgent."

"Hold on a minute. I'll go and see if he's in."

Alec held on. What was the meaning of it? If Major Wentworth had put through the call why was he not there to take it? However, the woman had gone to find him so the only thing to do was to wait. He waited and waited; he was still waiting for the woman to come back when he heard a car drive up the avenue and stop.

After a moment's hesitation Alec dropped the receiver, dashed into the hall and threw open the front door. He was just in time to see a tall, broad-shouldered man in a thick tweed overcoat coming up the steps. The man was bareheaded so his face was clearly visible in the light which streamed out through the open door — and there could be no doubt whatever as to his identity.

"Thank heaven you're here at last!" exclaimed Alec, too overcome with relief for any conventional greeting.

"You're Maclaren, I take it," said the newcomer, smiling and holding out his hand. "I got your message from old Whitehead — happened to see him at the theatre. I was rather surprised when he made violent signals to me; however, I went out and met him in the foyer . . . so here I am."

"I'll get your suitcase out of the car."

"I didn't bring one — I've got clothes here — I came straight here from the theatre. Bassett is in bed, I suppose."

"I expect so, but I can stir him up if you would like something to eat — something hot, I mean. There are drinks and sandwiches in the library. Oh, I'm sorry, Major Wentworth!"

"What's the matter?"

"Well, of course you'll order what you want yourself. The fact is I've had to take over the reins — there was nobody else to do it — and I seem to have acquired the habit."

"You had better carry on."

"No, certainly not. I've just been keeping things going until you could come and take charge. It has been very difficult for me; I can't tell you how pleased I am to see you."

"We had better go into partnership — or whatever you legal fellows call it."

"But I haven't explained who I am — or why I'm here. You must be wondering —"

"You're Katherine's husband," interrupted Major Wentworth. "That's good enough for me. Besides I saw you play for Cambridge in the Varsity match at Lords."

"That wasn't yesterday!" exclaimed Alec, smiling.

"No, but it was a damn' good show. I particularly remember a cut through gulley — very crafty. Simon told me you were giving him some coaching. Is he going to be any good?"

"He's going to be very good indeed."

"Lucky little beggar," said Simon's uncle.

It struck Alec that this was a very odd conversation. He ought to have started by explaining that he was Simon's guardian and gone on to commiserate with Major Wentworth on the death of his father; but perhaps it was not too late. He was about to begin his explanations when Major Wentworth took off his heavy coat, flung it carelessly on to a chair and said, "You mentioned drinks in the library."

"Yes," replied Alec, opening the door.

"Good," said Major Wentworth. He walked in and sat down on one of the easy-chairs.

Alec took the tray of drinks and sandwiches and put it on the table beside him.

"Oh, thanks," said Major Wentworth. "You had better have something yourself. I must say I could do with a little sustenance. I came down from town in record time. As a matter of fact I was absolutely thunderstruck when Whitehead told me that the old man had gone. When I was here last week he was in particularly good fettle."

"It must have been a dreadful shock. I'm sorry you had to hear about it like that, but I didn't know how to get hold of you. Bassett said you had gone back to Germany, but Sir Reginald Woodhall told me he had seen you in Regent Street and when I rang up your club the hall porter said you had been in to lunch."

"My leave isn't up until next Friday, but things were so uncomfortable here that I couldn't stick it a moment longer, so I told a little fib and went to stay with some friends who have a flat in Curzon Street."

"I see," said Alec. How simple it was when you knew.

"What's that buzzing noise?" asked Major Wentworth. "Oh, it's the telephone! Someone has left the receiver off."

"I did," admitted Alec, replacing it. "Somebody rang up and I thought it was you — I had been waiting for a call all day. The woman had just gone to find you when you arrived."

"I don't get it," said Major Wentworth frankly.

Alec was not surprised. The telephone call had been so mysterious that he did not understand it himself. He said, "Oh, it must have been a wrong number or something. Anyway it doesn't matter now that you're here, Major Wentworth."

"How about 'Peter'? I mean we're relations, aren't we?"

Alec agreed to Christian names — it made things easier — but he was considerably amused at the idea that he and Peter were "relations" for, although he acknowledged cousinship unto the third and fourth generation in the good old Scottish manner, he found this particular relationship a little difficult to swallow.

"Katherine is my sister-in-law," Peter pointed out. "And that reminds me that I haven't congratulated you. I do so now, most sincerely; you're a very lucky man."

"The luckiest man in the whole wide world."

Peter nodded, "I believe you! I only saw Katherine once, when I went up to Craig an Ron with a message from my father. I expected trouble and began by being rather rude, but Katherine wound me round her little finger and fed me on strawberries and cream. I thought she was a perfect darling."

"She is," said her husband.

"Katherine is lucky too," continued Peter, smiling in a friendly manner. "I never had much use for Gerald — why did Katherine marry him, I wonder. Women are queer, aren't they?"

Alec was unable to find any comment to make, so there was a short silence.

"You know, Alec," said Peter in a thoughtful voice, "this place has a funny sort of feeling. I felt it as I came up the avenue and I feel it more every minute. He filled this place — that's why. He has always been here and one felt he always would be here. I can't believe he isn't here any more. I keep on thinking that he'll walk into the room and ask what the devil we're doing, sitting in his library and having a meal at this time of night."

Alec said nothing but his eye fell upon the bookcase from which he had taken *Northanger Abbey* and he noticed that the glass door was half open. He rose and shut it.

"I'm sorry you had such a job finding me," said Peter. "Old Whitehead said you sounded quite desperate. I suppose I ought to have told someone where I was going but — well — I never thought of it. All I wanted was to escape."

"Miss Wentworth told me that things were rather unpleasant."

"Things were devilish unpleasant. My father was always difficult to get on with, and usually I gave in to him to keep the peace, but on this occasion I couldn't give in. He wanted me to send in my papers and come and live at Limbourne — live here, at Limbourne! The mere thought of it sent cold shivers up my spine."

Peter helped himself to another sandwich and continued, "There was a row. Of course there have been rows before — dozens of them — but this was the worst ever; it was an absolute Goliath of a row. It went on and on. Aunt Prissy got involved. The old lady took my part, you see; she's a courageous old bird and she saw my point of view. I'm due for promotion and I'm keen on my career — always have been keen."

"It seems very unreasonable to ask you to give it up."

"He didn't ask me to give it up, he told me to give it up. He was surprised when he discovered that he wasn't going to get his own way . . . and furiously angry of course. You don't know — I mean you didn't know my father so it's quite impossible for you to understand. When he was angry like that he was angry with everyone — like a mad bull, or something. He was even angry with poor old Nitkin who had the effrontery to mention my 'distinguished career.' You've no idea what it was like, Alec."

Alec had no words. He shook his head sadly.

"Well, to cut a long story short he sent for Fleece," said Peter.

"The lawyer?"

"Yes. I call him Fleece — and I don't mean the kind that grows on a sheep. The Bart sent for the horrible little creature and we had him to lunch (you should have heard him eat his soup, Alec; it was the most disgusting exhibition). The Bart got him to draw up a brand new will, cutting out most of his family and leaving the bulk of his private fortune to finance an expedition to Peru. Can you believe it?"

Alec was not quite so surprised as Peter expected, but he said, "How astonishing!"

"Is this boring you?" inquired Peter.

"Not at all, I'm most interested." He was deeply interested; he had heard most of this story from Miss Wentworth, but by no means all. Besides, he was not averse to hearing it from a different angle; his legal training and experience had shown him the desirability of hearing a story from as many angles as possible.

"Have another sandwich," suggested Peter. "Bassett is pretty good at sandwiches."

Alec took one. He said, "Do you happen to know if friend Fleece was a beneficiary under your father's will?"

"Funny that you should ask that! Yes, to the tune of five hundred quid."

"That explains a lot," said Alec thoughtfully.

"What does it explain?"

"I'll tell you later. Did you see the will?"

"Only the outside of it, but I heard all about it in detail."

"From whom?"

"From my father, of course," replied Peter, in surprise. "I thought you understood! We had the new will served up at every meal; we were told about it over and over again. The Bart enjoyed playing cat and mouse; good little Florence was played off against bad little Peter who was ungrateful for all the benefits bestowed upon him and wouldn't do as he was told. Aunt Prissy didn't hear about it so often because she usually feeds in her own sitting-room."

"Your father told you definitely that he was cutting you out?"

"Lord, yes! That was the object of the exercise. Wicked Peter was cut off without the traditional shilling, so was naughty Aunt Prissy. Good little Florence's legacy was doubled. Simon's share was reduced; he couldn't be completely cut out because that would have affected Limbourne . . . and so on and so forth, right down the list to Nitkin and old Nanny. I wasn't worrying really."

"You weren't worrying?" asked Alec incredulously.

"I suppose it sounds pretty crazy but it wasn't a real will, you know."

"Not a real will? What do you mean, Peter?"

"Oh, of course it was real — in a way. I expect Fleece had it all made out in the usual jargon — especially his

321

own little nest-egg — but the Bart never intended to sign it. I knew that all the time. He was just trying to force me to do as he wanted; he was trying to scare us into fits. It was nothing more nor less than a piece of bluff."

"He signed it the day after you left. Bassett and Mrs Sillett witnessed —"

"What!" cried Peter, leaping from his chair. "He can't have signed it! He never meant to sign it! It was an absurd document; there were all sorts of things in it — mad things! I can't believe he intended to leave Aunt Prissy without a penny to her name . . . Nitkin was docked of his miserable little pension . . . poor old Nanny, who was with us for thirty years, was never mentioned at all. As for me . . . Oh my goodness!" cried Peter, starting to pound up and down the room in a frenzied manner. "As for me — I'm properly in the soup. He never meant that will to stand — I know he didn't — he made it to give us a fright. It was a sort of practical joke — it was a trick — call it what you like! Look here, Alec, if he signed that will he was stark, staring mad. *He was, really.* He was mad with rage at being thwarted — so we can get it upset, can't we? Alec, we can get it upset. You're a lawyer so you know all about it — temporary insanity, that's the legal term, isn't it?"

Alec had been trying to get a word in, but it was not until Peter paused for an answer that he was able to make himself heard. "The will is burnt to ashes," he said loudly.

"Burnt? But you said he signed it."

"He signed it and then it was burnt."

"Does that mean the whole thing is cancelled?"

"Yes. I'm sorry I gave you a fright; I didn't mean —"

"Good lord, you did give me a fright," declared Peter, sinking into a chair. "It was signed — and then burnt. What an amazing thing! Who burnt it, by the way? Whoever burnt it deserves the V.C."

"Simon."

"Simon?" asked Peter incredulously. "How on earth did Simon get hold of it? Great Caesar's ghost, you seem to have been having some fun!"

"We've been — busy."

"You must tell me," said Peter. "But first of all *is everything all right?* It's vitally important to me because I don't mind telling you I'm absolutely on the rocks. I suppose I'm a bit extravagant but I find it quite impossible to live on my pay. Lots of fellows do, of course, but I was brought up in an extravagant sort of atmosphere — see what I mean? Besides I knew that there would be money coming along some day — or at least I thought I knew — so I didn't bother much. Duns don't worry you if they know there's money in the offing, but if there's any doubt about it they're on to you like vultures. I'd have been pretty well sunk if that will hadn't been burnt. You're sure it's burnt, Alec?"

"Quite sure."

"Well, in that case we're sitting pretty."

"I hope so," said Alec with native caution.

"You hope so? What do you mean? If the new will has been burnt the previous will comes into operation — or whatever you call it. That's right, isn't it?"

"Yes, if it's in existence."

"Oh, I see. You mean it may have been burnt too . . . but I don't think we need worry about that. I expect old Sandford has got it stowed away safely — no flies on old Sandford."

"Your family lawyer?"

"Yes, Riggs, Sandford and Wilkins have been our lawyers for generations. That's another reason why I was so certain that the new will was just a colossal piece of bluff. If the Bart had really intended to make a new will he would have sent for Sandford. Fleece would never have come into the picture at all."

Alec considered this point; he was not so sure about it. Sir Mortimer might have consulted his family lawyer about the changes in his will and been advised not to make them; he would have been annoyed with Mr Sandford and possibly quarrelled with him . . . in which case one might suppose that Sir Mortimer would take the just and generous will out of Mr Sandford's keeping and either put it away somewhere or destroy it. As a matter of fact Alec had had a case of a somewhat similar nature not long ago; it had given him and his partners a good deal of trouble.

"What are you thinking about?" inquired Peter.

Alec explained.

"Oh, that wouldn't be so good, would it?" said Peter in alarm. "I mean if there was no will at all."

"If Sir Mortimer has died intestate —" began Alec.

"Well, what happens then?"

"If this were Scotland his private fortune would be divided between his children — or the heirs of his children. In this case it would be divided into three portions; for you and Gerald and Mrs Godfrey. Gerald's share would be divided amongst his three children."

"That wouldn't be too bad," said Peter thoughtfully.

"But this isn't Scotland. In the matter of intestacy English law is slightly different and to tell you the truth I'm a bit hazy about it."

"We must get hold of old Sandford and find out."

"Yes."

"About Fleece," said Peter thoughtfully. "Does Fleece know that the new will has been burnt to ashes?"

"Yes."

"He must be pretty sick about it."

"He is. He's threatening to prosecute."

"Prosecute? Do you mean he'll bring an action against Simon for burning the will? Good heavens, that would be frightful — it would cause the most awful stink. There would be headlines in all the papers: *Baronet Aged Sixteen Burns Grandfather's Will.* Imagine it! We simply can't allow that, you know. Look here, Alec, I tell you what to do. Let's give Fleece his legacy and then he'll be satisfied."

"No, certainly not!"

"Send him a cheque and tell him to keep his mouth shut. That's the answer."

Alec looked at him to see if he were joking, but obviously he was not. He was sitting back in his chair and looking extremely pleased with himself.

"No, we mustn't do that," said Alec emphatically. "You see —"

"It isn't much," Peter pointed out. "I don't mind coughing up the money myself. It's worth it."

"It would be the height of folly."

"It would hush up the whole affair and that would be the end of it. I'm quite sure —"

"Listen to me for a moment. Fleece is a fool in some ways but he's extremely shrewd in others. You said yourself that he was a twister — or words to that effect."

"As straight as a corkscrew."

"Yes. Well, if you offer him money you will be delivering your family into his dirty hands."

"Why on earth —"

"Can't you see it, Peter? You would be giving him an open-and-shut case. He would only have to stand up in court, tell his story about Simon burning the will, produce your cheque and explain that the Wentworth family had offered him five hundred pounds to keep his mouth shut."

"Oh, I see. Yes, I suppose it wouldn't look too good . . . but perhaps if we offered him more and made him promise —"

"No," said Alec.

"Oh well, I suppose you know best," said Peter doubtfully.

There was a short silence.

"The funeral is on Monday," said Alec at last. "I was obliged to go ahead and fix it up — Mr Heath has been very helpful — but of course I didn't know who to ask or anything."

"Oh, I see! Yes, well, I can ring up some people to-morrow. There are one or two cousins who had better be asked, I suppose."

"What about Mrs Godfrey's son?"

"Lance is in South Africa and had better stay there. If he comes home there may be trouble with the police."

"With the police!"

"He was mixed up with a gang of lunatics who went about smashing things," explained Peter. "Adam Heath caught him, and was decent enough not to prosecute, so I got Lance shipped off to South Africa in the devil of a hurry. Then we managed to trap the leader of the gang, a revolting type —"

"Oliver Wade," murmured Alec.

"Oh, you know about it, do you?"

"A certain amount. Simon told me."

"Wade split," said Peter succinctly.

"You mean he —"

"I mean he gave the police the names of his confederates or whatever you like to call them. Lance was second on the list, but as he was in South Africa by that time, and doing fairly good work on an orange farm, the police took no action against him. I'm not a lawyer, of course, but I have a feeling that if Master Lance were to come home the police might be interested in him. That's all."

And quite enough, too, thought Alec. Aloud he said, "It depends what Lance did — or what Wade said he did — but we had better not risk it. In any case there's very little time; this is Friday night —"

"It's Saturday morning," interrupted Peter, pointing at the clock on the chimney-piece.

Alec took this opportunity to rise and say he was going to bed. He had done nothing all day except hang about and listen for the telephone; he was very tired and there was no reason why he should treat Peter Wentworth as a guest. "We were expecting you, so your room is ready," he said.

"But, look here, you haven't told me —"

"We can discuss everything to-morrow. Good night, Peter."

"Oh well, perhaps you're right. Good night, Alec," said Peter.

CHAPTER
TWENTY-FOUR

1

Alec and Simon were having breakfast together (there was no sign of Peter) and Alec was in the middle of telling Simon what had happened last night when Bassett came in and announced that Mr Sandford was on the telephone and wanted to speak to someone.

"I suppose I had better," said Alec, rising very reluctantly.

"Mr Sandford seems annoyed," said Bassett.

This news increased Alec's reluctance . . . but there was no help for it, of course, so he went into the library to take the call. He discovered that Bassett had understated Mr Sandford's condition; he was not annoyed, he was extremely angry. He had just seen the announcement in his *Daily Telegraph* and wished to know why he had not been informed of the death of Sir Mortimer Wentworth, who was not only a client of long standing but also one of his oldest friends.

"I'm sorry about it," said Alec. "I'm Simon's guardian, so it was really my business to let you know, but I'm a stranger here and it has been very difficult for me."

"You could have rung me up."

"Yes, I quite realise that you should have been informed but — but the fact is there has been a most extraordinary mix-up."

"Mix-up? What do you mean?"

"I can't possibly explain on the telephone. Would it be possible for you to come to Limbourne this morning, Mr Sandford?"

"No, it wouldn't. I always play golf on Saturdays and my car is being overhauled."

"We could send a car for you. I really think you should come if possible. Major Wentworth is here — he arrived late last night — and we need your advice."

"If you had let me know before —"

"I couldn't let you know before."

"Why?"

"Because . . . Mr Sandford, I can't explain this matter over the telephone."

"Is it really urgent?"

"Yes, it is."

"Very well, I'll come. You can send a car for me. The chauffeur has been here before so he knows my house."

When Alec had given orders for Mr Sandford to be fetched he returned to the dining-room to finish his breakfast. Peter had come down and was eating kidneys and bacon; Simon was explaining to his uncle how and why and when and where he had burnt the will. He had just reached the end of his story when Alec came in.

"Well, that's what happened," said Simon.

Peter produced his note-case. "Would a five-pound note be any use to you?" he asked.

"You bet!" replied Simon without hesitation. "Thanks awfully. It *is* kind of you, Uncle Peter."

"No need for thanks; you've earned it — and more!"

"It is merely a small token of your uncle's affection," said Alec clearly and firmly. He emptied his cup of cold coffee into the slop-basin and helped himself to fresh.

Peter hesitated, "But Alec, the boy deserves —"

"If the money is intended as a reward for anything that Simon has done I must refuse him permission to accept it."

Simon giggled and said, "It's because you love me, Uncle Peter," and taking the note put it away carefully in his pocket.

It was Alec's considered opinion that Peter was the right person to receive Mr Sandford and explain what had happened. Peter was one of the family, he had known Mr Sandford for years. When young, Peter had occasionally accompanied his father to Mr Sandford's office and had been given sticky jujubes to suck while his father and Mr Sandford talked business. This being so Alec put on his overcoat and crept quietly out of the side-door, taking care not to be seen.

Katherine had told him that the rose-garden was perfect (too perfect she had said) so Alec made for the rose-garden and sat down upon a wooden seat.

There was a cold wind this morning and the sky was overcast but the rose-garden was surrounded by tall hedges so it was quite pleasant sitting there. Needless to say there were no roses, but all the same there was something very attractive about the place: some of the beds were round, others rectangular and between them were grass paths — and as Alec had an orderly mind the symmetrical pattern pleased him.

He sat there for some time, thinking of Katherine. He was missing Katherine dreadfully. They had been married for less than four months but already she had become part of him — she had grown into his heart — he yearned to see her with an almost unbearable yearning. It was a definite pain — like toothache, thought Alec unromantically. Yes, it was exactly like toothache because, when he was very busy doing things, it let up a bit and then returned with increased virulence when he had leisure to think.

He watched a robin hopping about amongst the bare bushes and wondered miserably how long he would have to stay here; it might take weeks to inaugurate a new régime at Limbourne. Then the robin hopped on to a convenient twig, flew over the hedge and disappeared from view. Well, of course, thought Alec smiling to himself. That's what I'll do — fly home on Tuesday — no, it had better be Wednesday — and spend a couple of nights at The Cedars. I shall have to leave the car here — it will be quicker to fly — and I shall have to come back, of course. There's no reason why I shouldn't fly to and fro half a dozen times if necessary.

There were several reasons why he should; Katherine was by no means the only reason. Alec's partner, Andrew Firth, was worried about a case which was due to be heard in the near future and had written asking for Alec's opinion; there was a troublesome client near Selkirk who had closed a right-of-way with a barbed-wire entanglement and was exchanging unwise letters with the local authorities on the subject. Andrew had offered to go and see him and talk it over, but had received a reply stating that he would talk it over with Mr Maclaren — or nobody. It had been Alec's intention to sit down and write Andrew a long letter, but how much better it would be to see him and discuss these matters!

By this time the robin had returned and having found a very large worm amongst the rose-bushes was wrestling with it furiously. Yes, you've got the idea all right, said Alec to the robin.

Soon after this a gardener came through a gate in the hedge. When he saw that someone was sitting on the seat he approached and touched his cap.

"It's a nice morning, sir," he said.

"Are you Medlam? Did you get your barrows?" asked Alec.

"Yes, sir. I've ordered them, sir," replied the man.

Alec chatted to him and complimented him on the exquisite neatness of the garden.

"Sir Mortimer liked everything just so," Medlam explained. He looked round with a satisfied air and added, "You should see it in June and July. It's the best rose-garden in the county — and that's saying something." He hesitated and then added, "I've been wondering what's going to happen to Limbourne gardens."

It was natural that Medlam should be anxious to know what was going to happen to Limbourne — and incidentally to himself — so Alec explained that he was

Sir Simon's guardian and hoped to be able to keep the place running with a reduced staff until his ward was of age.

"Then you're the new master, sir?" asked Medlam looking at Alec with keen interest.

"Yes, I suppose I am," replied Alec, smiling. As a matter of fact he liked Medlam, the man seemed to have more nous than all the rest of Sir Mortimer's subjects put together (perhaps it's because he works in the open air — with plants, thought Alec vaguely).

Medlam was now talking eagerly, explaining that Limbourne gardens were known all over the south of England and, for this reason alone, he could get another job tomorrow; but he would rather remain at Limbourne and would be willing to look after the gardens with the help of one man if the greenhouses could be reduced.

"Sir Mortimer was very keen on orchids," said Medlam. "It's them that takes the time."

"What could we do with them?"

"Sell them, sir. It's a very fine collection; there's lots of people that would jump at the chance."

"That seems a good idea."

"With one man I could keep the gardens in fairly good trim — not like Sir Mortimer had them, of course."

Alec nodded. "I think I can promise that if you're willing to carry on at Limbourne with a reduced staff —"

"I am, sir. We've got a nice house — the wife likes it here — and the kids are at school. It would suit us to stay on. I'd be willing to take over extra duties and responsibilities — in fact I'd like a little more responsibility than what Sir Mortimer gave me."

Alec nodded. "Right. That's fixed, Medlam. We'll arrange all the details later."

"There's just one thing, sir. I'd like to keep Brown if that would be all right. Price wouldn't stay if things were reduced — and I wouldn't want him. He's a bit too uppish — that's what's the matter with Price; but he'd get another job quite easily."

"Right," repeated Alec. "Come and see me at the house on Tuesday morning and we'll talk it over. Meanwhile you had better keep all this under your hat."

Medlam grinned. "I won't say a word, sir. It's a great relief to have it settled. I've been wondering, you see."

2

The clock on the stables struck twelve, so Alec rose somewhat reluctantly and went into the house to see how Peter and Mr Sandford were getting on. He took off his overcoat in the hall and went into the library. A small, thick-set man of about sixty-five with a keen face, piercing eyes, dark eyebrows and iron-grey hair was standing on the hearth-rug with his hands behind his back. Peter was reclining in an easy-chair.

"Goodness! Here you are at last!" Peter exclaimed. "Mr Sandford has been here for over half an hour."

"This is Mr Maclaren, I suppose," said Mr Sandford.

"Yes, he's my brother-in-law; I told you about him," replied Peter.

Alec shook hands with Mr Sandford and said, "I expect you've heard all about it."

"I tried to tell him," said Peter plaintively, "but it wasn't much use because he didn't believe me. It would have been much better if you'd been here — you're both lawyers. I don't pretend to know anything about law; I'm a simple soldier, that's all. Show me a battlefield and I'll tell you where to place your guns, but don't try to cross-examine me about wills, because —"

"I didn't disbelieve you, Peter," interrupted Mr Sandford. "I was just trying to get things straight."

"You'll never get things straight as long as Fleece has anything to do with them," declared Peter. He turned to Alec and added, "Bassett has been looking all over the place for you. Where the dickens have you been?"

"I should think Mr Maclaren has probably been hiding in the tool-shed," suggested Mr Sandford.

"You're not far wrong, sir," said Alec, smiling.

Mr Sandford smiled too. "I don't blame you. As you said on the phone, it's a mix-up, but I've known Sir Mortimer for thirty years and there have been mix-ups before, so I'm not really as surprised as you might think."

"He has brought the will," put in Peter.

Mr Sandford gestured to his brief-case which was lying on the writing-table. "It is perfectly in order. Sir Mortimer signed it in our office last July while his heir was staying here; he was very pleased with the boy. It is an exceedingly good will, sensible and generous. I had no idea —"

"Anything in it about Peru?" interrupted Peter.

"Peru?" asked Mr Sandford in astonishment.

"Machu Picchu, the lost city of the Incas," Peter explained. He added, "All right, I can see there isn't. I just wanted to know for certain. Go on, Mr Sandford, you were saying you had no idea . . ."

"I was about to say I had no idea that Sir Mortimer had made another will."

"Alec thought the Bart might have asked you to make it."

"If Sir Mortimer had asked me to draft a document such as you have described I should have advised him most strongly against it," Mr Sandford declared vehemently.

"It would have come to the same thing in the end," said Peter. "I mean he would have been fed up with you and gone to Fleece just the same. However, we needn't worry; everything is all right — thanks to Simon."

"That rather depends upon Mr Fleece, doesn't it? You've seen this man, Mr Maclaren. What do you think of him?"

Alec sat down and said, "His real name is Friece. I think we should —"

"I call him Fleece," explained Peter. "It describes the fellow. He doesn't look you in the eye. I wouldn't have an N.C.O. in my battery who didn't look you in the eye."

"Yes, you told me that before," said Mr Sandford.

"I tell you it again," said Peter. "It's important. You can't trust a man who doesn't look you in the eye."

"I'm in agreement with you," said Mr Sandford. "But I think it would be a good plan —"

"And his table manners are revolting," added Peter. "I wish you could have been here the day we had him to lunch; then you would have seen what the fellow was like. Alec can bear me out, can't you, Alec?"

"I haven't a doubt of it," said Mr Sandford. "As a matter of fact I was going to suggest that Mr Maclaren and I should have a private talk. I feel we should get on quicker."

Peter rose and said, "Oh well, I can take a hint. You're both lawyers, of course. I'll go and see if I can find Simon, I expect he's in the stables, gassing to Nitkin." By this time Peter had reached the door; he turned and added, "You know, I still think it would be a good plan to buy Fleece off, but neither of you seems keen on the idea."

3

When Peter had gone and shut the door behind him Mr Sandford drew in a chair to the writing-table and sat down. He said, "I've known Peter since he was nine years old. Even in those days he was keen on the Army and he stuck to it through thick and thin. You didn't know Sir Mortimer, so it's impossible for you to understand how difficult it was for Peter."

By this time Alec was sick and tired of being told that he had not known Sir Mortimer; everyone said the same thing and then went on to explain that, this being so, he could not be expected to understand . . . but Alec had heard so many varying accounts of the late baronet's idiosyncracies that he felt as if he had known him quite well.

"Peter was always keen," continued Mr Sandford. "To his rage and despair he was too young for military service at the beginning of the war but he joined his battery as a subaltern in time for D-Day and was all through the campaign in France and Germany. He was slightly wounded twice and was decorated at the crossing of the Rhine. I happen to know from an outside source that he is very well thought of, and will probably go far. I just mention this so that you will understand why he refused to retire."

"It was most unfair of Sir Mortimer to ask him to give up his career," declared Alec. "I don't underrate Peter — if that's what you think. Even his idea of 'buying Fleece off' has its points. The fact is that, although Peter dislikes Friece and distrusts him, he hasn't come into contact with people like that before; therefore he doesn't realise that the man couldn't be trusted to keep his promise."

Mr Sandford nodded thoughtfully. "There would be no possibility of coming to an arrangement with him, I suppose."

"Too risky. The man is a scoundrel."

Mr Sandford's eyebrows rose slightly. They were dark and bushy and could express quite a number of

339

different emotions. "Really? That's a very strong term, Mr Maclaren. Supposing you start at the beginning and tell me all about it. Then we can discuss what action to take."

Alec told him. The story took some time to tell because he was anxious to leave nothing out; it was important that Mr Sandford should know every detail.

When it was finished Mr Sandford was silent for several minutes. Then he said, "It would be useful if we had some corroboration of the boy's story."

"There's the key," Alec pointed out. "The younger nurse, who seems to have some sense, saw it under Sir Mortimer's pillow when the doctor was there, just before Simon went in. It was not there afterwards. As nobody else had been in the room it's obvious that Sir Mortimer must have given it to Simon. She has gone now, but I've got her name and address."

"She's willing to swear to it?"

"Yes."

"Good. Then there's the point that neither you nor Friece was able to open the drawer. Have you got the key, Mr Maclaren?"

Alec produced the key and handed it over.

"What a curious little key!" exclaimed Mr Sandford, looking at it with interest. "I know a good deal about locks, but I have never seen a key with wards like this before. I've often seen Sir Mortimer use this key with its little gold chain — it was never out of his possession — but I didn't realise that there was anything peculiar about it."

"Try it, sir," suggested Alec.

The lawyer hesitated. "It would be better if I couldn't open the drawer, wouldn't it?"

"I don't see that it matters."

Mr Sandford slid the key well home and tried it this way and that; at first in a tentative manner and then more purposefully. He took it out, examined it carefully and tried it again. Then he handed it back.

Alec took it and opened the drawer.

"Extraordinary — and most satisfactory," was Mr Sandford's comment. He added, "I'd rather not know the secret. It would be better if you and Simon were to keep it to yourselves."

"I've told Simon not to mention it."

"Good."

"What is to be done about Friece?" asked Alec. "As I told you, he came down here with the object of finding the will. I refused him access to Sir Mortimer's papers and he went away in a rage."

"I wonder," said Mr Sandford thoughtfully. "Should I write to him or would it be better to go and see him . . . or perhaps take no action and allow him to make the first move?"

"I leave it to you, sir. My only suggestion is that if you decide upon an interview you should have a witness. As I told you, I shall be surprised if he takes the case to court. I suppose he has a case, but —"

"I doubt if he has any case at all. I shall take Counsel's opinion but I'm fairly certain what the opinion will be. The boy is sixteen years old; he was sent for by his grandfather, given a private key and told to burn a sealed envelope. His grandfather died and the boy was so upset that he forgot all about it. When he was undressing to go to bed he found the key in his pocket so he put on his dressing-gown and went downstairs and did exactly as he had been told. That's right, isn't it?"

"Yes."

"Just supposing Friece decided upon a legal action would the boy be able to tell his story clearly? He wouldn't be frightened to open his mouth?" asked Mr Sandford anxiously.

"Simon is longing to open his mouth. He told me that it would be fun to stand up and tell the judge the truth the whole truth and nothing but the truth — and I gather he would be a hero at school."

Mr Sandford chuckled. "I'm looking forward to meeting the new baronet; he must be a bit of a lad."

CHAPTER
TWENTY-FIVE

1

Mr Sandford did not meet the new baronet at lunch (he had ridden over to have lunch at Hurlestone Manor) and this afternoon was spent going through Sir Mortimer's papers. As might be expected everything was in perfect order; bills and leases and share certificates were neatly and clearly docketed. There was a file of private letters, which was laid aside for Peter, and a small file of unpaid bills which was put into Mr Sandford's brief-case. Alec had turned off the telephone in the library and given orders that they were not to be disturbed, so they had peace to get on with their task and by five o'clock they had finished.

Alec rang for Bassett and ordered tea.

"I wish the affairs of all my clients were in such good order," said Mr Sandford. He added, "Have you considered what to do about Limbourne? It would be a pity to shut up the place —"

"We can't," said Alec quickly. "There's Miss Wentworth, you see. She mustn't be turned out whatever happens. My idea is to put in a thoroughly competent manager and run the place with a reduced staff. I haven't mentioned it to Simon as I thought it better to wait until I saw the financial position clearly."

"It's an excellent plan and I can assure you that the financial position is — er — extremely sound, to say the least of it. No need to worry about that. As for a competent manager there's Mr Marsh, of course. He has been estate-agent for years — acting under Sir Mortimer's directions."

"Could he do it alone?" asked Alec doubtfully. "Most of Sir Mortimer's employees seem to have lost every ounce of initiative."

"I believe Marsh would welcome a little more responsibility; there would be no harm in giving him a trial. It would be an advantage to have a man who knows all about the estate; at least that is my opinion."

It was Alec's opinion also.

Mr Sandford continued, "You can decide which of the staff you want to keep. I happen to know that the head gardener is being offered a post at Wintringham Castle. The Earl is very anxious to get him."

"Medlam is staying on."

"He won't stay on with a reduced staff."

"It's fixed," said Alec. "I'm sorry to disappoint the Earl — perhaps he would like Price. I'm afraid Bassett will have to go; I like him and he's good at his job but I must have somebody with more gumption."

"He gets a pension."

"Oh, that's good. We shall keep Nitkin, of course; I believe he gets a pension but he can potter about and drive the car when necessary. Hurrell can easily find another job."

"You haven't wasted your time," said Mr Sandford in surprise.

"I haven't any time to waste," replied Alec. "I've got a great deal of work waiting for me in Edinburgh. I'm going north on Wednesday."

"Wednesday!" echoed Mr Sandford in horrified tones. "Mr Maclaren, you can't possibly! Surely you must realise the importance of these affairs. Sir Mortimer's estate is very large indeed and there will be a great many things to arrange."

"I'll come back. I shall have to fly to and fro," said Alec, smiling a little at the thought of the robin. "I can't possibly neglect all my clients."

"No, of course not! It was just . . . Oh well, we shall have to do the best we can."

Bassett came in with the tea and laid it on the small table. He said, "Excuse me, sir, but there are several matters. Hurrell asked me to inquire when Mr Sandford wishes the car to take him home and Mr Simon — I mean Sir Simon — has returned from Hurlestone Manor and would like to have tea with you. I told him you had given instructions that you were not to be disturbed."

"Oh, we've finished," said Alec. "Ask him to come in. Mr Sandford is anxious to see him."

"Yes, sir . . . and about the car?"

"I had better stay here over the week-end," Mr Sandford said. "If I might telephone to my sister to pack some clothes for me Hurrell could go over and fetch the suitcase."

345

Alec agreed and gave the necessary orders. He was glad that Mr Sandford had decided to stay; it would save time to have him on the spot.

2

When Simon came in to the library for tea Alec was interested to watch Mr Sandford's reaction; just for a moment he seemed to see Simon as Mr Sandford saw him: a tall, slender boy with dark hair and grey eyes, a very good-looking boy who would bear his newly-acquired title with distinction. As usual Simon's manner was perfect, he shook hands gravely and said, "How do you do, sir," and sat down without another word.

"You are extraordinarily like your father," said Mr Sandford.

"I'm glad you think so. I couldn't be like anybody finer," replied Simon. He hesitated and then added, "I've been wishing my father were here. It's an awfully big responsibility for me, but I'll do my best."

Alec was pouring out tea and inquiring about milk and sugar, so no more was said on the subject. Mr Sandford began to talk about Hurlestone Manor and to ask how the luncheon-party had gone off.

"It wasn't a party," replied Simon as he handed a plate of sandwiches to his companions. "It was just me — which was nice because I got to know them better. The D'Artingtons have a meadow down by the stream, where they practise archery. I had never tried it before, but Wilfrid took me there after lunch and gave me a lesson. It's a fascinating sport. Wilfrid is pretty good at it; he and his father often shoot. It's the only thing Major D'Artington can do because he's so lame. They have two big targets one at each end of the meadow and you walk backwards and forwards between them."

"I've watched people practising archery," said Mr Sandford. "I've never done it myself. Golf is my game."

"Have you ever tried it, Alec?" asked Simon.

"Yes, I'm a member of the Royal Company of Archers, sometimes known as the Queen's Bodyguard. I'm not a first-class shot by any means, but I enjoy the sport and I turn out in my green uniform with a feather in my hat when Her Majesty comes to Edinburgh."

"Really?" asked Mr Sandford, looking at Alec in astonishment.

Alec nodded. "I like the age-old traditions of archery; the sport has a long and interesting history. Mary, Queen of Scots, was fond of it and is supposed to have been a very good shot; she and Bothwell won a match against the Earl of Huntly and Lord Seton at Seton Castle. They shot at butts in those days — or at a popinjay, a coloured handkerchief hanging on a pole."

Mr Sandford did not seem to be interested in the unfortunate Queen Mary. He said, "I've heard about the Queen's Bodyguard but I had no idea that the Archers really practised the sport."

"Of course they do! It isn't just poodlefaking!" exclaimed Alec in horrified tones. "Many of the members are first-class archers and tremendously keen. We have competitions every year. Some of the trophies are very valuable; the Musselburgh Silver Arrow dates from sixteen hundred and three and there is another, undated, which is thought to be even older."

"You shoot at targets, I suppose?"

"Yes, usually, but occasionally we do clout-shooting as well."

"What is clout-shooting?" inquired Mr Sandford.

Alec helped himself to another sandwich and proceeded to explain the myseries of clout-shooting.

By this time Alec had made up his mind that something important had happened to Simon. There was a new dignity in his demeanour — a new poise — but it was not until tea was finished and Mr Sandford had gone upstairs to talk to Miss Wentworth that he discovered the reason.

Simon came and sat down beside Alec on the sofa; he said, "Major D'Artington talked to Wilfrid and me about Monday and told me exactly what I shall have to do. I hope I'll be able to do it all right — I mean not only at the funeral but afterwards when the people come here to lunch. He says I'm the head of the Wentworth family, so all the people who come to the funeral will be my guests; later on, when I come and live here, they'll be my neighbours. I felt a bit scared."

"They'll be very friendly."

"Yes, that's what Major D'Artington said. I shan't know any of them, of course, but he said that wouldn't matter. Wilfrid is to be my A.D.C.; he's to stick to me all the time (like my shadow, Major D'Artington said) and Wilfrid knows nearly everybody so he can keep me right."

348

"That's an excellent plan."

"Yes, Wilfrid and I talked about it afterwards. We went down to the meadow — I told you about that — and Wilfrid showed me how to stand and hold the bow and loose off the arrows. At first the arrows went all over the place but after a bit I began to get the hang of it; Wilfrid said I didn't do badly for my first attempt. Then my arm got tired so we went and sat in the little hut where they keep the bows and arrows and all the other paraphernalia and we talked about the future. You can't know what's going to happen in the future, but you can see what's likely to happen."

"You and Wilfrid are just about the same age so you'll be neighbours all your lives."

"Yes, that's what we thought. Wilfrid's position is different from mine; he has been brought up to this kind of life. I've been thrown into it suddenly — like a person who has never learnt to swim being thrown into the sea. I said that to Wilfrid and he understood. We made a solemn pact to stand by each other through thick and thin. He'll help me and tell me about things and I'll stand by him when things go wrong. He didn't say it straight out but I know what he meant."

"Is he worried about his father?"

Simon nodded. "Yes, that's it. Sometimes Major D'Artington is fairly all right — as he is just now — but other times he has a lot of pain. When he was wounded the bone of his leg was splintered — he has had five operations — and every now and then his leg flares up and causes trouble. He's terribly brave about it. It would be a lot easier for Wilfrid if he wasn't quite so brave."

"Why?"

"Oh, because he never complains, so Wilfrid never knows . . . at least he *does* know because he can tell from his face and sometimes he hears him moving about at night and sees the light under his door. Sometimes the surgeon comes down from town to see him. The surgeon is an old friend and they pretend it's just a friendly visit, but Wilfrid never knows if it means another operation. Wilfrid is absolutely devoted to his father."

Simon was silent for a few moments and then added thoughtfully, "It's funny how everybody seems to have problems and worries — all different."

Alec had often thought this himself. He said, "Is Wilfrid's grandfather any comfort to him?"

"No, he's old — nearly ninety. Wilfrid told me that he isn't really in this world any more."

"What did he mean?" asked Alec in surprise.

"Oh, he's not gaga," explained Simon. "They took me up to his room to see him and he knew who I was and talked to me very kindly but I could see that he had got past caring very much about anything. It was just as Wilfrid had said: he isn't really in this world any more — that describes his condition exactly."

"Wilfrid certainly has troubles and worries," said Alec compassionately. "It's a dreadful burden to bear alone; I'm glad you made the pact."

"I was afraid you might think the pact was rather silly."

"On the contrary, I think it's extremely wise."

When Alec went upstairs to dress for dinner he put through a call to The Cedars. It was answered by Daisy, who, recently, had become an addict to the telephone and rushed into Alec's study like a whirlwind whenever she heard the bell. She had been told to reply to the call by giving the number but she was always too excited to remember this injunction and to-night was no exception to the rule.

"Oh, it's you!" she squeaked breathlessly. "This is me."

"I thought it was."

"You sound quite near!"

"What have you been doing?"

"Well, it's Saturday so Den and I went to lunch with Aunt Liz and played Happy Families. That's what we did. Oh, here's Mums — she wants to talk to you — but I want to ask you something first. Listen, Alec, will you be home for our birthday? Den and I want you to be here."

"I shall come," Alec declared. "I may have to come back here again but I shall be with you on the day . . . with two large parcels."

"The parcels will be nice," said Daisy frankly. "But it's really you we want. You'll play bears, won't you?"

At this moment Katherine lost patience and removed the receiver from her daughter's hand. "Darling, I was just going to ring you up," she said. "How are you getting on?"

"Quite well. Peter came last night — so that particular worry is off my mind."

"You'll be able to come home after the funeral, won't you?"

"Not at once, I'm afraid. There's a good deal of business —"

"Oh, Alec! I'm missing you terribly much. There's nobody to watch me brushing my hair."

"I should just hope there isn't!"

Katherine laughed.

"You were going to ring me up. Was there anything special?" Alec wanted to know.

"Yes, a letter from Zilla — a very interesting letter."

"Has she seen the *Comtesse* yet?"

"She doesn't mention the *Comtesse*; the letter is full of Mr Guest. They went to Brighton together for the week-end and —"

"What!" interrupted Alec in horrified tones. "Zilla and Mr Guest went —"

"I'm afraid you've got a nasty mind," said Katherine with a little chuckle. "Mr Guest's mother has a house at Brighton. They stayed with her. It was a delightful rest and Zilla enjoyed the sea breezes."

"Oh, I see. All the same . . ."

"Quite," agreed Katherine.

"Do you think there's anything in it?"

"Your guess is as good as mine."

"I wonder what he's like."

"Zilla told me he was a wonderful man, 'highly cultured'."

352

"Oh lord! I wish I'd seen him when I was in London."

"You sound a bit worried, Alec."

"Yes, I am. We don't know anything about him. Zilla isn't a good judge of character; she's very gullible . . . and she's very well off," added Alec significantly.

"I see what you mean, but we can't do anything about it, can we?"

"Well, I might go up to town and see her — later on, when I've got things a bit more settled here."

"Perhaps you should," agreed Katherine with a sigh. She added, "But don't stay away too long."

"Not a day longer than I can help; I'm yearning to come home. What are you doing, darling? You should have some of your friends to lunch or tea to cheer you up."

"Aunt Liz is coming to lunch to-morrow and I thought of asking Isobel Fisher to tea on Monday."

"Good idea!"

"I've been star-gazing, Alec. Last night the stars were gorgeous and I'm going out again to-night."

In Alec's opinion this was not such a good idea. He exclaimed, "You shouldn't go out by yourself after dark."

"Oh, I enjoy it — besides it's important. I've written a long letter to a great friend of mine so I'm going to walk to the village and post it. I want him to get it on Monday morning."

"Him?"

"Yes, *him*." She was laughing — so of course he guessed.

"Oh, darling!" he exclaimed. "Of course it will be lovely to get the letter but I don't like you going out alone after dark."

"What do you think could happen to me?"

There were all sorts of things that could happen to her: she might be attacked by a hooligan . . . or trip and sprain her ankle and lie in the road all night. In fact, now that Alec considered the matter, he could think of half a dozen frightful things. He said anxiously, "Katherine, it really isn't safe. I would much rather you didn't walk to the village in the dark. I know you think I'm silly, but —"

"I like you to be silly."

"You like me to be silly?" he asked incredulously.

"Yes, silly like that — about me. For years and years I had nobody to be silly about me. See?"

"Darling!"

"And I promise faithfully not to walk to the village in the dark. I'll send Ellen and her niece to post the letter, so you'll get it on Monday morning. We had better ring off now. Good night, silly Alec."

"Good night," said silly Alec. "Take care of yourself. I'll come home as soon as I possibly can."

CHAPTER
TWENTY-SIX

1

After hearing so much about Wilfrid it was natural that Alec should be interested to see him in church next morning, sitting beside his father in the D'Artington pew: a tall well-made boy with fair hair and a healthy complexion. He was not in the least like his father (whom Alec secretly thought of as the crusader).

It was Peter who had suggested "Church Parade" and the rest of the party had agreed. They had walked to church together; Mr Sandford and Simon in front, Peter and Alec behind. As they neared the church they saw people streaming down the road and when they reached the lychgate there was a little group waiting for them to go.

"You had better lead the way, Peter," Alec whispered.

But there was no need for Peter to lead the way. Simon smiled at the little group, said good morning, and led the way, himself. He walked up the aisle and paused at the Wentworth pew to allow his elders to enter before him. It was done so naturally that at first Alec thought nothing about it, but afterwards he began to wonder whether Simon had thought it out and had done it because Major D'Artington had said that he was "the head of the Wentworth family." In either case it was very well done.

The church was of Norman architecture, with a barrel-shaped roof crossed by dark oak beams; the walls were of grey stone with brass tablets fixed to them; the winter sun streamed through the stained-glass windows making patterns of ruby and amber on the uneven flagstones of the floor and on the faces of the congregation. There was scarcely a vacant seat, Alec noticed. Presently the choir filed in: little boys in snow-white surplices with angelic faces followed by bigger boys and middle-aged men. Mr Heath himself was a small, thin, elderly man with clean-cut features and silver hair.

The service was surprisingly good for a small village church; the organ rolled out sonorously and the choir sang well. Alec enjoyed the service; he might have enjoyed it even more if he had not felt that he and his companions were being observed with a great deal of interest by hundreds of eyes. The Wentworth pew and the D'Artington pew were at the east end of the aisle, facing each other, so the eyes could stare at their occupants very conveniently . . . but they're looking at Simon, not me, Alec assured himself.

Certainly Simon did not mind; he had smiled at his new ally in a friendly manner and was now singing lustily, "making a joyful noise unto the Lord."

When Mr Heath went up into the pulpit he stood in silence, looking round the church, and then said a few words about Sir Mortimer Wentworth: the parish had

356

sustained a great loss — a sudden and most unexpected loss. Sir Mortimer was generous and open-handed, always ready to give freely in aid of a good cause. "As you know it was Sir Mortimer who paid for having our organ reconditioned, a most generous gesture which we all appreciate greatly. 'Freely ye have received, freely give'," said Mr Heath and added the usual expressions of sympathy for the bereaved family. He then announced his text and preached a very interesting and memorable sermon about brotherly love.

It had been difficult for Mr Heath — Alec realised that — he was bound to say something about Sir Mortimer and he was too highly-principled to eulogise a man who was a professed atheist. Perhaps the sermon about brotherly love was intended to make up for all the things he could not say about the late baronet.

After the service Alec had a few words with Mr Heath about the arrangements for to-morrow and then started to walk home. Simon was waiting for him — the others had gone on.

"I wanted to talk to you," explained Simon.

"What about?" asked Alec, somewhat apprehensively.

"About Mr Sandford. He's an awful snob, isn't he? I suppose that's why you gave him the works yesterday afternoon."

"I don't know what you mean."

"You do," declared Simon with a little chuckle. "I mean about the Royal Company of Archers — and all that. I couldn't understand it at first because I've never heard you blow your own trumpet before."

Alec smiled.

"The trumpet blast shook him up all right," continued Simon. "He was talking about you all the way to church, telling me that the Royal Company is a '*corps d'élite*' and explaining that only distinguished people are accepted as members of the Queen's Bodyguard. I think he must have found a book about it in Grandfather's library and mugged it up," added Simon thoughtfully.

Alec laughed.

"I knew you'd done it on purpose," said Simon. "It was clever of you, Alec. He'll pay more attention to what you say because you're a member of a *corps d'élite*."

"The end justifies the means," agreed Alec.

They walked on for a few yards in silence.

"Alec," said Simon. "Let's go for a ride this afternoon, just you and me. I want to take you up to the top of the hill. Grandfather took me one day; you can look down on Limbourne as if you were in the air and see the whole place spread out like a map. I want to show you."

Alec hesitated. Then he said, "I don't see why we shouldn't. I've been shut up in the house for days. I haven't got boots or anything, but —"

"Uncle Peter's boots will fit you," said Simon eagerly. "Do come, Alec. I want to show you — and it will be a lovely afternoon for a ride."

2

It was a lovely afternoon for a ride. Simon and Alec set off soon after lunch, they rode down the avenue and turned to the left up a steep, stony lane with beech hedges on either side. Here it was sheltered and remarkably warm, but presently they came to a wood of oak trees whose bare branches creaked and swayed in the breeze. The sky above was pale blue with large white clouds sailing across and disappearing one after another behind the hill.

Alec had not ridden for years but his mount seemed quiet and well-behaved so he was enjoying himself; he said so to Simon.

"Good," said Simon. "I wanted to get you out. You've been having a ghastly time, haven't you?"

"Rather worrying for us both."

"Frightful," declared Simon. "But it would have been a hundred times worse if I hadn't had you. Goodness knows what I'd have done if you hadn't come with me. You've come here when you would much rather have stayed at home; you've backed me up and managed everything. It seems silly to say thank you; if I knew anything better I'd say it."

"You've said more than enough."

"All right. I just wanted you to know."

They rode on in companionable silence and presently emerged from the little wood on to a moory piece of ground which sloped upwards to the crest of the hill. There were sheep here, wandering about and cropping the grass in a leisurely way; there was also a man with a bob-tailed sheepdog. The man touched his cap when he saw the riders approaching so they stopped to speak to him.

Simon said, "You're Colgate, aren't you? I met you one day when I was up here with my grandfather."

"Yes, sir."

"This is Mr Maclaren. He's my stepfather. He's going to look after Limbourne for me and — and manage things."

"The sheep seem in very good condition," said Alec.

"Yes, sir."

"It has been a mild winter — so far."

"Yes, sir."

They rode on.

"What an ass he is!" exclaimed Simon. "Shepherds are usually interesting, aren't they?"

"He was shy, that's all. I don't think Sir Mortimer encouraged people to chat. Perhaps when you've seen Colgate more often he'll open out a bit. The sheep are in very good condition; that's the main thing."

"They look nice and fat," agreed Simon. He hesitated and then asked, "Do you think I should try to make friends with these people — or not?"

"I'm quite sure you should."

"Right, I shall," nodded Simon.

By this time they had come to the top of the hill so they dismounted and tied the horses to a sturdy wooden stake, which had been placed there for the purpose and, walking on a few yards farther, found themselves in a sheltered hollow amongst some boulders.

"This is where I came with Grandfather," explained Simon. "It was his special place. He told me that he was going to have a seat put here . . . but it hasn't been done. Alec, do you think we could do it? I mean — well, because of him, really."

"I think it's a very good idea."

360

"You'll do it, won't you?"

"No, you'll do it," said Alec, smiling at his ward. "You will speak to the estate carpenter and tell him exactly what you have in mind."

"All right. That will be rather nice."

Having decided this they turned and looked at the view (as Simon had said, it was as if one were seeing it from the air); below them lay Limbourne, surrounded by its gardens and green parklands and fine old trees. At one end of the gardens there was a long row of greenhouses and several large sheds. To the left was the village, a cluster of little cottages most of which had red-tiled roofs; in the middle of the village was the green churchyard and the grey stone Norman church with its square tower. In the country round about there were several large farms with barns and out-buildings and stackyards. There were woods and chocolate-brown ploughed fields surrounded with hedges; there were meadows dotted with cows.

"How much of this belongs to you?" asked Alec after a long silence.

"Well, most of it . . . I suppose," replied Simon. "I can't really believe it, you know. It's quite incredible, but I suppose I'll get used to it in time." He added in a low thoughtful voice, "I wonder what Phil will think of it."

For a moment or two Alec was too surprised to make any comment. Then he said, "It's different from her own country but in its own way it's very beautiful."

"Yes, that's what I think. I told her about it, you know . . . and I wrote her a long letter yesterday and told her all that had happened, so I expect she'll write to me soon."

"I'm sure she will."

"I like Phil. She's very sweet and pretty and she's sensible too. She's the sort of girl you can discuss things with. I wish she could see Limbourne."

"No doubt she'll see it some day," suggested Alec.

"Yes, of course," agreed Simon, as if that went without saying.

This seemed to be the end of the conversation so Alec took out a pair of field-glasses, which he had borrowed from Peter, and surveyed Simon's property in detail. "What is that big house away to the right amongst the trees?" he asked.

"Hurlestone Manor," Simon replied. "The D'Artingtons were here long before us, so the village and the church belong to them . . . and those fields beyond the stream."

"There are three large farms."

"They all belong to Limbourne. Mr Marsh could tell you a lot more than I can; is he going to stay on?"

"I hope so. I haven't seen him yet."

Although Simon had indicated that he himself did not know very much about his newly-acquired property he seemed to know a surprising amount considering the fact that he had spent only ten days here. Some of it had been learnt from his grandfather, but more from Nitkin with whom he had ridden nearly every morning.

Alec listened with interest, picking out the different landmarks with the field-glasses. Presently he passed them to Simon and said, "It's a goodly inheritance, Simon."

"I know. It's a very big responsibility — but, thank goodness I've got you, Alec! Will you be able to stay on and fix up everything? I mean there's your own business, isn't there? And I expect you're longing to get back to Mums."

"Yes," said Alec with a sigh. The ache in his heart (which he had compared with toothache) was no better — in fact it was worse. He had made up his mind to fly home on Wednesday, but there were so many urgent matters requiring his attention that he could see no prospect of getting away before Friday at the earliest. He had written to Katherine giving her a full account of everything — or nearly everything — that had happened but fortunately he had not mentioned his plan to fly home so she would not be disappointed.

Meanwhile the new owner of Limbourne had been surveying his domain. "Oh, I say!" he exclaimed. "These glasses are marvellous. I've got them adjusted now and I can see all sorts of things. I can see old Parker leaning on the wall of his pigsty and admiring his prize sow. Nitkin says he gets lots of prizes for his pigs. And I can see Medlam, all dressed up in his Sunday suit, going into the orchid-house . . ."

There was a lot more of this. Alec listened and smiled and made up his mind that a pair of field-glasses would be an acceptable birthday-present for the new baronet, who was going to be seventeen next month.

The afternoon was so pleasant that Alec and Simon decided to ride home another way and have a canter in a meadow near the stream, so it was beginning to get dark when they turned in through the Limbourne gates and trotted up the avenue. Simon took the horses round to the stable and Alec went into the house. He had not ridden for years so he was tired. (I shall be frightfully stiff to-morrow, he thought apprehensively.) He was just going upstairs to have a boiling-hot bath when Bassett came through the green baize door which led to the kitchen premises.

"Excuse me, sir," said Bassett. "I would like some instructions."

Alec was heartily sick of Bassett's craving for instructions. He looked over the banister and said, "Won't it do later? I'm going to have a bath."

"It was Mrs Sillett, sir. Mrs Sillett would like to know which room should be prepared for Mrs Maclaren."

"What?"

Bassett repeated the message word for word.

"Do you mean she's coming?" asked Alec incredulously.

"There was a telephone call, sir. You were out riding with Sir Simon so I took the call myself. Mrs Maclaren said she was flying south this afternoon and would like to be met at the air terminus in London if possible."

"Great Scott! What time is she arriving? Have you sent a car?"

"The Major has gone to meet her, sir. The Major said he had to go up to town anyhow, to call at his club and get his clothes for to-morrow, so he could easily meet Mrs Maclaren."

Alec was still leaning on the banister, he felt quite weak with astonishment and delight. "Goodness," he said. "I can scarcely believe it . . . she said she wasn't coming. I wonder why she changed her mind."

He was speaking to himself, rather than to Bassett, but Bassett replied, "I understood Mrs Maclaren to say that her aunt advised her to come."

"Oh, I see. Thank you, Bassett."

"Mrs Sillett would like to know —"

"I'll see her! I'll tell her!" cried Alec joyfully and he raced upstairs two steps at a time, quite forgetting that he had been feeling tired.

Mrs Sillett had already chosen apartments for Mrs Maclaren and merely wished to have her choice confirmed.

"I thought you would like the grey suite," she said, opening a door which led to a large room with a double bed. Next door was a dress-room and a bathroom. Alec had a look round and confirmed her choice. Like everything else at Limbourne the grey suite was perfect; the carpet and curtains were silvery-grey; the furniture was mahogany, polished and shining; a touch of colour was provided by large pink cushions on the divan and a pink bedspread.

"Lovely," said Alec. "Perhaps a few flowers would —"

"Yes, of course, Mr Maclaren," interrupted Mrs Sillett in pained accents. "I have sent a message to Medlam asking him for pink carnations. I shall put an electric blanket in the bed and towels and soap in the bathroom. The Major told me that he and Mrs Maclaren would be dining in town so there's plenty of time to get everything ready."

"Dining in town?"

"That's what the Major said."

Alec was a little disappointed. It meant that he would not see Katherine as soon as he had hoped ... however, it could not be helped. He asked Mrs Sillett for a bottle of Scrubb's Ammonia and went off to have his boiling-hot bath.

3

There was a large party for dinner that night. In addition to Mr Sandford and Simon there were three male cousins, who had arrived to stay at Limbourne for the funeral; one of them had Wentworth features, the other two had not. Miss Wentworth was present looking very handsome in black velvet; Mrs Godfrey had emerged from her seclusion and appeared in black crêpe and jet ornaments.

Alec found himself sitting next to Mrs Godfrey with a male cousin on his other side — it was the one with the Wentworth face. Mrs Godfrey certainly had not a Wentworth face; she was a podgy little woman with a double chin and fluffy grey hair. Miss Wentworth had introduced him to her, saying his name and adding, "I told you about him, Florence. He's Katherine's husband." Mrs Godfrey had given him a flabby white hand to shake.

Alec had not liked her much but now that he was sitting beside her with the Wentworth cousin on his left he realised that he must try to make polite conversation. It was difficult because he was so excited at the prospect of seeing Katherine in a few hours' time that everything seemed a little hazy.

After a few moments' thought he said, "I'm so glad you're better, Mrs Godfrey."

"I'm a little better," she replied. "It's a great strain for me to come down like this but Aunt Prissy said I must make an effort. Aunt Prissy has very strong nerves; she doesn't understand what it's like to be sensitive." She turned and looked at him and added, "You're poor Clarence's son, of course."

"No, I'm Katherine's husband. Maclaren is my name."

"Oh, no relation at all!"

"No."

Mrs Godfrey digested this; then she said, "Katherine came and stayed here last summer; she was very pleasant but Papa thought she was too fond of having her own way. However, I dare say she will be different now that she's married."

"I don't want her to be different," declared her husband emphatically.

Mrs Godfrey took no notice of this pronouncement. She had begun to eat hors d'œuvre with obvious enjoyment and it was not until her plate was empty that she spoke again.

"You have heard about poor Papa, I suppose," she said. "It was a dreadful thing to happen. Sister Walsingham says it was all Simon's fault. Poor Papa would be alive to-day if Simon had not excited him."

"Oh no!" exclaimed Alec. "It wasn't that at all. Simon was —"

"Sister Walsingham said so. She's a very nice woman and an excellent nurse. She had been looking after me while I was ill. I was very ill — Papa's death was a great shock to my nerves. I'm very sensitive, you see, and of course Papa was a wonderful man. You didn't know him, did you, Mr Macfarlane? It's a great pity you didn't know Papa. He's a dreadful loss to the family — and to Limbourne, of course. I'm going to stay with my sister-in-law at Maidstone; it will be very sad for me to leave home but I couldn't bear to stay at Limbourne and see it going downhill. I don't know what will happen to Limbourne now that Papa isn't here to look after things. It would be different if Lance was here, but Lance is in South Africa and Peter wouldn't telegraph to him and tell him to fly home. It was very unkind of Peter and I told him so; he doesn't understand a mother's feelings."

Alec had been listening to the rigmarole with half an ear — so to speak. The monotonous voice had gone on and on but now it had stopped and its owner was looking at him with bulging pale-blue eyes so he was obliged to make some comment. "Yes, it's very sad," he said vaguely.

"Peter doesn't understand a mother's feelings," she repeated. "Lance ought to be here. Don't you agree?"

He did not agree, but as it was impossible to give reasons for his disagreement he held his peace.

Mrs Godfrey continued in plaintive accents, "They are all making a great fuss of Simon, but Lance is Papa's eldest grandson so he ought to be Papa's heir. I told Sister Walsingham about it and she agreed that it was most unjust. Those were her very words, 'It's most unjust, Mrs Godfrey,' she said."

"The property is entailed," Alec pointed out. "Simon is the son of your brother Gerald, so naturally —"

"But none of us liked Gerald," interrupted Mrs Godfrey. "He went to Italy and married an Italian peasant girl against Papa's wishes so it's most unjust that his son should inherit Limbourne. Papa was very angry indeed; he said Gerald had disgraced the family and wouldn't have anything more to do with him. That was the end of it, of course . . . at least we thought that was the end of it. Then Papa discovered that Gerald had a son." She sighed and added, "It was a great pity that Katherine and Simon came to Limbourne last summer and upset everything."

Alec could find nothing to say. The woman was so foolish — practically half-witted — that he could not even be angry with her. He changed the subject by inquiring after her daughter.

Mrs Godfrey's pudding-like face brightened. "I wish you could see Anthea, Mr Macfarlane; she's a most attractive girl, so pretty and graceful — and very clever indeed — but she's having such an amusing time in Austria that she has decided to stay on. She's with a party of young people and they are ski-ing every day and dancing in the evenings. Edward Ferrars is there — he's a charming young man. I told Anthea about poor Papa, but she's very sensitive — just like me — so she decided *not* to come home."

She stopped in order to give her whole attention to the casserole of chicken and mushrooms which had appeared between them. It was rather a long pause because she was poking about in the dish to find the liver-wing.

"Do you mean you wrote to your daughter?" asked Alec.

"Oh no, there wasn't time. I rang her up on the telephone. I had no idea you could telephone to Austria, but Sister Walsingham said you could and I have a telephone beside my bed so it was quite easy. Sister Walsingham helped me to get through to the hotel where Anthea is staying and we had a nice little chat. It was so delightful to hear dear Anthea's voice. She said the snow was fab — which means it is very good for ski-ing on. Then she asked me to send her some more money and I said I would. I can send her as much as she wants because Papa made a new will just before he died and left me twice as much money as he had left me in the old will. I shall be very well off indeed," declared Mrs Godfrey, nodding complacently. "Isn't that nice?"

Alec was speechless.

Somewhat disappointed at receiving no reply Mrs Godfrey glanced at her companion and, mistaking his embarrassment and consternation for surprise, she added kindly, "Of course you don't understand what I'm talking about, Mr Macfarlane. It was a family matter. Papa was a little vexed with Peter and Aunt Prissy and several other people, so that was why he made a new will and didn't leave them any money. It was never wise to vex Papa — Peter should have remembered that and done what Papa wanted."

"He's very keen on his career," said Alec feebly.

"That's what Peter said; but Papa said, 'the salary bestowed upon you by your grateful country is insufficient to pay for your neckties.' Those were his exact words," said Mrs Godfrey. "Papa had a very clever way of putting things. I remember it because it seemed unfair. Officers ought to be paid more than that . . . though of course Peter has a great many neckties," she added thoughtfully.

"It was a *façon de parler*," murmured Alec, who by this time was feeling like Alice in Wonderland (he had been reading the well-known classic to the twins as a bed-time story, so Alice's adventures were clearly in his mind).

"That's French, isn't it?" said Mrs Godfrey. "I used to know French — Mamma had a French maid at one time — but I've forgotten it now."

"I mean Sir Mortimer's reference to neckties was not intended to be taken literally."

"Papa was a very literary man," declared his daughter proudly. "You have no idea how many books there are in the library."

Fortunately at this moment Mrs Godfrey was offered a dish of chocolate mousse topped by a snowy mountain of whipped cream studded with crystallised cherries. She helped herself to a large portion and proceeded to eat it with avidity.

Alec decided that it was not a pleasant sight so he turned to his left. The Wentworth cousin had refused chocolate mousse and was sitting staring into space.

"I hope it will be fine to-morrow," said Alec.

"It always rains at funerals," replied the Wentworth cousin. After a moment's thought he added gloomily, "Or else there's a howling wind."

Alec tried to remember a funeral which had taken place in pleasant weather conditions but failed, so he gave up the unequal struggle and ate his chocolate mousse in silence.

CHAPTER
TWENTY-SEVEN

1

After dinner Alec escaped. He ran upstairs and moved all his belongings from the room he had been occupying into the dressing-room in the grey suite. Bassett would have performed this task, but Alec felt so restless that it was a comfort to have something to do. Unfortunately it did not take him long. When everything had been put away tidily he drew back the grey curtains in the bedroom, opened the window from the bottom and leaned out. There was no moon but the sky was full of stars.

The window looked out on to the gravel sweep so Alec stayed there, watching for Peter's car. As time passed and it did not come he began to worry. Supposing something had happened: an accident to the plane or an accident on the road on the way down from town! Was Peter a careful driver or the sort of man who takes risks? If only I hadn't gone out for a ride I could have met her myself, thought Alec miserably. I hadn't been out for days — but the moment I go out this happens! Why did Peter take her to dinner in town?

Why didn't they come straight down to Limbourne? Where are they having dinner?

He thought of them having dinner together, talking and laughing. He remembered that Katherine had said she liked Peter — he had sent her a beautiful handbag for Christmas. Peter had said, "I thought she was a perfect darling." At the time Alec had been quite pleased but now he felt differently about it: *what business had Peter to say she was a perfect darling?*

I'm being a fool, thought Alec, but for some reason the knowledge that he was being a fool did not help him to be sensible.

By this time he was feeling quite desperate; he was sure that there had been an accident and Katherine was lying in a ditch with a broken leg — or worse. He had just decided that he could bear the inactivity no longer and would go out and walk as far as the gates when he saw the head-lamps of a car lighting up the trees in the avenue and heard a distant hum. He waited a few moments to be quite certain — yes, it was approaching Limbourne — then he shut the window, drew the curtains and ran downstairs.

When Alec opened the front door the car had stopped at the bottom of the steps.

"Here she is, safe and sound!" shouted Peter cheerfully.

Here she was, coming up the steps! Alec took her in his arms and kissed her. He didn't care how many people saw him. She was his wife, wasn't she?

As a matter of fact there were quite a lot of people to witness the embrace. Peter was standing at the bottom of the steps, laughing. Simon was in the doorway and behind him were the boot-boy, Bassett and Mrs Sillett. Miss Wentworth was in the hall.

Katherine turned to greet Simon and received his usual bear's-hug; she emerged from it flushed and breathless and went into the hall where she shook hands with Miss Wentworth. Everyone was in the hall now, with the exception of the boot-boy whose duty it was to unpack the car. Mrs Sillett was inquiring whether Mrs Maclaren would like some refreshment.

"No thank you, Mrs Sillett, we had a lovely dinner in town," replied Katherine, smiling at her in a friendly manner.

Alec had hoped to get Katherine to himself; he had intended to take her upstairs to the grey suite and talk to her — but he couldn't, of course. Katherine was being lured into the drawing-room to talk to Mrs Godfrey, to meet Mr Sandford and the Wentworth cousins . . . and when Alec followed he found the whole gang standing by the fire with Katherine in the middle. She was wearing a black cloth coat with a grey chinchilla collar which Alec had not seen before — he had never seen the close-fitting black hat either. The grey fur collar stood up round her ears and framed her face; it was very becoming — no doubt of that — but it made her look different, somehow, and he didn't like it.

The others seemed to like it: Peter was standing beside her, smiling down at her in amusement at something she had said; Mr Sandford was preening himself like a little cocksparrow; the Wentworth cousins had clustered round like bees at a honey-pot; even the gloomy one had come to life and was gazing at Katherine as if she were something good to eat.

Alec felt shut out — it was not a pleasant feeling — he stood apart from the little group, watching the exhibition and frowning.

"Look at Mums," whispered Simon, putting his hand through Alec's arm. "She's doing her stuff all right — she's making them sit up and take notice. I like watching her, don't you?"

Quite suddenly Alec's feelings changed completely; he smiled at Simon and said, "She belongs to us."

"Yes, that's what I meant," explained Simon with a little chuckle.

2

Alec was sitting on the bed watching Katherine brush her hair. It was not quite such a good seat for the performance as the bed at The Cedars; he was obliged to lean sideways over the wooden panel at the foot of the bed before he could see her reflection in the mirror but that was a mere detail. At long last he had Katherine all to himself so he was happy and at peace. He saw the white sleeve of her peignoir fall away from her rounded arm as the brush swept slowly and rhythmically through her brown curls; he leant sideways and saw her face.

"Simon seems older, somehow," said Katherine.

"He's just the age to grow up all of a sudden — nearly seventeen — and a lot of things have happened to him lately: all that trouble at Christmas-time; then Sir Mortimer's death — it was a great shock to him, you know — and his new status and responsibilities as head of the Wentworth family."

"I hadn't realised that properly."

"Neither had Simon until his talk with Major D'Artington. I noticed he was much more grown up after that. He's thinking about getting married," added Alec with a little chuckle.

Alec had expected to surprise Katherine — but he was disappointed. She said, "It's Phil, of course. Well, he couldn't do better."

"Katherine, they're children!"

"You've just said he has grown up all of a sudden . . . and Phil is one of the most grown-up people I've ever met. I've known lots of women over thirty who aren't nearly as adult as Phil."

"Do you think Phil —"

"Oh yes," said Katherine, nodding emphatically. "Phil likes him. One day when we were talking about Simon she said in a very thoughtful voice, 'Of course I could never leave Daddy alone'."

"Oh no!" exclaimed Alec in consternation. "No, she couldn't possibly —"

"Don't be alarmed; her plans are made," interrupted Katherine, smiling in a mischievous manner. "She has decided that 'Daddy' is to marry Miss Finlay of Cluan Lodge. They like the same things; they enjoy each other's jokes; they have been friends since they were children — what could be better than that they should marry and grow old in each other's company?"

" 'The best laid plans of mice and men — ' "

"But Phil is neither a mouse nor a man and her plans usually come off. Think of the attic full of junk!"

"You're talking nonsense."

"Well, perhaps," admitted Katherine. "But it's fun to talk nonsense sometimes."

There was a short silence.

"You decided to come quite suddenly," said Alec at last.

"To-day at lunch-time," nodded Katherine. "Aunt Liz came to lunch. She was horrified — quite horrified — when she heard I wasn't coming south for the funeral. She said I was leaving all the dirty work to you — shirking my duty as a wife. Aunt Liz has no use for shirkers."

"But you weren't —"

"Yes, I was," declared Katherine, frowning at herself in the mirror. "I was shirking it — I was letting you down. I saw that quite clearly the moment she said it. I shirked coming to Limbourne because I was so miserable when I was here last summer; miserable, not only because the atmosphere of the place got me down but also because I felt I was losing Simon. I was so terribly miserable that I made up my mind I would never come back if I could possibly help it."

"I know, darling. That's why I told you that you needn't come."

She smiled at him in the mirror and said, "But you wouldn't want your wife to be a shirker. I felt sure you wouldn't so I came as quick as I could. It was a frightful rush because I had no suitable clothes — and

378

it's Sunday — but I rang up Isobel Fisher and she said she had just bought a new black coat and she had a black hat that she thought might do. She got straight into her car and brought them to The Cedars and they fitted me 'a treat.' Wasn't it kind of her?"

"I don't like them; they're not you, somehow."

"No, darling, they're Isobel Fisher," said Katherine, laughing at him. "Aunt Liz was there and she approved, so that was all right. As a matter of fact Aunt Liz wanted me to bring Denis with me; she said Denis was just as much Sir Mortimer's grandson as Simon. I saw her point, of course, and I thought about it seriously, but he and Daisy have never been parted for a single day and I was afraid there might be trouble. I couldn't bring Daisy."

"No, you couldn't," agreed Alec, smiling a little at the thought of his high-spirited stepdaughter.

"Now that I'm here you must make use of me. What about to-morrow?"

"It's fixed up," he told her. "After the funeral the people are all coming here for a fork-luncheon. Peter said that was the best thing to have; there will be too many for a sit-down meal. I left the catering to Peter and Mrs Sillett, so I needn't worry about that."

"Can't I do anything to help you?"

"Just be yourself," replied Alec seriously. "Look beautiful and be kind to everybody."

"You do say the nicest things!"

"True things. I'm no good at compliments. Oh, Katherine, I have missed you so dreadfully!"

"I've missed you dreadfully, too. It's only four days, but —"

"Four days? Yes, I suppose it is. How amazing!"

"Time is a very queer thing," declared Katherine, swinging round on the stool and looking at him. "Sometimes a day seems like a week and at other times it feels like five minutes — it rushes past so quickly that it makes you quite breathless. Do you realise that this time last year I hadn't met you, Alec? I was living in the flat with the children. I was lonely and — and a little bit frightened."

"Frightened?"

"Frightened of getting ill. There was nothing to come and go on, you see. I was pinching and scraping and worrying myself silly because I didn't know how I was going to pay the coal bill. I thought my life would go on like that until I was old and grey."

Alec nodded thoughtfully. "This time last year I was living at The Cedars with Zilla; trying to keep her happy, doing my level best to avoid ructions — but not succeeding. It was a wretched life and I thought it would go on like that until I was in my grave."

Katherine came over and sat down beside him. She leant her head against his shoulder.

Alec put his arm round her and felt the softness of her. He had felt her softness before, hundreds of times, but it still alarmed him; so soft and fragile . . . and so terribly precious.

"Don't think about the past," said Katherine. "We've got the present and the future. We've got each other. We've been married for four months —"

380

"Sixteen weeks — nearly."

"All right," she said, looking up at him and smiling. "I wasn't counting in weeks but I'll take your word for it. We've been married for sixteen weeks; I wonder what we shall feel like when we've been married for sixteen years."

Emily Dennistoun

D. E. Stevenson

Emily Dennistoun lives alone with her elderly tyrannical father at Borriston Hall on the Scottish coast. Her mother died many years before, and her younger brother is at Oxford, presented with opportunities that Emily can only dream of. She has few friends and lives through her writing. Then she meets Francis, and despite vicissitudes of fortune, despite uncertainties, loneliness and unhappiness, Emily holds steadfast to a love she knows is true.

ISBN 978-0-7531-8950-4 (hb)
ISBN 978-0-7531-8951-1 (pb)

The Fair Miss Fortune

D. E. Stevenson

Jane Fortune causes a stir when she arrives in the small community of Dingleford. She has bought an old cottage and plans to open a tearoom. Old friends Charles Weatherby and Harold Prestcott both fall for the newcomer, but her behaviour seems to vary wildly — she encourages first one then the other and at other times barely recognises them. Is there more to the fair Miss Fortune than meets the eye?

ISBN 978-0-7531-8948-1 (hb)
ISBN 978-0-7531-8949-8 (pb)

Mrs Tim of the Regiment

D. E. Stevenson

Vivacious, young Hester Christie tries to run her home like clockwork, as would befit the wife of British Army officer, Tim Christie. However hard Mrs Tim strives for seamless living, she is always moving flat out to remember groceries, rule lively children, side-step village gossip and placate her husband with bacon, eggs, toast and marmalade. Left alone for months at a time whilst her husband is with his regiment, Mrs Tim resolves to keep a diary of family life.

When a move to a new regiment in Scotland uproots the Christie family, Mrs Tim is hurled into a whole new drama of dilemmas. Against the wild landscape of surging rivers, sheer rocks and rolling mists, who should stride into Mrs Tim's life one day but the dashing Major Morley. Hester will soon find that life holds unexpected crossroads . . .

ISBN 978-0-7531-8608-4 (hb)
ISBN 978-0-7531-8609-1 (pb)

Miss Buncle's Book

D. E. Stevenson

The scene of this entertaining story is laid in a charming English village. The plot centres round Miss Barbara Buncle, a maiden lady who was obliged to write a book because — as she naively explained — her dividends were so poor.

Unfortunately, Miss Buncle had no imagination, so she wrote about her friends — quite kindly and truthfully, of course, for she was a benevolent and veracious soul. The reactions of her friends to Miss Buncle's book, however, were a little surprising, and the far-reaching and unexpected results of its publication caused quite a stir.

ISBN 978-0-7531-8552-0 (hb)
ISBN 978-0-7531-8553-7 (pb)

Miss Buncle Married

D. E. Stevenson

Marriage to her publisher, Arthur Abbott, has done nothing to stop Barbara Buncle from involving herself in the lives of her neighbours. The only difference this time is that she's trying to avoid writing about them too.

After leaving Silverstream and moving to London, Barbara and Arthur are enjoying their newly-wedded bliss, but not the city life. The only solution to their problem? Returning to the country. Silverstream is out of the question, but Barbara eventually finds the perfect candidate in the town of Wandlebury. After falling in love with the town, and the run-down Archway House, the Abbotts move in and make it their home. Barbara doesn't intend to get mixed up with those around her, again, but can't help falling into those scrapes, often with humorous consequences!

ISBN 978-0-7531-8554-4 (hb)
ISBN 978-0-7531-8555-1 (pb)

ISIS publish a wide range of books in large print, from fiction to biography. Any suggestions for books you would like to see in large print or audio are always welcome. Please send to the Editorial Department at:

ISIS Publishing Limited
7 Centremead
Osney Mead
Oxford OX2 0ES

A full list of titles is available free of charge from:

Ulverscroft Large Print Books Limited

(UK)
The Green
Bradgate Road, Anstey
Leicester LE7 7FU
Tel: (0116) 236 4325

(Australia)
P.O. Box 314
St Leonards
NSW 1590
Tel: (02) 9436 2622

(USA)
P.O. Box 1230
West Seneca
N.Y. 14224-1230
Tel: (716) 674 4270

(Canada)
P.O. Box 80038
Burlington
Ontario L7L 6B1
Tel: (905) 637 8734

(New Zealand)
P.O. Box 456
Feilding
Tel: (06) 323 6828

Details of **ISIS** complete and unabridged audio books are also available from these offices. Alternatively, contact your local library for details of their collection of **ISIS** large print and unabridged audio books.